"You need to teach D0711270

"Pardon me?" Olivia Mae asked.

"You need to give me dating lessons," Noah said.

"What do you mean?"

"You and me. We'll go on a few dates…three. That would be a *gut* number. You can learn how to do most things if you do it three times."

"That's a ridiculous suggestion."

"Why? I learn better from doing."

"Do you?"

"I've already learned not to take a girl to a gas station or a picnic, but who knows how many more dating traps are waiting for me to stumble into them."

"So this would be…a learning experience."

"It's a perfect solution." He studied her closely and then reached forward and tugged on her *kapp* string, something no one had done to her since she'd been a young teen in school with a crush on a boy.

"I can tell by the shock on your face and the way you're twirling that *kapp* string that I've made you uncomfortable. It's a *gut* idea, though. We'd keep it businesslike—nothing personal."

Vannetta Chapman has published over one hundred articles in Christian family magazines and received over two dozen awards from Romance Writers of America chapter groups. She discovered her love for the Amish while researching her grandfather's birthplace of Albion, Pennsylvania. Her first novel, *A Simple Amish Christmas*, quickly became a bestseller. Chapman lives in Texas Hill Country with her husband.

Dana R. Lynn grew up in Illinois. She met her husband at a wedding and told her parents she'd met the man she was going to marry. Nineteen months later, they were married. Today, they live in rural northwestern Pennsylvania with enough animals to start a petting zoo. In addition to writing, she works as a teacher for the deaf and hard of hearing and works in several ministries in her church.

VANNETTA CHAPMAN

A Perfect Amish Match

&

DANA R. LYNN

Amish Haven

LOVE INSPIRED

INSPIRATIONAL ROMANCE

LOVE INSPIRED®

INSPIRATIONAL ROMANCE

Recycling programs
for this product may
not exist in your area.

ISBN-13: 978-1-335-22986-1

A Perfect Amish Match and Amish Haven

Copyright © 2020 by Harlequin Books S.A.

A Perfect Amish Match
First published in 2019. This edition published in 2020.
Copyright © 2019 by Vannetta Chapman

Amish Haven
First published in 2019. This edition published in 2020.
Copyright © 2019 by Harlequin Books S.A.

Special thanks and acknowledgment are given to Dana R. Lynn for her
contribution to the Amish Witness Protection series.

This edition published by arrangement with Harlequin Books S.A.

For questions and comments about the quality of this book,
please contact us at CustomerService@Harlequin.com.

Harlequin Enterprises ULC
22 Adelaide St. West, 40th Floor
Toronto, Ontario M5H 4E3, Canada
www.Harlequin.com

Printed in U.S.A.

CONTENTS

A PERFECT AMISH MATCH

Vannetta Chapman

This book is dedicated to Beth Scott, a dear friend.
God blessed me when our paths crossed.

Acknowledgments

Continued thanks to my editor, Melissa Endlich,
for guiding me through the Love Inspired process. All
of the people at Harlequin have been a joy to work
with. A special thanks to my agent, Steve Laube,
for his wisdom, hard work and sense of humor.

I wouldn't even attempt to write without the help
of my family, pre-readers and friends.
You all are a constant source of inspiration.

And finally, "Giving thanks always for all things
unto God and the Father in the name of
our Lord Jesus Christ" (*Ephesians* 5:20).

Many waters cannot quench love,
neither can the floods drown it.
—*Song of Solomon* 8:7

By this shall all men know that ye are my
disciples, if ye have love one to another.
—*John* 13:35

Chapter One

Olivia Mae Miller had her hands covered in flour and was breading chicken breasts to slip into the oven when *Mammi* called out, "Someone's at the door."

It was late Wednesday afternoon, the first day of May. She'd opened the doors and windows to allow the spring breeze into the house. She could just make out the silhouette of a tall man through the screen door. Olivia Mae added dashes of salt, pepper and garlic to the chicken, then popped the baking dish into the oven. Finally she snagged a dish towel off the counter and hurried through the living room, hoping the sight of a stranger wouldn't upset her grandfather. Some days he could become quite agitated. Other days he was sure the person was a long-lost relative.

"Can I help you?" She peered through the screen, looking up to take the measure of the man on their porch.

"Are you Olivia Mae?"

"Ya." Still she didn't step outside. Maybe he would go away if she wasn't overly friendly. She had dinner

to finish preparing—potatoes and corn and salad. The doctors said small amounts of salad were very important for people her grandparents' age. She really couldn't afford to run behind on their schedule. Evenings were difficult when they didn't manage to tuck *Daddi* into bed early. She almost said, "We're not interested," to shoo away the man.

But then the stranger held up a wooden box that had been tucked under his arm. "I believe this is yours."

"Oh, my." Still wiping flour off her hands, she pushed through the door, forcing him to take a few steps back. "Where did you find that?"

He placed the box in her hands. "I'm an auctioneer over in Shipshewana, and it was in a lot—"

"From my grandparents' old house. I must have left it there, and then they moved. But I still don't understand how you ended up with it."

"I thought it was something that my *mamm* would like."

She must have looked alarmed, because he quickly added, "I didn't actually buy it. I couldn't. Since I'm the auctioneer, that wouldn't be proper. I asked my *bruder* to bid on it, which he did."

The man was rambling and refused to make eye contact. He seemed nervous for some reason. Olivia Mae pulled her gaze from him to study the box she was holding—cherry wood, sanded smooth, with a trio of butterflies carved in the bottom right-hand corner.

"After the auction, when I opened it, I saw the papers that had your name on them."

Her head jerked up at the mention of her letters. "They're still in here?"

"I didn't—didn't read them. Just saw your name, and my youngest *bruder* was standing there, and he knew you—knew of you. We both agreed it should be returned to the rightful owner. Didn't seem likely that you would intentionally auction it with the letters inside."

She moved over to one of the porch rockers, and Tall-Dark-and-Handsome followed her. Olivia Mae sank into the chair, opened the box and unfolded the top sheet. It was her handwriting all right, from so many years ago. Pain as sharp as any paring knife sliced through her heart. She shook her head, refolded the letter, gently closed the lid and turned her attention to her visitor.

"It would seem I owe you then."

"Of course not. We have a process for things like that—when something is auctioned but shouldn't be."

"So your *bruder* was refunded his money?"

"He was."

"What's your name?"

"Noah. Noah Graber." Instead of looking at her as he spoke, he stared out over the porch railing at her pitiful herd of sheep in the adjacent pasture—if you could call six a herd.

"And you live here in Goshen?"

"I do now. Just moved back." He didn't offer any further explanation about that, but he did add, "My youngest *bruder*, the one who was helping me, is Samuel."

"I know Samuel, as well as Justin."

"Seems everyone knows everyone around here."

"Justin Graber and Sarah Kauffmann. They were married last fall."

Dawning washed across Noah's face.

It was almost comical.

"You're the matchmaker?" He was still standing, and now he glanced at her before looking at his hands, the porch floor, even his horse and buggy. "I recognized your name, but I didn't remember…that you, well, put Justin and Sarah together."

Olivia Mae waved away that thought. "It was obvious that those two were a perfect match for each other."

"Wasn't obvious to Justin or Sarah. They'd known each other all their lives and never even thought of courting, to hear him tell it."

She'd dropped her gaze to the box and was again focused on it. To see it after all these years, it made her feel young again, made her feel seventeen. But it also reminded her of the painful times that came during and after that year. The deaths of her parents, moving to live with her brothers and then the problems with her grandparents. She could have never imagined then how her *mammi* and *daddi* would come to depend on her, and how inadequately prepared she was for the changes in their health. If she didn't find a way to stem their drastic decline, she knew it would mean a move, and she was convinced that would be the worst possible thing for them.

"I missed the wedding," Noah continued. "I was living in Pennsylvania at the time. Seems I've missed a lot of things around here, but to meet an Amish matchmaker… Well, I wouldn't have ever guessed that, and I wouldn't have thought she'd look like you."

There was something in Noah Graber's voice that pulled her attention away from the wooden box and to his eyes, which were a warm dark brown, like the best kind of chocolate.

"What's that supposed to mean?"

"What's *what* supposed to mean?"

"What am I supposed to look like?"

"Well—"

"Old, maybe. Using a cane. Peering at you over my glasses and shaking my knitting needle at you." She'd come across the stereotype before. She should be used to it by now. "Yes, I'm a matchmaker. Is that something you're interested in?"

"Me? *Nein.*" He shifted uncomfortably on his feet and jerked the straw hat off his head. She wasn't surprised to see that his brown hair curled at the collar. Over six feet, tall as a reed and brown curly hair to boot? Noah Graber could be a cover model for an Amish romance book. As she waited for him to explain why he wasn't interested in dating, a blush crept up his neck. He was easily embarrassed, too? He'd be perfect for Jane, or possibly Francine.

"I wouldn't think that you would need a matchmaker. No doubt you have women following you around at the auction." She motioned toward the other rocker.

He shrugged and perched on the edge of the seat. "Actually I'm single—happily single."

"Is that so?"

"It is."

"And why would that be?"

"Can't see as that's your business."

Olivia Mae laughed. "Fair enough. It's true that I enjoy setting up dates for those who haven't found the love of their life."

Noah shook his head in disbelief. "You believe in that?"

"*Ya.* Don't you?"

"Never really thought about it."

She doubted that was true, but she didn't call him on it. Instead she returned her attention to the box. Running her fingertips across the top, she marveled at the way just holding it took her back to a simpler time, an easier time.

"My *daddi* made it for me. He was quite good with small wood projects, when he was younger. Now…" She pulled in a deep breath. "He gave it to me when I came to visit one summer. I left it at their home, thinking I would be back the next year. But they moved and things…changed."

"I'm surprised it ended up at auction."

How could she explain what *Mammi* and *Daddi* had been through the last few years? She couldn't, and why would she try? This stranger wasn't interested in the particular burdens of their life, so instead she changed the subject.

"I don't remember seeing you at church."

"We didn't meet this past week, and I only moved back the Wednesday before that."

"And already working at the auction house?"

"*Ya.* It's the reason I moved here. They needed another auctioneer so I thought I'd come back home."

Olivia Mae searched his eyes for a moment, long enough that he began to squirm again. There was something he wasn't saying, but she had no reason to press him. As he'd pointed out, he wasn't interested in being matched and beyond that she was simply being nosy.

"Welcome to Goshen, then, though it sounds as if you grew up here."

"I did."

"If it's been more than a few years, I expect it's changed a bit since then."

"Yes and no."

A man of few words. Yes, he would match perfectly with Jane Bontrager. She was a real chatterbox, which would balance them out. She was tall, too—not as tall as Noah Graber, but tall enough that he wouldn't feel awkward. Was that why he'd never married? Did he tower over every woman he met?

He pinched the bridge of his nose, as if the entire conversation was painful to him. "Some things always stay the same—especially in Amish communities."

"Yes. I suppose so." She smiled, stood and said, "*Danki* very much for bringing this out to me."

Noah seemed to realize he was being dismissed. He nodded once and headed down the porch steps when there was a clatter of dishes inside the house.

Olivia Mae was already moving toward the door.

A woman shouted, and then a man hollered something in return.

"Do you need help?"

"*Nein*. We're fine." Which was categorically not true, but she wasn't about to reveal as much to a man she barely knew, and one that probably wouldn't last in town long enough to see the summer flowers.

She hurried inside, allowing the screen door to bang shut behind her. Matchmaking was good and fine, but it was what she did to relax. Her priority was the two dear old people who now looked up at her in surprise— as if she'd popped in from thin air.

"I've got that, *Mammi*."

"Turned my back on him for one minute…" *Mammi* had a dish towel and was attempting to clean up the coffee that had spilled on his shirt. The mug sat on the floor next to *Daddi*'s chair.

Olivia Mae went for the broom and dustpan. She returned to the sitting room and began sweeping up shattered pieces of a small dish on the opposite side of the room, where it had apparently been flung.

Mammi continued to blot at the coffee stains, but *Daddi* was having none of it. He captured her hands in one of his, which were still strong—they were the same hands that had felled trees and planted fields and carved Olivia Mae's letter box. "Don't bother me with that, Rachel. Did you see the size of that hog? Nearly knocked over my chair trying to get at your peanut-butter squares."

Olivia Mae and *Mammi* shared a look, but neither corrected him. They'd learned long ago that doing so only made matters worse.

Noah spent most of the drive home wondering if he should have gone back up the porch steps to make sure everyone was all right. As he'd walked away, he had distinctly heard an old man's shouting. Olivia Mae had clearly not wanted help—she'd practically slammed the screen door shut without a single look back.

His mood jostled between concern for this woman he didn't know, aggravation at his brother and curiosity over what was in the box. She had barely glanced at the top sheet, though plainly she'd recognized it instantly.

Noah was twenty-nine years old, and it wasn't lost on him that all the fine women—women like Olivia Mae

Miller—were taken. No doubt her husband had been out in the fields or in the barn with the animals, though he had wondered at the absence of children. Most Amish households had a whole passel.

She had struck him as quintessentially Amish. Thick brown hair pulled back under her *kapp*, with just enough showing that he'd been sure to notice how it was shot through with blond. Simple Amish frock covered with a clean apron. Brown eyes that seemed to be both laughing and taking in everything at the same time. She reminded him of a teacher he'd had his last year of school—she'd been young and seemed impossibly beautiful and even then he couldn't understand why she was teaching.

That was it. She'd reminded him of a teacher, and he'd felt like a schoolboy squirming under her gaze.

Teacher! Ha. Perhaps she read romance books when she wasn't tending to her children. That would explain her fascination with true love. He'd nearly laughed at her, but stopped when he saw the serious look on her face. She was a believer—no doubt about that. Why shouldn't she be? For Olivia Mae life had turned out the way it was supposed to. For him? Not so much. His mind threatened to turn toward his past failed relationships, but he shook his head and focused on the scene in front of him instead.

He pulled into his parents' farm, which was one of the larger properties in Goshen. It wasn't that they were wealthy, but with seven boys, his *dat* had made it a priority to purchase any adjacent property as it became available. The result was that they owned close to three hundred acres, which was enough for four farms.

Three of his brothers had built adjacent homes, two had moved to nearby counties and one had taken over the family place.

As for Noah, he had no intention of being a farmer.

He'd found his passion, and it was in the auction house.

He directed the buggy horse into the barn and jumped down from the seat as his two younger brothers emerged from the back stalls.

"Managed to miss most of the work," Samuel said, a smile playing across his lips. Samuel was the youngest of the boys. He'd inherited their *mamm*'s blond hair as well as her shape—short and stocky.

Justin was also short, though thin like Noah. He leaned against a bale of hay as Noah removed the harness from the buggy mare.

"How was Olivia Mae?"

"You sent me to a matchmaker? Really?"

Justin held up his hands in innocence, and Samuel began to laugh. "Can't blame us for trying."

"A matchmaker?"

"You're the one who wanted to return the box. You could have left it at the office, and they would have mailed it to her."

"I thought I was doing the neighborly thing. Instead I walked into a trap."

"A trap?"

"*Mamm* probably put you up to it."

"Now you're being paranoid. *Mamm* didn't even know about the box."

"I'm surprised our community tolerates such."

"Are you kidding? Olivia Mae has been a real asset

around here. No fewer than six marriages in the last year are a direct result of her—"

"Meddling?"

"Encouragement."

"Well, I'm not interested."

"Told you that's what he'd say." Samuel nudged Justin and held out his hand. "Pay up."

Grudgingly Justin pulled out his wallet and slipped a five-dollar bill into his brother's hand.

"Seriously? You're betting on my social life?"

Samuel laughed again as he pocketed the money, walked out of the barn and headed across the field toward his own family. Noah finished unharnessing the mare and set her out to pasture as Justin watched.

"Actually we're betting on the absence of your social life," he finally said. "Which isn't quite the same thing."

"So you admit that's why you sent me over there?"

"No. Not at first. Samuel didn't know when you asked him to bid on the box that it was Olivia Mae's."

"This wasn't a setup from the get-go?"

"We don't have the time or energy to be that manipulative. I was standing in the back watching—it being your first auction and all. You did well, by the way."

Noah rolled his eyes and tried not to be distracted by the praise.

"When we realized who the box belonged to, we figured it couldn't hurt for you to meet her."

"So it was more of a coincidence than a setup."

"We just saw it as an opportunity."

Noah grunted.

"But it couldn't hurt to talk to the woman."

"I did. She thanked me for the box, pried into my recent history, and then had to go because of some emergency in the house."

Justin took off his hat and scratched the top of his head. "You know *Mamm* and *Dat* worry."

"Because I'm not married?"

"Because you're not the least bit interested in getting married."

"Why should they worry about that?"

"They don't want you to be alone in your old age."

"I have the six of you, plus your wives and children to keep me company. Not to mention *Mamm* and *Dat* are in excellent health."

"It's not the same as having your own family."

"Says who? You? You've been married what…six months?"

"Never been happier."

"And I'm glad for you."

Justin let that comment slide, but as they walked out of the barn and toward the house he said, "You sound kind of crabby."

"Do I?"

"Maybe she got under your skin."

"Maybe you should mind your own business." The words came out crankier than he'd intended. Noah softened them by shoving his *bruder* and taking off toward the house. And suddenly it was like they were ten years old again and racing for the first hot biscuit.

They tumbled into the house, both laughing, and Noah wondered why his knee had begun to twinge after a short sprint. He was trying to rub it inconspicuously when he glanced up and saw Sarah walk into Justin's arms. He kissed her once and touched her stomach, then they both laughed. They might have only married six months ago, but they'd wasted no time in starting a family.

Noah was honest enough to admit the twinge of envy he felt. It was normal he supposed, not that it changed anything. Olivia Mae might believe in true love. His *bruders* might think he'd be better off married, and his parents might think of him as the last baby to be pushed from the nest, but Noah didn't see it that way.

He planned to establish himself as a good auctioneer.

Maybe he'd buy a small farm after that, something with a barn and a horse pasture—there was certainly no need for fields to cultivate.

He'd settle down all right, but on his own terms.

He understood what his future held, what kind of man he was. He'd be a dependable brother, an excellent uncle, even a good son. He had it in him to be a successful auctioneer. But a husband? *Nein.* That wasn't in his future, and he had the dating history to prove it. Something he didn't plan to share with Olivia Mae.

Chapter Two

Sunday morning dawned cloudy but warm. It seemed to Olivia Mae that *Daddi*'s moods reflected the changing weather. As a farmer, rain had always been a good thing—a sign of God's blessing. *Daddi* sat at the kitchen table, a smile on his face, shoveling scrambled eggs into his mouth as if they were the best thing he'd ever tasted.

"Maybe I'll have a chance to meet that nice young man who visited the other day." *Mammi* refilled their coffee mugs and sat down across from Olivia Mae.

"Nice young man?"

"You know very well who I mean."

"We have a new postman."

"*Nein.* Young *Amish* man."

"Our neighbors dropped by with their new baby."

"Olivia Mae, you know *gut* and well who I mean, though you've avoided talking about him all week." *Mammi* pointed a fork at Olivia Mae as if in warning, but there was a smile on her face.

"Hmmm. Oh, you mean Noah Graber?"

"Indeed. He seemed like a fine young man."

"How could you tell? You didn't meet him."

"Because you didn't invite him in."

"He was just returning something he'd found. There was no need to invite him in, plus I think he was in a hurry."

"Well, he won't be in a hurry today, and I have a mind to speak with him."

"Oh, please don't do that." Olivia Mae fumbled around for a reason. In truth she simply didn't want her grandmother to attempt setting up a date for her again. The last one had been a disaster. The man had been nearly fifty. She certainly didn't get her matchmaking skills from her grandmother. Thank goodness! In desperation she added, "He's rather the shy sort. I was thinking of maybe setting up something between him and Jane Bontrager."

"Why are you always matchmaking other folks together, but no one seems to catch your interest?"

Olivia Mae wasn't too surprised at the question. It was something *Mammi* tossed at her at least once a week.

"I have my hands full with you and *Daddi*. I have a family of my own. I don't need another."

"Pshaw." *Mammi* plucked a hot biscuit from the basket and broke it open with trembling fingers. The steam rose, and she inhaled deeply before adding a pat of butter. "You know what the Good Book says about taking a log out of your own eye before you worry about your *bruder*'s."

"My *bruders* are doing just fine, but *danki* for your concern."

She thought her grandmother would continue to bat

the topic back and forth, but instead, when she looked up, confusion clouded her features. "Elizabeth, I've told you before. It's past time you marry, and I don't think you should put it off. There are plenty of *gut* boys available."

Olivia Mae closed her eyes briefly, said a quick prayer for wisdom and forced a smile. "Yes, *Mammi*. I'll give that some thought."

"And prayer. Don't forget prayer, young lady."

Olivia Mae hopped up to clean the dishes so they could leave for church on time. But as she washed and rinsed, she wasn't thinking about the service, she was thinking about *Mammi* calling her by her mother's name. Olivia Mae didn't even look like her mother—she took after her father. Both of her parents had perished in an accident ten years ago and she missed them as sorely as if it had happened the week before.

Daddi's dementia was a terrible thing to watch, but it was *Mammi*'s slips into the past that frightened her more. She couldn't possibly care for her grandfather and grandmother by herself, not to mention that the house was starting to show signs of neglect. She would ask for help if she needed it. Of course she would, but she knew what her *bruders*' answer would be—they had wanted to move *Mammi* and *Daddi* to Maine years ago.

She couldn't imagine taking them away from what was familiar. As far as the house, she could ask the bishop for help and a work crew would be there the following week, but she hesitated to do that, too. Her church family had already done so much to help when *Daddi* was in the hospital last month. She knew they didn't mind, but she didn't want to be the type of person who only asked for help but never gave.

So she bought old sweaters at garage sales, unraveled and washed the yarn and used it for her knitting. She was able to scatter the shawls and sweaters and blankets throughout their community. That and matchmaking were the only ways she knew to give back.

And she prayed, but not for a beau. That would only complicate things. Who would want to take on a twenty-seven-year-old wife, a small farm, a dwindling herd of sheep that she thought of as pets, and tottering grandparents? It seemed too much to ask, in her opinion. Best that she keep her problems to herself and bury her own dreams. Sometimes life called on you to sacrifice.

Mammi and *Daddi* were definitely worth sacrificing for.

Olivia Mae didn't involve herself in someone else's life unless they asked. But during their church service Sunday morning, she couldn't help watching Noah Graber and Jane Bontrager. They sat as far from each other as possible. Noah was on the men's side of the aisle, closer to the front. Jane was near the back, helping with her nieces. Noah didn't seem aware of Jane at all, which wasn't unusual in Olivia Mae's experience. It was one of the reasons that older men remained bachelors. They weren't even looking for love.

What was it that Noah had said?

I'm single—happily single.

He wouldn't be the first man to think so.

Their opening hymn had ended and the ministers had filed into the barn. The doors were open wide, allow-

ing in the fresh spring air, but rain threatened so they'd
opted to have the church service under cover. Now they
all stood for the *Oblied*, and for a moment Olivia Mae
forgot about Noah and Jane and even her grandparents. She allowed the words of the praise song to flow
over her, to rise from her heart. She felt, in those few
moments, transported to a place without difficult days
and hard decisions. She felt like the young girl who had
written the letters to herself, the letters that were in the
box Noah had brought to her.

She'd tried to read them. The evening he'd given her
the box, she'd waited until she'd settled down for the
night and then she'd once again unfolded the top sheet.
She'd instantly been transported back to the summer
of her seventeenth year, when her dreams were still
fresh and hopeful. Each sheet contained a letter to herself that she'd penned quite seriously over the course
of the summer. Where had she come up with that idea?

But the words she'd written seemed to come from a
different person. The naiveté of her thoughts and hopes
and dreams was too painful.

So she'd folded the letter back up, and had gently
placed the box on top of her dresser, then flung her *kapp*
over it so she wouldn't have to stare at it.

She tried to focus on the sermons. The first was
something about Joshua and Moses and the lost Israel-
ites. Standing between her grandmother and her neighbor, Olivia Mae prayed, sang, kneeled and stood. She
felt as if she was going through the motions, but the
ritual soothed her nonetheless. After all, *Gotte* was in
control last week, and he was still in control.

Even though *Daddi*'s condition seemed to be worse…

Even though *Mammi* grew more unpredictable each day…

Bishop Lucas stood and startled Olivia Mae out of her daydreams. He'd been their bishop for over six months now, but still she was surprised that it wasn't Atlee who offered their blessing over the meal, who sent them out to be *the people of Gotte*, as he was so fond of saying. She was sure that Lucas would make a fine bishop, though he seemed awfully young at fifty-two. The truth was that in her heart she missed Atlee. He'd been like a wise old *onkel* to her. He'd been someone that she could be completely honest with.

Another hymn, and then they were dismissed and she was hurrying to check on *Daddi*, who insisted he was fine. Several of the men told her not to worry, they would take care of her grandfather.

Mammi was already standing behind the serving line when she joined it. She reached out and touched Olivia Mae's arm, and a flash of understanding passed between them. Being away from the farm was good, but being in public was always nerve-racking. There was just no telling what *Daddi* would do.

Her *mammi*'s look reminded her that they were among friends, among family. She could stop worrying, at least for a few hours.

So Olivia Mae made her way down the line to the table with the main dishes—cold crispy chicken, thick slices of ham, spicy links of sausage. First the elders came through, then the women with the little ones, followed closely by the men. Finally the *youngies*, who filled their plates high, never worrying about calories or fat content. The last group was what Olivia Mae thought of as her people—Amish men and women in their twenties, some recently married and without children, some courting and some who seemed caught in that in-between place.

Jane stepped up with Francine. The two girls were barely twenty and stuck together like peanut butter and honey, which sometimes complicated her matchmaking efforts.

"*Gudemariye*, Olivia Mae." Jane smiled at her brightly—expectantly.

"And to you."

Francine leaned forward. "We heard you were setting up a match for Noah Graber."

"*Nein*. Noah's not interested." Olivia Mae pushed a plate of sandwiches forward, trying to buy herself some time. "I would like to talk to you, though, if you have a minute."

"We'll save you a place." Their heads together and giggling, both Jane and Francine moved toward the dessert table.

She'd thought nearly everyone was through the line the first time, and was looking to make sure that *Mammi* had made herself a plate, when Noah stepped in front of her table.

"I heard the fried chicken is *gut* today."

"Did you, now?"

His hat was pushed back on his head, once again revealing the curly hair, and he was actually making eye contact with her. No doubt he felt safer with the table between them—she wasn't going to jump over it and drag him toward a woman he might feel pressured to court. She couldn't help noticing he was in a better mood, as well. Perhaps because he wasn't on her front porch. Men like Noah relaxed on what they thought of as neutral ground. She'd have to suggest he take Jane to a restaurant in town. A family dinner would be too much pressure.

"Too bad there's not any chicken left."

"I gather you'd like some."

"It's why I'm standing here with no meat on my plate—my *bruders* insisted that I had to try it."

"Smart guys, your *bruders*." Olivia Mae opened the cooler under the table, pulled out her large Tupperware container and scooted it toward him. "I always make extra."

The grin he gave her caused butterflies to twirl in her stomach. Yes, this one could be a charmer. She only needed someone who was willing to push past his disinterested facade, smooth the rough edges and convince him that he wasn't *happily single*.

He thanked her for the chicken and moved toward the dessert table. Tall and handsome. There was no way she was letting Noah Graber get away from their community. His family was here. He belonged here! He probably faced a contented future with a house full of children.

No woman can be happy with fewer than seven to cook for.

The old proverb danced through her mind. She didn't completely agree with it. After all, she was happy right now. But then, that was a different story. She didn't abide gender stereotypes, but she did believe that men were happier with families. Hadn't she read an article in the grocery checkout line about that very thing? Something about men living five years longer if they were married, and up to seven if they had children.

When she thought of it in those terms, she wasn't prying her way into Noah's life, she was looking out for his health. Isn't that what the *people of Gotte* were supposed to do?

She plopped a crispy chicken leg onto her plate, added a scoop of macaroni salad and a slice of cheese and chose a chocolate brownie for dessert. She was going to need the calories if she was going to be successful today. They might rest from their daily work on Sundays, but matchmaking was a seven-day-a-week affair.

She made her way to where Jane and Francine were sitting and enjoying their meal.

"Uh-oh. She has that glint in her eye." Francine bumped Jane's shoulder. "And I think it's your turn."

"Why do you say that?"

"Because I had a date two weeks ago, and you haven't had one in… I don't know—a month."

"*Ya.* I'm journaling about my good qualities, like Olivia Mae told me to."

Olivia Mae only raised an eyebrow and bit into her chicken. It really was good. She'd learned the recipe from *Mammi*. The trick was to use a good sprinkling of garlic salt but not too much, and to keep the fire high enough to render the coating crispy but not burnt.

"Just tell us who it is." Francine clasped her hands in her lap and leaned forward. "It is Noah? I bet it is. He's the only new person I see here, and you have a definite new-person glint in your eye."

"I didn't know my eyes were so readable." Olivia

Mae wiped at her mouth with her napkin. "Yes, it is Noah, and I think we should give Jane the first try."

"Because I'm taller. That's it. Right?" Jane slumped down in her seat. "Why do I have to be so—"

"Three things."

Jane rolled her eyes.

"I'm serious about this—you both know I am. Our first step toward progress is to defeat those negative thoughts in your mind. Now tell me three positive things about your height."

Francine giggled, but Jane screwed up her face as if she hadn't been presented with this question a dozen times. She had. Olivia Mae thought it was her biggest obstacle to finding a suitable man. Jane wasn't that tall, but in her mind she was an ostrich. It didn't help that her first few dates had been with very short men, which only served to reinforce the gangly image she had of herself.

"I can reach the top shelf in the pantry."

"Gut."

"I've stopped growing."

"Not sure that's a positive thing, but go on."

"It's something I inherited from my *dat*, who I adore. So it's… I don't know—nice to be like him in some way."

Olivia Mae put down her fork, which was filled with macaroni salad. "I think we've had a breakthrough. You genuinely meant that."

"*Ya*. Maybe the journaling is helping, because it occurred to me that even though I don't enjoy being taller than most men, I love the fact that I have something in common with my *dat*."

"I suspect you have a lot in common with him."

"Back to the dating thing…" Francine was much more invested in the matchmaking process, maybe too much. Her enthusiasm tended to frighten men. It was one of the reasons that Olivia Mae thought that Jane might be a better match for someone as shy as Noah.

"I only met Noah earlier this week."

"Tell us about him." Francine stole a glance over her shoulder at Noah.

He was sitting three tables away with his *bruders* and their wives. Was he the only Graber son who wasn't married? Olivia Mae thought he was, but she'd have to ask around to be sure. That could work in their favor, too.

"He's nice enough. Obviously he's easy on the eyes."

"I'll say." Francine grinned.

Jane blushed, but she was listening intently.

"He's working as an auctioneer in Shipshe."

"Is that why he moved back?" Jane asked.

"*Ya*, and it's *gut* that he knows what he wants to do. He won't be distracted by that question as some men are—"

"I still can't believe that Elijah took a job at the RV factory." Jane shook her head in obvious disbelief. She'd thought Elijah would settle down and work for the town farrier, but it apparently wasn't destined to be. "He told his *schweschder*, who told me, that working around the horses just wasn't challenging enough. What's not challenging about shoeing horses?"

"Let's focus." Olivia Mae picked up her brownie, took a bite and allowed the sugar and chocolate to work their magic. Why was it that things you weren't supposed to eat a lot of were so delicious? "Seems to me that Noah might be self-conscious about his height."

"How tall is he?" Jane asked.

"A little over six feet, I think. I didn't exactly measure him when he came by the house." She hadn't meant to say that. One glance at Jane and Francine told her she'd have to go through the entire story of how he'd returned her box, so she did so quickly. "Anyway. He's back in town, working at the auction house, and he says he's happily single."

"Uh-oh." Jane sat up straighter, which was another improvement. She used to always slump, trying to make herself shorter.

"That's what they all say," Francine reminded them. "His own *bruder*—Justin—told you that he wasn't interested in dating at all. That it was a waste of time! Look at him now. He's happily married and expecting a *boppli*."

"Sometimes that makes things easier, when another person in the family has been successfully matched. Other times…" Olivia Mae noticed Noah was being teased by his *bruders*. He glanced toward her table, shook his head, picked up his plate and walked away. "Other times it can make a man more resistant to change."

"Why am I not encouraged by this entire talk?" Jane began to chew on her thumbnail, but tucked her hands back into her lap when she noticed Olivia Mae watching. "Sounds like he's not interested at all. What's your plan?"

"My plan is to convince him that it's his idea."

Chapter Three

Noah made a point of avoiding Olivia Mae after lunch. His brothers had had a hearty laugh over the fact that he'd thought she was married. How was he to know? What kind of matchmaker couldn't find herself a husband? It would be like owning a buggy shop but no buggy. Regardless, he thought it best to avoid her.

It wasn't so terribly hard.

He played baseball. She sat with the women under the hickory tree.

He had more dessert. She seemed to be avoiding the snack table.

He saw her take two young girls into the sheep pen, then coax one of the new lambs over and show them how to pet the babes so that the mother wouldn't be frightened. He'd almost walked over to her then, just casually, to tease her about being a shepherdess. He'd even remembered a sheep joke that he thought would make her laugh.

But she'd said something to the girls, and they'd hurried out of the pen and toward her grandfather. At least Noah supposed the old guy who was gesticulating wildly was her *daddi*. Olivia Mae and an older woman—her grandmother?—had helped him into the house, and then he hadn't seen her again for a while. He'd almost put the idea behind him—of having a talk with her and setting her straight—when he literally bumped into her coming out of the barn and carrying a large ice cooler.

She juggled the ice cooler, and he plucked it from her hands.

"Leaving so soon?"

"*Ya, Daddi*'s tired."

"I can carry this for you."

She cocked her head and stared up at him.

He squirmed under her inspection. Why did she make him feel like his hat was on backward? "Since I almost ran you over, seems like the right thing to do."

"All right. *Danki*."

They talked about the weather as long as anyone possibly could and then fell into an awkward silence. Her buggy would be the last one in the line. Why had he offered to carry the cooler? It was obviously empty and weighed practically nothing. Fishing around for something to say, he remembered her standing in the sheep pen.

"Where do sheep go on vacation?"

"What?"

"Where do sheep go on vacation?"

"I'm sure I have no idea."

"The Ba-a-aa-hamas."

The look on her face was funnier than the joke.

"Do you do that very often?"

"Do what very often?"

"Tell jokes when you're nervous."

"Who said I was nervous?"

"It's sort of obvious."

They'd reached her buggy. She opened the driver's-side door, fished around inside and pulled out three bungee cords. He strapped the cooler to the back of the buggy, as he tried to think how best to answer her question.

"I'm not nervous exactly. It's only that I wanted to say something to you, and I wasn't sure how to bring up the subject."

"Oh. All right. I'm all ears."

"I'm afraid we started off on the wrong foot."

"How so?"

He knew she knew what he was talking about, but obviously, she wasn't going to make this easier for him. He leaned against her buggy and crossed his arms. "I didn't mean to dismiss what you do. Obviously you provide an important service to our community."

"You mean my knitting?"

"*Nein.* I do not mean your knitting. You know exactly what I'm talking about."

Now she smiled at him—a perky *got-you* smile that had him shaking his head. Was that why she wasn't married? Because she was feisty, with an attitude and a sense of humor? Perhaps she had the idea that she didn't fit into the submissive Amish-woman mold, though his own mother was the same in many ways. Regardless, the fact that Olivia Mae was not married was not his business.

"I'm talking about your matchmaking."

"Oh, that."

"Yes, that."

"You've decided it's an important service?"

"It could be. I see that now."

"*Englischers* have dating sites and apps on their phones," she pointed out.

"I wouldn't know about that."

"Of course you wouldn't."

"I've never even owned a phone."

"Neither have I." She was grinning at him now.

If he didn't know better, he'd think that she enjoyed baiting him. He forced his eyes away from her adorable face and tried to remember what he'd wanted to tell her.

"Your *bruder* seems happy enough."

"He does. He is, and that's what I mean. You obviously do what you do very well."

"Danki."

"I just wanted to remind you that I'm not on the market."

"Oh, you made that quite clear."

Was she being serious? Or playing with him again? Looking back toward the barn, he saw that more people were leaving. He couldn't keep her here forever. He needed to try a more direct approach.

"I saw you talking to the two girls—the tall one and the heavy one."

"Do you mean Jane and Francine?"

"I guess."

"They're *freinden* of mine. We often talk to each other."

"I'm sure, but as soon as you sat down, and you three put your heads together, the heavier one looked over her shoulder at me."

"Did she, now?"

"You're going to deny it?"

"Deny what?"

"That you were talking to them about setting up a date with me."

"I could set you up with one of them." She tapped her chin and scrunched up her eyes as if she'd never considered such a thing. "But I thought you weren't interested."

Noah laughed out loud. "You are twisting what I'm saying every which way. I'm *not* interested. I told you I wasn't on Wednesday, and I'm still not. I wanted to make sure we're clear about that."

"Crystal."

"Gut."

"Gut."

Another awkward silence followed. She'd caved easier than he'd thought she would. He'd expected her to list the reasons that either girl would be a good match for him. Didn't she think he was dating material? Did she think he was too old or too set in his ways?

He didn't want to talk about that, but he wasn't ready to walk away, either.

"What do you call a sheep that knows karate?"

Olivia Mae rolled her eyes, but a grin was spreading across her face.

"I don't know, Noah. What do you call a sheep that knows karate?"

"A lamb chop."

He walked away then, the sound of her laughter ringing in his ears.

* * *

Unfortunately his good mood didn't last. His father insisted Noah ride up front in the buggy with him on the way home. His mother sat in the back, surrounded by grandchildren. For the first ten minutes, Noah actually enjoyed the ride. Then his *dat* cleared his throat and glanced his direction.

"You know we're glad you're home, son."

"But…"

"No *but*. Your mother and I want you to know that we are grateful to the Lord for bringing you back."

Perhaps he'd misjudged his *dat*'s intent. Maybe he'd anticipated a lecture when there wasn't one headed his way. Noah rested his head against the door and looked out over the Indiana farmland. "I'm glad to be back. Goshen seems…better in some ways. Instead of it feeling like a shoe that's too small, it feels like one that fits just right."

"That's *gut*, but…"

Noah tried to suppress a sigh, without success.

"Just hear me out."

"Of course, *Dat*." It wasn't as if he had a choice. They were still ten minutes from home. It would be childish to ask to be let out and walk, though the thought did cross his mind. Instead he sat up straighter and clasped his hands in front of him.

"I know you enjoy your auction work…"

"It's why I'm here."

"However, I'd like you to leave some time free to learn more about the farm."

"Why would I do that?"

"Because you never learned it as a *youngie*."

"I grew up doing farm chores."

"That's true, but a young man's real training begins about the time that you left—was it when you went to New York or Pennsylvania?" He waved away the question before Noah could answer it. "I want to teach you about farming because every young man needs to know how to plant, grow and harvest a crop."

"*Dat*, I'm not a farmer. I never have been a farmer, and I have no intention of becoming one in the future. I'm an auctioneer."

That statement sat between them as the mare clip-clopped down the road.

Noah could just make out his *mamm* saying something to his nieces, but he couldn't discern her exact words. At least she was preoccupied so that it wasn't two against one, not at this point.

"I appreciate your offer. I do. But times have changed—"

"Every man has to eat and farming is what we do. It's the Amish way."

"Not every Amish man farms. Some are farriers. Others are cabinetmakers."

"And you're an auctioneer."

"A *gut* one, too, if I say so myself."

"It's only that—to me—auctioneering seems like a hobby, not a way to support yourself."

Noah slouched down in his seat. He honestly didn't know how to make his *dat* understand. He didn't know how to explain that there were more opportunities available to Amish folk now. Working in the auction house could provide a good, steady income. It was only that it was different from work that his father's generation had done.

"There's one other thing."

"Of course there is."

"We understand it may seem awkward to date because you're late getting started."

"I dated…"

"And sometimes these things need a little help."

"I thought you were happy to have me at home. Now you're trying to scoot me out of the nest?"

"You're twenty-nine, son."

"I'm aware."

Noah glanced at his *dat*, noticed a furrow of lines between his eyes. He was obviously bound and determined to have his say.

"It's easy at your age to believe that you have an endless number of days in front of you—to plan, to decide, to marry. But that's not true. Every man and woman has a limited amount of time on this earth, and it's our responsibility to put those days to the best use."

"What does this have to do with dating?"

"I'd hate to see you waste the best years of your life."

"Waste them?"

"A family is a *wunderbaar* blessing."

"For most, yes, it is."

"Your *bruder* Justin needed a little help, and your *mamm* and I just want you to know that we see no shame in that."

"Now you're talking about Olivia Mae."

"She's a *gut* woman, and she has a real knack for putting the right people together. I was skeptical at first, too, but seeing the couples she's matched… Well, it's a real gift that she has."

Fortunately their farm had come into view.

Noah's shoulder muscles felt like two giant knots, and a headache was pounding at his temples. How could a twenty-minute ride with his parents make him so tense?

At least he was able to keep his mouth shut for the remainder of the ride. No use telling his father that he had no intention of being matched. No use pointing out the obvious—that his dating life wasn't anyone's business.

At least his mother hadn't chimed in with her two cents. The last thing he needed was more pressure.

They pulled to a stop in front of the house, the lecture delivered. The evening's chores still waited to be done—even on a Sunday. Horses still had to be fed, cows milked, goats checked. He actually looked forward to the escape of farm work, though it was not what he planned on doing for the rest of his life.

As he was helping the children out of the back seat, his mother stopped beside him, reached up and kissed him on the cheek. "Give it some thought, dear."

He stared after her as she climbed the front porch steps, a grandchild holding on to each hand.

Life was so simple for their generation, with everything laid out in black and white. But Noah had traveled enough to learn two very important things.

He was not, nor would he ever be, a farmer.

And given his dating history, which they knew nothing about, he also wasn't the marrying type.

The only problem would be convincing his family of that.

It took longer than Olivia Mae thought it would. Exactly ten days later, a familiar buggy pulled down their lane. She was out with the sheep, so instead of hurrying toward the house, she waved her arms over her head, hoping that Noah Graber had come to see her and not her grandparents. He turned the pretty sorrel buggy mare toward her, and pulled up next to the pasture fence. He hopped out and joined her, though she was standing on one side of the fence and he was on the other.

"Where are the rest?"

"Rest of what?"

"Rest of your sheep."

"Oh. This is all we have."

Noah pulled off his hat, held it up to block off the late-afternoon sun and made an exaggerated motion of counting her ewes. "Six?"

"Ya."

"You have six sheep."

"I do, as you've so accurately counted."

"Why couldn't the little lamb play outside?"

Olivia waited, both dreading and looking forward to the punch line.

"It was being ba-a-aaad!" As she shook her head in mock disgust, he plopped the hat back on his head and crossed his arms across the top board of the wooden fence. "I honestly don't know a thing about sheep."

"Though you do know a lot of jokes."

"Tell me about your flock."

She didn't think he was asking for their names, though she had named them all. Instead she simply offered, "They're Lincoln sheep."

"I don't know what that means."

"They're large, as you can see. Ewes can weigh from two hundred to two hundred and fifty pounds."

"I thought they were just fat."

She slapped his arm. "Rams can get up to three hundred and fifty. They're a *gut* sheep to have if you're raising them for their fleece. Lincoln sheep are very long-wooled."

"I can see that."

Olivia Mae laughed. "Wait until you see them just before shearing. This is nothing."

"So you sell their fleece?"

"*Ya*, it's quite popular for spinning and weaving."

"Why do you only have six?"

Olivia Mae shrugged. Though she didn't want to go into it, she understood that making small talk made Noah comfortable, so she played along. "We lost two to predators…"

"Predators?"

"Probably a coyote. That was in January, and then we had another two that wandered off into the road during a late snowstorm in March. I check the fencing regularly, but they'd somehow found a way through. It was a hard winter."

"I'll say. So you had ten, which doesn't sound like very many, and now you're down to six."

"My initial plan was to slowly build the herd, but… sometimes life doesn't work out like you plan."

"Said with the wisdom of a matchmaker."

She waited.

"Speaking of that…"

"Of what?"

He tossed a look her way and smiled. Good teeth.

Wait. Did she just assess his teeth? That was terrible. But good oral hygiene was a plus in the dating world.

"Speaking of *matchmaking*, I have a problem that I was hoping you could help me with."

"Is that so?"

"My family is driving me crazy."

"Huh."

"My *dat* wants me to learn to farm."

"I thought you were an auctioneer."

"My *bruders* are all up in my business."

"Aggravating."

"But it's my *mamm* that is pushing me over the edge."

Olivia Mae knew that his mother was a sweet, if concerned, woman. After all, they'd had a good long talk on Monday, when Olivia Mae had taken over a blanket for Sarah's child. The baby wasn't due for another four months, so it had been perhaps obvious that she was making up a reason to visit, but Sarah had been thrilled with the knitted receiving blanket—yellow and green, made from Olivia Mae's own wool, and with a small sheep motif running across the edge.

Of course, she'd picked a morning when she was sure Noah would be at the auction house, and was it her fault that his mother, Erika, had brought up finding a match for Noah? Olivia Mae thought it was a completely natural concern. She might have suggested that Erika make a deal with Noah.

"You're awfully quiet over there," Noah said.

"Am I?"

"Where do sheep take a bath?"

"Let me guess…"

"In a ba-a-athtub," they said together.

She really did need to get him to focus or they'd be here all day. And while his jokes were cute, she had to see to *Daddi* and *Mammi* soon. "You were telling me about your *mamm*."

"She offered me a deal."

"Did she, now?"

"Her deal, or suggestion, is that I give you three chances."

"Excuse me?"

"Three chances to…you know." He twirled his finger in a circle. "Do what you do."

When she only raised her eyebrows, he laughed. "It's like you need to hear me say it."

"I do need to hear you say it. I can't read your mind."

"*Mamm* suggested that if I give you three chances to find me a suitable girl, which I guess you'd be happy to do—"

"Of course I would."

"And if by some chance those three girls don't work out—"

"No reason why one of them wouldn't."

"Then she and *Dat* will leave me alone."

"Leave you alone to—"

"Live my life in peace." This last sentence he practically growled.

Olivia Mae scratched the ewe closest to her between the ears, made her way out of the gate, being careful to latch it securely behind her, and finally turned her attention to Noah.

"I'm not sure that will work."

"What?"

"It sounds as if you're being coerced."

"*Coerced?* Who uses words like that? Did you read them in a book?"

"What book?"

"I don't know what book. I suppose you read *Englisch* romances. That's why you're so keen on this whole true-love business."

"I will admit to having a few sheep magazines as well as some books of knitting patterns. I don't have a lot of time for reading, though I do enjoy it when I have the rare hour to myself. I might have read a novel or two last winter when the weather was too bad to accomplish any work outside."

"Look, I'm not being coerced. I'm being worn down."

"Is there a difference?"

"I don't know."

The look on his face was so miserable that Olivia Mae couldn't help but feel a little pity for him.

"Nice sorrel," she said, walking up to the reddish-brown mare and allowing it to smell her. She then reached into her pocket for a carrot. "What's her name?"

"Snickers—like the candy bar."

She scratched the mare between her ears, causing it to nicker softly.

"Do you do that a lot?"

"What?"

"Take care of things—sheep, horses, people."

He'd stepped closer and she could smell the soap he'd used, and other things probably from the auction house—old wood and leather and some kind of oil. What was that like? To spend your day selling off people's memories? Maybe she was thinking of it wrongly. Maybe what he did was the ultimate recycling—making old things new again. She looked up at him and smiled, then took a step back.

"What did you mean when you said you're not sure it will work? Would I be such a challenge for you to match up?"

"Most people come to me wanting to find a suitable husband or wife."

"Ya."

"You're practically saying you hope it won't work."

The smile on his face grew. She hadn't known Noah Graber long, but already she knew him well enough to worry when he smiled that way. A girl could fall for that kind of charm, and she made it a point not to harbor romantic feelings about someone she was trying to match.

"You don't think you can do it."

"What?" Her voice came out like a screech owl. She smoothed down her apron and lowered her voice. "Why would you say that?"

"I'm too big a challenge for you."

"Oh, please. I've matched worse—" She almost said *misfits.* "I've matched more stubborn bachelors than you."

"Is that so?"

"It is."

"But younger, I'll bet."

"Matched a thirty-two-year-old last fall."

"Widower?"

"I don't see what difference that makes." She did. Of course she did. The widower had wanted a wife. He was desperately lonely, struggling to raise five children on his own and willing to do whatever she suggested.

No need to share all of those details with Noah Graber, though.

"Clearly this is what your *mamm* wants—"

"And my *dat*, my *bruders*, my sisters-in-law—even
the bishop."

"Lucas has spoken to you?"

Instead of answering that, he said, "Dating may not
be my primary concern, but I'll play along."

"How do I know that you won't sabotage my efforts?"

"Because I'm giving you my word that I won't."

The growl was back. Noah Graber was the full package—tall, handsome, hardworking and with just enough
humility to care that he not be called a liar.

She wiped her hands on her apron and then stuck
them in her pockets.

"Fine."

"You'll do it?"

"I will."

She began walking toward the house. Noah tagged
along beside her, as she'd known he would. Just like
teasing a fish with bait, she thought. Good thing *Daddi*
had taught her how to fish.

"What happens next?"

She stopped suddenly. "I'll call you."

"You'll call me?"

"Phone shack to phone shack, of course."

"I thought you'd just…give me a name or something."

"I need to think on it, prayerfully consider the situation. You wouldn't want me to rush."

"Kind of, I do." He rolled his eyes when she stared up at him. "As soon as this is over—"

"You'll be able to live your life in peace. I heard you the first time."

"I give you my word that I'm not going to sabotage anything, but you'll see." The grin was back. "I'm not the marrying type."

"You're not?"

"And as soon as this is over, I can get on with my life, establish my reputation as an auctioneer and hopefully make enough to buy a bachelor place."

She could have argued any one of those points. Instead she smiled again—what she hoped was a sincere smile and not one that conveyed how much she'd like to pick up the bucket of water sitting on the front porch and dump it over his head. Anything to erase that condescending grin on his face.

"Great. I'll call when I have some ideas."

And without a backward glance, she hurried up the porch steps and into the house.

Chapter Four

"She still hasn't called?"

Noah and Justin were eating lunch at the Subway sandwich shop in Shipshewana. He had two hours before the next auction, so when his brother had shown up, it had seemed like a good idea. Now he wasn't so sure.

"I already told you that."

"You told me that yesterday."

"And the day before."

"Did you check the recorder at the phone shack today, on your way into work?"

"I did."

"And still nothing?"

"Only a message for Widow King. Something about a crate of baby chicks she'd ordered."

Justin bit into his meatball sub and stared up at the ceiling as he chewed, as if he'd find the answer to their current puzzle written there.

Finally he dropped the sandwich onto the wrapper and admitted, "It only took two days for Olivia Mae to match me with Sarah."

"Two days?"

"Longer for us to court and all, but it only took two days from the time I first visited Olivia Mae. Does she still have that scrawny herd of sheep?"

"If you can call six a herd."

"I wonder what's up with that."

The bell over the door rang and a trio of Amish girls walked in.

"Maybe she needs to cast her net wider." His brother nodded toward the girls. "Plenty of fish here in Ship-she."

"Those aren't fish. They're girls."

"Women."

"And I don't think I specified a geographic location."

"Maybe you should, though. Maybe let her know it doesn't have to be a Goshen girl. Could be we have a shortage or something."

Noah didn't want to talk about his dating life—or his lack of one. He focused on finishing his sandwich, and thought they had moved on from the subject when his brother crossed his arms, sat back and cleared his throat.

"What happened to you?"

"What do you mean?"

"While you were gone. When you were on your extended *rumspringa…*" He waved toward the window. "Wandering all those years."

Noah shrugged. "I don't know what you're asking exactly."

"'Course you do. You just don't want to talk about it."

"If you're so astute, why bother me at all?"

"Because I think you need to talk about it. I think

whatever happened out there, it's going to follow you here unless you work through it."

"You sound like Bishop Lucas."

Instead of responding to that, to the fact that their bishop had already asked the same question, Justin plowed on.

"It was hard on *Mamm* and *Dat*, you know—your being gone, them not knowing when or if you were moving back."

"I don't need a lecture from you, little *bruder.*"

"And I don't intend to deliver one. Just making sure you're aware."

"Oh, I'm aware."

"*Mamm* probably thinks if you met a girl and married that you'd settle down, that you wouldn't leave again. That's her biggest fear at this point."

"I am settled down—married or single. I'm here to stay, Justin. I'm home, and I don't plan on leaving."

Justin searched his eyes for a minute and apparently found the assurance he needed. "*Gut.* I'd like my son or daughter to know their *onkel* Noah."

With that image planted firmly in his mind, all of Noah's defensiveness melted away. He wanted to be there when Justin's child was born. He wanted to watch all of his nieces and nephews grow up. In truth, he had missed his family more than he'd realized. How many nights had he gone to sleep in a strange town, knowing no one and depending on the kindness of strangers? How many times had he lain there envisioning his father's farm and wishing he was back in Goshen?

His pride had kept him away. He could see that now. In the end, he'd returned home because he didn't know where else to go, but he was staying because he realized this was where he wanted to be.

They finished their meal, threw their trash onto the tray, dumped it into the nearby trash can and refilled their drinks. Stepping outside, he relaxed. He loved working in Shipshewana, loved how busy it had become and yet it still managed to remain Plain in so many ways.

Sure there were *Englisch* vehicles, but there were also buggies in every direction he looked.

There were *Englisch* tourists—many probably there for the auction—but there were still plenty of Amish folk, as well.

Englisch restaurants abounded, but Jojo's Pretzels and Amish Frozen Custard were as busy as ever.

In short, northern Indiana was what he'd been looking for all along. It was a place where Plain could live beside *Englisch*. They didn't have to worry about ordinances that would require them to diaper their horses. They didn't have to be concerned about becoming less Amish, if there was such a thing.

He could be happy here. He could be content. If only his parents could understand that marriage wasn't for everyone.

If only they'd let him be.

As the brothers were walking back down the road to the auction house, Noah decided maybe Justin would be a good person to vent to. Maybe his brother would realize he was right and tell his mother to cancel the deal they'd made. Already he was regretting it. There had been something about the glint in Olivia Mae's eyes that made him uncomfortable.

It wasn't that he thought she would find the perfect match, but there was a marked look of determination in her eyes. He didn't want to be her pet project.

If he'd been pressed, he would have admitted that he didn't believe there was someone out there for him. Hadn't his past proven that? But between his mother and Olivia Mae, he was in for several weeks, maybe even months, of misery before they understood the futility of what they were attempting to do.

He needed someone on his side—someone who understood his position. Noah glanced back at the sandwich shop and then nudged Justin. "Those girls back there were very young—too young."

"For what?"

"For marrying."

"They looked old enough to me. One was carrying a *boppli*."

"Could have been a niece or nephew."

"They didn't seem too young to me."

"Seventeen, maybe eighteen." Noah jerked the hat off his head and ran his fingers through his hair. "I'm twenty-nine. That's part of the problem."

"Why is that a problem?"

"Because I've never been married before." He rammed the hat back on his head. "I'm like…"

"A freak?"

"An anomaly."

"Whatever."

"Think of me like a horse."

"A horse?"

Noah was warming up to this analogy. His brother

had worked around horses all his life. This was something he would be able to relate to and understand.

"Say you found out a horse was for sale, a buggy horse. Only when you went to see it, the horse had never been hitched to a buggy."

"How old is this horse?"

"I don't know. Say it's six years old."

"So a third of its life."

"More or less."

"I get it. You're nearly thirty, which is probably a third of your life."

"Exactly."

"And you've never been hitched to a buggy before."

"Now you understand."

"Is that it?"

"What do you mean?"

"Is that all you've got?"

"I'm just saying there's a reason Olivia Mae hasn't called. There's a reason this whole stupid plan isn't going to work. Old bachelors like myself... Well, young girls aren't interested in us. And everyone else is married."

"What about widows?"

"What about them?"

"Well, every community has a few."

"So you want me to have an instant family?"

"Nothing wrong with it. And the woman would be older, like you and that hypothetical horse."

"Widows are old."

"Not always."

"Even a young widow doesn't want a thirty-year-old who's never—"

"Been hitched to a buggy?"

They'd reached the auction house, and Noah wasn't sure he'd made one bit of progress. His mood plummeted as he realized the uselessness of trying to explain his way of life to his brother. Justin, however, looked thoroughly entertained.

"That was a good story."

"It wasn't a story so much as it was a comparison."

"*Ya.* I get it. I'm just not buying it."

"Meaning…"

"Meaning I know you, and you're hoping that Olivia Mae won't find anyone, but you're also afraid that she will."

With a slap on his back, Justin turned and walked off to where he'd parked his buggy. As Noah headed back into the auction barn, he slowed down to look at the advertisements.

Midwest's Largest Flea Market!
Shipshewana * Trading Place * est. 1922
We love Shipshewana, Indiana, USA
The Heart of Amish Country

He loved everything about the auction house. It, too, was full of Amish and *Englisch*. He knew the serious bidders by name, even after less than three weeks. From the group of *Englischers* he was able to distinguish between those there to bid and the ones who were stopping to watch.

Checking in at the office, he made sure of where he was supposed to be. They had him scheduled for half a dozen auctions that afternoon—proof that the boss was pleased with his work. They'd scheduled him in the livestock barn, which normally he would have enjoyed. Instead, with every group of animals, he kept thinking of Olivia Mae's pitiful herd of sheep.

Should he buy her the smaller Dorper sheep? Their black faces and white wool would make her smile. Did she even want more sheep? Was she getting into or out of the business? Why was he even thinking about her?

The next auction was goats, followed by donkeys. Hadn't she said she'd lost two sheep to predators? A donkey could help protect her herd, keep it from dwindling more. Somehow he continued calling out the bids, joking with the crowd, moving the animals through the pen, but his thoughts weren't focused completely on his work. Instead they pinged around like popcorn in a hot skillet.

Twice he closed a bid while people still had their hands raised. He needed to pay attention, but that wasn't so easy because his mind kept straying back to the woman who was searching for the love of his life. Why had he agreed to his mother's ridiculous deal? Why put himself through the humiliation?

Why hadn't Olivia Mae called?

Before the afternoon was half-done, he'd made up his mind that he'd stop by the phone shack again on the way home. If she hadn't called yet, he'd stop thinking about it. If he was fortunate, maybe she would have decided to call the whole thing off. Whatever Olivia Mae's decision, he was ready to get this over with. Honestly, it was worse than waiting for a dentist appointment.

Olivia Mae waited until Friday to contact Jane, and then she insisted they meet in person. They managed to get together that afternoon. Sitting on the front porch of Jane's home, or rather her parents' home, Olivia Mae couldn't help wondering what eligible man wouldn't want to be a part of her friend's life.

The fields were well tended, the barn in good shape, crops were coming in well and Jane's parents were genuinely nice people. The only problem was they'd had four other daughters, all of whom had married easily and at a young age. They didn't understand what was wrong with their Jane.

That's what her mother had said to Olivia Mae when she'd arrived at the house. "Are you here to set her up? Because we don't understand what's wrong with our Jane." The woman's demeanor suggested nothing but parental love. The family didn't fight, no one had a drug or alcohol problem, and none of the girls had gone through much of a *rumspringa*. Olivia Mae knew this firsthand because she'd gone to school with all of the older girls. Jane, being six years younger, had been in second grade the year that Olivia Mae had finished eighth.

She pushed away that uncomfortable thought.

After assuring Jane's mother that there was nothing wrong with Jane, she'd waited on the front porch. Best to do this away from curious ears, even if those ears were well-meaning.

Twenty minutes later, Jane had joined her and listened to her suggestions, but she still wasn't convinced.

"I thought he wasn't interested," Jane repeated.

They'd been through this once, but apparently Olivia Mae's assurances hadn't calmed her fears.

"It's his *mamm*'s idea for him to allow me to try to

make a match, but Noah agreed to it. If he agreed to it, then I think somewhere in his heart he wants it."

Jane nodded, but she didn't answer right away. Jane was a talker, so Olivia Mae wasn't sure how to interpret her silence. She repeatedly smoothed the apron covering her dress, and finally turned and looked at Olivia Mae directly.

"Is this it?"

"What do you mean?"

"Is it my last chance?"

"Of course not."

"Because I'm twenty-one."

"I'm twenty-seven." Olivia Mae tried not to take offense. It was true that most in their community considered someone past the age of twenty-five to be a late bloomer. And thirty? Well, by thirty most people simply accepted that the loved one wouldn't ever marry. Noah was dangerously close to that age, but Olivia Mae wasn't going to let that stop her.

"It's only that my *schweschdern*, they all married young, and my *mamm*, she worries. I even heard her talking to my *dat* the other night, asking how I would run the farm when they're gone, as if they're going to stride through the pearly gates any day now. They're not even sick. They're only in their fifties, and many people live to be older than that. Widow King turned ninety-one this year, and I think she's related to us in some convoluted way. Once my *mamm* told me..."

This was the Jane that Olivia Mae knew—a chatterbox with a propensity to worry. It was something they were working on. Olivia Mae sat forward and claimed Jane's hands in her own.

"Take a deep breath."

"Okay." She inhaled.

"Blow it out."

She rolled her eyes, but did as requested and exhaled.

"Relax your shoulders."

As she did, she sat up straighter and set the rocker slowly in motion.

"Feel better?"

"Ya."

"Jane, I know what it is like to be Amish. I am Amish. I understand the pressure you feel, but I want you to understand your worth as a person—as a single woman. *Gotte* has a plan and a purpose for your life, whether it includes a husband and children or not."

"I know." Her voice was small, tentative. She bowed her head and pulled in a deep breath, and then sat up even straighter. "I know that. I believe that, it's only… it's only that I want a husband and I want children."

"Wunderbaar. If that is the desire of your heart, then I believe that *Gotte* will provide a way." As an afterthought, she added, "But let's not spring all of that on Noah at once."

Jane nodded, and then she began to laugh, and then Olivia Mae started laughing. It took five minutes to pull the conversation back on course.

"I'll call Noah day after tomorrow."

"Sunday?"

"Ya."

"Not tonight?"

"Nein. I think it would be better if we wait. I'd rather your first date not be on a Friday or Saturday."

"Okay." Jane didn't ask why.

Olivia Mae understood that in matters of the *when* and *where* and *how* of dating, the girls she worked with trusted her to make good decisions.

"I think Tuesday would be good."

"Next Tuesday?"

"Less than a week away."

"That's true. What should I wear?"

"Your favorite thing, the thing that makes you smile when you pull it off the hanger."

"I only have four dresses and five aprons, but I do have that sweater you knitted me..."

"From the variegated blue yarn. It's lightweight and it matches your eyes nicely."

"I hardly ever wear it. I don't want people to think I'm putting on airs, but if we go out Tuesday night, well, there is a chill in the air on May evenings."

"Indeed there is."

Olivia Mae stood and started down the steps. When she looked back at Jane, she realized suddenly how much she liked her, how in some ways Jane and all the women she helped seemed like the younger sisters she'd never had. So instead of leaving, she walked back up the steps and squatted in front of Jane.

"We don't know—we can't know—if Noah is the man that *Gotte* intends for you."

Surprisingly Jane didn't interrupt.

"But we do know He has a plan, and we can trust Him. So Tuesday night, remember this isn't on you. It's not about what you do right or wrong. It's about finding out if Noah Graber is the man that *Gotte* intends for you to marry, and maybe you won't even know that right away. But I want you to just enjoy yourself, okay?"

For her answer, Jane leaned forward and enfolded Olivia Mae in a hug, reminding her again of the sister she'd never had.

Chapter Five

Olivia Mae loved that they only had church every other Sunday. On the off Sundays, she missed the hymns and the prayers and even the singing. But she loved the extra time that they had to rest and simply be with one another. Plus the gatherings on their off Sundays were usually small.

She didn't have to call Noah to tell him about his upcoming date because they ended up at the same family gathering on Sunday—this time at Bishop Lucas's house. Since *Mammi* and *Daddi* had no other relatives in the area, they often spent the Sundays when they didn't have church at the bishop's. It had started with Atlee and continued with Lucas. Olivia Mae was a tad surprised to see Noah and his family there, but she shouldn't have been. It was just that he had such a large family, so she figured they'd always meet at his parents' house.

"My *bruders* are spread out," he explained. "Samuel, Justin and George live here, but it was their week to visit their in-laws. My other two *bruders* live in Middlebury—close enough to visit a few times a month, but not usually on a Sunday."

"Which means your parents were home alone."

"Not completely. I was there." He grinned at her sheepishly. "But I'm not the best company."

"And why is that?"

"I don't want to hear the stories they've told a hundred times. I'd rather be up and moving about than sitting in a rocker. Every conversation seems to lead to a lecture. Take your pick of reasons."

They were walking through the bishop's back pasture. Olivia Mae was picking a bouquet of wildflowers—tiny clumps of blue-eyed Mary, the occasional pasture rose with its yellow center and something her mother had called bird's-foot violet. The memory made her smile. How she missed her parents, but it seemed that reminders of them were everywhere.

She gathered the flowers for *Mammi*, who claimed to enjoy the sight and smell of them. The small bouquets certainly brightened up the house considerably, and they cost nothing. Their house could use some brightening. Three new holes in the roof had shown up with the last rainstorm. Olivia Mae needed to think of a way to fix that, or she could hope they wouldn't have any more pouring rains. The lighter showers didn't seem to work their way through the roof.

"Where did you go?" Noah asked.

"Go?"

"I lost you there for a minute. I was complaining about my parents in a very entertaining way and you just…" He interlocked his thumbs and mimed a bird flying away.

Instead of boring him with details of how her grandparents' home was falling apart, she opted to change the subject.

"I was trying to think how best to tell you that I have a date for you."

He stopped in the middle of the field and crossed his arms. She thought that would make a pretty picture, if she had a camera or could even sketch. Most Amish didn't own a camera, though of course some on their *rumspringa* did. Sketching was allowed, but any artists among them usually stuck to landscapes. Still, Olivia Mae couldn't help thinking that Noah Graber looked like something in a picture, in his Sunday best, crossing his arms—a scowl on his face and wildflowers at his feet.

"We've been talking for a while. You could have led with that."

"Her name is Jane. She is a friend of mine."

"One of the girls you were sitting with?"

"Yes."

"Tall or chubby?"

She fisted her hands on her hips and scowled at him. "If that's your attitude…"

"I'm kidding. Relax. You take this thing very seriously, you know."

He walked over to a bunch of buttercups, pulled three out of the ground and handed them to her. "Peace offering?"

"I'm serious, Noah." She accepted the flowers, but kept her gaze on him. "These women are *freinden* of mine, and they deserve your respect."

"Why are women so sensitive?" The expression on his face told her that it was a serious question. "If we were looking at horses, it would be okay for me to ask about the tall one or the chubby one."

"Women are not horses."

"When I'm auctioning items, it's okay for me to describe things in details. It's what I'm supposed to do."

"But you would say *antique*, not *old*. You would say *lovingly worn*, not *falling apart*. You would speak kindly."

He grunted in reply.

They crossed the pasture and stopped at the fence line, where more flowers grew in abundance. It was a fine May day, and Olivia Mae should feel happy and excited that she'd found a possible match for Noah, and for Jane. Instead she felt worried.

"Jane is tall, yes."

"Do you know how many times I've been set up with the tall *schweschder*?"

"I wasn't aware you'd ever been set up before."

"When I was younger. Everyone seemed to think that tall people wanted to be around other tall people—like we were a tribe or something."

Olivia Mae craned her head back to get a good look at his face. "Do you dislike being tall?"

"Of course not. What good would it do? A giraffe doesn't dislike having a long neck."

"A giraffe?" She shook her head at the absurdity of their conversations. "Let's refocus. Jane is self-conscious about her height."

"She didn't look that tall."

"And yet beside other women, she's always the tallest, and some men—I won't mention names—have said disparaging things, perhaps because they were short and felt uncomfortable beside her."

"I won't call her Big Bird."

"Did you watch a lot of *Englisch* television as a child?"

"*Nein*. But I helped to build an addition on to a day-care center once, and just before nap time they'd play shows for the kids. Kind of gets stuck in your head."

"Another *gut* reason not to have a television."

"We can agree on that."

"Jane is available to go out with you on Tuesday."

"I thought you'd say Friday. Don't most dates take place on Friday?"

"Tuesday works better." She didn't explain her reasoning. "I suggest you take her to dinner in town."

"I'm not made of money, you know."

"You're living with your parents, and you're earning money at the auction house."

"True enough, but I'm saving up for my own place. It seems a waste of good money to go out to dinner when I could…"

"What? Let Jane cook for you?"

"I didn't—"

"Or maybe you'd planned on rustling up a meal on your own."

"That would be a terrible idea. I've been known to burn toast."

"Did you want to take her home to your parents and let your *mamm* cook for her?"

"*Nein. Mamm*'s a *gut* cook, but she'd be asking her about *grandkinner* before we made it to dessert." Noah scrubbed a hand across his face. "This is the problem with dating. There are too many details."

He looked truly frustrated—almost miserable if she wasn't mistaken, and that was not the way she wanted this date to begin. So she reached out and touched his arm. He stared down at her hand, then into her eyes.

Olivia Mae jerked her hand away, feeling as if she'd dared to touch a hot stove. "Dating can feel overwhelming at first. Think of it as an investment."

He snorted.

"If you want a relationship you have to be willing to spend the time and a little money."

"Fine."

"And it's a chance to enjoy yourself. You work hard. One dinner out a week isn't such an extravagance."

"We're supposed to do this every week?"

She hoped he was kidding, but one look at his face told her he was quite serious.

Olivia Mae jerked a few more flowers out of the ground, decided her bouquet was large enough and turned back toward the group of old folks enjoying the May afternoon. "Let's just deal with this one week at a time. Take Jane somewhere that you like. It'll help her to learn more about you."

She pulled a piece of paper out of her pocket and handed it to him. "Pick her up at five thirty."

She'd written Jane's name, address and the number to the nearest phone shack. At the bottom she'd penciled in a list of things to remember and added a note that read "Girls love flowers." It was what she did with every new match. Sometimes men needed a little prodding in the right direction. She had a feeling Noah Graber was going to require something much more obvious, like a good solid push.

* * *

Noah had thrown away Olivia Mae's list. Who needed instructions on how to go on a date? He wasn't a child. Noah had left home feeling confident that a relationship with Jane wouldn't work, but for mysterious reasons, not because he was going to mess it up. He did not plan to sabotage this. In fact, he thought that he'd done everything right.

Maybe Olivia Mae didn't know what she was doing, because he'd certainly met her expectations. He'd done it all except for the flowers, which, honestly, he had forgotten completely about.

Pick Jane up on Tuesday night—check.

Take Jane to his favorite place—check.

Don't mention Jane's height—check!

So why had the night felt like such a failure? Who was he kidding? It didn't just feel like a failure, it *was* a failure. He could tell as much by the way that Jane had stopped attempting to make conversation and sat quietly in the buggy with her hands clutched in her lap. When he had pulled up to her parents' house, she had murmured "good night" while still staring at her hands and literally fled inside without a backward glance.

He'd stewed over the situation while he was at work on Wednesday.

He'd vowed he wouldn't think about it while he worked around the farm on Thursday.

But on Friday he couldn't stand it any longer. This was Olivia Mae's fault. Why did people think she was a *wunderbaar* matchmaker? She was terrible! She was probably too embarrassed to call him, so it was up to him to call her—or better yet, stop by after work and see her.

It occurred to him as he rode the bus back to Goshen that perhaps he was worrying for nothing. Just maybe Olivia Mae would be ready to admit defeat and call off the entire deal. He changed into his everyday clothes and hitched up the buggy. Maybe she was ready to surrender! That thought cheered him immensely as he drove the buggy toward her house.

Olivia Mae was in the pasture tending to her buggy horse when he arrived. Standing ten feet away, looking dolefully at what she was doing, was a brown jenny mule. Good thing he hadn't bought her one of the donkeys at the auction.

He'd planned to start right in on discussing the date, but instead he asked, "Why the mule?"

Olivia Mae glanced up, then turned her attention back to the horse, brushing through its mane and stroking it with her other hand. "We only have the one horse."

"So?"

"Horses are social animals. This one was showing signs of depression."

"Horses get depressed?"

Instead of answering, she asked, "Are you sure you grew up Amish?"

He waved away her question. "That date you set me up on was a disaster."

"So I heard."

"What's that supposed to mean?"

"Jane came by Wednesday morning."

"And said what? I did everything that you told me to do."

"Oh, really?" She pointed the currycomb at him. "You promised me you wouldn't intentionally mess this up."

"I didn't."

He jerked his straw hat off his head, slapped it against his leg and then put it back on.

"I did not intentionally mess anything up," he said in a calmer voice. "Like every other date I've been on, it seemed to start out okay and then slid rapidly downhill."

"Maybe we should talk about your dating history."

"Maybe we shouldn't." He walked away from her then, because he couldn't stand the look of confusion on her face.

He didn't want to explain about Cora or Samantha or Ida.

Three different women from three different states.

Three different relationships that he thought might have been the one.

Three different kinds of disaster.

He didn't want to relive the humiliation and regret and guilt. He was home now and those experiences were behind him. All he wanted was a fresh start. All he wanted to do was be an auctioneer.

Of course, he had agreed to only three dates.

Maybe he was looking at this all wrong. Maybe he should be relieved the date with Jane was such a disaster. Two more nights of humiliation and his family would leave him alone. He'd be free to pursue his dream of being a successful auctioneer without wasting time and money on something that wasn't ever going to happen. He could start searching for his bachelor pad. In fact, he should purchase a paper on the way home and scan the for-sale ads. The thought cheered him immensely.

He turned back toward the pasture, nearly plowed into Olivia Mae and took a step back. "Didn't realize you were done with the horse."

"Why don't we go to the porch, have some lemonade and talk about this?"

He wasn't sure he liked the idea of having an extended conversation about Tuesday night. Then again, the thought of sitting on the front porch with Olivia Mae sipping fresh lemonade didn't sound terrible.

Glancing at her, he realized that she looked tired and a little defeated. Where was the spunky girl he'd met when he first brought over the letter box? Maybe the situation with her grandparents was difficult emotionally and physically. Maybe she needed to go out on a date—take a teaspoonful of her own medicine. The thought brought a smile to his lips, and then he remembered one of the jokes he'd memorized for her.

"Why was the sheep arrested on the freeway?"

"Oh, Noah…"

"Because she did a ewe-turn."

She didn't laugh out loud, but he thought maybe her shoulders looked less bunched up. That animal-joke book he'd bought in the gift shop next to the auction house was definitely worth what he'd paid for it.

Olivia Mae's grandmother insisted on bringing them two large glasses of lemonade as well as a plate of cookies.

"Danki," he said.

"Gem Gschehne." She smiled broadly at him, the skin around her eyes folding into a patchwork of wrin-

kles. He could see the similarity then—between Olivia Mae and Rachel. Their eyes were shaped the same and they both had brilliant smiles. "I hope you're enjoying Goshen."

"Oh, *ya*. I like Goshen fine." He almost added, "it's the meddling I hate," but since it was her granddaughter in charge of the meddling, that might sound a bit rude. So instead he raised the glass, sipped the cold drink and smacked his lips together. "*Gut* lemonade."

"Olivia Mae made it. She's a *wunderbaar* cook. You should try her fried chicken."

"Actually I had some at the church luncheon."

"And her pot roast is *gut*, too. Then there's the cakes she bakes—"

"Stop talking about me as if I'm not sitting right here." Olivia Mae nodded toward the living room. "*Danki* for the drinks, *Mammi*. We don't want to keep you from what you were doing."

Instead of being offended, her *mammi* laughed and said, "That's my signal to leave."

When she'd gone inside, he noticed the melancholy expression return to Olivia Mae's face. "Your *mammi* seems very nice."

"She's the best. Both her and *Daddi* are."

Suddenly she wouldn't look at him directly. Something was up, but he couldn't imagine what it was. The older couple seemed healthy enough from what he'd seen of them on Sunday. Was there something she hadn't shared yet? Why was she living here alone with her grandparents? And how hard was that?

Did Olivia Mae have trouble asking for help?

"Where do your parents live?"

"They died—ten years ago in a car accident." She rubbed the heel of her palm against her chest, though she seemed unaware that she was doing it. "You hear how dangerous buggies are, but they were in a van that they'd hired to take them to see relatives in the southern part of the state. An oncoming vehicle crossed the line, pushing them into a concrete barrier. They were killed instantly."

"I'm so sorry." It sounded like a stupid thing to say, and he regretted it immediately.

"Their life was complete."

She smoothed out the apron over her dress. It was a somber gray. He wondered why she always dressed like that. The blue sweater that Jane had worn on their date would have looked beautiful on Olivia Mae. Hadn't Jane told her that Olivia Mae had made it? Yet her own clothing was always so…plain. He pushed the thought from his mind, choosing to focus on the beautiful May afternoon, the sheep in the pasture in front of them and the tart sweetness of the lemonade.

Olivia Mae had other ideas. "Let's go back over what happened."

"I don't see how that will help."

"When did you pick Jane up?"

"Before dinner, like you said. I guess it was…" He stared up at the roof of the porch. "Six, maybe six thirty. Could have been closer to seven."

"We agreed on five thirty."

"What difference does it make?"

"The difference it makes is that Jane was sitting on her front porch waiting for you for nearly an hour and a half. That's a long time for her to wonder if you had perhaps changed your mind."

"I would never do that."

"Punctuality is a sign of respect."

"Look, I would have been on time, but my *dat* insisted that I walk out with him to look at the fields. He's clinging to the long-cherished idea that I'm going to wake up one day and have a sudden desire to take up farming. By the time we got back to the house, and I changed clothes and harnessed the horse, it was already six thirty. Then I lost the sheet with her directions and had to go back inside and ask my *mamm* for directions."

"You could have told your *dat* that you had other plans and that you'd be happy to go with him in the fields another time."

"I guess. In truth, it's easier to tag along when he asks rather than argue with him." He honestly did not see what the big deal was, and he said as much to Olivia Mae, but she started shaking her head before he was even finished.

"What time does your auction begin?"

"What?"

"Your auction. What time does it start?"

"What does that have to do with my dating?"

"Just humor me."

"I had three on Monday and four on Wednesday. Today I had nine." He couldn't help feeling proud that the auction house was giving him more responsibility, and he was relieved that Olivia Mae had moved on to a different subject. Talking about work was easier than discussing his feelings about dating. "On Mondays my lots start at ten, two and four."

"On the nose?"

"What? *Ya.* Of course. It would be unprofessional to start late."

Instead of responding, she stared at him, eyebrows raised, like a schoolteacher who was waiting for him to catch on to a lesson.

He dropped his head into his hands and tried to re-play her words in his mind. But instead of hearing what she'd said, he kept seeing her watching him, that small smile playing across her pink lips. Finally he glanced up and admitted, "I have no idea what point you're try-ing to make."

"Noah, think about it. You would never consider starting an auction late because it would be rude to the people coming to bid on the items."

"Eventually they'd stop coming to my auctions, then I wouldn't sell anything, and soon after that I'd be fired."

"Exactly. In the same way it's rude to show up an hour and a half late for a date."

"But a date isn't an auction." He guzzled the rest of the lemonade and then growled, "Women are so dif-ferent from men."

"Why do you say that?"

"I wouldn't care if my brother showed up late to go fishing."

"Then perhaps women are different than men."

She took another sip of the lemonade, and he sud-denly wondered what it would be like to kiss her.

Whoa.

Where had that come from?

She was the matchmaker, not the match.

"Why aren't you married?"

"What?" Olivia Mae's eyes widened.

"No offense, but if you're so good at this, why aren't you married yourself? Why haven't you found *your* perfect match?"

"We're not talking about me right now. We're talking about you. Now, why did you take her to a gas station for dinner?"

"It wasn't a gas station! Well, I mean they do sell gas, but they also have a *wunderbaar* barbecue place on the side. It's this little trailer, and there are wooden benches set up on the concrete pad—"

She held up a hand to stop him. "Most women don't enjoy eating at an establishment that sells fuel—"

"What does that have to do with the price of oats?"

"They want a nice dinner out or a romantic picnic."

"A romantic picnic?" He snorted. "How is eating in a park on a blanket romantic? At least we had an actual table to sit at."

"Let's move on."

"*Ya.* Let's."

"Apparently you talked to her about your auctioneering. You talked about that a lot, but you never asked her a single question about what she does during the day."

"Did she write you a report and hand it to you?"

"Don't get defensive."

"Of course I'm defensive. I didn't ask Jane any questions because I didn't want to seem nosy."

"When you ask questions about someone, you're showing an interest in them, not being nosy."

Noah slammed his cup of lemonade down on the table, grateful that neither was made of glass, and jumped up out of the rocker. He walked over to the porch railing, attempted a few shoulder rolls to loosen the knots in his muscles and tried to figure out how to call off this entire fiasco.

Why had he ever made such a stupid agreement with his mother? And how was he going to endure two more nights of humiliation? But it was only two nights.

Only two more women who would most certainly reject him.

So instead of explaining how unreasonable she was being, he turned to Olivia Mae with a smile pasted on his face. Leaning against the railing, he jerked off his hat, crossed his arms and said, "Okay. Be on time. No gas station. Ask questions. Got it. When do I take her out again?"

"It's not that simple."

"What do you mean?"

"Jane…doesn't think that you're compatible."

"How can she know that after one date?" He felt his cheeks burning and knew that he was blushing. He rammed the hat back on his head, hoping that Olivia Mae wouldn't notice. "How am I supposed to get better at this if she won't give me another chance?"

"We try with someone else."

"The chubby…er, wait. Don't give me that lecture again. The other girl that you were sitting with at our church meeting?"

"Her name is Francine, and yes—that is who I had in mind."

Noah ran his hand over his face. Two more dates, and he would have fulfilled his half of the bargain. "Okay. I'm in."

"Tomorrow night."

"That soon?"

"Sure. I don't want you to have time to forget what you learned."

He wouldn't forget, but he also knew it wouldn't matter.

She pulled another sheet of paper from her pocket. It looked just like the first one she'd given him. Same precise handwriting. Same list. Same smiley face at the bottom. What grown-up put a smiley face on the bottom of a note? It didn't matter. He didn't even need her instructions, but he stared at the paper, folded it up neatly and stuck it in his pocket all the same.

If Olivia Mae understood what she was up against, how many times he'd crashed and burned in the dating arena, she would surrender now. But she was as stubborn as he was, and he could tell by the look on her face that she would see this through to the bitter end.

He forced his voice to be pleasant. No use letting her see how crazy she was making him. "Fine."

"Really?"

"Sure. You're the matchmaker."

He walked back to his buggy whistling. Something would go wrong tomorrow night. He didn't know how he knew, but he did. Then Olivia Mae would search around for one more poor girl to throw his way, and he'd mess that up, too. This entire foolish plan to find him a wife would be over by the following week.

As he drove away, he glanced back and saw Olivia Mae standing on the porch, watching his buggy…or maybe watching him. He didn't know why he didn't tell her the truth—that Jane seemed like a nice young girl, but a girl. Why didn't anyone seem to realize he was nearly thirty years old? He didn't want to date someone who was barely out of their *rumspringa*.

He wanted to date someone who had a little experience in life, who understood that there was more to a person than the condition of their buggy or whether they arrived on time or not. He wanted to date someone who wasn't out looking for love but was involved in their own life—caring for others, pursuing their dreams, content whether they found a spouse or not.

What he wanted was to date someone like Olivia Mae.

Ha. Not likely. She could give sage advice, but didn't seem to be interested in following it.

Nein. Dating Olivia Mae wasn't going to happen.

She hadn't shown the least bit of interest in him—other than as a puzzle she needed to solve.

Still, he warmed up to the idea as he drove home. Someone like Olivia Mae was what would suit him best. He knew it—felt it in his heart. Didn't he feel more comfortable with her? And they had things to talk about. He didn't have to have a list of topics penned on his palm like he'd done the other night.

Olivia Mae was more his style.

Perhaps he should ask if she had a twin sister hiding somewhere.

Chapter Six

Olivia Mae knew that Jane had already spoken with Francine about Noah. She could have left her a message at the phone shack telling her about the date she'd set up for her with Noah. Somehow a phone message seemed too impersonal, though, plus there was the fact that it was happening in a few hours. They'd talked about the possibility, but Olivia Mae had promised to get back to her with the exact details. She wanted a chance to meet with Francine and answer any questions. It wouldn't hurt to calm her nerves a bit. So she'd left a message saying she'd like to see her the next morning, and they'd decided on a girls' trip to town.

They were at the thrift store in Goshen as soon as it opened Saturday morning. This particular store supported Habitat for Humanity, which Olivia Mae had heard a lot of good things about. The person who had told her about their work building houses for those in need was an older man who worked for Mennonite Disaster Services. Olivia Mae had once thought about going on MDS missions herself, but now with her grandparents' health worsening every day that wasn't going to happen.

Mammi had warned her earlier that morning about traveling alone to Goshen even though they lived in Goshen. She'd acted as if their farm was miles and miles away from anyone else. She'd acted as if they lived in the old days, when the Plain community was small and folks lived farther apart.

And as Olivia Mae had walked out the front door, Rachel had reminded her to stop at the apothecary for her herbs. Apothecary? Had they ever had one of those? Was her *mammi* losing it completely? Or was she simply confused? Maybe she'd even been misheard. Regardless, Olivia Mae didn't think that she'd be going on an MDS mission any time soon.

She caught up with Francine, who was looking for anything that she could cut up for quilt squares. She loved making salvage or, the more popular term, *scrappy* quilts. She would purchase curtains, sheets, even old clothes to cut into squares and triangles. Francine was an excellent quilter. Olivia Mae preferred to knit. She liked visiting thrift stores because she could sometimes find sweaters for a quarter, frog the yarn, wash it and make something brand-new.

"Frog?" Francine asked. "What does that even mean?"

"It's the sound you make when you—you know. Rip the yarn out."

Francine began to giggle, and Olivia Mae was reminded of Noah's silly sheep jokes. In one way, those terrible jokes proved that he had a caring personality— at least he seemed to care about making her laugh. She thought he was probably a very kind person, only nervous when it came to women. She remembered his red ears the night before and how he'd tried to cover them with his hat. Nervous and easily embarrassed—both qualities that she thought were endearing in a man.

The question was whether Francine would feel the same way.

They finished pawing through the bins, paid for their purchases and walked out into a perfect May afternoon.

"Let's sit for a minute—if you have time."

"Sure." Francine plopped onto the wooden bench, dropped her bags near her feet and turned toward Olivia Mae. "I guess you want to give me some tips, so my evening with Noah doesn't end in disaster like Jane's did."

"She told you about that?"

"Described every agonizing moment."

Olivia Mae fought to hold in a sigh and failed. "Perhaps it's best if you just forget all of that and give Noah a chance."

"Oh, I plan to. I don't care if we eat at a gas station."

"You won't be."

"Or even if he's late. What's the big deal?"

Maybe Francine was a better match, or maybe she was simply trying very hard to appear to be.

"It's okay to expect someone to be on time, you know."

"*Ya*, I know." She fiddled with the strings of her prayer *kapp* and stared out at the passing traffic—cars, horses pulling buggies and folks riding bicycles.

Goshen had certainly grown, even in the few years since Olivia Mae had moved there. *Mammi*'s earlier comments about the apothecary pushed into her mind, twisting her heart, but she shook her head and focused on Francine.

"I don't even mind listening to details about the auction. Anything different from the same old thoughts circling through my mind would be *gut*."

Francine lived with her *bruder* and his family. It was a crowded home with nine children. She'd confessed to Olivia Mae that often she retreated into her own thoughts, completely unaware of what was going on around her. It was a form of self-preservation, according to Francine. Otherwise the sheer number of children in the house would overwhelm her.

She also struggled with diabetes, which she'd been diagnosed with as a young teenager. It was hard to avoid carbohydrates in an Amish home, especially one full of children. Francine was very serious about her health, especially since she had an overactive sweet tooth. The two challenges—a love for sweets and diabetes—were a constant battle for her. Living in a houseful of children only made that worse.

Olivia Mae knew there were plenty of families with more than ten children, but she suspected that it was easier if you added one at a time. Francine had moved from another state to be with her *bruder*. Her family had hoped it would increase her dating prospects. So far, it hadn't done much more than cause Francine to question whether she ever wanted to have children. She'd once confessed she didn't want to take care of another thing—person, pet or plant.

"Jane is thinking of writing to Elijah," Francine said.

"What?"

"Ya."

"She told you that?"

"She did." Francine glanced at Olivia Mae and then

back at the street. "She said that the date with Noah opened her eyes. She doesn't need a perfect man, but she does need someone who is interested in her. That was her exact word—*interested*."

"Whatever does that mean? Of course Noah was interested. He's just out of practice as far as relating to women."

Francine was tapping her fingertips against her lips, as if she wasn't sure she should say what she wanted to say. Finally she shrugged and looked directly at Olivia Mae. "Jane said he wasn't interested and that she could tell. He was, you know…only going through the motions."

"She said that?"

"I know what she means." Francine sighed and rubbed at her elbow. She'd admitted the previous week that the hand-quilting tended to cause the joints in her right arm to ache. "My *bruder* set me up with one of his buddies once—this was before I knew you. It didn't go well, and it left me feeling like a shelter dog that no one wanted. He never looked directly at me, and it seemed he couldn't get me home quickly enough."

Just when Olivia Mae thought she knew all that these young girls had been through, she unpeeled another layer. "I'm sorry that happened to you, but Noah isn't like that. He's just shy, and he doesn't think there's anyone out there for him. It's not that he's uninterested, he's simply not a believer in romantic love."

When Francine didn't respond, she said, "Do you think Jane will do it? Write Elijah?"

"She might. She told me that she realizes it doesn't matter what he does for a living—that details like that will work themselves out. What matters is how they feel about one another, and she's beginning to realize how much she did care for him." She pulled more tightly on her *kapp* strings. "And before you say that she's confusing loneliness for affection, I think she might be right."

Olivia Mae sighed and stood up, gathering up the two paper bags full of sweaters she'd purchased. It would be enough yarn to last her at least a month.

"What do you think?" Francine asked.

"I think our Jane is growing up, and I think you need to head home so you'll be ready for your date with Noah."

Olivia Mae expected to go home and spend the afternoon worrying over Noah's date, but she never had the chance. She pulled into the yard and saw *Mammi* pacing on the front porch.

"What's wrong?"

"It's your *daddi*."

"Is he all right?"

"I don't know. I don't know where he is."

"Tell me what happened." She clasped her *mammi*'s hand in hers. They were cold, and it was obvious she'd been crying. "Why don't you sit down, here in the rocker. Take a deep breath. It's going to be all right."

When *Mammi* didn't answer, she reached out and tucked her hand under the dear woman's chin, forcing her to look up. "Do you believe me?"

"I suppose." The answer was a whisper, a prayer.

"*Gut.* Now tell me what happened."

"He was napping, in his chair. I thought I had enough

time before he woke, so I went outside to work in the garden. When I came back inside, he was gone."

"And you've looked in the barn?"

"Ya."

"And the pasture?"

"Ya, of course. I thought of running to the phone shack, but then… Well, what if he came back and no one was here and he got scared?"

"It's okay, *Mammi.* You did the right thing to wait here."

"I did?"

"Ya."

Mammi closed her eyes, clasped her hands and began to silently pray. Olivia Mae knew that was what she was doing because her breathing evened out and she slowly began to put the rocking chair into motion, plus she'd seen her do that very thing a hundred times before— maybe a thousand times. And wasn't prayer what they needed at a time like this? Surely *Gotte* would help them to find *Daddi.* She added her own prayers to her grandmother's, and then she turned toward the still-harnessed horse. That wouldn't work, though, because *Daddi* probably would not stick to the road. He'd wandered off before and it was always across a pasture, as he would forget where their land ended and another farm began.

Olivia Mae reached out and covered *Mammi*'s hands with her own. "I'm going to the barn."

Mammi's eyes popped open. "But the horse and buggy are right here."

"I need to take my bike. Can you unhitch Zeus?"

"Of course."

"Just leave the buggy here. I'll put it up later, and if you open the pasture gate, Zeus will follow you in."

"I know how to pasture the horse."

And there was a small miracle, because she could see in her grandmother's face that she did remember how and would be able to do it. The confusion of the morning and the panic of a few moments ago had both passed.

Olivia Mae broke into a run. The last thing she wanted to do was explain to *Mammi* that she didn't think *Daddi* would stay on the road. She'd be better off with the bicycle. She'd start at his favorite fishing spot—though he hadn't fished in over a year—then work her way around to the neighbors. If she didn't find him by dark, she'd call Lucas.

She prayed that wouldn't happen.

She prayed that *Daddi* was all right, that he'd simply sat down somewhere and was resting.

She prayed that she wasn't too late.

Noah thought that he'd done better.

He'd picked up a couple of cans of soda, some fried chicken, a bag of chips and a package of cookies while he was in town running errands for his *mamm*. Olivia Mae might be right about some things, but he thought she was wrong about choosing restaurants. Who wanted to eat in a noisy restaurant on a Saturday? The weather was beautiful, and Olivia Mae had mentioned romantic picnics in an offhand way. No doubt she thought that was beyond him, but the bag of groceries behind his seat proved she was wrong.

He arrived twenty minutes early, which for some reason seemed to fluster Francine.

Then he drove her to the park, which was where the trouble began.

"This is where we're eating?"

"*Ya.* I thought it would be nice to enjoy the beautiful weather."

The park was full of children of all ages, plus quite a few dogs. It looked to him like everyone was having a good time, and he silently congratulated himself on having such a good idea. Hopefully the natural setting would help them relax around one another.

"Where are we going to sit?"

He'd thought there would be picnic tables, but there weren't. He glanced into the back seat of the buggy and spied his old horse blanket. It would do.

He handed her the bag of groceries, then fastened the mare to the buggy post and went to the back seat to pull out the blanket. They walked down to the pond and he shook the dirt from the blanket, then laid it on the ground.

Francine had eyed the blanket suspiciously, but she sat down without comment. When he began pulling out their food, her eyes grew rounder.

"This is what we're eating?"

"*Ya.* Fried chicken is *gut*, and who doesn't like chips and cookies?"

"Oh." She seemed to think about that for a minute. Finally she shrugged and asked, "Do you have plates or silverware?"

"Don't need it, not really." He popped the top on a can of soda and handed it to her. She stared at the drink as if it was a snake, then set it down in the grass and said, "I'm not very hungry, but *danki*."

He had asked her about her day, and paid attention when she described her quilting. He learned what a scrappy quilt was, and how salvage quilting was a type of recycling, and even that nine squares in a certain order made it a nine-patch. He felt Francine was a virtual encyclopedia of quilting terms, and he was a student trying to catch up.

But the problems cropped up pretty quickly. They seemed to be opposites. He sensed it almost immediately, and he thought she did, too.

Francine couldn't wait to put Goshen behind her. Noah was glad to be home.

Francine was pretty sure she didn't want any children, or at least not very many. Noah had always imagined himself with a houseful of kids—when he imagined himself as anything other than an old crotchety bachelor.

Francine jumped if any of the dogs came near them. Noah thought he wouldn't mind having one when he bought his own place.

Worse yet—she didn't like his jokes. She had stared at him when he'd shared one about pigs.

What do you call a pig with no legs?

A ground-hog.

Hilarious!

But Francine only chewed on her thumbnail and glanced away.

He was going to say, "Even Olivia Mae would have laughed at that one," but at the last second decided to keep that comment to himself.

Then the mosquitos attacked. He slapped one that was feasting on her arm and left a trail of blood. "Guess that one already got you."

"*Ya*. I guess it did." She looked around for a napkin to wipe off her arm, but he didn't have any. She'd settled for a corner of the horse blanket, which left a red rash on her arm.

But the biggest blunder of the evening had come when he took her home. He parked at the corner of the house, where the light from the living room couldn't reach them. It wasn't quite dark, but the sun was setting. Now, this was what Olivia Mae would call a romantic moment, or so he thought. Then he'd turned to Francine, removed his hat and leaned forward and kissed her.

His timing couldn't have been worse.

She'd turned away as he was making his move.

The result was that he smacked her on the ear with his lips, which startled Francine so that she let out a squeal. Then what looked like twin boys popped up in front of his buggy and began making smooching sounds.

Francine had screamed at the boys in such a way that it had surprised Noah. After all, they were only boys being boys. Then she had started to cry, and he hadn't known what to do so he'd patted her shoulder and said, "There, there."

He'd never heard those words from someone under sixty. He couldn't believe they came out of his mouth.

Francine had scrubbed at her eyes, proclaimed, "I hate it here," and jumped out of the buggy.

He didn't know what had caused her to run off.

His kiss?

The boys?

His ineffectual attempt to comfort her?

Dating was simply too hard.

And demeaning. It was definitely demeaning. He felt like a fish out of water. He felt like he had to be someone else, only he didn't know who that someone else was.

By the time he'd driven home, unhitched the buggy and pastured the horse, night had settled across the fields. For that he was glad. Maybe he wouldn't have to answer the fifty questions that had greeted him after his date with Jane.

But his father was sitting on the porch, rocking as he clamped a rarely lit pipe between his teeth.

Noah tried murmuring good-night and slipping by, but his father called him back. He motioned to the chair beside him and said, "Your *mamm* is glad you're back with us, Noah. We all are."

"And I'm glad to be back."

His *dat* rocked for a few minutes, struck a match and lit the pipe. Finally he said, "Do you think you'll stay?"

"*Ya*. I told you that. I'm done wandering."

"Because it would break your *mamm*'s heart for you to leave again. That's why she's so intent on finding you a *fraa*."

"I thought it was your idea."

His *dat* held the pipe by its bowl, pointed the end at him. "Wouldn't hurt you. Personally I think a man is happier when he's married with a family."

"I know you do."

"You don't?"

"I don't know. I used to. I used to be able to picture myself that way, but life seems to have different plans."

"Life doesn't have plans at all. 'For I know the thoughts that I think toward you, saith the Lord.'"

"Well, maybe the Lord's plan isn't for me to be married."

"Have you prayed on it?"

"I guess."

They sat in silence, his father drawing on the pipe. Noah stared out into the darkness. Fireflies darted back and forth, and he could hear an owl call out to its mate.

"You're not the first in our family to wander, you know."

"I'm not?"

"My *bruder* Josiah."

"You never speak of him."

"What is there to say? He wrote, at first. I was only seventeen when he left, and he was twenty-two."

"A long time ago."

"Indeed."

"Where did he go?"

Instead of answering that question directly, his *dat* said, "Josiah was never happy. If it was winter, he longed for summer. And in the summer, he couldn't wait for the snows to come. There was something restless about his spirit, about his attitude toward life."

"So he left?"

"He did. The first couple of years, he would come back every few months. Long enough to raise my parents' hopes that he was staying. But he never stayed. Last I heard from him, he was in Nova Scotia living with the Mennonites. That was over twenty years ago."

"Nova Scotia?" Noah tried to imagine that. "Is he still Amish?"

"Couldn't say. I suppose some part of him will always be."

"You've never told me this before."

"You didn't need to hear it before."

"And now I do?"

"I'm not sure, son."

Noah thought about that a moment. He had no doubt that his *dat* cared for him, that he always had. He did question whether he'd ever be able to live up to his parents' expectations. So instead of trying to explain how humiliating his most recent venture into dating had been, he said good-night and walked into the house.

Chapter Seven

Olivia Mae sat at the kitchen table, her Bible open in front of her, clutching a cup of hot tea. On the floor beside her sat the bags of thrift-store sweaters. She'd intended to frog at least one of them, but then a heavy exhaustion had claimed her and she'd found herself unable to do anything but clutch the tea and occasionally take a sip of it. Darkness had fallen outside the window.

She wondered about Noah and Francine. Had their date gone well? Why did that thought not fill her with as much happiness as she'd thought it would? She wanted to find Noah a wife. She couldn't do anything about her bleak situation, but she might be able to help his. She told herself that maybe that was her purpose in life— to find love for others.

Mammi walked into the room, hobbled over to the stove and placed her fingertips against the teapot.

"Should still be hot," Olivia Mae said. "Want me to make you a cup?"

Mammi shook her head as she reached for the tin of tea bags and plopped one into a cup. She covered it with hot water, dunked it repeatedly and then dropped the tea bag into the trash. Finally she joined Olivia Mae at the table, her fingers interlaced around the cup, a smile on her face.

"We have much to be grateful for."

"I guess."

"You're worried about him."

"Of course I am."

"But he's home now, and he wasn't harmed. You did *gut*, Olivia Mae. You found him, and you brought him home."

Olivia Mae wasn't sure how to respond to that. When she'd found her grandfather, sitting with his back pressed to the neighbor's barn, unsure of where he was or why he was there, her heart had broken. It was past time that she stopped ignoring their situation and did something about it. If she didn't, someone else would. Their neighbor, Isaac, had looked terribly concerned when she'd stumbled out from behind the barn, guiding her bicycle with one arm and her grandfather with the other. "Isaac will speak to Lucas."

"Of course he won't. There's no reason—"

"There is a reason, *Mammi*." She raised her eyes and studied her grandmother. This was a *gut* evening. *Mammi* was in the present for now. Perhaps she could make her see how desperate their situation was becoming. "It's Lucas's job—every bishop's job—to look after the people in their community."

"We are fine."

"We're not fine."

Mammi had been staring into her tea, looking out the

window at the darkness, even studying the ceiling, but now she met Olivia Mae's gaze. "He frightened you."

"*Ya*, he did. *Daddi* didn't know where he was. He didn't recognize Isaac at all."

"We've known him for years, since before we moved to this house."

"Isaac is a *gut* neighbor and a *gut* friend. He'll speak to Lucas."

"And what will Lucas do?" *Mammi*'s chin came up defiantly, and Olivia Mae almost laughed. Eighty-eight years old and still stubborn.

"Lucas will come and speak with us. He'll want to know what he can do to help, and he'll insist that we take *Daddi* to the doctor."

"There's nothing the doctors can do. We both know that, and Lucas does, too."

"Maybe. Or maybe there are new medicines."

But *Mammi* wasn't listening.

"I wish you could have known your *daddi* when he was younger. I first met Abe when he'd come down to help his parents with the harvest. Have I told you this before?"

Olivia Mae nodded slightly, but she didn't mind hearing the story again. There was grace and mercy and hope in the telling.

"He'd moved to Maine, where your *bruders* are now. I suppose they heard the way he bragged about the land there, heard his memories of a different time and took them to heart." *Mammi* sipped the tea, smiled slightly. "Abe was a hard worker, always was. When I first saw him he was covered in dirt, sweaty and he smelled bad. But I lost my heart the first time he smiled at me."

Olivia Mae was listening to *Mammi*, but instead of imagining her grandfather, her mind drifted to Noah, standing on their front porch and handing her the letter box, smiling shyly... Yes, she could see how a girl could lose her heart over a single smile.

"He was so strong, and I knew... I was certain he would take care of me. I never..." Her voice wobbled. "I never imagined this."

"Daddi may have many years left, but we need help. This isn't the first time he has wandered off. What if he ended up on the main road? What if he accepted a ride with a stranger? How would we find him?" Her resolve hardened at that thought, and the look of fear on *Mammi*'s face. This was too much for her, too much for the both of them. Olivia Mae had thought she was doing the right thing by allowing them to stay in their home, to spend their final years in a place they loved and were familiar with, but now she wasn't so certain.

"I'll call Ben tomorrow."

"Tomorrow is Sunday. Your *bruder* won't be checking the phone shack."

"Then I'll call him on Monday. I'll call him and tell him how things are. Maybe he will think of something that we haven't."

Mammi nodded, but only slightly. They both knew that Ben would want them to sell the house and move to Maine. He'd mentioned it more than once, and he'd only agreed to let Olivia Mae move in with their grandparents as long as it remained a *healthy environment*. Those were his exact words, and the memory of them almost made Olivia Mae put her head down on the table and weep.

Mammi had been determined to stay in Goshen—
to cling to their old life. Moving to Maine wasn't what
she wanted. It wasn't what she'd envisioned all of those
years ago.

Daddi didn't seem to know where they were, and
there was at least that to be thankful for. As far as Olivia
Mae knew, he'd be just as happy living somewhere else.

And Olivia Mae? She didn't know what she wanted.
She only knew that she had somehow failed in her attempt to allow her grandparents to spend their final
years in the community where they'd always lived.

She dreamed that she was still searching for *Daddi*,
only in the dream she couldn't find him. The days and
nights melded together in the way of dreams, and she
wandered constantly, calling his name with *Mammi*'s
pleas in her ears.

Find him, Olivia Mae. Please find him.

She woke more tired than when she'd first lain down.

When she walked into the kitchen, she found *Daddi*
sitting at the table, smiling and talking about a wren
that he'd seen at the feeder. *Mammi* stood at the stove,
pretending that all was well.

The morning sped by in a blur of activity—preparing
for church, harnessing the mare to the buggy, helping
her grandparents make their way down the porch steps.
May sunshine splashed across the road, and birds sang
and the mare clopped merrily down the road, tossing
her head occasionally. Olivia Mae realized there was
much to be grateful for, even in these times of trouble.

Perhaps she was being overly dramatic. There would
be sunny days in Maine, as well. Or maybe Ben would

think of another solution. She was determined to speak to Lucas after the service, which was taking place at his house. She wanted a chance to explain things without her grandparents interrupting.

The service calmed her fears and strengthened her resolve. The first sermon was from the Old Testament—Genesis, Chapter 37. Ezra was preaching, and his voice was calm, confident, assuring. "*Gotte* provided for Joseph, even as he sat in the well that his brothers had thrown him in. *Gotte* hadn't forgotten Joseph, and he hasn't forgotten you."

Daniel King preached the second sermon. It was from the book of Acts, the twenty-fifth verse of the sixteenth chapter—the story of Paul and Silas in prison. Olivia Mae knew the passage well. She'd often marveled at the terrible things the apostles had endured. More than once, she'd read this particular passage and been inspired by the fact that Paul and Silas were singing hymns to God, even as they were shackled in a cell.

"We're shackled, too," Daniel said. "For sure and certain we are. Only our shackles are made of different things—our fears, our disbelief, even our past can shackle us. But *Gotte*, His eye isn't on our past, it's on our future."

If ever there was a service that spoke to Olivia Mae's heart, that calmed her troubled thoughts, this was it. After the final hymn and prayer, she helped in the serving line and decided she would eat later. Looking out across the tables that had been set up on the lawn, she saw that Lucas had finished eating and was speaking to a group of children. It was a perfect time to ask if he had a few minutes to talk. She was walking toward him, when the shouting started behind her.

She turned toward the voices and was shocked to see Noah and Francine nose-to-nose.

Everyone was staring as she hurried over to them, though no one had interrupted the argument yet. It wasn't unheard of to have a disagreement at an Amish gathering, though it was rare at a church meeting. Most people were on their best behavior at church, but the Amish were as human as everyone else. Apparently either Francine or Noah had reached the limit of their patience.

"A horse blanket, Noah. I'm still itching."

"I'm sorry that I'm not fancy enough for you."

"Fancy? We didn't even have silverware."

"What does that—"

"You didn't even ask me what I would have liked to eat, or where I would have liked to go."

Jane was tugging on Francine's arms. Olivia Mae expected to find her friend in tears, but that wasn't the case at all. Francine was angry, and she was bound and determined that Noah know it.

Olivia Mae put a hand on Noah's arm. "Let's go for a walk."

He jerked away his arm, his attention still on Francine, on defending himself. "You didn't even try the food."

"I couldn't!" Francine turned and stomped toward the barn, Jane jogging to keep up.

Noah finally seemed to realize that they'd caused quite a scene. "Women," he muttered, and strode off in the opposite direction—toward the horse pasture.

Olivia Mae stood there, unsure whether to go after Francine or Noah.

"Want me to talk to him?" Noah's brother Justin was trying to hide a smile as he spoke to Olivia Mae.

"You think this is funny?"

"I think it's typical."

"Of?"

"A man who's on unfamiliar ground."

Which made a certain amount of sense. "I'll talk to him."

She hadn't had time to find out how the date went the night before, but from what she'd just seen, it had been a disaster. Why was she not surprised?

By the time she reached Noah, he was sitting with his back against a tree, studying the horses cropping at the new May grass.

She sat down beside him and waited.

Finally he said, "I told you I wasn't any good at this."

"You might have mentioned as much once or twice."

He turned to her, and she thought that Noah would proceed to defend himself. Instead he shook his head, smiled sadly and said, "You certainly do say what you think."

"As do you, from what I heard back there."

Noah tore off his hat, as if he needed something to stare at, something to do with his hands. He twirled it round and round, pausing now and then to dust off some imaginary dirt. Finally he said, "I thought I was doing what you said."

"Such as?"

"Well, I thought a picnic would be nice. You know, instead of a gas-station date."

"What's wrong with a restaurant?"

"I don't know. Too many people watching you. You're trapped at a table with nothing to look at but each other. It's all very awkward."

"A picnic, it sounds good in novels…"

"Don't read many of those."

"But in reality a lot can go wrong."

"So I learned."

"Why don't you start from the beginning?"

He went through it all—how he'd arrived early, the food that he'd picked up, even the horse blanket and the kiss.

"Oh, my," she said, when he was finished.

"Ya." He smiled at her ruefully, like a schoolboy caught skipping class.

Telling the story seemed to have eased some of his tension. At least he was able to laugh at himself now. He stuck the hat back on his head and smiled at her. "So…"

"What?"

"Tell me what I did wrong."

"Are you sure you're ready to hear that?"

"You're the dating expert."

"Matchmaker—it's not the same thing."

"Whatever."

"All right. Well, as I said, a picnic is a chancy thing, especially for a first date."

"I should have stuck to a restaurant."

"Definitely. Then you don't have to worry about the food. You know it will be good, and your date can choose whatever she wants, which for Francine is very important."

"I don't understand."

Olivia Mae sighed, stared out at the horses and finally said, "Francine is diabetic."

Dawning spread across Noah's face. "All I had to drink was sodas."

"Plus fried chicken, potato chips and cookies—none of those things are good for a diabetic, and combined they probably would have sent her blood-sugar levels sky-high."

Noah sat forward and studied her. "I'm an idiot."

"*Nein*. You couldn't have known, but that's an important component of dating—you learn about the other person. For a fourth or fifth date, a picnic might be nice. But for a first date?"

"Chancy."

"*Ya*. I think Francine would have told you about her condition…eventually. She doesn't hide it exactly, and most of us know." Though as she thought about it, that alone didn't seem to explain the angry reaction that she'd seen from Francine earlier. "Was the park busy?"

"*Ya*. Kids everywhere."

"Oh."

"*Oh* what?"

"I'm sure she'd tell you herself if she was speaking to you, but Francine moved in with her *bruder* not so long ago, and she's been a little overwhelmed by the sheer number of children he has."

"She was probably hoping for an evening away from *kinder*."

"Probably. And then the kiss…to have it interrupted by two of her nephews, that was just a fine icing of embarrassment on top of an already overcooked cake."

Noah flopped back on the ground, staring up at the

white wisps of clouds that were scudding across the sky. "Dating is so complicated."

"People are complicated, Noah. Whether you're dating or working on a business deal or being a *gut* neighbor. Every single person you meet is dealing with something."

He rolled over on his side, propped himself up on his elbow and asked, "How did you get so wise?"

"Never said I was."

"I'm being serious. Don't look at me like that. I really am. How did you learn to navigate so seamlessly through these kind of interactions, and why aren't you married?"

Olivia Mae thought her eyes were going to pop out of her head. "Did you really just ask me that?"

"I did."

"A little intrusive."

"Meaning you don't want to answer?"

"Meaning it's none of your business."

"Fair enough, though it's like asking a horse salesman why he doesn't own a horse."

Which was so ridiculous that it eased the knot of defensiveness in her stomach. "My family situation is… unique."

"You mean with your grandparents?"

She nodded instead of answering and looked back toward the picnic area. She'd intended to speak to Lucas about *Daddi*.

"I've got it." Noah sat up and resettled his hat, looking quite pleased with himself.

"Got what?"

"The solution."

"To?"

"My dating disasters."

"Oh, that's *gut* to hear."

He leaned forward, close enough that she could smell the shampoo he'd used that morning. Close enough that she wanted to scoot back to calm her racing heart.

"You need to teach me."

"Pardon me?"

"You need to give me dating lessons."

"What do you mean?"

"You and me. We'll go on a few dates…say, three. That would be a *gut* number. You can learn how to do most things if you do it three times."

"That's a ridiculous suggestion."

"Why? I learn better from doing."

"Do you?"

"I've already learned not to take a girl to a gas station or a picnic, but who knows how many more dating traps are waiting for me to stumble into them."

"So this would be…a learning experience."

"It's a perfect solution." He studied her closely, and then reached forward and tugged on her *kapp* string, something no one had done to her since she'd been a young teen in school with a crush on a boy.

"I can tell by the shock on your face and the way you're twirling that *kapp* string that I've made you uncomfortable. It's a *gut* idea, though. We'd keep it businesslike—nothing personal."

Olivia Mae had no idea why the thought of sitting through three dates with Noah Graber made her stomach twirl like she'd been on a merry-go-round. Maybe she was catching a stomach bug.

"Wait a minute. Are you trying to get out of your third date? Because you promised your *mamm* that you would give this thing three solid attempts."

"And I'll keep my word on that," Noah assured her. "After you've tutored me, you can throw some other poor unsuspecting girl my way."

Olivia Mae saw Lucas walking away from the group. He was alone. She'd rather stay here talking to Noah, but now was her chance. She stood, brushed off the back of her dress and pointed a finger at Noah, who still sat in the grass as if he didn't have a care in the world.

"All right. I'll do it, on one condition."

Noah rolled his eyes, but motioned for her to continue.

"You go find Francine and apologize to her."

"I would have done that anyway. I'm not an ogre, just a bit clueless."

"You said it, not me."

Chapter Eight

Noah was cautiously optimistic when he checked the phone shack on Monday, felt a bit more cynical on Tuesday and grew positively aggravated by Wednesday. He wasn't asking Olivia Mae to marry him. He was asking for some in-person tutoring. Obviously he'd missed the lesson on how to act like a gentleman—according to Francine, who put it in those exact words. Where did men learn what women expected from them? It certainly hadn't been taught in his one-room schoolhouse.

Perhaps Olivia Mae was having second thoughts.

Why did it even matter to him?

So what if she had given up on him?

Maybe she'd found a more important match to make.

Good riddance. He could get on with his life—finally.

Or so he told himself as he clomped into the phone shack after work on Wednesday. He usually took the bus into work since Shipshe was eleven miles away—a bit of a long ride in a horse and buggy. At breakfast, his *dat* had asked him to drive the buggy and pick up a plow part on his way home. The sky was dark and broody, which matched his thoughts perfectly. He'd simply explain to his mother that no one was willing to give him a chance, so she'd understand that he was unmatchable and he'd be able to start looking for a bachelor pad.

He didn't want to live with his parents forever, but he wasn't quite sure what his new place would look like.

Obviously he needed a place for his horse and buggy. Something with a small sheep pen might be good.

He didn't need a sheep pen!

He didn't even particularly like sheep.

Maybe someone had a *grossdaddi haus* they'd rent to him. Amish might live simply, but they were usually on the lookout for ways to supplement the family income. He was making enough at the auction house that he could afford to pay a modest rent.

He stepped into the phone shack and saw the light blinking on the answering machine beside the flashing number 1. Probably it was a message for Widow King again. For an elderly woman with a large family spread out in Goshen who probably visited her once a week, she certainly did get a lot of phone messages. He picked up the pen and prepared to take down the name and number.

Instead he heard Olivia Mae's voice on the recorder. At the sound of her voice he felt a lightness in his chest as if a heavy burden had been lifted.

"This message is for Noah Graber. We could have your first lesson on Wednesday at five thirty if that's agreeable. No need to bring anything."

Five thirty? He glanced at his watch and confirmed that he had exactly fifteen minutes to get to Olivia

Mae's. He wouldn't have time to go home and change. He wouldn't even have time to warn his *mamm* that he wouldn't be home for dinner, but then that tended to happen a couple of times a week and he knew she wouldn't worry. Sometimes auction work ran late. She'd taken to leaving him a plate in the oven, covered with a pan lid, the temperature turned to low.

Which left him no good excuse to refuse Olivia Mae.

Why would he refuse her? This was what he'd asked for.

But suddenly he wasn't so sure. His mouth went dry, and he wondered if he'd made his predicament even worse than it had been.

He stomped back out of the phone shack as the rain began pelting the pavement. Great. Now his horse would wait in the rain while he learned which fork to eat with. His mood mirrored the stormy sky above him as he climbed into the buggy and called out to Snickers.

Twenty-five minutes later, he pulled into Olivia Mae's lane, his attitude actually worse than it had been when he'd received the message. The door to the barn was open, so he directed the horse inside. Olivia Mae had left an old towel to wipe off the mare, as well as a bucket filled with water and another that he could scoop oats into. After taking care of Snickers's immediate needs, he dashed across to the front porch, thoroughly drenched by the time he ran up the steps.

Olivia Mae was standing by the front door. He skidded to a stop a few feet in front of her, his throat suddenly dry. He was unable to figure out whether to cross his arms or leave them at his side. If she noticed his awkwardness, she didn't comment on it. Instead she smiled, her brown eyes reminding him of a cup of rich, delicious warm cocoa.

She offered him a towel.

"What's this for?"

"To dry off with."

"Oh, yeah." He accepted the towel, but simply stared at it. Turning, he scowled at the table she'd set up in the middle of the porch. "We're eating out here?"

"Ya."

"It's pouring."

"I can see that."

"You wouldn't rather go inside?"

"Nein. Here is *gut.* I've moved everything back so we won't get wet."

"More wet."

"Right. So you won't get *more* wet."

He grumbled a reply. Was she so embarrassed of him that he couldn't even go inside the house? He towel-dried his hair, took off his jacket, put it over the back of the chair and plopped down. "Fine."

"Let's try that again."

"Excuse me?" If he wasn't imagining it, she was actually trying to hold back laughter.

"You're here for a lesson, Noah. Remember?"

"How could I forget?"

"Well, sometimes dates are going to start off badly, like this."

"You mean because I'm soaking wet, and I had to rush to get here since I only heard your message half an hour ago? Or because I'm tired, I'm hungry and we're eating on the porch in a rainstorm?"

"See, that's exactly what I mean."

"What?"

"You're grumpy—out of sorts."

"I'm grumpy?" He nearly touched the top of his head to see if steam was coming out of it.

"Now, I don't intend to have you walk back to the barn—"

"Thank goodness for small favors."

"Let's just start when you were coming up the stairs."

"Fine. Do I need to put my coat back on?"

She waved away his suggestion and tugged on his arm. Her small hand on him caused him to break out in a sweat, even though the day had turned cooler with the rain. So why was he sweating? Why did he suddenly feel seventeen again?

"Stand over here, as if you're just arriving. Only this time try not to scowl at me."

"I'm scowling?"

"Maybe say hello and ask how my day has been."

He thought of walking away then. "This is a bad idea. This entire evening is a bad idea."

"I thought you wanted to learn." Now her voice was serious, and the look on her face seemed to dare him to find a reason to back out of his commitment.

That was it. She expected him to turn tail and run.

Well, he'd just see about that.

He could withstand one dinner in the rain. In fact, now that he could smell the food, his stomach had begun to growl. It would be foolish to leave before he had a chance to eat. So he stood straighter, walked back to the edge of the porch, where a spattering of rain still hit his back, and said, "Olivia, may I step forward three steps?"

"Now you're making fun of me and my name."

"Am not."

"Are too. You know my name is Olivia *Mae*, and you're playing on the word *may*..." She closed her eyes and pulled in a deep breath.

Ha! Mission accomplished. He was getting to her. He was testing her patience in the same way that she tried his. Two could play at that game.

"Try again, please."

"All right. Olivia Mae, you look beautiful tonight. How was your day?"

"It was *gut*. Nice rain we're having."

"Nice indeed."

She motioned toward the chair where he'd been sitting a few minutes earlier. "I thought we'd have a picnic outside, but since it's raining I moved it to the porch."

"*Gut* idea."

He started to sit, but when she shook her head, he froze.

"Problem?" he asked in a stage whisper.

"Pull out my chair for me. It's the gentlemanly thing to do."

"So now we're teaching me to be a gentleman?"

"It's a goal, *ya*."

He was still put out with her, but found it impossible to stay angry. Something about that impish grin she wore stole his irritation and sent it out into the storm.

"May I help you with your chair, Olivia Mae?"

She rolled her eyes, but allowed him to pull back the chair and then scoot it in.

"I've never seen my *dat* do that for my *mamm*."

"It would be awkward to do so the rest of your married life."

"It's our first date. We've already decided we're getting married?" He was enjoying teasing her, but Olivia Mae was all seriousness. He'd have thought she was a schoolmarm teaching advanced math.

"Many of the things you do on early dates are to set the tone of a relationship. Once that relationship, that bond, is established, some things are no longer necessary." She stared up at the corner of the porch ceiling as if she was trying to remember something, then added, "Though it's always kind to open a buggy door for a woman no matter how long you've been married."

"I thought today's women wanted more independence." The teasing had slipped away, replaced by his general confusion with the opposite gender.

"Women are not a deep dark secret, Noah. At the heart of it all, women want the same thing that men do—to be respected." She straightened the fork, which was positioned just so beside her plate. "As far as independence, well, I couldn't answer that."

The next few moments passed in an agonizing fashion.

He felt like a *youngie*.

She reminded him to put his napkin in his lap.

She told him to pick up the dishes and offer them to her first, then serve himself.

"Should I stand up and serve you?"

"You're kidding, but no, you shouldn't. You offer the dish to the woman first because she cooked the meal and you want her to have the first selection."

"Seems like my *mamm* always serves herself last."

"That's exactly my point. So take this plate of chicken, for instance. A woman might stand in a hot kitchen, frying chicken over spattering grease, and by the time the plate goes around the table, there's little left for her to eat but a wing."

"Maybe she needs to cook more." He smiled to show he wasn't serious. He passed her the mashed potatoes, hot rolls and salad. Both of their plates were now quite full, but she still hadn't picked up a fork, and his stomach was growling.

"My family usually prays silently. Does yours?"

"*Ya.*"

"All right. So once the food is served, simply bow your head. Your date will do the same."

He bowed his head but peeked at her.

"Don't do that."

"Yes, ma'am."

"Pray as you usually would and then a soft *amen* will indicate you're finished but not interrupt your date if she's still praying."

"Can I start eating now?"

"*Nein.* Wait for her to look up at you." She raised her head and smiled at him, and another piece of the ice that had formed around his heart melted away.

Olivia Mae did not like the way her pulse beat faster when Noah gave her that beseeching look. This was a lesson, nothing more. He'd said absolutely nothing to indicate he might be interested in her romantically. If anything, he'd made it rather obvious that he still didn't think she could find a match for him.

While she corrected his manners, which were as bad

as any bachelor's but no worse than some she'd worked with, she tried to remain detached and professional. It was hard, given what was going on in her personal life. Her thoughts drifted to the phone conversation with her brother and the doctor appointments for her grandparents.

"Where did you go?" Noah asked.

"Go?"

"I lost you there for a minute."

"I'm sorry. It's been a difficult week."

Noah cocked his head and waited. She'd noticed that he was good at listening once he conquered his initial battle of nervousness. But this evening wasn't about her or her problems. It was about Noah and helping him to prepare for his next real date.

"Tell me one of your silly jokes."

"Really?"

"Sure. Make me laugh. I could use a laugh today." She said it in a lighthearted way, but even she heard the pain beneath her words.

Noah sat back and rubbed his chin as if he needed to think long and hard, but he couldn't keep up the act for long. He pushed his plate forward—a plate that looked as if it had been licked clean—and crossed his arms on the table.

"What do you get if you cross an angry sheep and a moody cow?"

"A sheep with mad cow disease?"

"Moody, not mad. That was a *gut* answer, though."

"Okay, tell me. What do you get if you cross an angry sheep and a moody cow?"

"An animal that's in a ba-a-a-a-aad moo-oo-ood."

He sounded exactly like a sheep and then like a cow—or enough like one to make her laugh. "Your imitation is better than your joke."

"I'll take that as a compliment."

He smiled and seemed to relax for the first time since he'd arrived, causing Olivia Mae to realize he was quite a handsome man. He had nice hair, and a strong profile and beautiful eyes. She'd barely processed those thoughts, when her *mammi* pushed through the screen door.

"Elizabeth. What are you doing out here in the rain?"

Olivia Mae jumped up. "I'll be right back."

"Can I help?" Noah called after her, but she was already at the door, guiding *Mammi* back inside.

"I couldn't find you," *Mammi* said.

"I told you I was on the porch, remember? Giving Noah a lesson."

"Looked to me like you were giving him dinner." *Mammi*'s hands shook slightly as Olivia Mae led her back into the kitchen, stepping around the soup pot and basin that she'd placed under the leaks in the roof. The rain made a *pat-pat-pat* sound as it plopped into the containers.

"I don't know any boy named Noah. Where is Henry?"

Olivia's heart sank at the mention of her father's name. She'd hoped that when her grandmother called her Elizabeth it had been a slip, but it seemed that she was experiencing another one of her episodes that threw her into the past.

"Let me fix you some hot tea."

"*Ya*, all right. Then you can go back out to Henry, though I don't know why you're eating on the porch."

"It's a picnic, *Mammi*."

"In the rain?"

"Well, that I didn't plan on."

While the water in the kettle heated up, Olivia Mae checked in on *Daddi*. He was sitting in his favorite chair in the living room, oblivious to the rain splattering into a bowl next to his chair, trying to make sense of some article in the *Budget*.

At least he didn't appear agitated. She pulled a knitted throw from the basket in the corner of the room and placed it across his lap, righted the paper, which he was trying to read upside down, and kissed him on top of the head.

The kettle had begun to whistle when Noah rapped lightly on the screen door.

"Everything all right in there?" He'd cupped his hands around his eyes and was peering inside.

"Fine. It's all fine." She rushed to the door and pushed it open, forcing him back. "I just needed to help my grandparents."

"Did she call you Elizabeth?"

"I'll be out with dessert in just a minute. Just, um, take a seat and I'll be right back with some cake." Before he could ask any more questions that she'd have to ignore, she fled inside.

Daddi had turned the paper upside down again and was growing increasingly frustrated with it. She needed to get it out of his hands before he had a complete meltdown.

Her *mammi* called out from the kitchen, "Elizabeth, the kettle is ready… I'll just make us some tea."

Olivia Mae didn't think *Mammi* was steady enough

on her feet for tea making. She hurried back toward the kitchen and tripped over the soup pot, sending it sloshing across the floor. Dashing to retrieve it, she slipped on the wet floor, grabbed for the doorjamb and fell, landing hard on her backside. She sat there on the floor—wet, frustrated and unsure whether to run to her *daddi* or *mammi*—when a scream came from the kitchen.

She attempted to stand up, but the floor had become as slippery as an ice rink. Suddenly she felt two strong hands lifting her to her feet.

"Check on your *mammi*." Noah's voice was low, calm and steady. "I'll go and sit with your *daddi* for a minute."

Before she could answer, he'd retrieved the soup bowl, placed it under the biggest leak and hurried back toward the living room. Olivia Mae rushed into the kitchen to find the kettle on the floor and *Mammi* standing with a hot pad in her left hand, glancing around wildly.

"Elizabeth. Thank goodness you're here. I don't know what made me drop that kettle. It was as hot as a live coal."

"I'll take care of it, *Mammi*." Her grandmother was right-handed. Apparently she'd remembered to pick up a hot pad, but had put it in the wrong hand. "Let me help you to the table. Did you burn yourself?"

"*Nein*, I don't think so."

"Let me see." Olivia Mae sat in the chair next to her and pulled her grandmother's hand into her lap. The palm was a bright red, but it didn't look as if it would blister. She breathed a silent prayer of gratitude and smiled at *Mammi*. "We should put your hand in water."

"Seems to be plenty of that around here." *Mammi* glanced around the room, then met Olivia Mae's eyes. They both started laughing at the same time.

Perhaps it was relief over the fact that *Mammi* hadn't been burned more badly than she was. Maybe it was the look on Noah's face as he'd helped her up from the floor, or it could be that exhaustion had finally taken its toll. Whatever the reason, tears rolled down Olivia Mae's face. *Mammi* reached forward and thumbed them away. "You're a *gut doschder.*"

"*Danki.*"

She didn't bother to correct her grandmother, to explain that she was her granddaughter, not her daughter. Instead she snatched a bowl out of the drainer that sat next to the sink, stuck it under the nearest leak and brought the bowl filled with rainwater to the table. Gently she placed *Mammi*'s hand in it.

"Does it hurt?"

"*Nein.* It was a silly thing to do." She glanced down at the hot pad she still clutched in her other hand. "For some reason, I had it in my left and I always use my right. Getting old and forgetful, I guess."

Rather than agreeing or disagreeing with her, Olivia Mae patted her arm and made sure her hand stayed in the bowl of water. "I'm going to check on—" she almost said *Noah*, but at the last minute changed it "—*Daddi*. I'll be back in just a minute. Promise to stay put?"

"*Ya.* But you should pick up our kettle off the floor."

Olivia Mae accepted the hot pad, scooped up the kettle, placed it back on the stove and hurried into the living room. What she saw there stopped her in her tracks. Noah and *Daddi* were sitting at the small table near the window. Noah had moved it so it no longer sat under one of the leaks in their roof, and he and *Daddi* were engrossed in a game of checkers.

"Ha. Crown me," *Daddi* said.

"Got me again." Noah glanced up and smiled at her as she walked into the room.

Olivia Mae felt a surge of gratitude in that moment that threatened to overwhelm her. She'd put Noah through what must have been a difficult lesson on the front porch. She fully realized that no one liked being corrected and change—well, change was always difficult. Yet, here he sat, playing checkers with her *daddi* as if he had nothing better to do.

She skirted around yet another bowl and stopped beside the table. "How are we doing in here?"

"Gut." *Daddi* laughed. "Your beau isn't very *gut* at checkers."

She was about to correct him when Noah said, "Does that mean you're afraid to play me again?"

"I thought you'd be begging for mercy." *Daddi* proceeded to reset the checkerboard, his hands shaking only slightly and a smile playing across his lips. All the frustration from a few moments earlier had been forgotten, and he seemed to not have noticed the minor emergency in the kitchen.

Noah jumped up from the chair and pulled Olivia Mae a few feet away. Lowering his voice, he said, "We're doing fine here, but how is your *mammi*?"

"Okay. Only a little burn."

"Does she need to see a doctor?"

"*Nein.* I have her soaking her hand in water. I'd like to put some aloe vera on it. Could you stay with *Daddi* just a while longer?"

"Are you kidding? I couldn't bear to miss another thrashing at the checkerboard." He touched her arm as she turned away, and that—the simple act of him placing his hand on her arm—nearly caused the tears to spill over again. For some reason Noah's kindness cut her to her core, and that made no sense at all. Had it been so long since she'd accepted help from someone?

The next hour seemed unreal, as if it was happening to someone else. She cut two leaves from the aloe vera plant in the windowsill, washed them in the sink, then sliced them open and placed the jelly inside of each stem against her grandmother's palm.

"Does that feel all right?"

"*Ya.*" *Mammi* reached forward and cupped the side of Olivia Mae's face. "*Danki,* Olivia Mae."

Her grandmother calling her by the correct name righted her world and eased the last of the tension in her shoulders. They were okay. They'd made it through another event. She had no idea what brought on her *mammi*'s episodes, but since Lucas had insisted that she take them to the doctor, she might know more by the end of the week. For now, it was enough that her grandmother was back in the present.

"It must be hard, living with old folks like us."

"Not hard at all."

"*Daddi* is okay?"

"He's fine—playing checkers with Noah."

"There's some apple crumb cake left. Maybe we could have that with some hot tea."

"Cake and tea sounds *gut*."

They spent the next half hour all gathered around the kitchen table, enjoying the cake and the tea and one another's company.

The storm had moved on and the sky was clearing by the time she walked Noah out to the barn. "*Danki*, for your help."

But she could tell, even in the last of the summer evening's light, that he wasn't going to let her off the hook so easily. Instead of climbing up into his buggy, he sat down on a bale of hay near the barn door and patted the place beside him.

"Sit. Talk to me."

"About what?" she asked lightly.

"Talk to me, Olivia Mae."

Her shoulders sagged and she dropped down onto the bale of hay next to him. "You're here for a lesson, and I'm sorry it was interrupted."

"I'm not."

"What do you mean?"

"I mean, this is your life, and I'm not sorry I had a glimpse of it. But tell me what's going on. Obviously you're struggling."

The old defensiveness reared its head, and it took all of her control to stay put. "I don't know what you mean."

"You don't?" He shifted on the bale of hay so that he could study her. "Your grandmother called you by the wrong name, then burned herself because she couldn't properly pick up a kettle. Your grandfather was nearly in a state of panic sitting in the living room by himself, and if I'm not mistaken he thinks Eisenhower is still president. Lastly, your home's roof has more holes than a sieve."

"I was hoping you wouldn't notice."

"Which part?"

"All of it?" Olivia Mae sat forward and buried her face in her hands. Why was this so humiliating? Why was it so difficult to admit how desperate their situation was?

Noah was embarrassed. He'd actually thought he had problems, but he understood now that his were minor compared to Olivia Mae's. His biggest problem at the moment was whether he would continue living with his parents or strike out on his own. He'd had no idea that Olivia Mae was dealing with such a volatile situation. He hadn't taken the time to know, but he would now—that's what good friends did, they listened.

"No rush," he assured her. "Snickers seems quite content here in your barn."

"Don't you have somewhere you need to be?" She lowered her hands and smoothed out her apron.

"Me? *Nein*. I had a dating lesson tonight that went much better than I expected."

"It did go well. Didn't it?"

"No changing the subject. Maybe start with the roof. Why haven't you had it fixed?"

"No money? It seemed easier to hope it wouldn't rain? I wasn't sure who to ask?"

"The first two might be true, but not the last. If you'd told the bishop, he would have had a work crew out here before the end of the week."

"You're right. I know that—yes, but *Daddi* was in the hospital."

"When?"

"Before you were here, and the total of what we owed for doctors and the hospital was quite high. The benevolence fund paid his bill. I wasn't ready to ask for more help."

"Okay. We'll come back to that. What's going on with Abe? Does he have Alzheimer's?"

Olivia Mae flinched at the word. She and her grandmother hadn't discussed it, as if not saying the name of the disease could keep it at bay.

"I think so."

She told Noah how *Daddi* often had trouble dressing correctly, that he sometimes couldn't remember the names of common household items and other times he did things like put his reading glasses in the icebox. She told him about her grandfather wandering off the previous Saturday.

Noah could tell by the way that she wrapped her arms around her middle how terrified she was.

"It's what you were speaking to Lucas about on Sunday, *ya*?"

"*Ya*. After *Daddi* wandered off, I searched and called and prayed and searched some more. Then when I found him, he didn't recognize me, didn't know where he was. Worse, he was so frightened that it broke my heart."

"I can't imagine what that must have been like for you."

"It was a wake-up call, that's what it was. I knew then that I had to speak with Lucas. I had to come clean about all of this—though I didn't mention the roof. I planned to after we worked out the more immediate stuff."

"Such as?"

"Lucas insisted that I take them both into the doctor. We have appointments tomorrow."

"For Rachel and Abe?"

"*Ya. Mammi* doesn't have whatever *Daddi* has, but there's something wrong. I don't know what it is."

She stared down at her hands, and he forced himself not to rush her. From the way she was acting, he was the first person she'd talked to about this—other than the bishop.

Did that make them friends?

More than friends?

Finally she glanced up and admitted, "I don't know what to do anymore, so I called my *bruders*."

"They live in Maine?"

"Uh-huh. I told Ben everything. I'm supposed to call him back after we see the doctor, but regardless what we learn tomorrow, I know his answer."

"Which is?"

"That we move to Maine."

Noah felt a jolt of surprise for the first time since she'd begun baring her soul. "Do you want to move to Maine?"

"*Nein.*" Now she jumped up and began pacing in the doorway to the barn. "I do not, and I don't think it would be *gut* for them, either. I think they should be here, where they've always lived. Goshen is where they met and married. It's where things are familiar, and we have a church community that we know."

She stared across the yard at the house.

He could tell that she was exhausted and a little lost.

What she'd just described was a lot for a young woman to carry on her own, and the fact that she and Abe and Rachel had made it this long was testament to how strong she was.

Noah stood and moved behind her. He wanted to put his arms around her, but he didn't. He had the sense that she was like a newborn fawn—easily frightened and apt to dart away. When she turned to look at him, he couldn't help smiling.

"What?"

"Only that you look pretty standing there, rain still dripping off the leaves and the last of the sun's light pushing across the field."

She didn't respond, but her cheeks blushed a pretty rose color. He felt an irresistible urge to pull her into his arms and kiss her. Something told him he wouldn't make a mess of it this time, not like he had when he'd tried to kiss Francine outside her brother's house. He realized that had been foolish. He hadn't done it because he'd cared about Francine, but because he'd been curious, nothing more.

He almost asked, "Olivia, may I…?" but then Snickers neighed, and Olivia Mae plastered on a smile, and the moment slipped away.

"You should go. Your horse is growing impatient."

"And you need to get back inside with your grandparents."

She nodded in agreement, watched as he backed Snickers out of the barn and stood beside him as he climbed up into the buggy.

"I can't fix the situation with your grandparents, though I'll pray that tomorrow goes well."

"Danki."

"But I can fix your roof."

She'd been standing close to the buggy door, but now she drew back and crossed her arms. "There's no need—"

"To fix your roof? *Ya.* There is." Then, realizing that she might be worried he'd do a bad job, he added, "I did some roofing while I was in New York. Pretty sure my *dat* has some leftover supplies from when he redid our roof a couple of years ago. It's no problem."

"But…the storm is passed."

"Bound to be another. There always is. If it's okay. I'll come over after I do my chores in the morning."

"No auction?"

"Actually, it's my day off."

"Which you usually spend working at your parents' place. And don't bother denying it because you told me as much while we were eating."

"My parents would insist that I come over and help, and I don't mind, Olivia Mae. In fact, I'm happy to do it." He realized as he drove away that it was true—he was happy at the thought of easing her burden a bit.

But that part about her moving to Maine left him with a new kind of knot in his stomach.

Chapter Nine

Their doctor's appointment the next day was for three in the afternoon. Olivia Mae spent the morning baking, cleaning and trying to convince *Daddi* that it wasn't cold enough to wear his winter coat outside.

Noah arrived around noon and was nearly done with the roof when they left at two. The image in her mind as she drove the buggy down the lane was of him on top of the roof—straw hat pulled low against the afternoon sun, sleeves rolled up to his forearms, his hair curling and damp from the sweat running down his face.

She didn't know what she'd done to deserve a friend like Noah Graber, but she was grateful that the Lord had seen fit to send him her way.

Lucas must have explained their situation to the doctor, because they'd only been waiting twenty minutes when Dr. Laney Burkhart called all three of them into her office. She was a middle-aged woman, with purple-framed glasses and shoulder-length red hair. She had a kindly expression and looked straight at them as she spoke. She didn't act in a hurry, which immediately put Olivia Mae at ease.

"Your bishop explained a little of your situation to me over the phone, but I wanted to speak with you as a family before I begin my examinations. Then we'll meet back here when I'm done."

Mammi clasped her purse and nodded.

Daddi had become preoccupied with an old-fashioned slide puzzle that had been sitting on the corner of the doctor's desk. His suspenders were twisted and his hair was sticking up in the back, but overall he seemed to be having a pretty good day.

Neither her grandmother nor grandfather said anything, which left it to Olivia Mae to speak up. "There have been some…issues for a while now."

"And you're the primary caregiver for your grandparents?"

"I live with them, *ya*. I help out where I can."

"Olivia Mae has been a huge blessing to us," *Mammi* chimed in. "Our grandsons, they wanted us to move to Maine, but Olivia Mae and I, we both think it's best for Abe to stay in a place that he's familiar with."

Dr. Burkhart attempted to have a conversation with *Daddi*, but he simply looked at *Mammi* each time the doctor asked him a question. Once he looked out the window and said, "I bet it's cold out there." Dr. Burkhart jotted down a few notes and paged through the forms they'd filled out while they'd waited to be called back to the office.

Finally she turned her attention back to Olivia Mae and *Mammi*. "Have you noticed any recent changes or deterioration in Mr. Lapp's condition?"

"He forgets things sometimes, but don't we all?" *Mammi* attempted to make a joke of the situation.

But Olivia Mae understood that it was time they come to terms with what they were dealing with. They were well past the point of glossing over the truth of their situation. "*Daddi* has wandered off several times. When we find him, he seems confused about where he is and also when."

"When?"

"Sometimes, he thinks it's the past or he thinks it's winter when it's summer. It's as if his thinking process is jumbled in some way."

Daddi glanced up, perhaps sensing that they were talking about him. He seemed to notice the doctor for the first time. "Do I know you?"

"We just met, Mr. Lapp."

Daddi accepted that with the innocence of a child. He nodded, smiled and then leaned forward to confide in the doctor. "We're going for a treat after this—ice cream. I just love ice cream. Don't you?"

"I do," Dr. Burkhart said. "Strawberry is my favorite. What's yours?"

Instead of answering, *Daddi* glanced around the office and finally repeated, "We're going for a treat after this—ice cream."

The doctor nodded and continued with her questions. "Mrs. Lapp, how would you describe your health at this point?"

"Oh, I'm as fit as the buggy horse in the parking lot. Maybe not as strong as I once was."

The doctor allowed silence to permeate the room.

Olivia Mae cleared her throat and said, "Sometimes *Mammi* forgets who I am. Sometimes she calls me the wrong name."

"I do?"

Olivia Mae nodded, dying a thousand deaths at the look of confusion on her grandmother's face. "It doesn't last long, but sometimes she is confused. It's—it's different from whatever *Daddi* is dealing with. She might go for days without an episode, but then it comes on all a sudden with no warning that I can tell."

Dr. Burkhart scribbled a few additional notes, then as if on some secret signal, a nurse tapped lightly on the door and walked into the office.

"My nurse is going to get you both in a room," the doctor said. "Mr. and Mrs. Lapp, if you'll just follow Amy, I'll be with you in a moment."

Which left Olivia Mae alone in the office with the doctor.

She told her everything—her fears, *Daddi*'s growing confusion, *Mammi*'s unpredictability, their precarious living situation. By the time she was done, the doctor had pushed a box of tissues her way, and Olivia Mae was trying to dry her tears without making her eyes red and puffy.

"You've been dealing with a lot, but you did the right thing bringing them in today. Too many times, caregivers attempt to deal with a situation like this on their own. There are things that we can do to help—there are social services for the family, some new medications that might help your grandfather and support groups for you."

"I'm not sure how much of that they'd agree to."

"We're getting ahead of ourselves. I want you to go back out to the waiting room, make yourself a hot drink and try to lose yourself in one of the fabulous magazines on our coffee table. I think we even have the latest *People*, which, if I'm not mistaken, features Brad Pitt."

Olivia Mae wasn't interested in *People* or *Better Homes & Gardens* or even *National Geographic*. But the hot tea that she made from the Keurig machine did help to calm her stomach, and the thought of Noah— and Lucas and her brothers—praying for them calmed her fears.

By the time they all met back in Dr. Burkhart's office, she was ready to know what they were facing.

"You cannot escape the responsibility of tomorrow by evading it today," as Abraham Lincoln had said. She'd done a report on him in the fifth grade. She could still remember the tall black hat she'd made out of construction paper. She'd worn it as she read her report in front of the class. She remembered being so nervous that day and thinking that life as an adult would be much easier than life as a student. What she wouldn't give to go back and be young and carefree again—even for just one week.

Dr. Burkhart got right to the point.

"I want to caution you that I have only done a cursory exam today. My specialty is not geriatrics, though my colleagues and I see many older patients here in our offices. You might want to consult with a neurologist, a psychiatrist or a psychologist. I can give you referrals for any of those."

"But what do you think?" Olivia Mae asked. Already she felt comfortable with the doctor. She liked the way that the woman spoke to her grandparents, the way she waited for an answer and the amount of time that she was taking with them.

"I believe that Mr. Lapp is somewhere between stage four and five on the Alzheimer's scale."

"So he has it? You're sure?" *Mammi*'s eyes widened in fear.

Olivia Mae reached over and clasped her hand. As for *Daddi*, he'd once again taken to playing with the puzzle on the doctor's desk—sliding pieces left and then right, trying to create the picture of a boat.

"At this point, there's not a definitive test for Alzheimer's, but based on the things that you both have told me, as well as my exam of Mr. Lapp, I'd say that it's highly likely that he does have the disease."

Olivia Mae wasn't a bit surprised at what the doctor was saying. She'd known—probably for over a year now she'd known. She'd even gone to the library and used the computers to research the disease. She'd known what diagnosis the doctor would give them, but she hadn't wanted to face that truth.

These dear people were her responsibility, and there was no unhearing what the doctor had said. "Stage four and five. What does that mean?"

"Stage four is what we call mild and is characterized by decreased ability to manage complex activities of daily life—manage finances or prepare a meal."

"Abe never was a *gut* cook," *Mammi* murmured.

"Stage five is moderate—the inability to choose proper clothing, that sort of thing."

Olivia Mae and *Mammi* exchanged a knowing look. *Daddi* had insisted on wearing his winter coat and a wool cap when he'd dressed for the day. They'd only dissuaded him by bringing up the idea of ice cream as a treat afterward.

They spoke for the next ten minutes about what could be done to help *Daddi*'s situation, and the doctor gave them a folder with brochures and pamphlets in it. When Dr. Burkhart turned her attention to *Mammi*, she smiled and said, "I have somewhat better news for you."

Noah ran out of work to do on the roof an hour after Olivia Mae left with her grandparents. He could have gone home. He probably should have gone home. He'd told his brother that he'd try to get back in time to help him in the fields.

But he couldn't do that.

He needed to stay and talk to Olivia Mae.

So he packed the leftover supplies he hadn't used back into his buggy, and then he swept the front porch where his hammering had left piles of dust and debris. Satisfied it looked as clean as when he'd shared dinner there with Olivia Mae the night before, he went inside and picked up all the bowls scattered on the floor, shaking his head as he did so. Olivia Mae was one stubborn woman. She'd rather spread a half-dozen pots and bowls around the place than ask for help?

He knew the feeling, though.

It was more than embarrassment or pride; it was a sickening feeling that your problems were too big to admit to—certainly too big to ask help for. He'd felt that way personally for a long time. If he was honest with himself, he'd felt like a freak because he still wasn't married and everyone his age was. He'd convinced himself that there was something wrong with him and that such a future wasn't even possible.

But last night, his lesson with Olivia Mae had sent his thoughts veering off in different directions.

He'd actually enjoyed the time he'd spent with her, even playing checkers with her grandfather.

He'd thought about her a lot after he'd left.

And he found himself looking forward to their next *lesson*.

Not that he was getting emotionally involved with Olivia Mae Miller. He understood that she was out of his league, and besides that—she was probably moving to Maine soon.

He walked through the barn and noticed that the horse stall needed mucking out. After that, he checked on her sheep, though he knew nothing about the animals. He was just wondering if he should leave a note, when he heard the clip-clop of their old buggy horse coming down the lane.

Olivia Mae pulled up to the front porch and helped her grandparents out of the buggy.

"Go inside with them," Noah said, grabbing the reins of the horse.

"But Zeus needs—"

"I'll take care of the horse." He waited for her to nod in agreement, then he led the horse across the yard to the barn, unharnessed the gelding and set him out to pasture. By the time he was finished, Olivia Mae was walking toward him.

"Abe and Rachel doing okay?"

"*Ya.* They're resting. The afternoon was tiring for them."

He studied her a minute, wondering what he should do, and finally it occurred to him to simply ask. "Should I go? Do you want to be alone, or…"

"You probably have things to do at home."

He shook his head and waited.

"Then I'd like you to stay, if you don't mind."

"I don't mind at all."

He wanted to reach for her hand, but she'd already turned away and was walking toward the sheep pen.

"I haven't formally introduced you to my sheep. This is Ashlee, Gabriela, Izso, Loren, Joann and Alicia." She touched each on the top of the head as they crowded around her.

Noah couldn't help grinning. "Is there going to be a quiz?"

"Could you pass one if there were?"

"Nope."

They both laughed, and all the tension and the worry about Olivia Mae and her grandparents and her home melted away. Everything was okay for this moment, and that was enough. Unfortunately, Noah's feelings of tranquility lasted about as long as a sheep's attention span, which was apparently remarkably short.

As they scattered back out into the pasture, chasing something he couldn't see, Olivia Mae said, "*Daddi* has Alzheimer's."

"They're sure?"

"As sure as they can be without dissecting his brain. I think—I think I've known for a long time."

"I'm sorry, Olivia Mae."

"It isn't your fault." But she didn't smile the way she usually did. Instead she began walking down the length of the fence. He hurried to follow her. She picked up a soccer ball and threw it toward the sheep. She stopped to upend what looked like a piece of playground equipment that had been turned over, and she finally plopped down on a stool that was inside the three-sided shelter at the far end of the pasture.

They had a good view of the house from there—the house and the sheep and the entire farm really. It wasn't very large.

"Did you know one year's growth of fleece equals about eight pounds of wool?"

Noah shook his head and sank to the ground beside her. The littlest of the sheep—was it Izso or Alicia?—ran over, stopped short and then proceeded to nudge up against Olivia Mae.

"Is that a lot of wool?"

"To me it is. When I first bought the sheep, I had these plans of spinning the wool into yarn and having a little shop of things I'd knitted. I even learned how to card and spin. I had this entire future planned out."

"You could still do that."

Olivia Mae shook her head, swiped at her tears and sat up straighter. "On the way back from the doctor's, we stopped by the phone shack, and I called my *bruder*. He took the news pretty well, but he says we need to move up there, where I can have more help."

"We can help you here."

"He says *Mammi* and *Daddi* need to be around their family—their *entire* family. He says it's more than I should have to handle on my own."

Noah didn't know how to answer that. He only knew that he felt like a rock had landed in the bottom of his stomach.

"And what do you think?"

Olivia Mae shrugged. "I told myself I was staying here in Goshen, here on their farm, for them."

She looked directly at him now, and the misery in her eyes tore at his heart.

"But maybe I wasn't. Maybe it was for me, because I didn't want to move, because I like Goshen more than Maine. Maybe I was being selfish all along."

"You don't strike me as a selfish person."

She let out a sigh, pushed the sheep gently out of her lap, stood and brushed off her dress. When she squared her shoulders, he knew that Olivia Mae, Matchmaker and Caretaker Extraordinaire, was back.

"How long...?" Noah cleared his throat. "How long until you move?"

"*Gotte* knows."

"Yes, but do you have any idea?"

She laughed and started walking back toward the pasture gate, toward her responsibilities.

"Ben is going to put an ad in the next issue of the *Budget*. He thinks we have a *gut* chance of selling the place before fall. He thinks someone will be looking for greener pastures and snap it up even though it's small. You know how it is with *Plain folk*..." She emphasized the last two words and wiggled her eyebrows.

Unfortunately he understood that her bravado was merely a show. Underneath, he suspected her heart was breaking.

They'd reached his buggy when he remembered to ask about her grandmother.

"That wasn't the only news today. Dr. Burkhart thinks *Mammi* is having a reaction between her blood-pressure medicine and the statin she takes to lower her cholesterol. She's going to change one of them, and hopefully the bouts of forgetfulness will stop. She didn't think that *Mammi* has Alzheimer's."

"That is *gut*." Suddenly Noah had an overwhelming urge to do something, anything, to ease Olivia Mae's burdens. Fixing her roof wasn't enough. Members of their church should have done that long ago, and they would have—if they'd known.

"How about I take you out to eat tomorrow?"

"I don't think I can—"

"Leave them for a few minutes? I could ask my sister-in-law to come and sit with them."

"*Nein*. It's not that."

"What then?"

She'd been standing beside Snickers, running her hand up and down the mare's neck. Finally she turned to look at him, a twinkle in her eyes. "We're not dating, Noah. You don't have to take me out to eat."

"Oh, *ya*. Sure. I know that. But the thing is…" He stepped closer and lowered his voice as if he was sharing a secret. "I've heard that I'm pretty bad at restaurant dates, and I'm supposed to be learning from you because you're an expert and all."

She swatted his arm, blushed prettily and looked at him in a way that caused his heart to soar. "Okay, Romeo."

"Who's Romeo?"

"Romeo and Juliet. Shakespeare."

When he shook his head, she laughed and said, "Honestly. Did you pay attention at all in school?"

"I don't remember reading Shakespeare."

"Maybe we didn't. Maybe I checked that out from the library. Anyway, it was a compliment."

"In that case, *danki*." He climbed up into the buggy. "Pick you up at six?"

"Sure."

He was about to call out to the mare when she leaned in and said, "And *danki* for fixing the roof."

Her eyes met his, and he thought for a moment that she was going to kiss him, but instead she stepped away and waved as he pulled off down the lane.

Since Noah had missed out on helping his brother in the fields, he offered to muck out the horse stalls after dinner.

"You won't see me turning down that offer."

Which was a nice enough thing to offer to do, but once he was out there doing it, he wondered if he'd lost his mind. It seemed like he'd spent all day around manure—first in Olivia Mae's barn and now in theirs. The job was messy and smelly and he was sweating by the time he'd finished.

He was surprised when Justin and Sarah walked into the barn, hand in hand. She was smiling as if Justin had just caused the sun to set for her viewing pleasure. Justin wasn't wearing his hat, and his hair stuck up in the back with a cowlick that he'd had for as long as Noah could remember. His nose was sunburned, his pants a bit ragged at the hem and he'd spilled something from dinner on his shirt. Sarah didn't appear to notice any of those things.

It was obvious to anyone with eyes that they were crazy about one another, but since he'd been home Noah had come to understand that what these two shared went deeper than that. Neither was perfect, and he'd seen them argue a time or two. Regardless of the reason, within a few hours they'd be holding hands again. Maybe that was what Olivia Mae had meant. What was it she'd said when they were eating on her front porch? That all women want the same thing that men do—to be respected.

There was an obvious respect for each other between Justin and Sarah. Noah felt a twinge of envy. Who wouldn't?

"I thought you two were going to town."

"Already did. You've been out here awhile, bro."

Noah glanced around. The stalls were clean, fresh hay had been laid, all the buckets had water and the tools had been put back on their pegs. When had he done all of that? How long had he been in the barn? He glanced through the open door and saw the sky darkening, so it must be after eight. Yeah, he'd been in the barn a couple of hours.

Instead of explaining that he'd lost track of time, he said, "It's been a long day. Think I'll go in and clean up."

"Actually we wanted to talk to you." Sarah nodded her head toward the chairs set out under the tall sycamore tree. "Maybe over there, where there's a breeze?"

"I can't be in trouble. I haven't been home long enough today to do anything but eat and muck stalls."

"Don't be so defensive," Justin said.

"*Ya*. Maybe we just like hanging out with you." Sarah bumped her shoulder against his.

He'd only known his brother's wife a few weeks, but

already he could tell that she was good for Justin and easy to get along with. The three of them sat under the tree, Justin and Sarah in the bench swing, and Noah in the metal lawn chair. He realized that he hadn't really taken the time to do this since he'd been home—to just sit and be with his family. It seemed that he'd spent the last ten years running away from things, or running toward them, but never being still.

A firefly sparked in front of him, then another.

Somewhere near the porch a bullfrog croaked.

A songbird called out to its mate—short, urgent notes that were quickly answered. Noah tipped back his head and studied the stars that he could see through the branches of the tree.

After a few moments, he said, "This is nice, but I suspect there's something you want to say to me."

"Well, now that you mention it…" Sarah placed her hand on top of her stomach. "We know that the family has been pushing you to court."

"*Pushing* is a *gut* word for it."

"Yup. They're 'all up in your business.'" Justin laughed at the phrase that even Amish *youngies* used. "But you know it's because they care."

"Uh-huh." He was getting a bad feeling about this talk.

"Don't look so defensive," Sarah said.

"How does a person look defensive?"

"Like that…crossing your arms tight and frowning so hard I'm pretty sure there's a wrinkle between your eyes."

Which made him laugh. The last thing he was worried about was wrinkles.

Sarah cleared her throat and smiled. "We just want you to know that we approve of Olivia Mae."

"What?" He nearly came out of the lawn chair, then eased back and forced himself to not cross his arms tightly. "What are you talking about?"

"Only that we think you two would make a good match." Justin put his arms across the back of the swing. "We want to be encouraging."

"And offer to help, so if she, you know, needs help with her grandparents so that she can get away, we'd be happy to sit with them."

Had they been eavesdropping on his and Olivia Mae's conversation? But that was impossible. He'd been at her house. The Amish grapevine was good, but it wasn't that good. Only the sheep could have overheard them. Sarah was a good guesser, or maybe she'd read the situation better than he had. Maybe it wasn't a guess after all.

"Actually, we are going out tomorrow."

Sarah looked up at Justin. "See? I told you."

"Uh-uh. It's not like that. It's another lesson."

"A lesson?" Justin shook his head, as if he wasn't about to fall for that.

"Didn't you just have one of those?" Sarah reached her foot forward and pushed the swing into motion. "Must be going really well."

"And you two must be awfully bored if you want to spend your free time teasing me."

"We're not teasing." Justin glanced at his wife. "And it was her idea, to offer to sit with Abe and Rachel. After what you shared at dinner, it sounds like Olivia Mae could use some help."

He had mentioned the doctor's assessment at dinner. He'd forgotten about that.

"I'm sure she could use some help," Noah admitted. "And I don't know why she hasn't asked for it up until now—embarrassed, I guess."

"Or in denial." Sarah nodded her head so hard that her *kapp* strings bounced. "I know a little about that."

He suddenly remembered the situation Sarah had been in before Olivia Mae had matched her with Justin. She'd been the sole caretaker for an elderly *aenti*. When the *aenti* had passed, Sarah hadn't known what she was going to do. She didn't have any other family, and she'd tried maintaining the home by herself. It was only when Olivia Mae had stopped over for a visit that the community had understood how in need Sarah was.

Justin had shared all of this when Noah had first come home, but he hadn't really thought about it until now. Maybe Sarah did know something about what Olivia Mae was going through. Perhaps the two of them would make good friends.

"I appreciate your vote of approval, but Olivia Mae and I are just friends."

"So that's why you spent all day repairing her roof, because you're *gut* friends?"

"Was I supposed to leave it like it was, leaking?"

"We have groups who do home repairs for those who can't. You could have let Lucas know, and he would have seen that it was taken care of—"

Noah shook his head before Justin could finish. "It only took a couple of hours."

"But you were gone all day," Sarah said softly.

"Yeah, I know I was. I wanted to wait and see what

the doctor had to say. I was worried about her." He lifted his hands, palms out. "I was worried about my *friend*."

Sarah and Justin shared a look between them that he couldn't read. Pushing herself to her feet, Sarah stood, stretched and walked to where he was sitting. She put a hand on his shoulder, and said, "Just don't wait too long to make up your mind."

Make up my mind?

Maybe Sarah had spent too much time in the sun today. She wasn't making a lot of sense.

Justin hopped up to follow her in, but held back a minute. "I don't know how she knows things like that."

"Like what?"

"You being in love with Olivia Mae."

"I'm not in love—"

"Women. It's like they have a sixth sense about these things." He slapped Noah on the back and followed his wife into the house, leaving Noah to stare up at the stars and wonder if they were right.

Was he in love with Olivia Mae Miller?

Chapter Ten

It was past nine o'clock when Olivia Mae finally went to her room, pulled off her *kapp* and unbraided her hair. Massaging her scalp, she tried to relax, but she was too keyed up. Too much had happened in one day. She would never be able to sleep if she went to bed now.

So she tried knitting. When she'd dropped a stitch three different times, she frogged the row she'd been working on, reinserted her needles in the previous row's loops and put the project back in her bag.

Perhaps she should try reading, but when she picked up the book from the library with the Christian romance sticker on the side, she simply held it and stared out the window. The man and woman on the cover caused a deep yearning to stir in her heart. She loved matching people together, but she was rather practical about it. When the people she put together were meant to be a couple, it seemed that the emotions followed. But what did she really know about falling in love? How did it feel to trust someone else with your hurts and dreams and feelings?

She put the book back on her dresser and picked up

the one *Mammi* had given her the previous Christmas. But even the book on sheep trivia didn't hold her attention. As Olivia Mae paged through it, she kept thinking of Noah and his silly jokes.

She thought of him on top of their roof, his hat pulled low over his eyes.

Could practically see him as he reached for the reins of Zeus and said, *I'll take care of the horse.*

She could see him smiling at her as she told him about the sheep.

Why was she thinking about Noah Graber? He was a friend, a fellow church member, someone she was trying to match. She had no reason to let her thoughts drift off any of those paths.

So instead she jumped up and began straightening items in her already tidy room. It was while she was dusting off the top of her dresser that she found the letter box Noah had brought to her house nearly a month ago.

Sinking onto her bed, she pushed back the covers, sat cross-legged and held the box in her lap.

She ran her fingers over the soft wood, the engraved butterflies and finally the clasp.

Pulling in a deep breath, she opened it and upended the letters in her lap. She still remembered how clever she felt at the time that she'd written them. All of the other girls her age were keeping a diary, but she had decided to write letters to herself. In the back of her mind, she'd pictured herself years in the future—sitting in a new home with her husband and children scattered throughout the rooms. In the daydream, she'd occasionally receive a letter from herself, as if she could have mailed it from the past.

Powerless to resist the pull of her own handwriting,

the words of her younger self, she picked up the first
sheet, unfolded it and began to read.

June 8
Staying with Mammi and Daddi is my favorite
part of summer. It's so much better than being at
home, where my bruders roughhouse and fart and
laugh at stupid jokes. It's no easy thing being the
only girl in a house full of boys. When I get married, my husband is going to have good manners
and enjoy the things I enjoy—like reading and
taking walks and watching sunsets.

June 17
Suzanne told Martha who told me that Suzanne's
brother likes me. I'm not sure how I feel about
that, but I'm keeping an open mind.

June 18
Suzanne and Martha and I were sitting in the back
of the barn during the singing tonight. Richard
came over and asked if he could sit beside me. He
held my hand during the last song, but afterward
he went back to his friends. They were laughing,
and he looked over at me a few times.
    Does he like me?
    Does he want to be my beau?
    I wish I had an older schweschder to talk to.
Mammi's too old to remember courting.

June 25
Richard kissed me tonight.
    I think I might be falling in love.

June 28

Today might have been the worst day of my life. I didn't mean to eavesdrop, but that didn't stop me from hearing, and as Mammi is fond of saying, you can't unhear something so be careful what you listen to.

How I wish I had followed that advice.

Only I am glad that I heard. Otherwise I would have gone on believing that Richard actually liked me. Instead I know it was just a dare. I was coming back from using the outhouse. As I came around the corner, I saw them all standing together and heard someone mention my name. I jumped backward, curious and embarrassed at the same time. I was close enough to hear, though—to hear and recognize who was speaking.

Richard's friend laughed and said, "You should date her. Honest. I hear a plump wife and a big barn never did any man harm."

I thought I might die right there, but I knew boys could be rude. Don't I have five bruders? It didn't bother me, what Richard's friend said. But then I heard Richard speak over their laughter.

"Nope, the slender kind is more my type. Now pay up. I kissed her like you dared me to."

I should have known he couldn't really be interested in me.

No one our age wants a plump wife.

No one wants me.

I want to go home.

The letters weren't in any particular order. She relived that summer in random sequence, relived the hopes and dreams and disappointments. Finally, she read the last one, folded up the letters, slipped them back into the box and closed the lid.

But she didn't put the box up.

Instead she turned out her light and sat there in the dark, moonlight spilling in through her window, her mind traveling back to that summer when she'd written the letters to herself, when she'd first fallen in love, when she'd felt beautiful and womanly.

She'd thought the letters would be like writing to a best friend or a sister.

She'd thought it would be fun—that someday she'd look back and laugh at her younger self. That she'd be amazed at how young and bright and witty she was.

She could see now that she'd been a young girl with a fragile self-image. She had allowed a boy she barely knew to break her heart. She'd allowed her opinion of herself to be changed because of what a teenaged boy said to one of his buddies.

Was that why she'd never dated?

Why she'd always pushed away men?

Was that why she'd become a matchmaker?

She gently placed the box on top of the dresser and climbed back into bed, this time lying down and staring up at the ceiling.

She'd struggled with her weight as a teenager. As a young adult, she'd told herself it didn't matter. She remembered the year her mother had to sew new dresses for her because she couldn't let out the old ones she had any more. It wasn't a big deal. Many Amish girls carried an extra twenty pounds, though by that time all of Olivia Mae's friends were dating or married.

She flopped over onto her side and stared out the window.

When she'd moved in with her grandparents, she'd worked harder than she ever had before. She'd also changed her diet—not from any misguided notion of attracting a beau, but because she'd been worried about her grandparents' health. The pounds slipped away, but the image she had of herself had remained the same. She was no longer heavy, but neither was she *slender*—Richard's word caused her to cringe.

She could see now that in some ways she was still a young girl, on the brink of womanhood, pining away for Richard Hofstetter.

She jumped up, snagged her brush from the top of her dresser and sat down in the single rocking chair in her room. Pulling her hair over her shoulder, she stared down at it. As a young girl, she'd loved to watch her mother brush her own hair each evening. It had reached well past her waist, and Olivia Mae thought it was the stuff of fairy tales. She'd thought of her mother as an Amish Rapunzel, only she didn't need to be saved because she had a happy home, a loving husband, a family.

Remembering her mother didn't bring the pain it once had. She still missed her parents, still wished she could speak with them, but she knew she would—one day. They'd be reunited in the next life. She didn't doubt that for a moment, and it eased the loneliness in her heart.

Her hair was now longer than her mother's was then, though most of the blond strands had darkened to brown. She brushed it, one hundred strokes, the same as her mother had always done, then she plaited it into a loose braid.

She'd changed.

She wasn't the young girl who had written those letters. She was a woman now. Maybe it was time—past time—to accept that she wasn't a chubby young girl that no man would want anymore.

Maybe it was time to stop being a matchmaker, to stop focusing on finding happiness for others and to start living her own life.

Just maybe it was time to allow herself to dream.

A home health-care nurse came by the house the next afternoon. Jeanette Allen was a large woman, wearing loose-fitting blue jeans and a top that was a soft purple and featured cats playing with balls of yarn. It was soon obvious to Olivia Mae that Jeanette was comfortable with herself and very good at her job.

She had a checklist and went through the house marking things on her clipboard. When she'd finished, she joined *Mammi* and Olivia Mae in the kitchen.

"You have a beautiful home."

"Danki." *Mammi* placed a platter of oatmeal cookies on the table.

Olivia Mae fixed a cup of coffee for each of them.

"So did we pass?" Olivia Mae asked.

Mammi was more specific with her question. "We don't have to move him, do we? Because Olivia Mae and I, we're determined to keep Abe here as long as possible, and—being Amish and all—we don't often resort to nursing homes."

"It's not a pass-or-fail thing. I understand that you'd

rather keep him here, and that isn't my call, anyway. If I were to find your home to be a neglectful or unsafe environment, then I would be required to report that to my supervisor, who would report it to the authorities, but it's obvious that isn't the case."

She smiled at them both, waited for her words to sink in and then continued. "I can tell that you're doing your very best to care for Mr. Lapp."

She sipped the coffee and accepted a cookie when *Mammi* pushed the plate toward her. "There are things that you can do to make life easier for Mr. Lapp. Would he like to join us as we discuss those?"

"He's resting," *Mammi* said. "Days when he takes a nap, well, they're better for all of us. He seems less… aggravated."

"Understandable. All right. Let's see what I've checked here."

Most of the items were obvious, and Olivia Mae was a little embarrassed that she hadn't thought of them earlier.

Remove the rugs so that *Daddi* doesn't trip.

Place red tape on the floor around the stove they used to heat the living room in winter and also on the handles of the stove and oven in the kitchen.

Keep all medications out of reach and make sure they have child-resistant lids.

Avoid stacks of old newspapers or other clutter that cause anxiety and represent a tripping hazard.

Install a handrail on both sides of the front-porch steps and in the bathroom.

"It's a lot," *Mammi* said.

"But most of these things are small." Olivia Mae felt

empowered by the list. Finally, she understood that there were things they could do to make life easier and safer for all of them, to make living here possible—if only her brothers would agree to it.

Jeanette stayed another thirty minutes, going over dietary suggestions and support for caregivers. When Olivia Mae walked her out to her car, she said, "You're doing a good job here, Olivia Mae."

"I don't know about that."

"Trust me. I've seen all sorts of home situations. What you've done here, without any guidance, is very good."

"I have five *bruders* in Maine. They all think we should move closer to them."

"It might be a good idea. I don't recommend that you—or any caregiver—try to handle such a situation on their own, and your grandmother is going to need additional care as the years pass. They both will."

"One day at a time," Olivia Mae murmured.

"Yes, that's a good thing to keep in mind, but we also have to keep an eye on the future. You know, too often I see situations like this wear down a caregiver—women who are forty and look sixty, women who were in good health suddenly dealing with back problems and anxiety and sleeplessness." She opened the door to her car, but she didn't get in. "If your brothers are willing to help, let them. Anyone who is willing to help, they're a gift from God."

Winking, she got into her car. "I'm not supposed to make religious comments, but I didn't think I'd offend you."

"*Nein.* You didn't."

"Good. I'll see you next week."

Olivia Mae watched the sleek gray car drive away. One more person who thought they should move. It seemed everyone thought it was a good idea but her. So maybe she was being stubborn. Maybe she was too close to the problem to see things clearly.

Noah directed Snickers down Olivia Mae's lane at exactly six o'clock. He was having second thoughts about inviting her out to dinner. Olivia Mae was dealing with a lot right now. Why did he think she'd like to go out for a night on the town? No doubt she'd accepted out of pity for him.

Unless…

But his mind froze as soon as the word *unless* entered. He simply couldn't see beyond his doubts and bad experiences.

She was waiting on the porch, wearing her customary light gray dress and white apron. She was smiling, though. Surely that was something. As soon as he stopped the gelding, she walked down the steps, but he hopped out of the buggy before she reached him.

"Would it be okay if I go inside a minute? Just to say hello to Abe."

The old guy had been on his mind nearly as much as Olivia Mae had. Noah had never seen anyone enjoy a game of checkers so much.

Olivia Mae seemed surprised at his request, but she nodded and walked back up onto the porch. When they stepped into the living room, something looked different, something he couldn't put his finger on. Of course, the pots and bowls were gone, but there was something else that had changed.

Then he snapped his fingers. "You took out the rugs."

"Apparently they're a tripping hazard," Rachel said. She glanced at Abe, smiled and then turned her attention back to Noah. "I have some coffee on the stove. I could heat it up if you'd like a cup."

"*Nein.* We're about to go and eat. I just wanted to say hello."

Abe looked up from peas that he was shelling. "Hello. I'm Abe Lapp."

Noah stepped forward, taking off his hat as he did so. "Noah Graber."

"Do I know you?"

"*Ya*, I believe you do."

"Sometimes I can't remember."

"I'm the one who wants to forget—you thrashed me at checkers the other night."

Abe cocked his head as if he could capture the memory. Finally, he shrugged and said, "I was always *gut* at checkers."

Abe returned his attention to the peas, and Rachel picked up her knitting. "You two go on now. Have a nice evening."

"You're sure—"

"Olivia Mae, we'll be fine. Now shoo."

Olivia Mae turned to look at Noah, one eyebrow arched slightly higher than the other. "Did she just shoo me?"

"I think she did."

"I guess we should go then."

"We might as well."

Noah liked teasing Olivia Mae. He liked when she smiled and the worries she wore like a shawl fell away. He liked making her happy, and at the moment she definitely looked as if she was looking forward to the evening.

He started toward the door and then turned back toward Rachel. "My *bruder* and his wife are going to stop by in an hour or so, just to make sure everything is okay."

"It'll be nice to see them," Rachel said.

On the drive into town, he asked Olivia Mae about the nurse's visit. She told him the things they were going to change around the house and asked if he knew anyone who could install handrails for the porch and bathroom.

"I'll take care of it tomorrow."

"That's not what I meant."

"But I want to." The matter seemed to be settled. He was suddenly glad he hadn't accepted the offer to work one of the Saturday auctions. While the money probably would have been good, at this point he didn't need the money. But Olivia Mae did need the help.

When they reached the downtown area of Goshen, he said, "Where would you like to eat?"

"You haven't already picked the place?"

"*Nein*. My dating instructor says it's best to let the lady choose."

"Smart instructor."

"So I've heard."

Olivia Mae pretended to have a hard time deciding, but finally she leaned toward him and said, "I'd love pizza."

"Would you, now?"

"Not typical Amish food, I know, which is why I'd like it."

"You're not picking pizza because it's cheap?"

"We'll share a dessert if you just want to spend more money."

"Deal." He directed Snickers down Main Street and pulled into the parking area across the street from the town's most popular pizza spot. The place was packed, which wasn't surprising considering it was a Friday night. For some reason, that didn't irritate him like it had the last time he'd tried to eat there.

Instead he snagged two chairs at an outside table as soon as a couple left, and he waved wildly at Olivia Mae, who was standing in line. She shrugged, indicating she wasn't about to get out of line, and he couldn't leave the table.

It was a predicament! Then he remembered he was wearing a light jacket. He took it off, draped it over one of the chairs and accepted two glasses of water from the worker who was walking by. Orders were placed at the window, but several teens bussed tables and distributed glasses of water, silverware and napkins. Satisfied that no one would mistake their table for an empty one and grab it, he hurried over to Olivia Mae.

"How about you hold the table, and I'll place the order."

"I could place the order."

"But I want to pay."

"You don't have to pay. This isn't that kind of date."

"*Ya*, I know, but I want to."

An *Englisch* couple in front of them couldn't help overhearing their conversation.

"Sounds like our first date," the woman said.

The man nodded in agreement. "And our second."

"We finally agreed to take turns."

"*Gut* idea," Noah said. "I'll take the first turn."

"Fine. I'd like Canadian bacon and pineapple."

"Sounds disgusting."

"It's *gut*, I promise."

"We'll do half and half."

"What are you putting on your half?"

"Anchovies, of course."

She wrinkled her nose, then leaned forward and lowered her voice. "Never order anchovies while you're on a date."

He matched her tone, as if they were sharing an intimate secret. "I was kidding."

"You're sure?"

"*Ya.*"

"*Gut.* Your dating score is improving by the minute."

"Not so fast. You're not getting out of my third lesson." Whistling, he moved forward in the line, as she hurried back toward the table. Instead of paying attention to the menu posted overhead on a chalkboard, or the people in front of him, he kept peeking over at Olivia Mae. When she caught him watching her, he smiled, offered a little wave and turned to study the crowd.

About half of the teenagers—both Amish and *Englisch*—were tapping on their cell phones. People thought Amish teens didn't have cell phones, but of course many of them did. The difference was that their parents didn't pay for them. If a *youngie* wanted to work an extra five or ten hours a week to afford a phone, that was up to them. Noah didn't know a single family that allowed them in the house, though, so most teens kept them out on the porch or even in the barn. Noah had better things to spend his money on, like a bachelor pad or dinners with Olivia Mae.

Quite a few tables were occupied by families with young children. He glanced over at Olivia Mae again. She'd begun talking to a mother who was holding a young baby. If he wasn't imagining things, a look of yearning passed over Olivia Mae's face.

Why had she never married?

She would make a good wife, a good mother. Any man would be happy to have her by his side.

He shook away those thoughts as he stepped forward to place their order. He was helping a friend who needed a night away. It was nothing more than that, even if he wanted it to be.

The wait for their pizza passed too quickly. They never ran out of things to talk about, but they would occasionally lapse into silence, which was just as comfortable.

Dating was easy when he was with Olivia Mae. He felt none of the awkwardness that he'd suffered through with Jane and Francine.

It seemed they'd barely arrived, but already their dinner was finished, and he found himself looking for ways to avoid taking her home.

"Let's go for ice cream."

"I'm too full. I shouldn't have eaten that last slice of supreme."

"I told you that you'd like it."

"You did, and you were right, especially since it didn't include anchovies." She patted her stomach as if it was huge, which it wasn't.

"Ice cream would be *gut*. We can even share a scoop." When she looked at him like he was wearing his hat backward, he backpedaled. "Or get a small. We'll get a children's cone. Come on. I haven't had ice cream in ages."

She finally relented, declaring he was more persistent than a child. It was while they were sitting in front of the ice-cream shop—Olivia Mae holding a cone with strawberry ice cream and chocolate sprinkles, Noah enjoying a double dip of butter pecan—that she became serious about the subject of his dating.

"You know, Noah, I think I understand your problem."

He'd been chasing a dribble of ice cream down his cone, but now he froze and raised his eyes to hers.

"Don't look at me that way. I just meant I think I understand your issues with women." She rushed on when he tried to interrupt. "It's not that you need lessons. It's that you're an introvert."

"A what?"

"An introvert." She bit into the crunchy cone. "You know. Someone who is more comfortable alone."

"I don't know if that's true."

"Does being around a large group of people wear you out?"

"Like an Amish gathering, you mean? *Ya*. Sometimes."

"Do you prefer a few close friendships to a lot of casual ones?"

He thought about that a minute and finally admitted, "The only real friends I've ever had are my *bruders*."

"You're a *gut* listener, and you seem to think before you talk—usually."

"*Danki.* I guess."

"It's not bad to be an introvert."

"What are you?"

"Maybe a mixture of the two, but if I had to choose? Introvert. I tend to look at life from the inside out."

"I don't know what that means."

"You know." She tapped her chest. "I think about what people are feeling before I think about what they're doing or saying. Of course, we can't always know what someone else is feeling, so life can be hard for an introvert."

"Are you saying it's hopeless?"

"I'm saying that when you're comfortable with someone, like I think you're comfortable with me, then you act normal. You don't feel as if you have to cover every silence with words, and you haven't told a single animal joke tonight."

"I thought you liked my jokes."

"Uh-huh."

"I see what you mean, I guess." In truth he knew that his *problem* wasn't that simple. If Olivia Mae knew the truth about him, if she knew his past, she wouldn't think the *problem* was as simple as what personality type he was.

Chapter Eleven

Olivia Mae had been enjoying herself for the first time in a long time when Noah's mood suddenly changed. He tossed his unfinished cone into the trash, said it was getting late and walked her back to the buggy without another word.

She didn't understand what had happened.

She'd thought he was enjoying the night as much as she was.

As they drove back to her house, an uncomfortable silence filled the buggy. Noah drove as if the road required every ounce of his attention.

He didn't smile.

Didn't speak.

Didn't tell a single joke.

Could it be that she'd misread the entire situation? It had started to feel like a real date, but perhaps he didn't think of her that way. Perhaps he was just slogging through his commitment to the deal he'd made with his mother. Maybe, just maybe, he wasn't interested in a plump wife.

Nein.

Whatever had changed his mood, she was pretty sure it had nothing to do with her and Noah, and it certainly had nothing to do with her weight. That insecurity was her past, exerting itself into her present. She didn't have to allow that. She didn't have to let her old fears and old hurts ruin a perfectly good evening.

When they reached her grandparents' farm, Noah helped her out of the buggy, murmured "good night" and then strode back around to the driver's side.

She thought about letting him go.

But something told her that tonight was a chance she didn't want to let slip away. A chance for what, she didn't know, but she followed her instinct. "If you have a minute, I'd like you to stay."

"Stay?"

"Sit on the porch with me. I need to run inside and check on *Mammi* and *Daddi*, but I'd like… I'd like to talk to you a minute."

If anything, Noah looked more miserable than he had on the buggy ride home, but he nodded in agreement so she hurried into the house.

Daddi was already in bed sleeping.

Mammi was sitting in her rocker, an open Bible in her lap and a cup of tea on the table beside her.

Telling her grandmother to holler if she needed anything, Olivia Mae grabbed a dark green shawl from the hook by the door and walked back outside. She almost took a lantern, but she had a feeling that Noah would be more comfortable speaking if he didn't have to look directly at her.

She stopped to close the screen door quietly, stood

there in the pool of light and Noah said, "That color looks *gut* on you."

Her heart tripped a beat. *"Danki."*

"Did you make it?"

"Ya."

"From your sheep wool?"

"Nein. I never did buy a spinner. The whole thing was too expensive. So I sell the wool, and use the money to buy more yarn." She didn't add that this was a sweater she'd purchased from the thrift store, frogged and re-worked into a light shawl. Admitting that a week ago might have stirred the old ache in her heart for what could have been, but now it seemed trivial. It was un-important. She understood that Noah meant the com-pliment, but he was stalling.

She sat down in the rocker beside him and said, "Ex-plain to me what happened."

"When?"

"Earlier. At the ice-cream shop, when you went quiet."

She thought he might refuse her. He set the chair to rocking, stared out at the night and finally ran a hand up and across the back of his neck, massaging the mus-cles there.

"What you said about my being an introvert, that might be true. It might be part of it, but it's not all of it."

"What do you mean?"

"If you knew my history, you'd understand that it's nothing as simple as personality type."

"So explain it to me—explain what you mean by your *history*."

Instead of answering, Noah dropped his head into his hands.

Olivia Mae waited a minute, then two. Finally she said, "It's not that bad, Noah."

"How do you know?"

"Because the moon is still shining."

His head jerked up, he looked out over the porch railing, out into the cool summer evening, and then back at Olivia Mae. "You're saying the world goes on."

"I'm saying that sometimes things seem worse when they're stuck in our head, going round and round." She thought of the letters still in the box in her room. She'd let those doubts and fears and hurts trouble her for too long. Why was she free of them now? What had changed?

She couldn't say.

She only knew it felt good not to carry that weight any longer.

"Tell me," she said. "Not because I need to know, but because I think you'll feel better when you do."

He stood up, walked to the railing, turned to look at her, then strode back across the porch and plopped into the rocker. When he began to speak, she understood that it took all of the courage he had to do so. She understood that the trust he was showing in her was a precious thing.

"When I first left Goshen, I was young—only nineteen. I had some vision of myself traveling from community to community, enjoying the free life. In Maine, I worked on a farm helping with the harvest. The farmer had a daughter…"

He must have sensed her smile, because he said,

"I know. Sounds like a bad country song. Cora was younger than I was at the time—only seventeen. I didn't want a serious relationship. I wasn't looking for that at all, and I thought I'd made my intentions clear. I was still seeing myself out on the road with no obligations, able to pack up and move whenever the mood struck me, which I did a few weeks later when the harvest was done."

"You broke her heart?"

Olivia Mae could only see the outline of Noah, the shape of him. But a lot could be observed from a person's posture, the way they held their head, the tightness of their shoulders. At her words, Noah looked up, sharply, but then it seemed to her that the tension in his features eased. She could have imagined that, but she didn't imagine his voice, which was softer now, softer and tired.

"*Ya*. I suppose I did. The bad part is that I think I knew I was doing it as I was doing it, but it was just such a heady thing to have a girl like me, to have her want to spend the rest of her life with me. Here in Goshen, I'd always been Caleb's younger brother."

"I haven't met Caleb," she said softly, just to keep him talking.

"He's the oldest. Lives in Nappanee now—close enough to visit. All my *bruders* live close enough to visit. Maybe that's why I wanted to get away. Here, I was always going to be just another one of those Graber boys. There? Well, there I was something special." He sat back, again set the chair to rocking. "But it wasn't enough to convince me to stay in Maine. I didn't even tell Cora a proper goodbye. I told myself that it would be better that way. I just left."

"Introverts avoid confrontation."

"I guess. Maybe I was just a coward."

"You're being a little hard on yourself."

"Then there was Samantha." He sat forward, elbows on his knees, fingers interlaced. "She was *Englisch*, and I pretended I was, too, which was a joke. Anyone could tell from the way I talk that I'm Amish, but Samantha... Well, she just accepted whatever I said. I even bought some blue jeans and T-shirts, let my hair grow out, wore a fancy pair of sunglasses that must have looked ridiculous. It was almost as if I needed to be someone else, something else."

"Why do you think that was?"

"It was like I was running from who I was. What did I know? I was probably twenty-one or twenty-two, and at that time I really had no idea what I wanted my future to look like or who I wanted to be. So who knows what I was running from? Shadows maybe."

"You're not the first *youngie* to have an identity crisis."

"Sure. I guess that's true, and it's kind of you to say so. But that doesn't explain Ida. I was old enough to know better with her. It was only two years ago."

"You don't have to talk about this if you don't want to."

"Maybe you were right, though, when you said I'll feel better if I do. Maybe confession is good for the soul." He stood again, paced up and down the porch and finally stopped in front of her, leaning back against the porch railing, arms crossed, eyes studying her. It was as if he needed to see her response more than he needed to hide because of his embarrassment.

"Ida was an Amish girl I met when I was working at an auction house in New York. It was a *gut* community, and I learned quickly that the auction work was something I was able to do well, something I enjoyed."

"And Ida?"

"Daughter of the main auctioneer." He crossed his legs at the ankles, recrossed his arms as if he could get more comfortable, stared up at the ceiling and finally shook his head. "It would have been a nice place to settle, and Ida—she was a sweet girl. I don't actually remember asking her to marry, but suddenly we were pledged and attending classes with the bishop."

"You didn't ask her? But you were pledged?"

Noah only shrugged, as if even he didn't understand what had happened. "Before I knew it, the big day arrived. I thought I could do it. I thought everything would be all right afterward, that my feelings for her would be what they were supposed to be."

"What did you do?"

"What I always do—I ran. The morning of our wedding, I crept out of the house before dawn and hit the road—hitchhiked to Kentucky. That's what I'm telling you, what I've been trying to tell you. There's something wrong with me, and it's not just that I'm an introvert."

Olivia Mae had been sitting, patiently listening. But she couldn't sit any longer when she heard the desperation in Noah's voice. She smoothed out her dress, stood, walked across the porch and stopped next to him, mirroring his posture, which meant they were both staring back into the house. She watched as *Mammi* set aside her Bible and walked into her bedroom, leaving the lantern on for her.

"So let me get this straight." She ticked off the items on her fingers. "You're a heartbreaker, you avoid confrontation at all costs and you run whenever you feel backed into a corner."

"*Ya*, I guess that sums it up."

She stared at her three fingers. "I think we're each allowed a few flaws—at least three."

"You're making light of this and you know it."

"Actually I'm trying not to lecture you."

"Is that so?"

"Yes." She turned toward him, studied his profile. "Noah, there is nothing wrong with you. Cora and Samantha? You were too young to know what you wanted or how you felt. I know. Don't even say it. I know that many of our friends marry that young."

"Or younger."

"But many don't. And many, like you and me… Well, it takes longer. Some people are older when they fall in love and maybe that's because it takes a while for them—for us—to know their hearts."

"But what of Ida? I was older by that time, certainly older than her. I should have known better."

"Sometimes we end up in situations that we don't know how to get out of. The way you left, that was wrong and you should write her an apology. Whether she accepts it or not, that's her choice. But not marrying her? If you didn't love her, then you shouldn't have married her."

"Not everyone marries for love."

"That's true. Sometimes those relationships work out and sometimes they don't, but you knew you didn't love her. That's a form of dishonesty and basing a marriage on that? Never a *gut* idea."

He finally turned toward her, searched her face in the little bit of light that spilled out through the window.

"Why are you doing this?"

"Doing what?" She tried not to react to the way he was looking at her, to the way his eyes searched hers.

"Trying to make me feel better."

"Isn't that what a friend is supposed to do?"

"Is that what we are—friends?"

When she didn't answer, he stepped closer. Olivia Mae's heart rate accelerated like one of her sheep tearing across the pasture.

"Olivia, may I…"

This time she didn't admonish him for playing with her name. Instead she nodded. He reached out and touched her face, and she thought she might melt right into the floor of the porch. And then he did what she'd been hoping for some time he would do. He kissed her softly, gently, and then more urgently. When she thought that her knees would give way completely, he pressed his forehead to hers.

Then without another word, he turned and walked out into the night.

Noah thought about that kiss for days.

He thought about it on Saturday as he installed railings next to her grandparents' porch steps and then in the bathroom adjacent to their bedroom. He thought about it on Sunday when he sat next to Olivia Mae at the church gathering. Then later, as they walked around Widow King's property, he thought about it and found the courage to hold her hand.

The widow's home was actually across from Noah's parents'. He had known her all his life. Known her when all of the children were still there. By the time her husband died, the eldest son had already taken over the working of the farm. He'd married and they now had a full household of children.

"Why doesn't she live in the *grossdaddi haus*?" Olivia Mae asked.

"She did, when her husband was alive. I guess she got lonely. A few years ago she moved back into the main house."

"So the *daddi* house is empty?"

"Looks like it."

They'd reached the small front porch, which was just big enough to hold two rockers. The door was unlocked—Amish rarely locked their doors and never their outbuildings. Olivia Mae threw a smile back at him and then walked into the house.

"Cute," she said.

"Small."

"Only two people in a *grossdaddi haus*. It's big enough."

The place was well laid out, built with large windows and high ceilings. The open windows caught the summer breeze and stepping inside was like stepping back into spring.

There was a fine layer of dust on the furniture, but overall the place was surprisingly clean. Of course, with only four rooms that couldn't have been too hard.

They walked through the sitting room, the bedroom, peeked into the bath and ended up in the kitchen.

"It's a *gut* house—nice and solid." Olivia Mae smiled up at him.

"No leaks in the roof."

"Ha. And no steps out front. It's designed for grand-parents. They did a *gut* job."

He wanted to stay there with her—sit on the couch and pretend the place was theirs. The thought surprised him. Had he fallen in love with Olivia Mae? Could he see himself spending the rest of his life with her?

The next two days passed with excruciating slow-ness, though he was plenty busy. Their date—their final lesson—was scheduled for Wednesday night. He wanted to do something special, but he kept coming up blank.

They'd had dinner at her place.

He'd taken her out to pizza.

And she'd warned him against picnics.

So what was left? He was stewing over it as he worked in the family garden on Tuesday evening.

Justin came up behind him and let out a long low whistle. "What did that trowel ever do to you?"

"What do you mean?" Noah stared at the tool in his hand, then the row, then his brother.

"You're using it like a hammer. Thought maybe it had offended you in some way."

"Guess my mind was elsewhere."

"Did you and Olivia Mae have a fight?"

"What? *Nein.* It's just that… Well, we're supposed to have our final lesson tomorrow, and I can't decide where I should take her or what I should do. I want it to be special." He didn't add that he wanted it to be a real date and not just a lesson.

"Take her to your work," Justin said.

"Why would I do that?"

"She probably doesn't get out of Goshen much. I bet she'd enjoy a trip over to Shipshe. She could walk through the market and shop, maybe after she watches you auction."

"I don't think she'll leave Rachel and Abe for that long."

"I can take Sarah over to stay with them a few hours."

"She would do that?"

"Of course. She's been a little restless the last few days. It would probably cheer her up."

He had to admit the idea had merit. When he said that he'd run it by Olivia Mae, Justin grinned as if he'd stumbled upon the golden goose.

"What?"

"Nothing. Just nice to see you falling for someone."

Was he?

Falling for Olivia Mae?

He didn't know. He only knew that when he wasn't with her, he thought about the next time he would be with her. And when he was with her, he didn't want the time to end. But their date was the following evening. He couldn't count on her checking the phone shack, so he harnessed Snickers and drove over to her place.

He didn't want to show up empty-handed, so he stopped at the local farmer's market and purchased a basket of strawberries. She'd said something about needing to serve her grandparents more fruit.

She was standing in the kitchen, thanking him and

washing the strawberries in the sink, when he brought up the subject of their next date.

"I was thinking you could come to the market."

"Market?"

"The flea market and auction house—in Shipshe."

"Why would I do that?"

"To see where I work. To get out for a little while."

"Oh, I don't know. That would be a long time for *Mammi* and *Daddi* to be alone."

"We're not children," *Mammi* said from the kitchen table, where she was cutting up slices of peach pie for each of them.

"I know you're not, but what if something happened?"

"Like what?" Noah winked at Rachel and she grinned back at him.

"*Ya*, like what? We're old people. We can't exactly get in trouble anymore. Takes more energy than I have, and Abe, I'm not sure he remembers how."

It was good to hear her joke about their situation. At least, Noah thought it was a good sign.

"See? She wants you to go, and Sarah offered to come by. Something about asking your *mammi* to show her how to bind off a blanket. I have no idea what that means."

Olivia Mae rolled her eyes, obviously not buying the idea that Sarah needed help with her knitting. But she also hesitated, as if she was considering going.

"I have to leave early in the day," Noah added. "But another bus heads that way just after the noon hour. You could catch that one, watch my auction at two o'clock, and then we could walk around through the flea market and have an early dinner. The last bus leaves Shipshe at six. You'd be home by seven."

"Never know what you might find," *Mammi* chimed in. "I like the idea. You might even come across more sweaters to buy on the cheap and frog."

Frogging made no more sense than *bind off* to Noah, but he nodded in agreement.

"Okay. Fine." Olivia Mae raised her hands in surrender. "Now let's eat some of that pie before the ice cream melts all over the table."

He hadn't meant to stay for two hours, but he did.

They talked about a number of things: her *daddi*'s health—it seemed to have stabilized. Her *mammi*'s episodes—she'd only had two since changing her medications. The sale of the farm—no one had expressed an interest yet.

Noah didn't want to think about Olivia Mae moving. So he told her about the newborn calves at his brother's place, how well the hay was coming in at his *dat*'s, and that he'd written letters of apology to Cora, Samantha and Ida.

"That's *gut*, Noah. That's really *gut*."

He kissed her again before he left.

And as he drove away he felt, finally, as if his life was on the correct track again—the track he'd deviated from over ten years ago.

Olivia Mae was ridiculously excited about her afternoon in Shipshe.

She dug out one of her cloth shopping bags and put it next to her purse. She counted the money she'd been saving from her sheep's wool and decided she could afford to spend twenty dollars. She made an early supper for her grandparents, set it in the icebox and left Sarah instructions for how to warm it up. As if Sarah didn't know how to warm up a chicken casserole.

At a few minutes before the noon hour, Justin showed up to drop off Sarah and also to take Olivia Mae to the bus station.

"It's nice of you to do this," she said to them both.

"Happy to." Sarah grinned and held up her knitting bag. "I really do need help with this project."

Mammi had taught Olivia Mae everything she knew about yarn, patterns and stitches. More important, she'd taught her to love knitting and, although her arthritis sometimes kept her from doing as much as she would like to do, she still enjoyed every aspect of it. Her eyes were sparkling as she told Sarah, "Come in. Come in and let's sit around the table."

Daddi was taking a nap, so Olivia Mae didn't wake him. She pushed the list of emergency instructions into Sarah's hands, whispered *"Danki"* and hurried out to the buggy.

Thirty minutes later she was on the way to Shipshewana.

When was the last time she'd taken an entire afternoon off for herself? She always tried to limit her errands to an hour, two at the most. The thought of an entire afternoon and evening to do with as she pleased made her positively giddy. And the thought of spending it with Noah? Well, that was icing on the cake.

The market had grown since she'd last been there. Of course, it had been years, but still she was surprised. She hopped off the bus and hurried toward the auction barn. Noah had told her that he'd be working the live-stock auction. When she stepped into the cool shade of the auction area, she was nearly overwhelmed by the earthy smell of animals and hay and even manure. She saw crates of chickens, goats, several donkeys and, of course, sheep.

Then she heard his voice, and hurried toward the northeast corner of the barn. Noah was just beginning the afternoon auction. Olivia Mae's heart felt as if it had lodged itself in her throat when she saw him. He was dressed the same as always—straw hat, white long-sleeved shirt rolled up at the sleeves, dark pants and suspenders.

He noticed her, tipped his hat and then turned his attention to the people gathered around. He greeted everyone, said they'd be starting with a nice set of rabbits and then he began the opening bid.

And in that moment, when she first heard his auctioneer voice, Olivia Mae fell so hard and so completely that she knew resistance was a fool's game. The rhythm of his auctioneer's chant, the obvious fun he was having and the fact that she could stand back and watch everyone watch him shed an entirely new light on Noah Graber.

"Who'll give me ten? Ten-dollar bid?" he began. "Now twenty, now twenty, who will give me more?

"Twenty-dollar bid, now thirty, now thirty, will you give me forty? Thirty dollars for two breeders—how about thirty-two? Thirty-five? I got it! How about forty? Forty? Forty? I've got thirty-five. And these bunnies are hopping straight toward the fella in the Cubs base-ball cap."

Laughter rippled through the growing crowd. Before it could die down, Noah was opening the bid on half a dozen goats. That was followed by crates of chickens, including a rooster that they let out to strut around as Noah called out to the crowd, "Don't be shy, don't let these big birds pass you by."

The auction passed so quickly that Olivia Mae looked around in surprise as people began to move away. Had she really been standing there for an hour? Noah had a break before his next auction so he walked around the flea market with her, bought her a snow cone and insisted on carrying her bag of yarn. The variegated blue cotton was on clearance and she'd spent her entire twenty dollars in one booth, but the joy of it washed over her.

How long had it been since she'd splurged on new yarn?

How long had it been since she'd purchased something merely because the color caught her eye and the feel of it sent her imagination running off in new directions?

Amish and *Englisch* walked alongside each other, peering into booths, enjoying homemade samples of salsa and bread and peanut butter.

"We're going to be too full for dinner," she said as she scooped the last dollop of peanut butter out of the tiny cup with the tiny spoon. It reminded her of the miniature ice-cream cups they used to buy from the truck that drove around their neighborhood.

"Maybe you'll have to help me in the next auction." Noah bumped his shoulder against hers. "Then you'll be hungry. Auctions always give me an appetite."

"That's because you're working hard."

"Do you think so?"

"*Ya.* You make it look like you're not working. You make it seem like you're up there having fun, but it's hard work to keep an auction going and keep everyone involved. Your auctions—they draw the biggest crowds."

Noah looped his arm through hers. "I like it here. I like this kind of work. But you know what I like even more?"

"What?"

"The fact that you came with me today."

Which seemed to sum it all up.

When they were together, Olivia Mae felt as if the world had suddenly been filled with possibilities. Her problems faded into the background, and she forgot to worry. Instead she started thinking about her future.

Chapter Twelve

Noah finished his second auction for the day and tried not to stare at Olivia Mae, who was standing in the back smiling like she was at the state fair.

When the auction was over, they left the flea market and walked through some of the shops in downtown Shipshe. He realized that he liked being with her. He liked the way that she smiled at *Englischers* and waved at their children. He liked how she stopped to hold a door open for an elderly Amish woman. He liked everything about her.

"Let's eat at the Blue Gate," he said to her.

"You're kidding."

"I'm not."

"They serve huge plates of food."

"I worked up an appetite today. Didn't you?"

She started to laugh, and he realized he liked that about her, too. "*Ya*. You got me there. I did, too."

So they made their way into the Blue Gate restaurant, a place that Noah had only been to a half-dozen times in his life. It was somewhere his family went to on special occasions—to celebrate someone's birthday or someone graduating from their little one-room schoolhouse. Once they'd even come to celebrate his parents' twentieth anniversary.

But this day was just as special as those.

They hadn't once referred to their time together as a *lesson*.

And something told Noah that this day, a plain old Wednesday in the first week of June, would be one he'd always remember.

He ordered the Amish country sampler, and they had a good laugh over that. Olivia Mae ordered a grilled meat-loaf sandwich with fries and a side salad.

When they were done, he insisted they split a piece of pie.

"I'm going to burst. Honest, I can't eat another thing."

But he'd caught her looking at a piece of chocolate peanut-butter pie that the waitress was carrying to a nearby table. So he ordered one. "And two more forks, please." The waitress had taken away their silverware when she cleared off their dinner plates.

It seemed curiously intimate, sharing a piece of pie.

Noah found himself wishing that the night could go on forever, but, of course, it couldn't. They had to hurry to catch the bus, then sat together laughing about different parts of their day.

When the bus pulled into Goshen, Justin was waiting for them, as he'd said he would be.

But something was wrong.

Noah knew it the minute he saw his brother's face.

Justin met them halfway between the buggy and the bus. "Abe's at the hospital—here in town."

"What happened?" Olivia Mae's voice shook and her eyes widened and she reached for Noah's hand. "Is he okay? Where's *Mammi*? When did this happen? How did it happen?"

"He fell. Tried to get out of bed by himself, and he fell."

"Is he okay?" Noah asked.

"I think so. They had to put in a dozen stitches—"

But Olivia Mae wasn't listening now. She was hurrying toward the buggy. Noah and Justin caught up, and Justin said, "I'll take you there. Sarah's with him, and my *mamm* came, too. Lucas was on his way."

Olivia Mae sat there, back ramrod straight, eyes blinking rapidly, staring out the window but not seeing a thing. Watching her nearly broke Noah's heart. She might seem just fine to anyone else, might look as if she had pulled herself together quickly, donning the role of responsibility once again. But Noah understood how afraid she was and how much she was hurting. Her grandparents were everything to her.

They were the parents that she'd lost, the brothers who lived so far away. And in some ways *Mammi* was the sister she'd never had. In other words, they were her family—her immediate family. The people she shared coffee with each morning, a prayer at every meal and the daily ups and downs of life. Olivia Mae understood that her grandparents wouldn't live forever, but she loved them and she would miss them terribly when they were gone.

Not that Abe was in the grave just yet. If there was one thing Noah was sure of, it was that the old guy was tough and would fight through anything to stay with his family.

They rode in silence.

Justin drove.

Noah sat in the back with Olivia Mae.

He didn't ask if she was okay. He could tell that she was afraid and worried and upset—but she was also calm after the initial shock.

He didn't tell her everything would be fine.

How was he to know that it would be?

But he held her hand, and when they reached the hospital, he jumped out of the buggy and hurried with her into the emergency room. Olivia Mae rushed straight to the information desk as if she'd been there before.

"I'm here to see my *daddi*—Abe." Her voice shook and her hands had begun to shake. She glanced at Noah, then back at the person manning the information desk, and tried again. "His name is Abe Lapp. He was brought in earlier tonight. Can you tell me where he is? Can you tell me if he's okay?"

Sarah must have heard Olivia Mae's voice. She must have been waiting for them because she came hurrying toward them before the receptionist could answer Olivia Mae's questions.

"We're down the hall," Sarah said. "All of us are… waiting just down the hall."

When they turned the corner into the main waiting room, Noah understood what she meant. He'd expected his *mamm* and Sarah and maybe Lucas—like his brother had said. But it seemed that word had traveled quickly. Ezra Yoder and Daniel King, their two preachers, were sitting near the window playing checkers. Half a dozen older folks occupied chairs along one wall—all Amish, all there to wait and pray. They must be friends of Rachel and Abe. This show of support was a testament to what a difference Olivia Mae's grandparents had made in the community. They were obviously well liked.

The expressions were somber, and he noticed several folks had their heads bowed in prayer.

Jane and Francine were also there. They rushed toward Olivia Mae and put their arms around her. Noah thought that perhaps she'd like to be alone with her friends, but when he turned to step away, she reached for his hand and led him toward Lucas.

"Is *Daddi* going to be okay?"

"*Ya*, he is." Lucas motioned to the seat beside him. Olivia Mae sat, but Noah remained standing.

"What happened? Justin said he fell. Said he needed quite a few stitches."

"Abe was trying to get out of bed, and apparently he wasn't quite awake yet. He lost his balance and went down hard. The cut on his head is a long one, and they had to shave his hair to stitch him up." He patted Olivia Mae's hand. "Sarah and Justin, they acted quickly. Sarah stayed with your grandparents while Justin ran to the phone shack and called an ambulance."

"How long ago was this?"

"A little over an hour ago, maybe closer to two."

So Abe had been riding in an ambulance as they had been eating pie and laughing about the day. Olivia Mae looked up and met Noah's gaze, and he knew she was thinking the same thing.

"Can I—can I see him?"

"I'm sure you can. Let me go and tell the nurse that you're here—and that you're next of kin." Lucas winked, which did more to ease Noah's worries than anything he'd said. If Abe was in any sort of danger, Lucas would be somber and proper. The fact that he was kidding around was a good thing.

As Lucas walked away, Sarah and Justin made it over to where they were waiting.

"I'm sorry, Olivia Mae. I thought I was watching closely, but…"

Instead of answering right away Olivia Mae stood and put her arms around Sarah. They hugged and cried and finally pulled apart when Justin suggested they might need some fresh air.

"You two are acting *narrisch*. Lucas said Abe's going to be all right. What's all the tears for?"

"Men," Olivia Mae said.

"We're *gut*," Sarah said. "I am so sorry…"

"Don't mention it again. He could have fallen anytime." Olivia Mae wiped at her tears, the first that she'd allowed to fall since receiving the news about her *daddi*. "It could have happened while I was there. It's just… he's a little wobbly at times."

Noah saw Lucas trying to catch their attention. He touched Olivia Mae's shoulder and nodded toward where their bishop was waiting, motioning for her to join him.

"I'll be praying, and I'll wait right here."

"Danki."

And then she was gone, disappearing through the double doors and down the hall.

* * *

Olivia Mae walked beside Lucas, her heart hammering in her chest. She trusted what he said. She believed that *Daddi* was going to be okay, but she needed to see him for herself. She needed to see with her own eyes that he was fine.

And what about *Mammi*? How was she handling the emergency?

When they made it to the room with the name *Abe Lapp* scrawled on the whiteboard beside the door, they paused outside the doorway. Lucas touched her arm, then turned and silently made his way back down the hall. Olivia Mae stood there, studying her grandparents through the small window. Fear and relief and joy and sorrow coursed through her veins all at the same moment. So many thoughts and feelings collided within her that for a few seconds the hall began to spin and she had to reach for the door frame.

She closed her eyes, swallowed twice, prayed for the peace that passes all understanding.

When she opened her eyes again, she pushed her nose right up to the glass—still not ready to enter, still needing to see.

Daddi had his head bandaged, but his eyes were closed and his color was good. She could tell by the numbers on the digital screen that his blood pressure and heart rate were both in acceptable ranges. She'd been through this before—several times now. She'd learned her way around a hospital.

It was the image of *Mammi* that she thought she'd never forget. Sitting beside *Daddi*, her back was to the door, her head bowed, her hand covering his. Olivia

Mae knew without a shadow of a doubt that her grandmother was praying—for his health, his recovery, their time together, even for Olivia Mae.

She knew her grandmother's heart like she knew her own.

They were that close to one another.

They shared the same fears and hopes and memories.

And suddenly standing in that hospital doorway, Olivia Mae felt a shower of gratitude cascade over her. She understood that she'd been given a great gift once again—the gift of another evening with the people she loved. She bowed her head and thanked the Lord that He had once again seen fit to keep *Daddi* here with them a little longer, that they had so many friends waiting back in the little room down the hall, that Sarah and Justin and Noah were a part of her life.

But the prayer of thanksgiving clashed with another—as her heart cried out to God to see her through the next few weeks and months. Because she knew, without a doubt now, that they would be moving to Maine. She couldn't handle this alone anymore. She'd been a fool to try. And anything she felt for Noah? Well, it would have to wait.

Pulling back her shoulders and breathing deeply, she pushed the door open and stepped into the room. *Mammi* glanced back over her shoulder. Her expression broke into a smile and she stood. "*Gut*, you found us."

"Of course I found you, *Mammi*." The tears came fully then. The tears that she'd been holding back streamed down her cheeks. "I was so scared, when Justin told us—"

Mammi had stood and wobbled over to where Olivia Mae was waiting. "He's fine. Your *daddi* is fine."

"I should have been home."

"You know that isn't true."

Mammi placed her hands—hands that were as soft as a newborn's skin, though wrinkled and spotted and frail—on both sides of Olivia Mae's face. Olivia Mae closed her eyes for a moment and willed herself to remember this feeling, this love that was so precious.

"It could have happened while you were there. Abe could have fallen anytime and anywhere." *Mammi* hugged her, then returned to *Daddi*'s side to check him again and pull the covers up a bit. "We're old is all. Old age isn't something to be avoided at all costs, Olivia Mae. But it does have its challenges."

Instead of sitting back down, she motioned Olivia Mae toward the chair and whispered, "I think I'll step down the hall—say hello to folks and let them know that Abe is going to be fine."

Olivia Mae took her place and did the same thing that she'd been watching her *mammi* do—she prayed. For her grandfather, for the doctors, for her brothers and even for the people who would purchase their little farm. She prayed for the new home waiting for them in Maine. She prayed for herself and for Noah.

It was while she was sitting there, alone in the hospital room, watching the monitor's numbers flash on the small screen and the IV fluid drip into the tube that led to his arm, that *Daddi* opened his eyes.

He didn't seem to notice where he was or that there was an IV attached to his arm. He certainly didn't seem in pain, though that may have been because of some medication they gave him. Instead he simply smiled at her, reached for her hand and said, "Olivia Mae, it's *gut* to see you."

"*Ya?*" She once again found herself blinking back tears. How long had it been since he'd called her by her name? Why now, tonight of all nights, was he lucid?

Perhaps because she needed him to be.

Maybe because he was relaxed from the medication or the brief rest.

Or possibly this was one of those moments of grace that *Gotte* sent to calm her soul.

It was several hours later before she walked back out into the waiting room and headed toward the front of the hospital. Her *mammi* had sent everyone home, insisting they get some rest and come to see Abe when he was released from the hospital.

Everyone had done as she'd suggested—everyone except for Noah. He jumped to his feet and waited, his eyes searching hers. He didn't pepper her with questions. He didn't rush her. He simply waited.

She stopped in the middle of the room, her eyes taking in the empty chairs and then coming back to rest on him, her heart understanding that he had waited for her. She felt strong now and unafraid, and still she walked straight into his arms.

He let her rest there, and when she finally pulled away, he asked, "Are you okay?"

"*Ya.*"

"Abe?"

"Resting, and they brought *Mammi* a blanket and

pillow. The chair makes out into a bed. She wouldn't leave him."

"You're going home?"

"She insisted."

"May I take you? Justin and Sarah left me the buggy. Lucas took them home."

"*Ya*. That would be *gut*."

"I'm a little surprised you're not staying," he said as they walked toward the parking area. "You're nearly as stubborn as Rachel."

"I didn't think she'd rest as long as I was in the room, and there was only the one chair. So I pretended to agree with her. Honestly I'm not sure how I planned to get home, now that I think about it. I'd completely forgotten that I'd ridden here in Justin's buggy. I guess I would have called a cab, if there'd been no other way…"

"Glad I can be of service." Noah opened the door on her side of the buggy and faked a bow. "Welcome to Snickers's limo."

"Fancy."

"*Ya*, I know." He brushed back a lock of hair that had escaped from her *kapp* and kissed her softly. "You look exhausted. I'm glad you're going to get some rest."

"Actually I'm going to see to Zeus and the sheep."

"I would have done that."

"I know you would have." She squeezed his hand and then climbed up into the buggy.

"Sarah feels terrible about what happened."

"Nothing about tonight was her fault, and this isn't the first time he's fallen. That's one of the reasons we picked up all of the rugs."

"You're fortunate he didn't break a hip."

"I read once that elderly people don't fall and break a hip. What usually happens is they're standing, the hip breaks and then they fall."

Noah glanced at her in surprise. "I didn't know that. You know a lot about this sort of thing."

"What sort of thing?"

"Caring for your grandparents. You're a *gut* granddaughter."

"I've done my best, but I think—I think my opposition to change caused me to wait a little longer than I should have."

"He could have fallen in Maine, too."

"It's true. I only mean that *Mammi* could use more family around her—more than just me. And there's something else that occurred to me while I was sitting beside his hospital bed."

"What's that?"

"I've been dragging my feet—not wanting to move, not wanting to upset their daily routine. And I think I had good reasons for doing that."

"You love them."

"I do, and I'm concerned—always concerned for them." Olivia Mae stared out at the streets of Goshen as they drove toward the farm. The clip-clop of Snickers's hooves on the pavement soothed her nerves, and the night air felt good after being cooped up inside the hospital. She glanced back at Noah, who was still waiting patiently for her to finish her line of thought.

"At the same time I think that putting off moving them was a bit selfish of me. My *bruders* and their wives, my nieces and nephews, they deserve a chance to spend time with *Mammi* and *Daddi*. These final years—they're precious."

Instead of answering, Noah reached across the seat and covered her hand with his.

"If you don't mind, I'd like to stop by the phone shack."

"Call your *bruders*?"

"I'll leave a message. They need to know."

What was left unsaid between them was that most likely this would escalate the efforts to sell *Daddi*'s farm. And what did that mean for their relationship, their growing feelings for one another?

They traveled in silence, the gentle sway of the buggy nearly lulling Olivia Mae to sleep. The next thing she knew, Noah was standing outside of her open door, touching her arm. He said, "We're here. At the phone shack."

She nodded, rubbed her eyes and stumbled into the small building. She'd forgotten her purse, but Noah fetched the required change out of his pocket and dropped it into the coffee can on the counter.

She left her message—rambling a bit but managing to convey the basic facts.

Daddi had fallen.

He was in the hospital.

Both he and *Mammi* were fine.

She'd call the following evening, at six if possible, and give them an update.

When she walked back out of the phone shack, Noah was sitting on the steps. Though she knew she needed to get home, though every muscle in her body was suddenly exhausted and screaming for sleep, she sat beside him, her head on his shoulder, and together they watched the stars come out.

The next three weeks flew by. *Daddi* came home after just two days and much of their life returned to normal. It was Olivia Mae who had changed. She finally understood and accepted that they would be moving—and sooner than later if her brother had anything to say about it.

She continued to see Noah at church functions, and he stopped by the house at least twice a week to check on them. But she felt herself pulling back. Why lose more of her heart to this dear man who had become so important to her?

She couldn't make their future come together in her head.

They would be moving to Maine.

Noah had an excellent job here in Indiana—not to mention all of his family was here.

She couldn't see it working, so instead she focused on preparing for the move. Her biggest concern was what she'd do with her sheep, but Noah told her not to worry.

"That's like telling a mother not to worry about her children."

"Oh, they're children now, are they?" He could always make her laugh and never failed to point out the lighter side of things exactly when she needed to be reminded that all was not somber and gray. "What do you call a sheep covered in chocolate?"

Olivia Mae pretended to groan.

"A candy ba-a-a-aaa." Satisfied that he'd at least

made her smile, Noah grew suddenly serious. "I'll take care of the sheep, Olivia Mae. If that's what you're worried about, if you're sure that you're going to move—"

"What choice do I have?"

"If that's the way you feel, then I will take care of the sheep."

"You don't know anything about sheep, and I know you don't want to be a farmer."

"I could auction them."

She must have looked horrified because he quickly added, "I'm kidding. I'll learn. I don't mind learning— for you."

She would miss him terribly when they moved. She realized now what a precious thing friendship was. And love? Well, love was a blessing from *Gotte*, plain and simple. Each time she saw Noah, she pushed aside her fears and worries and tried to enjoy the minutes they had together.

And then, one month later, when a string of rainy days was broken by bright afternoon sunshine, she walked to the phone shack and saw the recorder blinking with the number 1. She knew then, before she even pressed Play, that it was her brother. They'd found a buyer. Someone who wanted to expedite the process. It was time for her to begin to pack.

That evening, she broke the news to Noah.

Chapter Thirteen

He drove around for more than an hour—not ready to go home, not sure exactly when he'd lost his heart to Olivia Mae Miller. But the fact remained that he had, and now it was time to step up and decide what to do about it.

He unharnessed the horse and tossed some feed into a bucket. He might have gone to his room and tossed and turned all night, but when he walked into the kitchen he was surprised to see his *mamm* there, her hands wrapped around a steaming cup of what he knew was herbal tea. On the table was a plate of peanut-butter squares that she pushed toward him. "Cold milk in the fridge," she said.

He poured a glass and made his way through two of the squares before he found his voice.

"She's leaving earlier than I thought."

"To Maine?"

"*Ya.* Her *bruder* has already found a buyer for the place. He'll be here to move them next week."

She didn't say anything, didn't offer an opinion or a

suggestion, simply waited for him to work through his thoughts and emotions.

Finally, he sighed and pushed the plate of sweets away. "I love her."

"And that's bad?"

"This situation—*our* situation—is problematic."

"How so?"

He sat back and studied her. His mom had always been the listener of the family, perhaps because she was the only female. Growing up, it had helped tremendously for him to know that he could trust her, that he could share with her the things that were bothering him. When he'd become a teenager, he'd suddenly grown shy about that, and perhaps that was when his problems had started—when he'd stopped sharing his hurts and fears and dreams with the people who loved him. So instead of shrugging, and offering a noncommittal response, he stared up at the ceiling and tried to articulate what was standing between him and the love of his life.

"Her family situation with her grandparents is difficult."

"Because of their health."

"And because she feels responsible for them, in the way a parent is for a child." He held out his hand, palm up, then turned it palm down. "Things have reversed."

"Not an easy situation."

"But that isn't the worst of it."

His *mamm* crossed her arms on the table and leaned forward.

"The worst of it is that I want what's best for her, what's best for Olivia Mae, and I don't know what that is. Is it moving to Maine? Starting over? Having help with Abe and Rachel? Or is it staying here? Do I even have a right to ask that of her?"

"It's a *gut* thing that you realize you love her now, before she leaves."

"Is it? Because at the moment it only feels miserable."

She patted his hand, picked up his glass and her mug and rinsed them in the sink. By the time she returned to the table he was sitting there with his head in his hands.

Her next words surprised him because they weren't about love or marriage or families—things that he knew she held dear. Instead she said, "I'm proud of you, Noah. You've turned into a fine young man."

"I'm twenty-nine, *Mamm*. I've been a man for a long time now."

"In some ways, I suppose that's true." She sat next to him and waited for him to raise his eyes to hers. "But in other ways it's happened in these last few weeks. When you learn to put others' needs first, over your own. When even in the midst of your own dreams and desires, your heart is set on easing the way for the person you love. Well, that's the difference between a boy and a man."

She stood, kissed him on top of the head, as she'd done for all of his life, and walked out of the kitchen.

He was left with her words echoing through his mind.

He supposed what she'd said was true, because he no longer felt like a *youngie*. He felt as if his heart were breaking in two, but that seemed almost minor compared to what Olivia Mae was facing. The thing that twisted his stomach into a knot was admitting that he didn't know what was best for her. How could he know? Those decisions were hers to make.

One thing he knew for sure—he wouldn't make the mistake of waiting to find out. His only regret would be not asking her what she wanted for her future.

If it was staying in Goshen, he would find a way to make that happen.

If it was going to Maine, then he'd help in any way he could to make that transition smooth.

And if she wanted him in her life, then he would give up anything because sacrificing something for Olivia Mae wasn't really a sacrifice at all.

Her happiness was what mattered the most to him. Olivia Mae was a *gut* person. She deserved her own family and her own home, but she also felt a strong responsibility to her grandparents. She wasn't a young girl, but a woman with all the emotions and needs and responsibilities of a woman.

And he loved her beyond anything he could imagine.

He took off his shoes and crept upstairs to his room, trying not to wake anyone. He needn't have worried. Justin was walking out of the bathroom, drying his hair with a towel.

"Sarah asleep?"

"Nearly. The baby was kicking a lot this afternoon so she didn't get a nap."

Noah nodded toward his bedroom. He turned on the lantern, and his brother sat on his bed while he took the chair.

"I have one week."

"What do you mean?"

"I mean I have one week…to convince Olivia Mae that we're meant for each other."

Justin had continued drying his hair with the towel, but now he let it drop around his neck. "I thought you had a month."

"So did I." Noah picked up a pen from the desk and twirled it in his fingers.

"What happened?"

"Her *bruder* called this afternoon. Told her he'd found a buyer for the house, and that he'd be down in one week to move them."

"Wow."

"Uh-huh."

"So what's your plan?"

"I don't have one. That's why I'm talking to you."

Instead of answering, Justin finished drying his hair, stood and returned the towel to the bathroom. Walking back into Noah's room, he asked, "So are you sure?"

"Sure about what?"

"That you love her?"

"*Ya.* I don't know when it happened. Maybe when I was sitting on her porch having our first lesson. Maybe when I walked into her house and saw the roof leaking like a sieve. Or maybe that first day when I gave her the letter box."

"This isn't you wanting to rescue her, is it? Because I don't think that's the same thing as love."

"She's the one who rescued me." It came out more of a growl than he intended, the admission piercing his heart but also firming his resolve.

They both turned toward the open window as an owl

hooted from a nearby tree. The storms of the recent days had passed, leaving the evening cool and pleasant.

"You're going to need a plan."

"Like what?"

"I don't know. What did you learn in those lessons she was giving you?"

They sat there for another half hour, as Noah explained the things he'd learned about dating, women and how to relate to someone else. By the time they were done, Noah understood that he'd learned about more than romantic relationships. He'd learned how to connect to people in general. While he might always be an introvert, be more comfortable around a few people than a crowd of them, he no longer had to avoid someone that he could care about.

And with that knowledge came the certainty of what he needed to do next.

When his brother left for his own room, Noah turned the lantern up to its brightest setting. The small desk in the corner of his room was well-stocked. His *mamm* must have been using it when he'd lived away, because he'd never needed pen, paper and envelopes. Now all that he needed was there—another example of *Gotte*'s provision. He pulled out a clean sheet of paper and began writing a note.

It took him three tries to get it right—to put his hopes and dreams on that sheet of paper without scaring off Olivia Mae. He understood that she was afraid of putting her heart on the line. She was also strong and kind and wise beyond her years. But change, especially big change, was always frightening.

So his first goal was to calm that fear.

His second was to pique her interest.

And his third? Well, his third was to win her heart. Which was expecting a lot from a one-page note.

After he'd done his best, he folded it neatly, stuck it into an envelope and scrawled her name across it.

Olivia Mae Miller.

If things went as he hoped and prayed they would, that would change. Personally he thought Olivia Mae Graber had a much nicer ring to it.

Olivia Mae hurried in from the barn as the sun was popping over the horizon. She hoped she hadn't made her grandparents wait too late to eat. She'd told them time and time again to start without her, but they never would.

Mammi was placing an egg casserole on the table and looked up to smile as Olivia Mae paused at the mudroom door to knock any dirt off her shoes. As she walked to the sink to wash her hands, she stole a glance at the table. Her *mammi* was following the nurse's instructions to a *T*. A bowl of fruit and a platter of hot biscuits sat in the middle of the table—along with butter and jars of peach, apple and strawberry preserves. Olivia Mae said good morning, poured herself a cup of coffee and plopped into her seat, which was when she noticed the envelope with her name on it. How could she not notice it? The envelope was positioned across the middle of her plate.

"What's this?"

"Looks like a letter."

"*Ya*, but—"

"Noah brought it by earlier."

"Noah Graber?"

"Don't know any other Noah." *Mammi*'s eyes twinkled as she sat down across from her.

"Earlier this morning?" She glanced up at the clock. It was only a few minutes past six thirty, and she hadn't heard a buggy. Then again, she'd been in the back of the barn mucking out stalls.

"We invited that nice young man to stay to eat, but he said he had to get to work." *Daddi* reached for a biscuit and broke it open, releasing steam and a scrumptious yeasty scent. "Do we know him?"

"*Ya*, for sure and certain we do. Let me put some butter on the biscuit for you, Abe."

Olivia Mae couldn't imagine why Noah would drop off a letter for her before going to work. That meant he'd harnessed the horse to the buggy, driven to their house, dropped off the letter, and driven back home in time to unharness the horse and catch the shuttle to the auction in Shipshewana.

"This came while I was in the barn?"

"It did." *Mammi* scooped a helping of eggs onto *Daddi*'s plate and then another onto hers. She pushed the casserole dish toward Olivia Mae, who shook her head. She was still holding the envelope as if she was afraid to open it.

Why would Noah Graber write her a letter?

What was he up to?

And why was her heart galloping like a mare set free in the pasture?

She had precious little time to get ready for the move and a long list of things to do today. She did not have the luxury of pining over what might or might not be in a mysterious envelope. Gulping down half her mug of coffee for courage, she stuck her fingernail under the envelope's seal and ripped it open.

Dear Olivia Mae,

I would like to ask for the pleasure of your company this evening at 6:00 p.m. for a picnic dinner. I realize you are quite busy this week packing the house, but everyone needs to eat. More important, we have only a few days left until your move, and spending what time we have together is important to me.

Of course, I will bring all of the necessary supplies. You only need to be on your front porch at 6:00 p.m. And before you say you need to eat with your grandparents—remember you will have all of the weeks and months stretching out into the future to spend with them. Our time is slipping away.

We won't be gone more than a couple hours, but if you'd like a sitter for your grandparents, I can arrange that. And I promise to have you home by nine so you won't be too tired tomorrow.

If you're agreeable to this, call the phone shack near my house and leave a message. However, if you feel you can't get away, there's no need to take the time to go all the way to the phone shack. I understand how busy you are, especially as you prepare for your journey to Maine.

Sincerely yours,

Noah

She read it once and then again. The first time through she was sure that she must refuse him. The second time through she wondered if she dared to take a few hours for herself. But when she raised her eyes and looked at *Mammi* and *Daddi*, who were both smiling at her, she knew what her answer would be.

Pushing back her chair, she said, "I'm going to ride my bike down to the phone shack. I won't be long."

As she pedaled down the lane, the letter tucked in her apron pocket, the tension that had been building since her brother's phone call melted away.

While it was true that her life was changing, the sun was still shining brightly, there was a pleasant breeze, and she felt young and healthy.

Did Noah Graber want to court her?

Did she want to be courted by him? She poked at the feelings that she had for Noah, like one might poke at a toothache. It was true that he was handsome, nice to be around and a *gut* person, but nothing in the letter suggested he felt as she did. He hadn't even tried to kiss her again in the last week.

Noah was a *gut* friend; that was the reason for the dinner invitation.

Or was there something more going on?

Did Noah care for her?

Was he actually asking her out on a date now that she was moving? His timing was terrible! But his letter was spot-on.

He'd appreciated what a stressful time this was.

He'd given her an easy out if she wanted to decline.

He'd respected her time, and he'd understood her need for a break from her grandparents.

Noah had come a long way from the clueless guy who thought he was happy being a bachelor. The night before she'd made a list of possible women he could date, wanting to fulfill her promise to give him three solid chances and wanting to do so before they moved. But each name she'd listed, she'd crossed out.

Oh, they were nice girls, but for some reason each one had seemed wrong for Noah.

So who was the right woman for him?

Why did the thought of matching him with someone else cause her heart to sink?

She let that question roll around while she parked her bike, hurried into the phone shack and left her message, which was short and sweet. "This message is for Noah Graber, and my answer is yes. Yes, I'd love to."

She stepped out of the phone shack into a summer morning that was as close to perfect as any she'd ever seen.

The sky was blue, the day promised to be warm and a light breeze stirred the trees.

And she was going on a date with Noah Graber.

How long had it been since she'd stepped out with a boy, since she'd done something for herself? For years now her very existence had been focused on two things—caring for her grandparents and matching others to their true love. Suddenly that seemed short-sighted. In fact, it seemed as if she'd neglected something very important.

She'd turned her back on her own hopes and dreams.

It was all good and fine to care about your family, but Olivia Mae wasn't one to encourage being a martyr. *Gotte* had a plan for every life, and it was possible—yes, it was actually certain—that He had a plan for hers. The question was, did it include Noah Graber?

The day passed quickly. Jane and Francine arrived with packing boxes and insisted on staying until lunch, helping her pack dishes, linens and clothes they wouldn't be needing in the next week. Everything was carefully labeled and then carried to the barn and stored. She didn't want the boxes in the house, where *Mammi* might trip over them and *Daddi* continually asked, "Is someone moving?"

It was when they were taking a break on the front porch, each holding a cold glass of tea and a snack, that Jane broached the subject of dating. "I've stepped out three evenings now with Elijah."

It was the first time she'd brought Elijah up in front of Olivia Mae, who asked, "How did that go?"

"*Gut.* He…he's enjoying working at the factory, or at least enjoying the pay."

They all three laughed about that. It was common knowledge that the factory paid well.

"More important, he's learning to use the modern equipment for the woodworking. Elijah says what he really wants to do is start his own business specializing in custom-built cabinets, that sort of thing. He knows that some of the modern tools wouldn't be allowed, but others would—many are now powered by batteries, which he could charge with a generator in the barn if the bishop allows it."

"I can see him being *gut* at that." Francine bit into the apple she'd chosen over a cookie. The tea—of course—was unsweetened.

"Do you have feelings for him?" Olivia Mae asked.

"*Ya.* I do." Jane wiped the condensation off her glass and rubbed it on the back of her neck. "Now that I understand him better, I realize that he has a real talent for working with wood. He never would have been happy as a farrier. I don't know why I couldn't see that before. Somehow, I took his rejection of his *dat*'s plans for his life as a rejection of me. Now I know he was just trying to find himself."

"Aren't we all," Francine murmured.

Olivia Mae almost let her comment slide, but she had six days left in town and while they would continue to write letters to one another, writing wasn't the same as speaking face-to-face.

"What do you mean by that, Francine?"

"Oh." Her gaze jerked up, as if she didn't realize she'd spoken aloud. "I guess while we're confessing, I might as well do the same."

"I thought we were just talking." Jane's grin widened. "But I like confessions, too."

Francine sat up straighter. "I've applied for a position with MDS."

"Mennonite Disaster Services?" Olivia Mae leaned forward and squeezed Francine's hand. "That's *wunderbaar.*"

"It's fantastic," Jane agreed.

"Do you think so? Because I haven't told my *bruder* yet or my parents. But I think—I think I'll like it. They do important work for people affected by disasters. And they need a cook for a crew in Texas, where they're still helping folks with hurricane recovery. It would be a three-month job, but possibly renewable for as long as they're in the area."

"You're a very *gut* cook."

"It doesn't pay, but they provide lodging and meals are free. More important, I think it would give me time away from Goshen, which is what I feel like I need right now."

"They would be fortunate to have you," Olivia Mae said.

"The question is whether they'll approve me, because of my diabetes."

"I don't think you have to worry about that, and it's because of your diabetes that you know so much about nutrition." Olivia Mae set her rocker into motion. The two women in front of her had become more than friends—they were like sisters—and she realized in that moment how much she would miss them.

"Why are you smiling?" Jane asked.

"She looks like she knows something we don't."

"Looks like she wants to share a secret."

"And now she's blushing."

"Okay, you can stop. It's not that big a deal, only that... Well, Noah asked me out for dinner tonight." When she told them it was for a picnic, they all three burst into laughter. It did Olivia Mae's heart good to see that Francine could laugh about Noah's ill-conceived date and the argument that had ensued. Both seemed like they'd happened long ago rather than earlier that summer.

"Just watch out for the horse blanket," Francine said, draining her glass and then standing. "Now let's get back to packing so you have time to prepare for your date."

Olivia Mae had used that phrase so often in her role as matchmaker—*prepare for your date*—as if it was a recipe that needed to have all the ingredients set out on the counter. But in truth she had been ready for tonight since the first day Noah had stepped on her grandparents' porch. She had no idea where the evening would lead, or if she was making too big a deal of it, but she knew with a deep certainty that it felt good to look forward to something for a change.

Noah arrived at Olivia Mae's place a few minutes early. Instead of turning into the lane, he pulled to the side of the road and waited. Arriving early would only make her feel rushed, and that was the last thing he wanted to do.

When his watch said five minutes before six, he called out to Snickers, who tossed her head and then trotted down the lane. It was almost as if the horse understood this was an important evening, or perhaps she was picking up on Noah's enthusiasm.

He thought he was ready for just about anything, but then he drew close to the porch and saw Olivia Mae standing there. She wore her light gray dress, clean white apron and a shawl the color of the summer sky across her shoulders. Noah's heart felt as if it stopped beating completely, then stammered and then galloped forward. He raised a hand to wave, murmured to the horse and jumped out of the buggy.

"Noah."

"Olivia Mae."

"Beautiful evening."

"Ya." It was as if the thoughts in his head had decided to shut down, but then he remembered sitting on the porch with her as she explained that women were more like men than different from them. Women liked to be appreciated, cared for, admired—same as anyone. So he stepped closer and said, "You look *wunderbaar.* That shawl, it's a nice color."

"This?" A smile tugged at the corners of her mouth.

"Did you buy it in town?"

"I made it."

Now her smile had broadened and any anxiety he felt slipped away. This was Olivia Mae, his friend, and the woman he hoped to marry. He didn't have to worry about being someone he wasn't. He only had to find the time and place to share his feelings.

"I'd like to say hello to your grandparents before we leave."

"Of course." Her voice had dropped to a whisper, and he thought her eyes looked bright with unshed tears. Before he could think that through, she'd turned and led him into the living room.

"Where are the packing boxes?" he whispered.

"Stacked in the barn. Bothers *Daddi* less that way."

"Evening, Abe."

The old man looked up in surprise. He'd been shelling peas, but he stopped, cocked his head and said, "Do I know you?"

"Ya, I'm Noah. Noah Graber."

"I knew some Grabers once. They own a farm closer to town."

"That would be my parents." They'd had this conversation before, several times, but Noah understood that the present often slipped away from Abe while the past anchored him to a safe place. "My *dat* helped you to build the barn. I was a young lad then, but I remember us all meeting early on a Saturday morning."

"And finishing it by evening." A look of contentment spread over Abe's face as he returned his attention to the peas. "We appreciate that. The barn, it's going to be a real help for our first winter here."

"*Ya*, I suspect it will."

Noah met Olivia Mae's gaze and she mouthed a silent *danki*.

Rachel walked into the room, carrying two steaming mugs. "Noah, I didn't hear your buggy."

"Let me carry those for you." He was across the room in three steps, taking the mugs and carrying them to the small table between the two rockers.

"We're just settling down for a little snack. Abe, he likes to go to bed early."

As if in agreement, Abe yawned, but he continued shelling the peas.

"Is there anything I can do to help this week?" He meant with the move, but he didn't want to upset Abe by mentioning it. "Anything you need?"

"The best things are not things." Rachel smiled at the old proverb. "If there is, I'll let you know. Now go, both of you. It's a beautiful summer evening. You don't need to spend it inside with two old people."

Noah reached for Olivia Mae's hand. Entwining his fingers with hers, he led her out to the buggy, helped her climb up into the seat and then hurried around to the other side.

The best things are not things.

How true that was. He'd thought that his life goal was to be an auctioneer, to have his own bachelor pad, to be free of others' expectations. But those things paled in comparison to the woman sitting beside him.

They spoke of the weather, Jane, Francine and general happenings within their community. He let Olivia Mae drive the conversation and when they fell into a comfortable silence, he enjoyed it rather than worrying what it might mean. When they were a mile away from his brother's place, he started to laugh.

"Care to share?" She adjusted herself in the buggy, waiting, one eyebrow raised and a smile on her face.

"I was just remembering my first date, with Jane. Did I ever tell you that I penned talking points on the inside of my hand? Thought I should have them there in case I couldn't think of anything to say."

"Oh, my."

"Uh-huh, and as she said, I barely let her get a word in edgewise. Silence—especially silence when I was with a woman—sort of scared me."

"And now?"

"Now silence feels comfortable, like we're sharing something without the need to put it into words."

Her cheeks blossomed pink, and he had to fight the urge to pull the buggy over on the side of the road and kiss her. Instead he turned his attention to the mare, intent on not missing the turn into his brother's back pasture.

"Where are we going?"

"Private little place I heard about."

"Heard about?"

"Okay. It's my *bruder*'s place—Samuel's. There's a nice pond near the back, with shade trees around it."

"Is that so?"

"And I have the owner's word that we'll have the place all to ourselves."

He pulled into the back entrance of the property, called out to Snickers to *whoa* and hopped down to open the gate. When he'd pulled through, Olivia Mae offered to close the gate, but he shook his head and took care of it quickly. The lane was a little bumpy, but the horse seemed happy to be on a less-traveled road.

When they pulled up to the pond, he knew that his brother had picked the perfect spot. Justin claimed he took Sarah there for all their important occasions—when he'd first kissed her, when he'd proposed—and she'd taken him there when she told him about the baby. It was quiet and private and peaceful. Perhaps the area would become a sort of living testament to their families and their love for one another. That thought cheered him immensely and calmed the nerves in his stomach.

The pond was full due to recent rains, large trees shaded the east and south side, and a small dock reached out a good ten feet into the water.

After setting the brake on the buggy and tying Snickers's lead to a metal rail his brother had installed for just that purpose, he helped Olivia Mae out of the buggy. Reaching into the back seat, he snagged the picnic basket and quilt.

"Can I help you carry that?"

"*Nein.* I've got it." He didn't let go of her hand as they walked to the far side of the pond. Though his heart was pounding in his chest he felt good—better than he'd felt in a very long time. He didn't know what turns their relationship might take over the next few hours, but he knew that he was where he wanted to be at this moment, and he planned on enjoying that instead of worrying.

He'd done enough worrying the night before to last him a lifetime. Now that he was with Olivia Mae, he knew that whatever happened would be what *Gotte* intended. But he certainly hoped that he and the man upstairs were seeing eye to eye.

Chapter Fourteen

Olivia Mae ran her fingers over the old quilt as Noah pulled food from the basket. The design was a double wedding-ring pattern. Had he chosen it on purpose? Did he understand the symbolism of the quilt? Though Amish didn't exchange rings, the idea of interlocking circles, intertwined lives, was one they could appreciate.

She glanced at him and caught him watching her.

"I brought salad." He held up a container. "I remembered you saying how every meal needs one."

"You were listening."

"I was. Also have some sliced ham and turkey—wasn't sure which you'd want—along with cheddar and Swiss cheese, fresh bread and all the other stuff you put on a sandwich."

"A well-planned meal," she teased.

"Which isn't complete without dessert." He held up a container of cookies. "Chocolate pecan. Your favorite, right?"

She lunged for the cookies, but he jerked them away at the last second and held them over his head. Then they were laughing and acting like two teenagers. His hand on hers caused goose bumps to dot her arms. She thought he was about to kiss her, their faces so close she could smell spearmint on his breath. Instead he pressed his forehead to hers and said, *"Danki."*

"For what?"

He pulled back and studied her a minute, as if he was weighing his answer. Finally he said simply, "Agreeing to come to dinner with me."

"I should be thanking you. This is a *wunderbaar* meal you've put together, and you were right—it does help to take a few hours away from the packing."

She began to relax as they put together two sandwiches that looked cartoonish in their height. He'd packed silverware for the potato salad, cloth napkins, bottles of water and cans of pop, as well as a thermos of coffee.

"Don't know how you fit so much in that basket."

"It's very special."

"The basket?"

"Ya. For sure and certain. Bought it from the auction, and thought to myself that this basket would be perfect for a picnic with Olivia Mae."

"So you've been planning this for some time."

"Maybe. In the back of my mind." He took a bite of the sandwich, but held up his hand as if he had more to say. When he'd finished chewing and taken a long pull from a bottle of water, he added, "Truthfully, it threw me for a loop when you told me your move is in a week."

"Ya. I felt the same way. I still do."

"I've been trying to gather my courage to do this, to take you on a real date and not an instructional one."

She shook her head, trying not to laugh. "That first lesson, on my porch…"

"Rainstorm nearly blew the table over. And you weren't going to let me inside."

"I was embarrassed." She stared out over the pond. "And proud. I suppose that was part of my problem."

"Didn't know a roof could leak that much and still hold together."

"The look on your face when you walked inside." She dared glance at him now and was relieved to see that he found the memory as funny as she did.

"Roofs are easy to fix. I know the situation with your grandparents is more complicated."

"It is."

"As far as overcoming my shyness and *learning I can be comfortable in someone else's presence…*"

"I shouldn't have suggested otherwise."

"*Nein.* It was true. I'd never thought of it that way. I always told myself there was no point because it wouldn't end well."

"Sometimes that's easier than trying."

"Agreed." He took another bite from the sandwich, then a few moments later added, "But knowing that our time is limited, that spurred me to action."

Olivia Mae didn't answer right away. She had so many thoughts spinning around in her mind that she didn't know which to say first, so she gave herself a minute. She couldn't believe that she—Olivia Mae Miller, Matchmaker Extraordinaire—felt so completely off-kilter by a simple date. It was one thing to teach something to someone, to advise others, but it was another thing entirely to experience it herself. She'd forgotten so much.

The heightened emotions.

The way that every minor touch felt like a jolt of electricity.

The anticipation and dread that mingled together.

"I'm glad I came tonight."

"Ya?"

She echoed his earlier sentiment. *"Danki."*

"For?"

"Inviting me. Being thoughtful. Knowing what would help. Take your pick."

He cocked his head and seemed about to answer, but instead he shook his head and took another sip of the water he'd opened. They finished the meal watching the birds swoop down over the pond, then a doe and fawn appeared at the far side of the water.

The fawn was only a few weeks old by the look of its wobbly legs. It hid on the far side of the doe, trying to nurse as she drank from the pond. It was covered with spots and occasionally it would stick its head out from behind the doe—all ears and eyes, spots and knobby legs. Olivia Mae thought it might be the most beautiful thing she'd ever seen.

One last drink from the pond and then the mom walked away, though not so quickly that the fawn couldn't follow.

She glanced up to see Noah watching her. "I've seen hundreds of does, but I've never watched one from across a pond as the sun set."

"We're making special memories, *ya*?"

"I suppose we are."

"Care to go for a walk?"

"A walk would be *gut*."

They stored everything back into the hamper except for the container of cookies and thermos of coffee. Then Noah pulled her to her feet, but he didn't release her hand. Instead he again laced his fingers with hers and she marveled at the warmth of that gesture, how it seemed to anchor her world.

Could a small touch do such a big thing?

They walked around the pond, stopping at the dock and then walking out on the wooden planks. The setting sun was sending color across the sky, though they still had probably an hour before darkness settled. The summer evenings in Indiana took their leave gently and slowly.

"Have I ever told you how nervous I was the first day I met you?"

"When you brought me the letter box?"

He nodded as they both sat on the edge of the dock. Olivia Mae pulled off her sandals. Noah laughed as he unlaced his shoes. They could just dip their toes in the water if they stretched.

"I knew you were nervous. You kept twirling that hat."

"If I close my eyes I can still see you standing there. At first I'm pretty sure you just wanted to send me away, and then you saw the box. You stepped out onto the porch and…"

He ducked his head, but still she didn't interrupt. He raised his eyes to meet hers. "You looked like you walked out of a dream. At that moment, all I wanted was to get to know you better."

"I remember you telling me that you were a happy bachelor, and I thought there was no such thing. I might have been wrong about that. Some people…well, I suppose some people are happier alone."

"I'm not one of those people, though. The past weeks with you, they've been the best of my life." He again reached for her hand. "I realize this isn't the best timing with your move and all, and I don't want you to feel pressured. But I need to say it…"

"Say what?"

"That I love you."

Her eyes widened. She hadn't expected this, though she'd known that his feelings for her had grown. The way she cared for him had certainly changed over the past few weeks.

"Olivia Mae, I…"

"Yes?"

"May I ask a question?"

She nodded, unable to talk now, her heart thundering in her chest.

"What are you doing for the rest of your life?" He reached forward, tucked her *kapp* strings behind her shoulders. "When I look at you, I see the girl I'm meant to love for my whole life. I see the woman that I want to eat breakfast with and raise children with and watch sunsets with."

When she didn't answer immediately, he stammered, "I know I won't… I won't always get it right, but I'll try."

She was speechless, utterly dumbfounded. In her wildest dreams she'd thought that perhaps they would begin to court. They'd exchange letters and maybe even visit, though it was a long way from Maine to Indiana. She'd never envisioned a marriage proposal, not on their first date. But it wasn't their first date, not really. And it wasn't sudden. What they felt for each other, it had grown naturally since that Wednesday afternoon when he'd brought her the letter box.

The Noah sitting beside her wasn't the same man who had shown up on her porch. He was confident, or at least hopeful. Even now, he waited patiently for her answer.

"Did you just ask me to marry you?"

"*Ya.* I did." He claimed both of her hands. "We can do this…"

"This?"

"Find our own future, the lives we're meant to live."

She still hadn't answered him. She understood that she needed to say what was in her heart, that now was the time to do that, but the words were frozen in her throat and her hands were shaking and she thought she might be about to have a panic attack.

"Maybe I'm wrong or maybe I'm right, but I had to try."

"You're not wrong."

"Do you love me?"

"*Ya*, Noah. I do." And suddenly the pressure on her heart eased. "I think I've loved you since you walked into my grandparents' house and claimed you were going to fix their roof."

"I've never seen so many pots scattered across the floor."

"And then you followed through—and Noah, it

wasn't only that you helped us, but you did it like we were doing you a favor. Like you were happy to help us."

"I was. I *am*."

She looked down at their hands, realizing that she was clutching his as if he was her life preserver in a storm-tossed sea. "And then when you offered to take care of my sheep…"

"I love sheep."

"You're an auctioneer, not a shepherd."

"But I would do it for you."

"I know." The words were a whisper. "And that made all the difference, knowing that you would sacrifice your dream for mine."

"Nein." He rubbed the backs of her hands with his thumbs. "First, it's not a sacrifice, and second, your dreams are as important to me as mine. We can find a way to have both."

"My grandparents…"

"I don't know the answer, but we'll handle it—together."

He jumped up, helped her to her feet and then stepped closer—close enough that there was only the smallest amount of space between them. He still held her hands, and when he leaned forward, when his lips touched hers, Olivia Mae thought she'd never known such happiness.

They stood there under the final remnants of a glorious sunset, and Olivia Mae stepped into Noah's arms.

The sale of the farm was finalized the week after Noah proposed, but Bishop Lucas was able to find Olivia Mae and her grandparents a place to stay for the rest of the summer. Olivia Mae's brothers came and helped with the move, brought their entire families and promised to return every year. The grandchildren needed to know their grandparents. The *grossdaddi haus* on Widow King's place was small, but there was a pasture for the sheep, and living there gave them the time that they needed.

Noah's *dat* bought a small strip of land across the road from their family farm. It had been for sale for over a year but, at twenty acres, it was too small to farm. It was, however, perfect for raising a small herd of sheep and pasturing a few horses. A ramshackle house sat on the corner of the property.

Noah and his *bruders* decided it would be quicker and less expensive to pull down the old homestead. They left the foundation and the chimney, then expanded the foundation because a single story would be easier for *Mammi* and *Daddi*. The new home was raised on a Saturday in late August, and a small barn quickly followed.

Daddi continued to have *gut* days and bad days, but he had no problem with the move. *Mammi*'s occasional lapses into the past disappeared completely. Perhaps it had been a way of dealing with stress. Perhaps she'd been more worried about their situation than she'd let on, or maybe as the doctor had suggested it had been a result of the medications that she was taking.

Regardless, both of Olivia Mae's grandparents seemed to have improved by the time they moved into the new home, and they all agreed that living across the street from Noah's parents would be a real help. Olivia Mae hadn't realized how much she'd let her pride stand in the way of accepting help that they desperately needed.

She and Noah were wed on the second Saturday in October.

Jane was there with Elijah. The Sunday before, they'd announced their intention to wed in the spring.

Francine had been accepted for the MDS cook position in Texas, and she was scheduled to leave the following week.

All of Olivia Mae's brothers attended the wedding, as well as all of Noah's family, including his new baby nephew, Silas. Their church family brought the number to nearly two hundred. Looking out over the crowd, she was surprised to see so many couples that she had helped to find one another.

"The matchmaker finally gets matched," Noah whispered.

Olivia Mae wore a forest green dress with a matching apron, and Noah looked so handsome in his new suit that Olivia Mae had trouble taking her eyes off him.

After the singing and sermon, Bishop Lucas called them to the front of the group and they recited their vows, repeating after him and staring into each other's eyes. So much of the day seemed like a blur, like something happening to someone else. Olivia Mae felt as if she was walking through a dream.

Then Lucas presented them as Mr. and Mrs. Noah Graber, and she knew it wasn't a dream. It was her life and her future and her hopes all tossed together into something beautiful—a marriage.

Later that day, as they were about to eat the second

meal, Noah tugged at her hand and whispered, "Let's go look at our house."

"But, we're supposed to…"

"Sit at the corner of the table. I know. I promise to have you back before Francine sets down the first plate of chicken casserole."

Instead of going into the house across the road, they walked around to the back, where her sheep were grazing.

"What do you call a dancing sheep?"

"Oh, Noah…" She was standing at the fence, looking at the herd, which would soon grow to nine. When he walked up behind her and put his arms around her, she felt as if she was the happiest woman in the world. She could even forgive him the terrible jokes.

"You know you want to know," he murmured, kissing her cheek.

"Okay. What do you call a dancing sheep?"

"A ba-a-a-llerina."

She covered his hands with hers, wrapping his arms even more tightly around her. "How many of these jokes do you have?"

"Enough to last us a lifetime." He turned her gently so that she was facing him. "I want to say, in case I forget or we get busy with—with living, I want to say that when I saw you standing there this morning, the sunlight shining down on you…" Tears filled his eyes, but he didn't bother to brush them away. "No one ever looked so beautiful."

"Beauty is only skin-deep."

"Not yours." He thumbed away her tears. "Yours

goes all the way to the center of your heart. That's what takes my breath away."

"I love you, Noah Graber."

"And I love you, Olivia Mae."

She glanced around at their small farm where they would build their life together, hopefully have children, care for her grandparents and her sheep, and her heart swelled with the joy and hope of their future together.

She and Noah were the perfect match—not because they were the right height for each other or had the same hobbies or even because they felt a very real physical attraction to one another. They were the perfect match because they'd taken the time to truly know one another, and when they did, they'd forged an emotional bond that blossomed into love.

That was *Gotte*'s doing, and Olivia Mae knew in her heart that He was the perfect matchmaker.

* * * * *

AMISH HAVEN

Dana R. Lynn

To my family. Thank you for giving me the love
and support I need to follow my dreams.

And now abideth faith, hope, charity, these three;
but the greatest of these is charity.
—*1 Corinthians* 13:13

Chapter One

"You don't need to be concerned. I have it covered."

Tyler Everson heard his boss's voice as he walked past his office. He frowned. What was Gene doing here? Gene Landis, one of the most sought-after lawyers in the city of Chicago, had supposedly left three hours earlier to attend one of his wife's benefit dinners. He shrugged. It was none of his business. Tyler knew as well as anyone that law was a demanding career. Those who wanted to succeed had to be willing to make sacrifices.

He should know that. He'd lost his wife and child because of his job. Annabelle. He missed his wife still. And his sweet little Bethany. She'd be five by now. Did they ever miss him? A familiar ache spread through his chest. Unbidden, the memory of Annabelle leaving him came to mind. Her accusations of how he had become withdrawn and was no longer the man she had married echoed in the recesses of his mind. She was right, but not for the reasons she had thought. Tyler had wanted to run after her, to plead with her to stay. But he hadn't.

Because due to his job, there was the possibility that she and Bethany could be put in danger. Tyler could never prove it, but he believed that her life had been threatened once before. There had been an accident that had left her with severe injuries. He had never believed it was an accident. Tyler had received threats after he had sent a man to prison for life. Threats that culminated in a runaway truck smashing into their home and injuring his wife. He still had nightmares about it. Annabelle had been horribly injured. Her legs had suffered extensive damage. Every time he had looked at the scars on them, he knew he had been to blame for not taking the threats seriously until it was too late.

She had been in the hospital while the police had investigated the incident. The police had looked into the threats, as well, but had been unable to find evidence against the man he suspected. In fact, they had concluded that the threats and the accident were unconnected. Annabelle had accepted their findings.

Tyler believed differently. Six months later, the man who had threatened him died of a heart attack. He still couldn't get over his fear.

What if someone else came after him? He had made a lot of enemies on the job. Tyler knew that he couldn't allow his family to be in danger. And so, even though they lived only an hour away, he stayed away.

He shook his head, trying to clear the dark memories. They were better off without him. He couldn't change what had happened. Most days he worked so hard that he could barely think by the time he reached his apartment. And that was the way he preferred it. Otherwise, the memories of the family he'd lost would hound him.

He couldn't regret his decision, though. He knew that he'd done what he could to protect them.

No, it was better this way. How many people got the opportunity to be up for partner at a prestigious firm such as Landis Law at the age of twenty-nine?

Tyler continued to the parking garage, his mind full of the case he was preparing to prosecute. It would be a tricky one. Would the witness's testimony hold up? He had his doubts about the woman. She'd waffled on a couple of details. Part of him dreaded putting her on the stand. And not only because of her weak testimony. In his gut, he wondered if she was being honest. Having someone swear under oath was a serious thing— at least it was to him. His reputation depended on his providing credible witnesses.

Arriving at his car, he unlocked it and placed his briefcase on the passenger seat. Then he remembered the brief. He unlatched the black briefcase and searched through it. His heart sank. The brief he'd printed out to review that night before tomorrow's court case was still on his desk.

With a sigh, he shut the car door and jogged back to the elevator. It would only take five minutes to go and retrieve it, but he hated inefficiency. His schedule was too jam-packed for him to be wasting time.

Tyler returned to his office. There it was. He picked up the brief he'd printed out and flipped through it to make sure all the pages were present. If he had to come back for something else, he would not be pleased.

Finally, positive that he had everything, Tyler switched off his light and headed out again. Gene's light was on. That man worked even harder than Tyler did. He could hear the murmur of Gene's voice. He was probably on the phone.

I'll just stop in and remind him that I'm going directly to the courthouse tomorrow morning.

Sauntering to the open doorway, he popped his head in.

Crack!

Stunned, Tyler watched as his boss fell back in his chair, red blossoming like some obscene flower across the once pristine shirt he wore. Gene was still, his eyes staring vacantly. Was he dead? Tyler jerked his gaze to the man standing across from Gene. His back was to the doorway. But Tyler knew exactly who it was. He recognized the dragon tattoo rising up from the collar of his dark jacket. Wilson Barco. The most wanted man in town. The man suspected of running a crime syndicate that was involved in everything from money laundering and drug trafficking to murder.

He hadn't seen Tyler yet. That was the only thing that was keeping Tyler alive.

He had to get out of here. Backing away from the door slowly, Tyler moved as quietly as he could. It wasn't quiet enough. Spinning around, the killer snapped the gun up and aimed.

Tyler ran. The bullet meant for him smashed into the wall where he'd been standing. A watercolor painting crashed to the floor, glass skittering across the surface.

Tyler didn't give it a second glance. His only hope was to make it to his car. He kept his head low as he ducked around a corner. Another bullet, but this time it made a solid *thunk* as it was embedded into the wall. He bolted past the elevator. No way was he risking waiting for it to open. Even if he made it, he'd be a sitting duck once it arrived at the bottom. The stairs. No other choice.

Another gunshot. A hot pain shot up his arm. He'd been shot. Despite the pain, he kept running. A little pain was better than being dead. Which was what he'd be if he slowed down.

Darting through the empty lobby, he grabbed his lanyard with a shaking hand and swiped his badge in front of the security panel, unlocking the door to the stairwell. It beeped, and the light turned green. He yanked open the door and jumped through the entrance, pulling it shut as the killer burst into the lobby.

He hit the stairs as the next bullet pinged against the metal door. He didn't slow down. Even though the door automatically locked when it shut, he wasn't taking any chances. He had no idea how Barco had made it into the building after hours. For all he knew, he could have already figured out a way to bypass the security system.

His feet made loud clanging noises as he rushed down the stairs to the basement. It couldn't be helped. He had just hit the second landing when he heard another set of shoes racing down the stairs behind him. He didn't have as much time as he'd hoped.

Reaching the bottom of the stairs, he whipped open the door to the parking garage and ran to where his four-door sedan was parked. It was still unlocked. Tyler hopped in and started the car, just as Barco burst out of the doorway.

Without fastening his seat belt, Tyler shifted into Drive and yanked on the gearshift harder than he had in years. The car jerked forward. Spinning the wheel, he drove toward the exit. His rear passenger window shattered. A second bullet hit the side of the car.

"God, help me!"

Tyler hadn't talked to God since his wife had packed up and left, taking their toddler daughter and his joy with him. He'd been so angry at God for not intervening. For not opening his eyes to what was happening. But even if God had shown him, would he have been able to change? He was a workaholic, just like his father had been. Plus, his work was his private mission. God hadn't helped him then, so he had decided he didn't need God.

He needed God now.

Tyler careened around the parking ramp leading to the exit. Glancing up into the rearview mirror, he sighed. The killer wasn't there. Yet.

The street was just ahead of him. All that separated him from the outside world and the parking garage was the long wooden gate arm. Out of habit, he slowed. The gate started to lift as the sticker on his windshield was registered. Another glance in his rearview mirror. His blood froze.

Barco was running up the ramp.

What was he doing? He stomped on the gas pedal. The engine roared, and the car shot forward. The boom barrier splintered as his car broke through it. He could hear an alarm sound as he pulled onto the street. The car he cut off braked and skidded, and the driver blared his horn at Tyler.

"Sorry, buddy," Tyler muttered.

Where did he go now? He had to go to the police. And then home.

Home. He couldn't go there. Barco had seen him pull out of his parking space. His very prominent parking space with his name on it. In this day of technology, it would be easy for anyone to find his identity and address. He had no doubt that if he went home tonight someone would be waiting for him.

He couldn't worry about that now. He had to go to the police. A vision of Gene flashed through his mind. What had he done to deserve being murdered?

He turned into the police station so fast that he barely missed sideswiping a police cruiser. He threw open his door and raced up the steps, holding on to his injured arm. The clerk at the window gaped at him for three seconds before rushing to assist him.

Two hours later, Tyler was sitting in a conference room at the police station. His arm had been cared for by the paramedics, and he'd been given something to take the edge off the pain. Fortunately, it wasn't a bad wound.

Officers had taken pictures of his arm and the side of his car. A team had been dispatched to the law firm. He'd heard something about an ambulance being sent there, as well. He remembered Gene's blank stare. He feared the ambulance was too late to do Gene any good.

An officer entered the room. Officer Cale. They'd worked together on cases before. Tyler had always liked the quiet officer. "Tyler, our men have caught Barco. They're bringing him in now. I hate to tell you this, but your boss—"

"He's dead." Tyler's voice was flat.

Cale nodded.

"Where did they catch Barco? Surely the man wasn't dumb enough to hang around the crime scene when you caught him."

Cale hesitated. Sensing more bad news, Tyler tensed.

"You were right that he would find out who you were. He was in your apartment."

Stunned, Tyler stared at him. Then some of the tension drained out of his shoulders.

"Good to know they caught him. Though I don't like that he was in my place." Tyler took a long drink of the bottled water they had brought him. He hadn't realized how thirsty he was.

Cale gave him a funny look.

"What?"

"You know it's not that easy, Tyler."

Before he had time to think about Cale's words, the door opened. A man who looked to be close to his age entered the room. Officer Cale straightened. The new arrival nodded at the officer before his gaze zeroed in on Tyler. His face was hard to read, but Tyler thought he could detect some sympathy in his eyes.

I'm not going to like this.

"Mr. Everson. I'm US Marshal Jonathan Mast."

Tyler's gut clenched. It couldn't be good if the US Marshals were getting involved.

"You're in a precarious position right now. Wilson Barco has his fingers in just about every crime venue you can imagine. But he could never be prosecuted because we could never find witnesses to his crimes."

Tyler nodded, not liking where this was going. He'd known that Barco had slipped through the cracks before.

"We believe that Gene Landis was on his payroll."

"No way. Not Gene!" He shook his head vehemently. Gene had always been a stickler about doing everything the proper way. And now to find out he'd been living a double life? He couldn't wrap his mind around it.

"Yes, Gene." Mast pulled out a chair and sat across from him. "Sorry, but that's what the evidence is adding up to. Barco is a man with vast resources. You are the first reliable witness we've ever had who could incriminate him. If we were to allow you to remain in your apartment, there's no doubt in my mind that you would be killed or simply vanish before you could testify."

For a moment, there was silence as Tyler thought through the matter. Finally, he spoke. "What's your plan? Will I get police protection? Go to a safe house?"

Mast shook his head. "Neither of those options would be enough. Barco's reach is too vast. No telling who we can trust. We're putting you in witness protection."

A sick feeling overwhelmed him. He knew all about witness protection. Those who went in lost all connection with their families. His daughter, Bethany—would he never see her again? Would she even know about him, or would she grow up and forget he even existed? And what about Annabelle? He had no hope of ever winning back his wife again, he knew that. He couldn't change who he was, and she had already shown that she couldn't accept that. Not to mention the danger he'd put her in if they were to get back together. But he'd never imagined a life where he could not even see her or hear her voice again.

The future that loomed ahead of him was dark and empty.

* * *

The hair on the back of Annabelle Everson's neck rose. Was she being watched? She glanced around the grocery store, but no one appeared to be paying any attention to them. She must have imagined it. She shivered, then blamed it on the air-conditioning.

Even though she knew it wasn't the cold that was making her shiver. This was the second time today she'd felt like someone was watching her. The first time had been outside the library, where she took her daughter every Wednesday afternoon for the reading hour. Today the library had been busier than normal. The local fire department had sent several of the firefighters and a truck to talk about fire safety. The children present were thrilled to get to touch a real fire truck.

After the library, she and Bethany went shopping. It was their weekly routine.

Annabelle pushed the cart down the aisle, listening as Bethany chattered on about the letter she'd received from her kindergarten teacher. Annabelle could hardly believe that her baby would be starting school in a month. Where had the time gone?

"Mommy, Tasha and Nikki said that their daddy is taking them swimming tomorrow."

Annabelle braced herself. Tasha and Nikki were the twins who lived two doors down from them. Since they had moved in three months ago, Bethany had started to talk about their daddy constantly. Which nearly always progressed to "Why doesn't my daddy do that?"

In truth, Annabelle wasn't even sure that Bethany remembered Tyler. It had been three years since she'd left him. He'd seen Bethany a few times after that, but not since she was three years old. She had seen pictures of him, though.

Her heart ached for her baby.

"Mommy, when will I see my daddy again?"

And there it was.

"Honey, I don't know. You know that. But I can take you swimming or to the playground with your friends if you want to go. I always do."

It didn't help. Bethany crossed her arms across her thin body and pushed out her lower lip. Oh, no. The last thing Annabelle wanted was for her daughter to go into a full meltdown in the middle of grocery store.

"Don't even think about throwing a tantrum, Bethany Jane. Or you won't be going swimming with your friends tomorrow."

Bethany glared, but wisely kept silent. Annabelle never proposed consequences she wasn't prepared to follow through on. It was one thing she'd learned as a single parent—something she'd never planned on being.

"Mommy, why is that man watching us?"

Forgetting her daughter's near tantrum, Annabelle swung her head in the direction that Bethany pointed. Her heart pounded at the thought that she'd finally see who was watching them. No one was. A young man in his early twenties was reading the label on a soup can. After a second, he dropped two cans into his shopping cart and moved past her to continue shopping.

"He's just shopping, Bethy. Like us." Despite her words, she couldn't relax. Her gut tightened. Her maternal instinct was on full alert. A mother knew when danger was near her child.

"Let's finish up and get home, okay? If we hurry, we can stop and get pizza for dinner."

Bethany's eyes lit up and she grinned. "Yay! Pizza! Can we get ice cream, too?"

Annabelle tousled her daughter's blond hair and smiled back. "Of course! What's pizza without ice cream for dessert?"

Happy again, Bethany skipped beside the shopping cart.

Annabelle hurried as much as she could. She couldn't shake the thought that someone was watching again. She turned her head suddenly. Her eyes were pinned by the stare of the young man she'd seen earlier.

Bethany had been right. That was not the face of someone shopping. The cold stare she encountered made her shudder. All thoughts of shopping left her mind. She needed to get her daughter home, where they'd be safe.

"Bethy, come with me." Grabbing her daughter's hand, she abandoned the shopping cart and made for the exit. A glance over her shoulder confirmed her fear. The man was on his cell phone, watching her. She moved quicker.

"Mommy, what about the ice cream?"

"Honey, I will see if we can get it somewhere else. But we need to leave. Now."

Bethany was a very bright girl. She didn't argue with her mom. Looking down at her daughter, Annabelle could see that she was pale and her eyes were wide. She hated that her daughter was afraid. Better scared and safe. That was the important thing.

She tightened her grip on Bethany's hand and left the

store. The little girl was trembling now. Who was that man? An image of him grabbing Bethany and running off flashed through her mind. Annabelle paused to lift her daughter in her arms. Bethany didn't question it but wrapped her legs around her waist while winding her arms around her mother's neck.

The parking lot was crowded. Annabelle ducked between two cars, crouching low. She set down Bethany, motioning her to keep low. Bethany squatted next to Annabelle. "Shh. Don't make a sound. Okay?" she whispered in Bethany's ear. The child nodded, burying her face in her mother's shoulder. Moving as if in slow motion, Annabelle raised herself enough to peer across the parking lot through the windows of the car on her left. The man was standing outside the store, talking on the phone while his eyes searched the parking lot.

For her.

What did he want?

Settling back down, she considered her options. Her car was three rows away. It would be practically impossible to get there without being seen. Or worse.

She peeked again. Oh, no. He was heading this way. Now what?

Putting her finger to her lips to let Bethany know to keep silent, she crouch-walked away from the row, heading toward the next one. Her daughter stayed close to her side. She glanced back. Not good. He'd seen them and was picking up his pace. His eyes were glued to her as he moved toward her.

"Run, Bethany!" Grabbing her daughter's hand, she ran as fast as she could with a five-year-old in tow. "Please, God. Keep us safe. Protect my baby."

A police car turned down her aisle and pulled in two cars away from her.'

"Thank You, Jesus!"

The officer stepped out of his car.

"Officer!" She ran up to the man. "Help! We're being followed!"

She pointed to the man who'd been following her. He was gone.

"Ma'am?"

She shuddered. "There was a man. He'd been following us around the store. When we left, he followed us out here. We hid, and tried to get to our car, but he saw us and was chasing us."

Her cheeks heated. The officer probably thought she was being paranoid.

"I was scared," Bethany offered in a shy whisper.

Fortunately, the officer seemed to believe them. "Ma'am, do you think you could give me a description of the man?"

An hour later, they arrived home. Bethany was happy. They'd stopped and picked up pizza and ice cream. Annabelle wanted to sleep for the next ten hours, she was so emotionally drained. Fear for her daughter still swirled in her head, but she wasn't panicking anymore. Going around the house, she locked and dead-bolted all the doors and windows. She was probably overreacting, but she didn't care. The whole situation had freaked her out.

She was cleaning up the dishes when her cell phone rang. She didn't recognize the number.

"Hello?"

"Annie, it's me." There was only one person in the world who called her Annie.

Tyler.

Her husband. The man she hadn't seen in two years.

"Annie? You there?"

She shook her head. "Yes, I'm here. It's been a frazzling day, Tyler. What do you want?"

A pause. "Something happened last night, Annie. I can't tell you everything, but the US Marshals are involved. I'm being put into witness protection."

"Witness protection?" Stunned, she lowered herself into a chair at the kitchen table. "Tyler, people in those programs have to completely disappear."

In her mind, she heard Bethany ask when she would see her daddy again.

"I know. It won't be forever. At least I hope it won't. I need to testify against someone. Maybe after that, I can go back to being me."

A sudden thought occurred to her. "Tyler, the reason you're going into witness protection… Would it affect me at all?"

"What do you mean?"

"Someone was following me today."

Chapter Two

"Someone's following you?" Tyler exclaimed, horrified.

"Hey, don't shout at me!"

"Sorry." *Keep it together, Tyler.* "Where are you now?"

He heard an aggravated sigh. "I'm at home. I just put Bethany down to bed, and I'm exhausted."

She sounded irritated, but he hadn't lived with her for the first four of their seven years of marriage without learning something. She was frightened. She was covering it up, but he heard the tremble in her voice. Man, he hated that. She had always seemed so fearless.

"You never answered me. Could the man following me be related to what happened to you?"

That was a good question. He had the feeling she wasn't going to like the answer.

"I don't know. Annie, I will call you back." He disconnected the call and went to the door of his room. He had no idea where he was. All he knew was that Marshal Mast and his team had hustled him out the back door of the police station the night before and driven for over an hour to this house.

An agent was coming down the hall. Tyler had met him briefly earlier. What was his name? Kurt? No. Karl. Karl Adams. That was it. "Could you tell me where I could find Marshal Mast?"

"Sure. Come with me."

Tyler walked beside the agent, his nerves on edge. What was happening at Annabelle's house right now? Was someone watching her? What about his daughter? Fear rose up inside him. How much danger was Bethany in? He was helpless to protect her, and it ate at him. He followed Karl Adams. A female agent with a tight dark bun smiled at them as they passed. He saw her gaze lingering on Karl. Karl left him at the office, then retreated to talk with the woman.

Marshal Mast was sitting at a laptop in an office at the back of the house. He glanced up from the screen as Tyler entered. Pushing back the headset, he allowed it to settle around his neck. "Something on your mind, Tyler?"

"Yes, Marshal Mast."

The marshal waved his hand. "We're going to be working together, Tyler. You need to get used to calling us by our first names. We don't want to announce to others that we're US marshals."

Tyler nodded. "Jonathan, then. I called my wife to tell her I was going into witness protection."

Jonathan frowned. Tyler had told the man that he and his wife were separated and wouldn't be getting back together. He could practically read the man's mind: *So why is he calling her?* He quickly headed off any questioning.

"She informed me that she and my daughter were being followed today."

At this information, Jonathan jumped to his feet. "Karl!"

Feet pounded in the hallway. Karl Adams entered the room at a brisk pace. "Jonathan? What did you need?"

Jonathan glanced up at Karl, a frown creating grooves in the flesh beside his mouth. "Karl, I need you to make a trip for me to pick up Tyler's wife and daughter. They may be in danger. Take Stacy with you. What's the address, Tyler?"

Tyler recited the address. Would Karl and Stacy get there in time? How he wished he could go with them.

"Call her back, Tyler. Let her know he's coming."

She wouldn't be happy. Nevertheless, Tyler dialed the number. Annabelle answered on the first ring. He knew at once she was steamed.

"What's going on, Tyler? You call me out of the blue, tell me you're going into hiding, hang up on me and now you're calling me back? Do you know what time it is? What have you gotten yourself into?"

"Annie—"

He stopped. Jonathan held out his hand for the phone. Fine. Let him deal with her. She was too stubborn to listen to him, anyway. And too angry.

"Mrs. Everson? This is US Marshal Jonathan Mast. I am in charge of your husband's case. He tells me you thought someone was following you today?" He listened for a minute. It drove Tyler crazy not hearing her side of the conversation. What exactly had happened? Had it been an actual threat, or some freaky coincidence?

He didn't believe in coincidences. And he doubted that the marshals would buy that theory, either.

"Mrs. Everson, I need you to listen. I am sending a marshal to come get you and bring you to a safe house. Yes, it's necessary. I have every reason to believe that your life and the life of your daughter are in grave peril."

Grave peril. He'd failed his family again. Despite his best efforts, he'd brought danger to their door. If Annabelle was scared, his daughter was probably terrified.

The daughter that he hadn't seen in two years. Guilt swamped him. He knew why he'd made the choice not to be a part of her life. It had hurt more than anything he'd ever done to distance himself from his family, but he knew it had been for their own good. He was saving them from heartache and disappointment. And possibly from danger.

Except now he wasn't sure if he'd done the right thing, because danger had found them, anyway.

Jonathan got his attention when he set the phone back down.

"So, what's the plan?" Tyler asked. "You're going to protect them, right?"

"Let's bring them here first. Then we'll decide. I will do my best to see that you are all protected."

It was a long night, waiting for Annabelle and Bethany to arrive. His nerves were stretched tight as he paced through the house. He couldn't eat, and he was too wound-up to relax. He forced himself to try to sleep, but it was useless. In his mind, every possible scenario played out, each one worse than the one before. Finally, he gave up trying to sleep and decided to watch a movie to help pass the time.

It was a little after two in the morning when a car pulled up the lane. He shot to the window and peered out. Was that Karl? It was too dark to see, but who else would it be? The grating noise of the garage door opening seemed overly loud in the silent house. Jonathan walked out of the office.

A minute later, the door connecting the kitchen to the garage opened up. Stacy walked in, her dark brown hair starting to escape from the bun at the nape of her neck. She held the door open. Karl walked through the open door and flashed her a tired smile as he passed her. He was carrying a sleeping Bethany against his chest. Tyler was startled by the surge of jealousy that shot through him. That should have been him carrying her. Immediately, he felt ridiculous. The man was protecting his daughter, after all. He should feel grateful, not jealous.

His attention shifted to the woman who had entered behind Karl.

Annie.

Even exhausted and scared, she was beautiful. Her hair was shorter than it had been the last time he'd seen her, brushing her shoulders in straight waves. But it was still a lustrous deep brown with hints of red in it. And her eyes… He'd never forgotten those toffee-brown eyes. Eyes that were guarded as they met his.

He'd hurt her badly during their marriage. How could he expect her to understand, much less forgive him?

"Tyler." Just that one word, said in a voice devoid of emotion, told him that forgiveness wouldn't come easy. As she stepped farther into the room, she swayed once.

Jonathan moved forward. "Annabelle. We can talk in the morning. I have you and Bethany in a room in the back." He led them away, glancing back once at Tyler sympathetically.

Tyler was left standing alone. He was always alone. But at least he could sleep now.

The next morning, Tyler was reunited with his daughter. Unlike her mother, Bethany was overjoyed to see her daddy. She was a little shy at first, hanging back. A tight sensation crept into his chest. She didn't know him. Why should she? After a few minutes, though, her natural curiosity and her happiness at seeing her father overruled her bashfulness. His heart melted as the bright child snuggled up to him and told him all about her two best friends, identical twins who lived down the street, and her excitement to begin kindergarten.

He glanced at Annabelle. She listened, her face strained. She didn't have to say that she wasn't pleased with the turn of events. It was clear on her face.

Karl Adams stepped into the kitchen, a fierce frown on his face. Stacy approached Tyler and attempted to persuade Bethany to leave Tyler's arms. No easy task. The child wanted to stay with her father. Eventually, the marshal succeeded. Holding Bethany's hand in hers, Stacy led her from the room. Her eyes met Karl's as she passed him. Something was going on with those two, but Tyler was too concerned about his daughter and Annie to give it much thought. Karl turned his eyes back to meet his. Tyler tensed.

As soon as the child was out of earshot, Jonathan indicated that Karl should go ahead and speak.

"Jonathan, you were right. Barco has put a price on Everson's head. Every criminal within a hundred-mile radius will be gunning for him." Karl shifted, his gaze sweeping over Annabelle. "He's also offered money for Annabelle and the child. Probably to smoke Tyler out of hiding."

"Can't you stop it?" Annabelle blurted.

"No, ma'am. Barco has more resources at his disposal than we know about. He has managed to escape capture for years. Every potential witness has been compromised or disappeared. Evidence has disappeared. Plus, he's always managed to have an alibi. It's been impossible to prove his guilt. Until now. Which means he'll be pulling out all the stops to eliminate Tyler."

The ticking of the clock on the wall was unnaturally loud in the silence.

"What's going to happen to my daughter and me?"

The quiet whisper from his wife made his heart ache.

Karl answered. "You're in danger as a result of your association with Tyler. The US Marshals will help you go into the witness protection program, as well."

"No."

Any other time, the sight of all these big men sitting with their mouths open would have been amusing. Right now, she was just trying to keep herself from panicking. It took all her effort to keep the tremors that were making her stomach quake from showing up in her voice.

"Annie—"

"No, Tyler!" She swung back her gaze to her husband. He hadn't changed much since she'd seen him last. Still handsome. His brown hair was on the longish side, blue-gray eyes that reminded her of the ocean on a cloudy day, and that square jaw, now covered with several days' worth of whiskers. Once, he could persuade her to do anything. Not anymore. She was through letting him bother her. She was in charge of her life. It was by his own choice that he wasn't a part of their lives anymore. "I understand that you are in trouble, but that has nothing to do with me."

"Ma'am." One of the agents stepped forward. She was so upset, she couldn't remember the man's name. "It would be safer for you if you came with us."

"I'm not going into hiding. I can go on vacation for a bit with Bethany. Leave the area. Then when this all blows over, I can come back."

"I don't think—" the man began.

But she was done. "I don't care what you think. Tyler and I haven't lived together for three years. He hasn't been to see us, including his daughter, in over two. If anyone was searching for him, we wouldn't be the people to go to. I am not disrupting my life again for him. We'll go to my mother's house. She lives in Southern Illinois, five hours from where I live. My brother is a cop. He lives a little over ten minutes from her. He can protect us."

The marshals tried to convince her to change her mind. She wouldn't budge. Tyler tried to talk with her, too. Every time he moved toward her, she glared at him. Finally, he seemed to get the message. He wasn't happy about it, but she didn't care. He'd made his choice when he'd let them go. She quickly squelched any pity she might have felt for him.

They couldn't hold her against her will. She knew it,

and they did, too. Nor could they force her to go into the witness protection program. That didn't stop them from giving her disapproving frowns. She ignored them all.

Strangely, while their frowns didn't bother her, Tyler's silence did. The way his eyes followed Bethany around. He stuck close to his daughter.

Annabelle couldn't take it. If she didn't know better, she'd think he really was concerned. A sliver of guilt tried to wedge itself into her mind. Guilt that she was going to be separating a father from his daughter. Maybe forever. She shoved aside the guilt. She didn't have time for this.

She walked into the kitchen to demand that they either put her and Bethany in a taxi, or take them home.

She never got the words out.

Marshal Mast, who'd insisted she call him Jonathan, leaped to his feet as his phone went off. Not the phone he'd been talking on throughout the day. Annabelle figured that was his work phone. This one had to have been his personal phone. Especially since it was playing a popular song for the ringtone.

"Celeste?" he blurted into the phone.

She watched, amazed, as the calm US marshal paled. Her brow furrowed. Hopefully it wasn't too serious. Instinctively, she glanced at Tyler to see his reaction. His eyes were narrowed as he watched the marshal. Obviously, he had no clue what was going on, either.

That could have described their whole situation. It was surreal.

"Okay, honey, relax. Do what the paramedics tell you. I'll be there as soon as I can." Jonathan's finger trembled as he disconnected the call. "Karl, you're in charge. My wife just went into labor at the shopping mall. They are taking her to the hospital in an ambulance."

"She'll be okay, Jonathan." The female marshal she'd met earlier, Stacy, stepped forward. "We know what to do here."

He nodded, then rushed to the back of the house. Within minutes, he ran past them and out the front door. She heard his car start up and pull down the lane.

"Remember when Bethany was born?"

Annabelle jumped. When had Tyler moved up beside her? She had been so fascinated by the escaping marshal that she hadn't seen Tyler moving.

Memories of happier times flooded her brain. She smiled. "I thought I was going to have her in the car."

"Me, too! I was terrified. I'm still shocked I didn't get a speeding ticket."

She turned to face him. As she did so, she noticed for the first time the corner of a gauze bandage peeking out from the sleeve of his T-shirt. "What happened to your arm?"

He hesitated. "Wilson Barco shot me. While I was running from him."

Her blood ran cold. No way. She needed to get her daughter away from him. Even as she cringed at being so coldhearted, she hardened her resolve. She had to put Bethany first. There were some things her daughter shouldn't be exposed to. Bullets were one of them.

Something of what she was feeling must have shown on her face. Tyler hastened to explain. "It's not a bad wound. Seriously. I need to keep it clean for a few days, but it should heal fine."

She shook her head. "Tyler, I know what you're trying to do. And I'm not changing my mind. If someone doesn't drive me home, I'll call a cab. I'm sorry you're in this mess. I truly am. But it's your mess. And I don't want any part of it."

She turned her head away so she didn't see his reaction.

Karl Adams wasn't happy. "Look, Annabelle, if you won't go into the witness protection program, will you at least let us drive you to your mother's house? It would be safer than driving you to your own house."

Annabelle thought about it. What did she really need to get from her house? It would be nice to have her own car, but it wasn't worth their lives. Nor did they desperately need anything from inside the house. She already had some bags packed from when Karl and Stacy had picked them up.

"I will agree to that. A marshal may drive us to my mom's house."

Karl visibly relaxed at that. It was a safer and smarter decision, and she knew it.

In a remarkably short time, Annabelle and Bethany were in a car with a younger marshal, heading to her mother's house. Talk was scarce on the drive. Although the marshal, Rick, seemed like a nice man, Annabelle's stomach was in knots. What if she was making a mistake? She clenched her teeth, refusing to second-guess her resolve.

A couple of times, Rick tried to engage her in small talk. She did her best to answer but found herself distracted.

After an hour or so, she allowed herself to lean

against the door and close her eyes. Every time she would begin to drift off, though, a noise or the motion of the car would jerk her awake, her pulse racing.

The third time it happened, Rick glanced at her out of the corner of his eye.

"Ma'am, it's not too late to turn back. We would keep you safe."

Shaking her head, she sat up.

"Thank you, Rick. I mean it. But I really think we'll be fine at my mother's house."

Even as she said it, Annabelle suppressed a shudder.

Recalling the events of the past two days, she wondered if she would forever be looking over her shoulder.

Chapter Three

Exhausted was too weak a word to describe how Annabelle felt as Rick finally pulled into her mother's driveway Thursday evening.

Nerves had her continuously checking her side mirror to make sure that no one was following them. A couple of times, she got spooked by a car driving too close. Rick took no chances, to her relief. If he thought a car was suspicious, he would turn off the road, or see if it would pass them. Every time, the cars would pass them or keep going straight. It didn't help her relax. The danger was still very real.

When they were an hour away from her mother's house, Rick allowed her to call her mother on a burner phone.

"If they are tracking you, using your cell would be too dangerous."

Her mother didn't pick up. The answering machine kicked on. "Mom, are you there? Mom?"

"Annabelle? I didn't recognize the number."

"I know. Listen, I'm going to be at your house in an hour. A friend is driving me."

The last hour of the trip dragged on and on.

Her mother was up waiting for them. Annabelle had told her as much as she dared on the phone. She didn't mention Tyler. Even if she wasn't going into witness protection, he was. It wasn't a good idea to broadcast that information, even to her mother. Instead, she told her that someone had been bothering them at home and she needed a safe spot for a few days, so that she could figure out her next move.

Rick waited until she was inside before he left.

"Thanks, Mom." Annabelle leaned into her mother's arms as she stepped through the door. Bethany hovered at her side, blue eyes bleary with sleep.

Nancy Schmidt kissed her daughter's cheek. "You know you're always welcome, sweetheart." She turned to her granddaughter. "Bethany, do you have a hug for your grammy?"

Bethany lifted her arms to her grandmother, yawning as the woman pulled her close. "Tired, Grammy."

"You should have invited your friend in for a few minutes." Curiosity burned in Nancy's eyes.

"He couldn't stay," Annabelle replied, not meeting her mother's eyes. Thankfully, the older woman allowed the subject to drop.

"Have you eaten?"

Annabelle and Bethany both shook their heads.

Nancy bustled them toward the kitchen. "I heated up some mac-'n'-cheese. Eat, then you can go to bed. We can talk in the morning."

A gentle sigh slid from Annabelle. She should have known that her mother would have something ready for them to eat, no matter what time they showed up.

Forty-five minutes later, Annabelle was in her old bedroom, staring into the darkness. Her mind wouldn't settle down. Had she made the right decision? At the time, she'd been so angry, so scared. Now? Now she was worried that she might have brought danger to her mother's doorstep.

Maybe the people after Tyler would leave her alone once he disappeared.

Or maybe they'd become more aggressive.

Lord, grant me wisdom. Help me to do the right thing and protect my little girl.

Around midnight, she finally dropped off into a fitful sleep. Her rest was interrupted by nightmares. Nightmares of a stranger taking Bethany. She ran after him, but he kept running. Just when she thought she'd catch him, he'd vanish right in front of her. Bethany was crying out for her to save her, but she was always too far away.

Bolting straight up into a sitting position, Annabelle panted like she'd been running, sweat clinging to her skin. The sun was just starting to peek through the windows. It was early. No other sounds stirred in the house. She slipped out of the bed, welcoming the familiar comfort of the shag carpet under her bare feet. She could do with more sleep, but the thought of returning to bed made her shudder. Instead, she headed toward the shower.

When she emerged, she followed the aroma of fresh coffee and cinnamon rolls to the kitchen. Her mother was awake, but Bethany was still in bed. Poor thing, she had to be wiped out after all they'd been through in the past couple of days.

"Hey, Mom." Annabelle helped herself to a cup of coffee, added some mocha creamer, then slid into a chair at the table.

"Annabelle." Nancy scooped a warm cinnamon roll onto a plate and placed it in front of her daughter with a fork. "I would ask if you slept well, but I can see you didn't."

Annabelle sighed. While she considered what to say, she forked a bite of the pastry into her mouth, closing her eyes to savor the sticky-sweet flavor. "Mmm. Delicious. I had trouble sleeping. Too many things happening." She raised her eyes to her mother's concerned face. "I keep worrying if I should have come here. I hate to think I put you in any kind of jam."

Her mother clucked her tongue. "Now, don't you be worrying about me. You and my granddaughter are my priority. Always have been."

"I know, Mom. I just—" She broke off as her cell phone rang. Tensing, she looked down at the number. "Hold on, Mom. It's Danielle, a woman on my block. Bethy was supposed to go swimming with her daughters yesterday."

She didn't comment on the obvious reasons why they hadn't.

She tapped the screen to answer and took a deep breath. "Danielle? What's up?"

"Annabelle, are you and Bethany okay?" Danielle's normally peppy voice was nervous.

How to answer that? *Oh, yeah. Just being followed. Oh, and my estranged husband is going into hiding after seeing his boss get killed. Not.*

Trying to be upbeat, she said, "We're fine. On a little trip, that's all. Why? Is something wrong?"

A slight pause. When Danielle's voice came again, it was softer, like she didn't want anyone to hear her. "Listen. I don't want the girls to worry, but something weird is going on. Mike said there was a car parked across the street from your house yesterday morning. And someone was sitting inside it. There's no house across the street from you, so why was he there? Mike was walking the dog at lunch and they went right past the car. Mike thought he had surprised the guy. He wasn't positive, but it looked like the man was looking at your house through binoculars."

A shiver worked its way up Annabelle's spine. Danielle might not have been sure, but she had no doubt Mike was right. They were waiting for her.

What would have happened if she had gone home first, the way she had planned?

"Thanks, Danielle. I will call the police. I appreciate your letting me know."

"There's more." Of course there was. "Yesterday afternoon, someone was going around the block with a picture of you and Bethany. He was insisting that he was your cousin and trying to reach you on urgent business."

Her stomach turning, Annabelle closed her eyes.

She didn't have any cousins. Where did the man get the pictures?

Annabelle couldn't get off the phone fast enough. As soon as she hung up, she dialed Tyler's number.

"The number you have reached is no longer in service." She wanted to cry at the automated message. Tyler's phone must have been disconnected so he could disappear. Now what?

Wait a minute. Karl Adams had given her his card.

Jumping to her feet, she ran back to her bedroom to grab her purse. This was not a conversation she wanted her mother to hear. Shutting the door, she began rifling around her purse frantically. After a few seconds, she found the item she was looking for.

Her fingers shook as she tapped his number into her smartphone. When Karl answered, she breathlessly repeated her conversation with Danielle Johnson.

"Hold on, Annabelle. I will call you back as soon as I know something."

He hung up quickly. Sinking down on the edge of her bed, Annabelle fought to control her emotions. The urge to cry battled with the urge to throw something. She did neither. Instead, she sat tensely, clasping her phone between her hands like a lifeline. *Please, Lord,* she repeated over and over and over in her mind.

She checked on Bethany. She wasn't awake yet, which gave her a little more time. Returning to her bedroom, Annabelle paced as she waited. Every minute or so, she looked at the screen on her phone to see the time.

When her phone rang forty minutes later, she nearly dropped it.

"Y-yes?" she gasped.

"Annabelle? You were right to call. I sent someone to your house. It's been ransacked. I have the feeling that the pictures that man was showing your neighbors were from your wall. There were several empty picture frames on the floor, and it was obvious pictures had been taken from the walls. No doubt someone was trying to find something that would lead them to you. The problem is, there are bound to be many people after you because of the bounty put on your head. Who knows how many people are watching your house. Whatever you do, don't leave your mother's house. And stay inside. The last thing we want is for you to be recognized."

"I won't! Oh, I'm just so scared right now. What if my mom's in danger because of me?" She shouldn't have come. Oh, why had she been so stubborn?

"I understand your concerns. We're coming to get you. What?" the marshal said to someone on his end. "Here."

A moment later, Tyler came on the phone. "Annabelle, can you convince your mom to go stay with your brother for a while?"

She nodded. Oh, wait. He couldn't see her. "Yeah, I think I can do that. I'll see if she can stay at Ethan's place."

"Do it. She'll be safer at Ethan's house."

"Tyler—"

He was no longer on the phone. "Karl Adams again, ma'am. Someone's on the way. I agree with Tyler. Your mom needs to get out of the house. We'll see that she's safe. But you and your daughter need to go into hiding. They won't stop coming for you."

Six hours later, she and Bethany were led into a house in Iowa. She'd never been to Iowa before. Now that she was here, though, she had zero interest in looking around at the scenery. Guilt over the disruption to her mother's life weighed heavy on her. Inside the house, Karl was there. And so was Tyler.

"Daddy!" Bethany ran to her father, throwing herself into his arms as if she hadn't just seen him for the first time in years a little over a day ago. Her sweet daughter apparently harbored no bitterness toward the man who'd always chosen business over family.

She couldn't be so blasé. The bitterness she'd shoved deep down inside, for her little girl's sake, erupted.

"What are you doing here?"

Tyler blinked. "What do you mean? I'm going into witness protection, just like you."

A familiar tall woman stood up from the table. For a brief moment, Annabelle paused, trying to recall the woman's name. Ah. Stacy Preston. That was it. Stacy smiled at her and intervened in what promised to be a heated reunion. "Why don't I take Bethany to see if we can find something fun to play." She gave Karl a meaningful look.

"Excellent idea, Stacy."

She wasn't sure, but Annabelle thought she saw the man wink at his colleague. As she watched, the very efficient female marshal blushed and ducked her head.

Annabelle waited until Stacy left the room with Bethany chattering beside her, then turned to her husband again. "You and I are both going into witness protection. But we are not going together. It's your fault we're even in this mess."

Tyler felt as if he'd been punched in the stomach. Her words knocked the wind right out of him. Not that he could deny her accusations. He couldn't. It was all his fault. While he might not have asked for any of it to happen, he had once again brought danger to his family.

But this time, he wasn't going to walk away.

"I can see you are put into separate placements," Karl began slowly.

Uh-uh. No way.

"Could we have a moment, please?" Tyler shoved his hands deep into his pockets. He needed to convince Annabelle of his sincerity.

A slight smile touched the marshal's mouth. "Of

course. There's a small dinette off the kitchen. Why don't you go in there? I'll make sure you aren't disturbed."

Tyler motioned for Annabelle to precede him. She crossed her arms in front of herself and glared. "Please?"

Huffing, she tossed her brown hair over her shoulder and marched in the direction the marshal had indicated. When they arrived in the room, she didn't sit, but faced him. Her chin raised a notch, as if she was daring him to speak. If the situation hadn't been so serious, he might have been tempted to smile. She was as adorable as he'd remembered. As it was, there was little cause for humor. Their very lives were being ripped apart.

"Annie—" he began.

"Annabelle," she interrupted. "No one calls me Annie. Not anymore."

"Fine, Annabelle. Look, I know I screwed up. I put my work ahead of you and Bethany. I left you alone when I should have been with you. I made it impossible for you to stay. I get that. And I know I don't deserve a second chance."

"You're right." Her nostrils flared. "Do you know how many times she's asked for you these past two years? Of course you don't! Because you weren't there. But I'm used to that. Even when we were together, you were never there. And now you show up again, but only because you've dragged yourself, and us, into danger. It infuriates me knowing that it took someone gunning for you to bring you into your daughter's life. And what happens when this is over? You disappear again?"

Annabelle stepped closer to him. He could almost feel the energy of her anger crackling off her skin. Her rich brown eyes shimmered with her rage. "She was too young to remember being abandoned before. If you distanced yourself again, it would wound her deeply. I have to protect her from that."

Would it wound Annabelle, too? He knocked that thought out of his head. He had no right to expect to be welcomed back into Annabelle's life. They were strangers now. But his daughter… He couldn't bear the idea that she would grow up and not know him.

"I wouldn't abandon her."

Annabelle snorted, cutting her eyes at him. Her scorn made him wince.

"I'm serious. Annie… Annabelle." Tyler ran his hands through his hair and breathed in deeply. He needed to think. To make her see reason. "There's no way to tell how long this case could drag out. It could be months. It could be years. None of us would be safe until it's over. If we go into separate placements, I would never see my daughter again. Please, Annabelle. This is my last chance to be a father to her. I don't want to disappear on her again."

He could see her jaw tensing. She didn't immediately say no. A bubble of hope swelled in his heart. For the second time in less than a week, he turned to God and pleaded for help and guidance.

"I need to think." Annabelle walked out of the room, without giving him another glance. His heart sank.

A minute later, Karl appeared in the doorway. "Well?"

Tyler sighed. "She needs to think. I can't blame her."

"We can't let her think too long. I'm sorry, Tyler, but time is something we just don't have."

Right. Tyler hadn't felt this helpless in a long time.

"Karl!" Rick, another marshal, rushed into the room. "You need to see this."

"Coming now, Rick." Karl nodded once at Tyler, then left the room.

Once again, Tyler was alone with his thoughts. He was tempted to go after Annabelle again and try to reason with her, but really, what was the point? She'd obviously made up her mind. And he couldn't say he blamed her.

If only she knew about the reason he'd pushed her away. How it had been for her safety. Somehow, knowing that she was in danger even though he'd kept away from her made his reasoning back then seem ridiculous.

A sudden flurry of action caught his attention. Karl marched out to the garage, his phone to his ear as he barked out questions. His intense expression didn't bode well for the current situation.

Karl called a meeting with Tyler and Annabelle. A couple of other marshals were in the room. He could hear Bethany squeal with laughter in the other room, where she was playing. A smile spread across his face at the sound. When he considered that he might never hear that joyful sound again, his chest grew tight. Rubbing his chest, he turned his head to find his wife staring at him, frowning slightly, her head tilted like she was trying to solve a puzzle.

A throat cleared. Tyler reluctantly removed his gaze from Annabelle and turned it on Karl. He didn't like the look in the marshal's eyes. Karl was worried about something, and the way the man continued to watch him told Tyler he strongly figured in whatever was on Karl's mind.

"Tyler, there's been a complication," Karl said finally, confirming his fears. "Jonathan had planned to place you in Colorado. He had a job lined up for you and your new identity was in the works, but we have to change our plans. It seems that Wilson Barco has doubled the bounty on your head. There have already been reports of men resembling you being attacked in ten states, including Colorado."

Annabelle gasped, her eyes showing her shock. "So what does that mean? What happens now?" Annabelle's voice was quiet. He knew that voice well. It sounded calm, but it really signaled that her emotions were spiraling very close to the surface.

Karl turned to her, his expression smooth.

"It's not unexpected," Karl told the group. "We have been monitoring the airways and computers for anything. An undercover contact has informed us that the bounty has stirred up interest in several states. Plus, Barco has apparently called in favors from all over the country. There's no way for us to know all the people who are out to get to you. We're working on a different placement right now. One that will take you farther off the grid and out of Barco's reach."

Tyler felt as though he was sinking in quicksand. He had heard much about Wilson Barco during his time as a prosecuting attorney. The amount of power the man wielded was terrifying.

Was there any place they could go that he wouldn't find them?

Chapter Four

Off the grid?

Annabelle stared at the marshal, appalled. What exactly did Karl have in mind when he said "off the grid"? Mentally, she envisioned them living in a rustic shack in the middle of the woods. *Little House on the Prairie*–style. She quelled a shiver of distaste. She was not a woman who enjoyed camping. Too many creepy crawly things. If it wasn't for the danger to her daughter, she'd back out now. However, since her daughter's life was at stake, she held her silence. There was nothing she would not endure to protect Bethany.

She regretted thinking that she would be able to protect her little girl without the protection of the marshals.

"Annabelle?"

She turned her head and met Tyler's eyes. The concern in them was clear. "I just want to go back to a normal life and forget that all this happened, Tyler. I want to wake up in the morning and know that Bethany is safe. Instead, I know that from this point on, I am going to be constantly looking over my shoulder. I hate that."

"Annie—" Tyler began. He broke off when Stacy entered the room. Without Bethany.

"Where's my daughter?" Annabelle winced at the harsh note in her voice. She'd always thought of herself as someone who could keep calm in an emergency. This whole experience was testing that theory.

Stacy, fortunately, seemed to understand. She flashed a sympathetic smile at the nervous parents. "She's fine. Really. She fell asleep while I was reading to her. I'm guessing she was pretty worn out from the past couple of days."

Annabelle felt a small niggle of guilt. Her baby girl was suffering because of her stubbornness. If she had just given in gracefully when the situation had first come up…

No! That was not productive. She had been doing her best to protect her child. That was never the wrong thing to do. Now she was starting to second-guess her choices, and she wasn't going to go down that road. She had second-guessed herself for months after she left Tyler, but when he never made any effort to get her back, she realized that she had been right.

She'd also realized that she hadn't wanted to be right. Not that time.

The conversation drifted into more logistics. She doubted that she'd be able to add anything. Solitude. That's what she needed. Just a few minutes to herself, so she could think.

Pushing her seat back, she stood. Immediately, all conversation stopped and the marshals and Tyler all focused on her.

"Is it all right if I excuse myself for a bit?" She wasn't

really asking but thought she should be polite. Out of the corner of her eye, she caught the small grin that crossed Tyler's face. Ah, apparently, he was on to her.

"Of course!" Karl stood, deep furrows digging into his forehead. "Are you all right? Anything we can do for you?"

She felt ridiculous.

"Relax, guys. She just needs some time to herself to process. She'll be fine."

Annabelle felt her jaw drop as she turned to look at Tyler. She was amazed that he had realized that about her. Granted, they had been married. But it had seemed back then that his attention was always on other things. She'd often wondered if he was truly listening to what she had been saying.

He had just proven that he had been. She wasn't sure what to think about that. And that scared her. Because she needed to keep up her guard around him. She had given him her heart once, and he hadn't appreciated it, choosing his job over her and their daughter. She couldn't allow herself to make that mistake again.

It was getting hard to breathe in the room, being so close to him.

She walked into the living room area to check on Bethany. The blanket from the couch was on the floor. Bethany, however, was not on the couch. Annabelle frowned. She had thought that Stacy had left her in the living room, but maybe she had put her in one of the bedrooms.

Stomach flipping like she had swallowed a couple of frogs, Annabelle ran to the first bedroom and opened the door. Her heart raced as her fear spiked. She had to swallow past the scream that had lodged in her throat. Spinning around, she checked each bedroom. They were all empty. Where was her baby?

She wasn't going to stand here, though. She had a house full of US marshals to help her.

And Tyler.

Running back through the house, she burst into the room. "Bethany's gone!"

Tyler jumped to his feet so fast that his chair tipped over. No one even glanced at it.

"I'll check the rest of the house!" Stacy charged off. Annabelle could hear her feet pounding down the hallway.

"The rest of you, check the perimeter. Rick, check the garage. If she's not there, join us outside."

Without another word, the search began. Annabelle ran outside after Karl. When he turned to her, she shook her head. "Don't you dare tell me it's safer inside. No one is going to keep me from searching for my daughter."

Wisely, the lawman let the subject drop.

The group spread out. Within a few minutes, Stacy and Rick had rejoined them and were helping to comb the yard for Bethany. Annabelle had barely held back a sob when she had told them. She had been holding on to the hope that Bethany was playing in the house and she just hadn't seen her. Now that hope was gone.

The air was suddenly split by a child's shout.

"No! I want my mommy!"

Bethany.

"Quiet, kid." The cold voice sent ice through her veins.

"No! Let me go! Let me—"

Annabelle's knees turned to water as her daughter's shout was suddenly cut off. She couldn't allow herself to falter, though. Her baby needed her. Karl waved his gun in the air, indicating that they should follow him. He pointed at Rick and signaled something. Without breaking stride, Rick turned the corner and disappeared on the other side of the house.

She understood. They were going to try and box in the villain who was taking her daughter. What if they were too late? "Hurry," she whispered.

A hand touched her back. She didn't scream. She knew that touch. Tyler was right behind her. For some odd reason, his familiar touch was comforting. She drew in a deep breath as they continued to follow Karl around the side of the house. He was moving so slowly. Even though she knew in her heart they had to move with care, she found herself practically stepping on the heels of the marshal's black shoes.

As they turned the corner, her horrified eyes met with a sight that would haunt her for the rest of her life. A young man in his twenties was dragging her struggling five-year-old daughter across the lawn. Bethany was small, but she was also wiggly. And she was putting all that wiggle to good use now. The man was having trouble keeping hold of him.

"Halt!" Karl bellowed, snapping his gun up.

Annabelle clutched the man at her side. Dimly she was aware it was Tyler, but she couldn't help herself. What if he shot and hit Bethany? It took all her will not to say something. She had to trust that he knew what he was doing. It was the hardest thing she had ever had to do. So hard, she tasted blood from biting her lip in her agony. Needing to be strong, she released Tyler. She swayed briefly, but his hand touched her on her back and steadied her.

The young man did halt. He swiveled, putting himself behind Bethany. He strapped the young girl against him with a muscular arm and yanked a knife out of his pocket. Instead of showing fear, a sneer slipped onto his face.

"You ain't gonna shoot me. 'Cause if you do, you might hit the kid. She's my insurance. There's a lot of money riding on me bringing her daddy in. And unless you let us go, and he comes with me, then she might get hurt. It's that simple."

"Please." Was that strangled voice hers? Annabelle swallowed the fear that clogged her throat. "Please. She's just a little girl."

He laughed. She shuddered at the sound. Stacy placed a hand on her shoulder. She had been so wrapped up in the scene playing out before her that she hadn't realized the marshal was beside her.

"Now, bring her daddy out to me."

Wait. What? She glanced over her shoulder, where her estranged husband had been standing mere seconds ago. There was no one there now. Her heart chilled in her chest. Had he abandoned them, right when they needed him?

No, she couldn't believe that. Yes, he had chosen work and his life over them before. But she had seen the caring in his eyes when he interacted with his daughter.

But she couldn't deny what her eyes were telling her.

Tyler was gone.

* * *

There was no way he was going to let that man hurt his daughter.

Tyler crept back into the shadows and stole up behind the man holding the knife. He saw a thick branch, about a foot long, and grabbed it. Stepping carefully, he concentrated on making a minimum amount of noise as his feet inched closer to his goal. It was a good thing it was summer. The lush green grass cushioned his steps and softened any noises. He could clearly make out the man's voice through the shrubbery. And he could hear the pleading voice of his wife.

He winced, remembering the man who'd promised to hurt his family years ago. He had hoped that when he had disappeared from their lives, they would be safe. And yet, they were once again at the mercy of a madman. But this time, he refused to sit back and let the criminals chase him away while those he loved were hurt. He would gladly sacrifice himself if it meant that Bethany and Annabelle would be well and protected.

But the world didn't work that way. Danger was everywhere.

He could see the man's head now. The man still held the knife. It wasn't touching Bethany. In fact, the knife was being held almost six inches away from her. Finally, something was going his way.

Glancing over, he knew the moment that Annabelle became aware of his presence. Her eyes widened slightly. Quickly, she jerked away her gaze. She again began to plead with the man. *Good girl.* Tyler knew that she was distracting the punk so he could act.

Karl was glaring. It was hard to tell if his hard stare

was aimed at Tyler or at the criminal, but he would guess that the glare was pointed to him. He didn't have time to care. Not when his daughter was in trouble.

The young man was growing angry. "Stop your crying, lady! I want you to go get this kid's dad or there's going to be trouble."

Tyler took the final two steps forward. "I'm right here."

The villain jerked around in shock. Bethany wiggled from his loosened grasp and ran to her mother's arms. Annabelle took her daughter in her arms. Immediately, Stacy stepped in front of mother and child, shielding them from harm. Tyler saw Karl glance their way. His gaze locked on Stacy for a moment. It might have been his imagination, but Tyler was certain that fear lurked in Karl's eyes at the sight of the female marshal in the line of danger.

The man with the knife glared in Annabelle's direction. There was nothing he could do. Bethany was firmly out of his range. Fury crossed the man's face. Raising his knife, he charged at Tyler.

A shot cracked out. Howling, the man dropped his knife from his bleeding hand. He didn't pause long. Tyler was ready for him. The moment he started forward again, Tyler swung his branch like a club. The man went down, stunned.

Within seconds, the marshals swarmed over him and had him restrained. Karl pulled the phone out of his pocket and demanded extra marshals at the house. Tyler heard him say something about the safe house being compromised. Duh.

"What were you thinking, Tyler?" Karl growled. The

cords on his neck were strained. He was probably fighting not to holler.

"I was thinking that I needed to save my daughter."

Karl didn't say anything as the dazed would-be kidnapper was loaded into the back of Rick's car. In silence, the group watched Rick bend his tall frame down to get behind the wheel and drive off.

"Annabelle, let's take her inside." Stacy gathered Annabelle and Bethany and herded them toward the house. Tyler watched them go. Seeing them safe was worth any chastising he might receive from Karl. Before she disappeared from his view, Annabelle threw a look over her shoulder at him. Gratitude shone in her eyes. Tyler stood taller. Karl might have thought he acted rashly, and perhaps he had. But his wife appreciated what he had done.

The moment the women were gone, Karl turned back to him.

He was in for it now.

"Tyler. Man, I don't even know what to say. What you did? It was all kinds of stupid. You could have gotten hurt. Bethany could have gotten hurt. It—"

"You watch your daughter being kidnapped and tell me that you wouldn't try to save her." Tyler tightened his jaw. The memory of that dude dragging his daughter away made his blood boil again.

Karl sighed, running his hand through his hair. "Look. I understand why you did it. I do. I get it. But, Tyler, that could have gone seriously wrong. You have to let us do our jobs."

Tyler didn't say anything. What was there to say? He couldn't promise not to act if his daughter, or if Annabelle, was in danger again. Shaking his head, Karl sighed.

"Come on, Tyler. We need to get inside and get mobilized. Obviously this safe house is no longer safe. We'll have to find a new place to hide you and your family until the details are final."

Tyler and Karl reentered the house. Soon after, new marshals and the state police were patrolling the perimeter. No chances were being taken with the safety of his family. He did appreciate the effort they were going to for them. The marshals went into action and searched for evidence that the house had been bugged. They checked every room, the cars, even the cell phones. Nothing.

He just had to stay alive until he could testify. Would the threat disappear then? Barco seemed to have so many resources, Tyler wasn't sure if he could ever return to normal society.

What would he do if, even after today, Annabelle decided to go into the program separately? He would have no more chances if she did that. He rubbed his chest, trying to soothe the ache that had formed. Karl disappeared into his office, his phone once again at his ear. Tyler sat by himself for the next half hour, trying to get a handle on his emotions.

He stood when Karl emerged from the office. The marshal strode with purpose down the hall. Curious, Tyler followed.

Karl marched into the kitchen. Annabelle was sitting at the table with Bethany and Stacy. The marshal motioned for her to come. Warily, she stood and went with him. Karl led them into the office. When they entered, he turned and shut the door behind them. Gesturing to the chairs in front of the desk, he seated himself behind it. Tyler had no idea what he was going to say. But he braced himself for the worst.

"Did Bethany say what happened, how he got to her?"

Annabelle bit her lip. He had to look away momentarily. He couldn't be distracted by her right now. "She said she woke up and heard a dog barking outside. Bethany has been wanting a dog for a long time. When she went out the back door, she couldn't find a dog. She found a man who tried to coax her into his car." Annabelle threw a haunted look at Tyler. His gut clenched. "She knows she's not supposed to talk to strangers. When she turned to go back inside, he grabbed her."

Tyler shuddered as the reality of how close they had come to losing their daughter rippled through his mind. Too close. They needed to go into hiding as soon as possible. Whatever wiggle room they'd had, it was gone now.

Karl seemed to be on the same page. He turned a grave expression toward Annabelle.

"Annabelle. You have to decide what you want to do," Karl stated. "We are running out of time. Once you are placed, you will have no further contact with anyone from your past or from your current life. Not friends or coworkers. Not even your family. That's the only way that I can protect you. Do you still want a separate placement? I can find you one. That wouldn't be a problem. However, if you decide that you do still want that, it means after today, you and Tyler will have no more contact with each other until the threat against you ends."

"If it ever ends." Tyler hadn't meant to voice the thought. But now it was hanging in the air between them. Karl acknowledged the truth of the statement with a nod.

"Unfortunately, there is that possibility."

Tyler held his breath. He couldn't believe how much it hurt to have it spelled out that way.

The marshal wasn't finished. "Or, I can place you together. If you want, I can even place you for a short trial period. If it doesn't work out, we can consider a new placement. Whatever you decide, I will do. But you have to decide now."

Annabelle dropped her head. From where he sat, Tyler could see her clasp her hands together tightly. The knuckles whitened. Finally, she lifted her head and leveled her stare at Tyler.

"I am so angry with you, Tyler Everson." His heart sank. She was going to ask to be placed separately. He was going to lose his daughter. "But even though I am angry, it would be wrong for me to deny you your daughter. If I was positive you didn't care for her, I wouldn't hesitate. I think you do care, though. Especially after seeing you trying to save her."

Annabelle switched her gaze to the marshal. "I will agree to our being placed together." She held up her hand to stop them from speaking. Like he would. His emotions were too high. "I don't want to commit. I will agree to go on a trial period."

Karl stood. "Excellent. I need to make some calls. Get everything set up. Everything should move fast from here on out."

"Do you have any thoughts as to where you'll put

us?" Tyler stood. Visions of a cramped apartment or a small house in mainstream suburbia rolled through his mind.

"I know exactly where I'm placing you. You'll be going somewhere no one would ever think to look for a high-powered lawyer and his family."

That was good, right? Just what they wanted.

"Where?" Annabelle asked.

Karl Adams smiled. "You're going to be living with the Amish."

Chapter Five

"Do you know where you're going?"

Annabelle shut her eyes and squeezed the bridge of her nose with her fingers. She had tossed and turned all night. Saturday morning had dawned bright and clear, in direct opposition to her mood. It was agony listening to her mother's tearful voice quavering over the phone. As much as she wished she could comfort her mother, she knew there was nothing she could say to make the situation more acceptable.

"I'm sorry, Mom. Karl didn't say where we were going. And even if he did, you know I can't tell you any of that."

She flinched as her mother sniffed. This was so hard. Tyler had taken Bethany to another room with Stacy to keep the fractious child occupied while she said good-bye to her mother. Possibly forever. It hurt so much to think about that. She had gotten used to talking with her mother every day on the phone. Or Skyping with her mom and Bethany. How was she supposed to not talk with her at all? How would her mother handle it? Ethan wasn't married, so Bethany was her only grand-child. The woman doted on her.

"It's cruel. Can't the marshals protect you from here?"

That worried her. She knew her mother. The woman was independent to a fault. She hadn't been happy about moving in with her son, no matter how temporary a situation it was. "Mom, you're not staying in your house, are you? I thought you were planning on going to stay with Ethan for a little while."

Her mother hesitated. "Well, I don't know, honey. I am used to my own ways. Besides, I have been in this house since before you were born."

Uneasy, Annabelle held the phone tighter, as if she could force her mother to see reason. "Mom, you have to go. Please. I would be constantly worried about you if I thought that you weren't safe."

She heard a muffled conversation. Then Ethan's voice came on the line.

"Hey, little sis. Don't you worry about Mom. She's stubborn, but so am I." That was true. When they were children, Ethan's stubborn nature had caused them to butt heads more than once. As an adult, however, his stubbornness had transformed into a determination that had served him well in his capacity as a lawman who was sworn to serve and protect. He would never let his mother remain in danger. He would use every argument he could to get her to agree to go stay with him.

She huffed a laugh, some of her tension draining. "So you'll make her go to your house?"

"Yeah. You don't need to be concerned about that. She might not be happy, but she won't want you to worry, so she'll do it."

That was probably true.

Tears again clogged her throat. "Oh, Ethan, I'm going to miss you guys so much."

His voice was slightly unsteady as he answered. "None of that. We'll miss you, too, but we will see each other again soon. Mom and I will be lifting you guys up every day in prayer." He paused. "Are you sure you want to go into hiding with Tyler, Annabelle? He isn't exactly the most trustworthy guy."

She bit her lip. She knew what Ethan's opinion of her husband was. She'd used Ethan's shoulder to cry on too many times for him not to be skeptical now. "I do. It'll be okay. He's changed. I can't really describe it, but I think this is the right decision. And I want Bethany to have a chance to know her father."

"Hmm."

Clearly, he didn't share her confidence. But she was sure that the change she had seen in Tyler was real.

She let the silence dangle between them, unsure of what to say to ease her brother's mind. What could she say? The situation was deplorable. A man had murdered someone, and Tyler had seen it happen. Now that man was willing do anything to make sure Tyler couldn't testify.

Including harming a five-year-old child.

That, more than anything else, was the deciding factor for her. She couldn't stay when her baby was in danger.

She hung up with her family, feeling alone. This was going to be the hardest thing she'd done since the day she'd walked out on Tyler. He had changed so much since they had gotten married. Missed important events, including her father's funeral. And he had gotten so withdrawn, she felt she was sharing her house with a stranger. Tyler had even stopped communicating with her. They would go through an entire evening without talking.

But she had still loved him. Had ached for the man she had married to return. But she could not continue to live in a house filled with such tension and silence. She had grown up with a distant workaholic father. The toll it had taken on her mother was painful to watch. She refused to be that woman.

She now knew that deep inside, she'd hoped that her leaving would have been a wake-up call to him and that he would have come after them. When that hadn't happened, she'd been devastated. Thankfully, she had Bethany to be strong for. And she had her mother's shoulder to cry on.

Now, however, she was going into the unknown. What did she really know about the Amish? She'd seen them, sure. The women always wore dresses and they had white bonnet-type hats on. And they didn't use electricity or drive cars. That was the extent of her real knowledge. She'd never actually met anyone who was Amish.

Looking down at her jeans and sneakers, Annabelle frowned. She'd have to wear a dress. All the time. She hadn't worn a dress in years. She even wore dress slacks to church. Skirts would allow the horrible scars—scars that she kept hidden at all times—on her legs to show. Part of her had always wondered if Tyler had been repulsed by them. It was after the accident when he had started to really withdraw. What other reason could there have been for the change in his behavior?

And now she was going to be wearing a dress. Would

the scars show? She tried to remember how long the dresses worn by Amish were.

Feeling slightly panicky, she wished the marshals had let her keep her cell phone so she could search the internet to research Amish clothing. She thought back to the Amish women she had seen in Indiana once. She recalled the women wearing dresses that were calf-length or longer. And most of them wore black stockings, too. So, even if she was forced to wear a dress, her scars would remain hidden. Cautiously, she inched her jeans up above her ankles and a couple of inches up her calves, about the length she thought an Amish dress might be. She twisted to the side to try and see if her scars peeked out below the denim hem.

"Annie? Are you ready to go?" Tyler walked around the corner.

She looked up at him guiltily, letting her jeans drop back down. They were all waiting for her, and here she was wasting good time. Where was her good sense? Not to mention her common courtesy!

Had he seen what she doing?

His face was softer than normal. She flushed. He knew what she was doing.

Only Tyler knew how much the scars bothered her. Only he would understand why she was looking up Amish dresses. A strange look crossed his face. Was it guilt? He looked almost haunted. But that didn't make any sense. The expression was gone so fast, she wondered if she was misreading him. After all, it had been several years since she'd last seen him.

"No one will see them, Annie," he said softly, almost whispering. "Even if they did, you have nothing to be ashamed of."

She shrugged, her cheeks still warm with embarrassment. "Why would I feel ashamed?" She hedged. "These scars are old news. I should be grateful that I survived the accident. Not worried about some scars."

Pain flashed in his face, although she had no idea why. He opened his mouth. Shut it. Paused. Finally, he sighed. "It's time to go. Have you done everything you needed to here?"

"Yes-s-s." She dragged out the word, disturbed by his attitude. Tyler had been going to say something different. She knew it. But she wasn't sure she even wanted to know what it was.

She needed to be careful. Being in his company again was affecting her more than it should. Oh, she was still angry at him. She wasn't sure if she could ever forgive him for giving up on her so quickly. For putting work and money ahead of her and their child. But seeing him now, watching him risk himself for Bethany, well, it softened the edge of her anger. If she wasn't careful, she was worried that she'd become emotionally involved again. She couldn't afford to do that.

Turning from him, she picked up her and Bethany's suitcases. All of the worldly possessions they'd be bringing into their new life were in the two red cases. Her lips twisted. She could probably leave most of the clothes behind. After all, once they arrived at the place Karl was taking them, they wouldn't be needing them.

Tyler couldn't get the image of Annabelle's face as she looked at her scarred legs out of his mind. She still harbored insecurities about her scars. Tyler wanted to tell Annie the truth—the accident had been a deliberate act of malice, and a warning. A direct result of his job.

Tyler had always believed that it was a warning for him. The runaway truck that had smashed into their front window and pinned his wife to the wall a week after he'd been threatened by the son of a man he'd sent to prison was too much of a coincidence.

Unfortunately, that man had an airtight alibi for the time of the accident. Tyler had understood the message. His family would suffer, just as the guilty man's family was suffering. Tyler had been in torment about what to do for weeks. Until the man had died unexpectedly and he could breathe again.

Eventually, the thought that he needed to save his family from himself had grown in his mind. When Annie had left him soon after, he'd taken it as a sign that he needed to let them go. Only then could he be sure they would be safe. And only then could he freely work to prove what the police had been unable to. It was a task he'd only recently been able to do.

The idea of telling Annie the truth crept into his mind. He scoffed at the idea. Yeah, right. Tell her that it was his fault she carried the scars, inside and out, that still bothered her. He finally had a chance to be with his daughter. He knew that he had destroyed all his chances to have a relationship with Annie. But he could still be a father to Bethany.

A few days ago, he didn't even have that.

"Let's move out," Karl ordered.

Rick slid behind the wheel of the car taking Tyler and his family. Tyler hadn't had a chance to speak with the man since he'd returned the night before from hauling Bethany's would-be kidnapper to the proper authorities. He wanted to ask him if the man had said anything more, but that would have to wait.

Karl led the way in his car. Stacy brought up the rear. The convoy was made less obvious by the fact that the cars were all different. Rick was driving a dark-colored SUV. Karl was in a midsize pickup truck and Stacy followed behind in a Jeep. Tyler sat in the front seat, next to Rick. Annie sat behind the driver's seat, and Bethany was securely fastened into her booster seat behind him. Tyler opened the mirror on his visor to look back at his daughter.

"You doing okay, bug?"

The smile she shot his way warmed his heart. "Yeah, Daddy. This is fun! Isn't it, Mommy?"

Annabelle rolled her eyes. "Absolutely. A blast."

Rick chuckled. Tyler winked at his daughter in the mirror. She was precious.

Rick's phone rang. He frowned when he glanced at it. Tyler went on full alert. "Something wrong?"

"Huh?" Rick checked the mirror, then switched lanes, following Karl. "No, not really. This girl I dated a couple of times, she keeps calling me. I am not sure why. We went out to a movie and to dinner. I told her that I would be busy with work for the near future."

Annabelle made a face behind him. Uh-oh. He knew what she was thinking about. When they'd still been together, he'd often been too busy with work to do things with his family. Even before he'd withdrawn.

"As long as we're okay."

"Yeah, I think we're fine. It'll probably be a boring trip. Sorry, but this isn't a very exciting drive."

Tyler settled down to enjoy the peace of the drive. It was a warm day outside. As the day heated up, Rick turned the air conditioner on higher. Around noon, Bethany started to whine about needing to use the bathroom. Rick called Karl and told him that they needed a restroom break.

Tyler turned around partially in his seat. "We're gonna look for a place to stop, bug, okay?"

The smile she had given him earlier was gone, replaced by a definite pout. "Wanna stop now. I don't like this car ride anymore, Daddy."

"Bethany Jane," Annabelle said, her tone a clear warning.

"Two named. That sounds serious," Rick murmured. Tyler held back a grin. He knew Annie's tone all too well. It wouldn't go well if she thought he found his daughter's attitude entertaining.

Bethany gave up her whining, although her pout became more pronounced. Tyler winced, wondering how long they would have to wait for a full-out meltdown. The kid had had a rough couple of days. She was about due for one. Not that it would be acceptable. But it would be understandable.

Ten minutes later, they pulled off the interstate and headed for a rest area. Bethany nearly leaped out of the car when he opened her door. Even Annie groaned as she exited the vehicle and stretched. She caught him watching her and grimaced.

"You okay?" He stepped closer to her.

"Fine." She waved her hand dismissively. "Just ready to get there. Wherever there is."

That, he understood.

"Mommy!"

"Okay." She reached out for her daughter's hand and threw a tired smile at the men. "We'll be right back." Stacy joined them, and the three females headed off together.

Karl walked over to where Tyler and Rick were standing. "We should be there in about four hours."

Tyler groaned. Four more hours in the car. They had a portable DVD player. He'd gladly listen to kid videos if it meant his daughter would be entertained.

"Here come the women," Karl said, halting his discussion with Rick.

Tyler turned to see Stacy leading the way back, followed by Annabelle and a much happier Bethany skipping at her side. He heard a heavy sigh behind him. Glancing over his shoulder, he was astonished to see the wistful expression on Karl's face as he watched the women. Eyebrows rising, he slid his gaze back toward them. Stacy's eyes skittered away from the men, her cheeks flushed. He tightened his lips so he wouldn't smile. They might think they were playing it cool, but anyone with eyes could see that there was something going on between those two. He shot a glance over at Rick and snickered as the marshal rolled his eyes. Yep. They weren't fooling anyone.

Absently, he rubbed his arm where he had been shot. The bandage was off now, although his arm was still tender. He thought about his relationship with Annabelle. He missed the way they used to be so close. Shaking his head, he closed down that line of thinking. He shouldn't waste time on what was. What they had was gone. They were not going to be together forever. Only until they could leave witness protection. Then they'd go back to their separate lives. Although, this time, he would keep in touch with his daughter.

A car squealed into the parking lot. Tyler took one look and his blood ran cold. The speeding car headed straight for them, showing no hint of slowing down. When the window rolled down, he was running before the first shot blasted through the silence.

"Get down!" he yelled at Bethany and Annie. Behind him, Karl echoed the command.

Tyler reached the women and put himself directly in front of his wife and daughter. He pushed them behind another vehicle. He felt Annie flinch when the car door was hit. He pushed Bethany's head down and covered them as well as he could with his body. Bethany's whimpered sobs broke his heart, but he made himself block them out.

More shots rang out around them. How many came from the marshals and how many from the people who wanted him dead, he had no idea. Stacy landed beside them, her Glock in her hands. Her pretty face was drawn and serious. She was every inch a US marshal, protecting those in her charge.

"If we could get you into my Jeep, we might be able to escape while Rick and Karl are keeping them busy. I have called in the state police. They are on their way."

She led the way to her car, motioning for them to keep low.

Tyler put Annie in front of him and sandwiched Bethany between them. Slowly, they crawled to the Jeep. Another shot rang out and this time, it was ac-

companied by a loud cry. They had almost reached the
Jeep when it was hit. Twice. Both rear tires hissed as
the air left them. They weren't going anywhere fast in
a vehicle with two tires deflated.

"You guys have to get to shelter." Stacy kept her eyes
firmly on her targets as she spoke to them.

Tyler swiveled his head from side to side, searching
for a safer place.

"Let's head to the trees. Run!" Tyler scooped up his
daughter in his arms and ran, keeping Annie in front
of him.

They had almost reached the trees when he heard a
shout. Instinctively, he slowed and looked back. Karl
was squared off against the villains, who had spotted them. One of them started up toward them. Stacy
stepped behind a tree for cover and held her Glock in
front of her. "Keep going," she ordered them. "I will
hold them off. The police should be here soon. Then I
or Karl will come and find you."

Tyler opened his mouth.

"Move, now! I need to focus."

Tyler turned and pushed his family behind the trees.
He managed to glance back over his shoulder. Karl and
Stacy were standing near each other, doing their best
to keep the bad guys at bay. Rick was standing to their
left, his face grim in his determination.

As he watched, Rick tumbled to the ground, his
hands clutching his side. From where he stood, Tyler
could see blood seeping between his fingers and covering his hands. His mouth went dry. A gasp at his side
reminded him of Annabelle and Bethany. He needed to
get his family to safety.

Chapter Six

"Do you think Rick is dead?"

Tyler sighed at Annie's softly spoken comment. He had wondered how much she had seen. If she hadn't seen Rick go down, he had every intention of telling her, once Bethany was not paying attention. He just knew that there were some things one couldn't unsee.

"I don't think he was dead." He flicked his gaze toward Bethany. Good. She didn't appear to be paying attention to them. "He was still moving. I have no idea how badly he was hurt, though. I imagine that the police will be there soon, and they'll call an ambulance." He glanced behind him. No sign of Stacy. Or Karl. Where were they? Were they safe?

He winced at the sorrow on Annabelle's face. The urge to put his arm around her, to comfort her, was strong. But he knew that she wouldn't accept comfort from him. He was fortunate that she was talking to him. He could expect nothing more than that, though.

"I think we need to keep going, Annie. I wish we still had our cell phones. We could try and contact them later."

"I still have Karl's card," Annie murmured. "Maybe we could find a business that would let us use their phone."

He pursed his lips, considering. It was a good idea. "I think that would work. If we can't reach them, we could contact Jonathan Mast. Although I would hate to disturb him right now."

She thought about it for a few seconds, then nodded. "Sounds like a plan. Which direction do we head?"

"We're close to La Porte, Indiana. At least, I think we are. I seem to recall signs for I-80. We would have taken that next. I am guessing that we want to keep heading east toward Ohio."

"Mommy, I'm hungry."

They exchanged glances. The food was back in the car. "I have a protein bar in my purse, baby doll. That will have to do for now."

It wasn't the best choice for a five-year-old, but it was better than nothing. Especially since they had no idea how far they would have to walk before this adventure came to a conclusion. Annie opened her mouth to say something—he had no idea what—when he heard something. Holding a finger to his mouth, he listened. Annie froze, then she bent down and whispered to Bethany to be very quiet. His heart ached when his baby girl opened her eyes wide, her lower lip trembling. The poor little girl had been through enough that she realized they were not playing a game.

"Mommy, I'm scared."

His throat tightened.

"It's going to be okay, sweet pea," Annie whispered back. "Daddy knows what to do."

He did? That was sure news to him. Right now he

was winging it. But he would do whatever he needed to if it would keep them safe.

Another patch of white noise. Followed by a burst of speaking. Like a pager.

Or a walkie-talkie.

They were being tracked through the woods. For a moment, he hoped that they were being tracked by the cops or the marshals. If so they would be safe for the time being.

"We have tracks in the dirt here," an unfamiliar masculine voice said. The white noise followed.

"Go ahead and shoot on sight. If you can catch the kid or the woman, they can be used as bait."

Nope, definitely not the cops. He looked down at the ground, and irritation with himself grew inside. They were leaving all kinds of tracks in the dirt, scuffing up the path. That would never do. He leaned closer to Annie, so he could whisper in her ear. The scent of her hair threatened to distract him, but he refused to allow that to happen.

"We need to get off the path. Head into the brush and try to keep from leaving clear tracks." His old Boy Scout motto of Leave No Trace came to mind.

Annie nodded. Tugging gently on Bethany's hand, she indicated which way they were going. Thankfully, his daughter seemed to grasp the urgency of the situation. She followed her mother's lead without question. It was another plus that they'd all worn jeans that day. Otherwise, their legs would have been scratched up from the shrubbery. A couple of times, thorns caught at his ankles.

Without pausing, he bent over and picked up his daughter. "So she doesn't get stuck with thorns," he murmured in response to Annie's raised eyebrow.

She nodded and kept going. The voices were coming closer. Though they were still on the path. There was no way that they could get far enough away to safely avoid them, judging by the pace with which the voices were catching up to them.

Tyler stopped and glanced around. A little farther on, there were two trees that had been toppled. There was an opening between them. If they could squeeze down in there, maybe they could get low enough that they wouldn't be seen as the men went past.

"This way!"

Moving as quickly as the prickly bushes and briars would allow, the small group slogged through the growth and arrived at the tree.

"Let's get you in there first, and then I will lift Bethany to you." Tyler assisted his wife over the first tree. It was enormous. When he handed his daughter over to her mother, Annie set the child down. The top of her head barely cleared the tree. Perfect.

Placing a hand on the top of the fallen tree, he vaulted over and landed with a slight *plop* next to them. Annie had already coaxed Bethany to crouch down. He got down as low as he could. In the close confines, he could hear them breathing. He placed his hand on Annie's shoulder to urge her to crouch lower. His hand tingled where he touched her. She flushed. Did she feel it? He removed his hand and focused on listening.

"Lord, protect us." Annie's whispered prayer resonated within him. When was the last time he prayed, really prayed? Would God even hear him now, after he'd ignored Him for so long? He had nothing to lose. And he and his family could use all the help they could get.

God, please be with us. Keep us safe. Amen.

It was all he could think of to say. Hopefully, it would be enough.

By now, the men were practically on top of them. Their voices were growing louder. Even a bit angry. It suddenly struck Tyler that they were making no attempt at all to keep quiet as they tracked his family. Were they so confident in their ability to catch Tyler that they didn't put any effort into sneaking up on him? Could they really be that arrogant?

"Jim, they had to have left the path," one of the men said.

Jim. He now knew that one of them was named Jim. He would, of course, relate that to the police or the marshals. Not that it would make much of a difference. Jim was a very common name.

"Cut through here."

Lowering himself farther, Tyler put an arm across Bethany's shoulders, just in case she decided to stand for some reason. He didn't think she would, but she was only five. She whimpered softly in his ear. He tightened his arms around her.

"Steady, bug," he breathed. "I've got you." He placed his lips against his baby girl's soft blond curls. Over her head, he met Annie's wide eyes. She was frightened, but she was strong. He had always known that.

Then the men were right over them. If one of the men glanced down and to the side in just the right way, there was the chance that they would be seen. And there was no way to escape from their present hiding place. Had he put them in an impossible situation?

Another prayer whispered through his brain. *Distract*

them, Lord. Please draw them away from us. Something crashed in the underbrush on the other side of the path.

"That way!"

He held his breath as the men dashed off, their voices loud and surly as they continued the search in the opposite direction. Tyler and Annie remained still and kept Bethany quiet for an additional ten minutes.

When it seemed that the men were gone, the tired group rose again. Tyler assisted Annie over the tree, then handed Bethany to her mother. When he had joined them, they started off again.

"I don't wanna do this anymore," Bethany whined. "I want to go home."

"Bethany, we are going on a little adventure, honey. I need you to be my brave girl for a little while longer."

How Annie could turn this horrific experience into an adventure was just part of what made her so amazing. However, the child wasn't buying it. Her bottom lip pushed out and her thin arms crossed her chest. He might not have been around her much, but he knew stubbornness when he saw it.

So did Annie. She glanced at him. He shrugged, as if to say, "Don't look at me, I got nothing."

"Bethany," Annie said, "I know that you're tired. I know that you are hungry. But there are bad men who are after us. We need to keep going so that they won't catch us."

That pushed-out lip started to tremble again. "But why are they looking for us?"

How did one tell a five-year-old that people were trying to hurt her family and it was all her father's fault?

Chapter Seven

She didn't like the bleak expression that had entered Tyler's eyes. The sudden urge to hug him caught her by surprise. It also concerned her. At some point, her anger had cooled, leaving her vulnerable to other emotions. She needed to keep her emotional distance. Still, seeing him hurting was uncomfortable for her. He was doing his best to protect them.

It had taken some coaxing, but Bethany had given in and they were once again headed east. Most of the conversation had ceased. Annie didn't even try to talk. Partly because they were listening for the men to return, partly because they were all too tired and hungry to talk and partly because the thoughts whirling around inside her head were too heavy and chaotic for her to try to voice them yet.

They pushed on. Tyler was carrying Bethany, who had grown too tired to continue walking. Her thin arms had looped up and were clinging around his neck. He dropped a kiss on her head. Annabelle looked away, her eyes stinging at the tender action. She swallowed past the lump in her throat.

"Annabelle, do you have any water in that bag?" Tyler asked, his voice a soft rasp in the stillness.

Nodding, she slipped her purse over her neck so that it hung diagonally across her body. She opened it up and rifled inside the bag until her hand bumped into the bottled water she had placed in it earlier. It was slightly damp from condensation and cool to the touch. She pulled it out, quickly unscrewed the top and held it out to him. He carefully hoisted Bethany closer and removed one hand so he could drink. Then he offered the bottle to Bethany before handing it back to Annabelle. When their hands touched, she felt a subtle zing of electricity. She sucked in a breath. Her face warmed. Turning her head to hide her reaction, she took a drink then put the water back in her bag.

A little after six, they came into a small town. They took advantage of the rural setting to get something to eat at the gas station and freshen up. The man at the gas station looked at them suspiciously when they asked to make a phone call, but a couple of college students in the store heard them asking.

"You can use my phone, man." One of the young men handed Tyler his phone. Annabelle dug out Karl's card and handed it to him. She waited, nerves stretched taut, as he went to stand a bit apart from them to make the call. She could hear him talking but couldn't make out what he was saying.

A minute later he returned. "Thanks. I appreciate it." He handed the phone back to the college kid.

"No problem, dude."

They had done everything they had set out to do.

Continually looking over their shoulders, they headed east again.

"Were you able to talk with Karl?"

He shook his head, his eyes continuing to roam their surroundings as they walked. Bethany walked between Tyler and Bethany, holding on to their hands. "No. I left a rather generic message telling him we were fine and heading east."

"I hope they are okay," she commented. He nodded but didn't say anything. He didn't need to. She saw his mouth tighten. He was as worried as she was.

"We need to find a place to stay for the night," Tyler said, his gaze still scouring the horizon.

Annabelle felt her shoulders slump. She was beyond exhausted. "I'm open to suggestions. I don't know that we want to use a credit card. And I don't think I have enough cash on me to spring for a hotel room."

"I might have enough. But I don't know if I'm comfortable with something as obvious as a hotel room, either."

They walked for a bit longer. Annabelle muttered prayers under her breath. *Just a place to sleep, Lord. Please. That's all we need.*

A few minutes later, she looked ahead and sucked in a breath. "How would that work?"

Tyler swung his head around to see what she was talking about. The grin that stretched across his face made her want to grin and laugh along with him. They were walking along the backyard of a house that had obviously been long abandoned, judging by the state of disrepair. That wasn't what she was looking at, though.

She didn't think it would be safe to set foot inside the house.

The tree house, however, was another matter all together.

"Can we get up there safely?" Annie asked, her eyes glued to the little wooden house sitting majestically in a tree. It was perfect. It was also high in the air. She swallowed. Her gratefulness was dampened only by her fear of heights.

Tyler placed Bethany on the ground. His face considering, he walked around to the other side and ran his gaze up and down the tree in slow sweeps. "The ladder is still intact. We can take turns sleeping and keeping watch."

"Daddy, are we really going to get to sleep up there?" Bethany was wide-eyed with excitement, practically bouncing on her feet. Suddenly the weariness had been replaced by childish excitement. Annabelle smiled. Apparently a tree house topped her daughter's list of fun things to do. She eyed the tree house again. Sweat was starting to break out on her forehead. It wasn't her idea of fun. She couldn't see any other options, though.

Annabelle stepped next to Tyler and looked at the ladder. She wasn't as convinced as he was. True, the ladder was still there. Mostly. It was made up of slats of wood that had been nailed to the tree. There were two large gaps, but it should be passable.

"I'll go up last." Tyler narrowed his gaze and tipped his head. His thinking pose. She remembered it well. "Annie, you go first. That way one of us will be at either end."

He didn't complete the thought. He didn't need to.

She was thinking along the same lines. That way there would be a parent at either end to assist Bethany, whose short legs might have trouble reaching the places where a board was missing.

"Oh, Annie. Are you going to be all right with this?"

So he had remembered her slight aversion. Okay, that was an understatement. She wouldn't let that get in the way of finding a safe place to rest during the night. Instead of answering, she moved to the tree, inhaled deeply and said a prayer in her mind. Then she climbed the first rung.

Tyler's hand dropped onto her shoulder. A tingle vibrated where he touched. "We can keep looking."

She sighed. Then she set her jaw and climbed up the next rung. Then the next. The higher she climbed, the tighter her lungs felt. She ignored them. *One more step, Annabelle. Take another step.* By the time she arrived at the top, sweat was running down her back. She crawled off the ladder and onto the platform, gasping as she collapsed onto the wooden floor of the tree house. She took three calming breaths, then hauled herself to her hands and knees and crawled to the opening. Looking down, she slammed her eyes shut, fighting the swirling sensation behind her eyes.

You can do this. Focus on Bethany.

Peeling her lids apart, she looked down into Tyler's blue-gray eyes. Tenderness and concern stared back at her. Somehow, she found steadiness there. Which was ironic, considering their history.

"I'm okay. I'm good." She called down, "Bethy, come on up, sweetheart."

Annabelle held her breath as her tiny five-year-old

wrinkled up her face in the most adorable expression of concentration and began her ascent. Tyler was right behind her, ready to catch her. The little girl struggled with the first gap. Tyler steadied her as she breached it. Why hadn't she ever noticed how strong he was?

Watching Tyler assist their daughter was surreal. She had thought the man didn't care, but caring was steeped in every move he made. The gentleness and love in his expression as he watched over Bethany tugged at her heart.

Which was the real Tyler?

Her thoughts were interrupted as Bethany reached the top. Annabelle lay on her stomach and stretched out her arms, assisting her daughter over the top. Tyler surged up after her.

Annabelle sat up, exhausted. Tyler plopped down next to her and hauled her into his arms for a brief hug. For a second, she allowed herself to relax against him, inhaling the familiar scent of mint and Tyler. It was comforting. She had the urge to snuggle deeper.

What was she doing? She stiffened and backed away, giving him a forced smile, ignoring the disappointment on his face. And the pulse pounding in her ears. "I'm okay. Really. Thanks."

For the first time she surveyed the inside of their lodgings and wrinkled her nose. A layer of dirt covered the floor. And a few leaves. Fortunately, the previous owners hadn't left anything. She wished she had her phone still so she could use the flashlight app to check for any other inhabitants. Like snakes. She shuddered at the thought.

Bethany was over the moon. She ran from one corner of the tree house to the other, peering out the windows, almost bouncing in her excitement. "This is so cool! Tasha and Nikki are going to be so jealous when I tell them."

If she tells them. Their situation pressed down on Annabelle again. Her daughter might never again see the twins. Or her grandmother and uncle. The knowledge latched on to her heart and tightened, like a fist. How did she explain that possibility when her little girl decided that she had had enough "adventure" and wanted to go home?

She pushed the worry from her mind. She just couldn't deal with it right now.

"We need to get some rest while we can," she whispered to Tyler.

He nodded. "You sleep first. I will stay awake and listen."

She took her purse off and used it as a pillow. Then, stretching out an arm, she bade Bethany to stretch out with her. Her daughter snuggled close, resting her head on Annabelle's outstretched arm. The sweetness of having her daughter safe and snuggled close overwhelmed Annabelle with gratitude.

"Thank You, Lord," she whispered, then closed her eyes to sleep.

Next to the wall, she heard a faint "Amen."

Chapter Eight

Bethany was making little sniffling sounds as she slept in her mother's arms. He'd expected more of an argument from her when Annabelle had called her over to lie down. The day's events had really tuckered out the poor kid. She didn't make a single protest.

He leaned back against the wall of their tiny shelter, his mind going back to watching Annabelle climb the ladder. He had been filled with worry that she would fall or faint or something. And pride. Because no matter what she was afraid of, Annie was a fighter. She always had been. He hadn't been at all surprised that she would put others ahead of herself. She had done that so many times in the past. Times he hadn't always appreciated. He could admit that now.

When he had hugged her earlier, he had only meant to tell her how proud he was of her, and how sorry he was that she had to do it at all. Those thoughts had melted away the moment she had relaxed against him. All at once, the memory of the years they had been in love overpowered him. Sadness that he had let life come between them seared into him. Not just life. His life. His choices. Choices that had robbed them of their love. Their marriage. And stolen his opportunity to watch his beautiful little girl grow up.

He'd missed so much. If they somehow survived this, he wanted the chance to be a part of her life again.

He'd destroyed his chances with her mother. He had known that, but the feeling had only been reinforced when she had pulled back out of his arms earlier. The cold that had made him shiver at the distance she put between them had nothing to do with the weather. The frustrating thing was he had been sure that she had felt something, too. But that was probably all in his mind.

Well, so what? The fact that his marriage was over in every way but legally came as no surprise. It was painful to admit it, but he did. He could still be a father, even if he couldn't be a husband.

Enough. He needed to stop being so maudlin. They were in a tough pickle right now, and he needed to use his time alone to think it through. Somehow, contract killers had found their way to the safe house where the marshals had been operating. Then, they had been ambushed.

The question was how? He knew that the place and vehicles hadn't been bugged. He remembered watching the marshals check everything for bugs. And he knew that the people employed to keep them safe had been thoroughly vetted. So the idea that one of them had been careless was ludicrous.

The marshals had also made it clear that everything was on a need-to-know basis. Karl hadn't even told the other marshals where exactly they were headed, just in case. Thinking about them brought back the memory of the recent events. He couldn't get the image of Rick slumped on the ground out of his mind. How was he? Had the police arrived in time to save him? And what about Karl and Stacy? Quietly, he said a quick prayer for their safety, feeling like a fraud. He had ignored God for so long, would He still hear Tyler's prayers?

He pondered their current circumstances for a few minutes. He was so deep in thought, in fact, that he almost missed the sound of approaching voices. One of those voices he recognized. Jim. The man who had chased them earlier was near.

Moving quietly, he reached over and placed a hand over Annie's mouth at the same time as he whispered, "Annie! Wake up!"

She jolted awake and jerked her elbow into his gut. He doubled over slightly. She was stronger than she looked. Bethany stirred, but didn't waken. Annie moved his hand off her mouth, and then kept holding on.

"Tyler?" she whispered fearfully. "What's—"

"Shh!"

She stilled. He could feel the tenseness of her body in the dark. She was listening. Her breathing was shallow and fast.

"Are you sure they came this way?" Tyler strained to hear the voices. The first man was obviously feeling out of sorts. "We've been walking and searching for hours. They have probably already been picked up by the police or the marshals by now."

So, the marshals were still alive. Or maybe he was talking about different marshals.

"Quit your complaining," a rough voice growled

back. He knew that voice. Jim was standing right below them. "The man at the gas station said they had been through there. He recognized the kid's picture. They were headed this way. We know that they were going east. We'll just keep going and flashing the pictures around. Sooner or later, they are bound to mess up."

"I told you that going through the woman's house was a good idea. We got the pictures and we got the address for her mother."

Annie shifted beside him. He could feel the concern radiating off her. These men had been watching her mother. He put an arm around her, to comfort her. It felt natural to have her in his arms again. She didn't protest. Instead, she leaned into him. Her breathing grew harsh. Her shoulders trembled under his arm.

"It's a good thing the man watching the mother's house took note of the car that picked the woman up. But it would have been nicer still if we had an idea where they were heading."

The voices grew farther away as the men continued their search.

By the moonlight filtering in through the opening, Tyler could just barely make out the outline of Annie and Bethany. Annie's silhouette sat up, bringing her face into clearer focus. It was still mostly in shadows, but he could see the glint of her eyes. She looked mysterious. And angry.

"Those men, they were the ones who ransacked my house. And they were watching my mother? What kind of people are they, Tyler?"

He didn't hear any blame in her voice. She didn't ask him what he'd gotten them into. Although, he felt she would have had the right to ask that question. He was glad that some of her anger at him seemed to be dissipating. He also noticed that she hadn't moved away from him.

"This is why I have to testify," he murmured. "Men like that, men who would shoot someone in cold blood or threaten a child, they can't be allowed to go free. It doesn't matter how much we might fear them or what is happening."

She was so still in the darkness, he wondered what she was thinking. When she spoke again, he could hear the steel in her voice. "We have to do the right thing. Even if it costs us."

"Hopefully, this ordeal will be short, and we can return home." Although he had no idea what would happen then. For now, he had to live each moment as it came.

"What should we do?" she whispered now.

Good question. "Well, we know that those two guys are still heading east, searching for us. If we keep heading east, then we might run into those dudes again. That would be a huge mistake. Probably fatal for us."

Annie winced at his blunt words. "I don't know where Karl was taking us, but we've been heading east most of the journey. I'm worried if we don't go in that direction, how will we ever meet up with the marshals again? I'm sure that Stacy and Karl are still searching for us."

If they were alive.

Frustration bit at him. All he wanted to do was protect his family and put Wilson Barco behind bars for good so that he couldn't mess with people's lives anymore. Why was that so hard to do?

They spent the rest of the night taking turns watching. He didn't think either of them really got too much sleep, even if it was their turn. Near dawn, they both gave up the pretense and talked about their options.

"I think we have no choice but to head west. Or south. Definitely not east," Tyler said, leaning his head back against the wall again. Man, he was so tired, he wasn't sure if he was making any sense.

She bit her lip, bruising it. He fought the urge to lean over and kiss her. What was he thinking? Kissing? Really? With all that was happening, he needed to be clearheaded.

"I don't know, Ty." She pressed the heels of her palms against her temples. "It kind of feels like we are giving up if we head a different direction. Like we don't think we have a chance of being found again."

He hated to hear the defeat in her voice.

"If you have any other ideas, Annie, I would absolutely consider them." He wasn't being snarky. He was completely out of ideas. Annabelle had always been quick under pressure.

The horizon was starting to lighten up. They had made it through the night.

She blinked. Her lovely brown eyes widened. They sparkled with excitement. Just seeing that look come over her face was enough to send the adrenaline coursing through his veins. He knew what it meant.

Annie had a plan.

Annabelle could almost feel the excitement hopping off Tyler's skin as he waited to hear her plan. She'd forgotten how much she'd missed having someone listen to her like this. Tyler had never tried to talk her out of things. No, he had enjoyed the way her mind worked.

When had that stopped?

"What's your plan, Annie?"

She was right. No one knew her like Tyler did. Or had. She shifted slightly. She didn't have much of a plan, just an inkling of an idea.

"It's like this," she began, keeping her voice low so that she didn't wake up Bethany. It took some effort, because she was feeling so nervous and excited at the same time. "Those guys, they know we ran. They even have an idea of what we look like. And it's true we don't have a phone. But what if we were to go into a store and pick up one of those phones that you pay for by the month? We could get a phone, hold a conversation about heading to a specific place in front of the clerk. That way, if they happened to go in there, they would be led off track. We could call Karl and tell him where we are and get a place to meet. Even if we have to leave a message again, he'd have a way to contact us. And it wouldn't matter if we have to head in another direction, it will give them time to regroup and come for us."

She could see he was considering it. "That should work. And if we keep to the side roads, and watch out for any traffic, it might just be workable."

"Plus, we would have a way to call the police if we did get into trouble."

They waited in the tree house for an additional two hours, just until the sun was up and Bethany had awakened. They ate quickly, finishing off a bottle of water bought from the gas station. Annabelle was torn between relief that they hadn't seen anyone else and frustration at not knowing where danger could be lurking. She absolutely had no desire to encounter the men who wanted to kill her, her daughter and her husband. However, it was nerve-racking needing to keep up constant vigilance.

Climbing down the tree house was easier than getting the nerve to go up the thing had been. The fact that she had a case of cabin fever might have had something to do with it. All she wanted to do was move.

They started hiking, keeping themselves off the most well-traveled roads. The sense of adventure had long since faded. Even Bethany was quiet this morning. Every now and then the little girl would heave a sigh of giant proportions. As serious as the situation was, Annabelle couldn't help but smile at her daughter. She was so cute when she was feeling the need to be dramatic.

After several hours, they came to a small town. They entered a drugstore and picked up some food and some more water. And a small pay-by-the-minute cell phone. As they stood in line, Tyler and Annabelle held a conversation, as planned.

"I think we should head toward Fort Wayne," he said.

She nodded, wincing slightly at his overly loud voice. Really, he was a horrible actor. "We could do that. That seems to make sense."

By the time they reached the bored clerk, Annabelle was clenching her teeth. They were so out in the open here. Yes, it had been her plan, but she wanted nothing more than to bolt out of the store and hide with Bethany and Tyler. Any moment now, one of the men after them could waltz right through those sliding doors. What would they do then? She doubted if the men would hesitate to shoot. Or kidnap Bethany. A shudder worked its way done her spine.

Tyler casually reached over and grabbed her hand. She startled. Forcing herself to calm down, she squeezed his hand to let him know she was all right. He raised an eyebrow at her, concern radiating from his blue-gray gaze. She smiled at him. He watched her for a minute before nodding and releasing her hand. Immediately, she wanted to reach out and grab his hand again. Which was ridiculous. She curled her fingers into her palm and focused her attention on her little girl.

Finally, they were on their way.

"Let's get a few miles between us and this store before we try to set up the phone and call." Tyler hefted up Bethany into his arm and grabbed Annabelle's hand again. She allowed him to lead them back into the shadows.

They walked for another twenty minutes in silence. Annabelle's thoughts whirled chaotically in her mind. Tyler's voice broke through.

"You are not going to like this." Tyler's statement came out of nowhere.

"What? I've not liked a number of things recently. Can you be a bit more specific?" She allowed the sarcasm to drip in her tone, knowing that Tyler would find it amusing. Sure enough, he chuckled softly.

His chuckle dwindled, though, as he nodded his head to the right. "You're not going to like that."

Annabelle followed where he was indicating. The pit of her stomach dropped out.

There. Was. No. Way.

But she knew that he was right. The bridge that stretched out across the fast-moving stream was the best way to continue heading east and putting distance between them and the people who wanted to cash in on their deaths.

It was also the flimsiest excuse for a bridge that she had ever seen.

Chapter Nine

Her heart rate went into overdrive as they approached the bridge. The stream was only about thirty feet across. And it didn't look that deep. Beneath the surface of the rippling, clear water, the rocks settled on the bottom were visible. What really bothered her was the speed at which it roared past. She was a good swimmer, but she knew that she would be swept away in that current. And what about Bethany?

The little girl had just started to learn to swim this summer. Before that, she'd been afraid to get into the water.

"I am sorry, Annie. I think it's our best option. We can move on, though, and try something else." Tyler. Trying to be understanding.

Her guilt shot up a notch. She was not going to be the one holding them back.

"No. You're right. This is our best option. I need to get over myself and do it." She clenched her jaw tight. She could do this.

"That's not what I meant. You know that." Now he sounded offended.

She cringed. She knew that wasn't what he had been getting at. Facing her fears made her snap. "No, really. I need to do this."

Without another word, they approached the bridge. A stiff breeze would rattle it. A cold sweat broke out all over her. She had no idea how she would manage this.

"Look, it won't be that bad," Tyler insisted. "There are handrails. And most of the wood is intact. Step over the parts that look rotted."

That looked like most of the bridge.

She looked at him. He must have seen her fear. He stepped up to her and rubbed his hands up and down her arms. "You can do this, Annie. I will do whatever I can to help you out. Let me get Bethany across and then I will help you."

Without thinking, she leaned forward so that her forehead rested on his chest. His hands gently squeezed her arms. Sucking in a fortifying breath, she stepped back.

"I can handle a bridge, Tyler. Fear or no fear. I will be right behind you." The words sounded good. She hoped that she could go through with them.

He glanced deep into her eyes, but finally he nodded. He turned and held out a hand to Bethany. "Okay, Bethany, let's see if we can cross this bridge together, honey. I want you to hold my hand, do you understand?"

Bethany had apparently caught some of the vibes. Her eyes were round with fear as she nodded. "I don't wanna."

Her favorite phrase lately.

"I know you don't, bug. I wish you didn't have to. But I need you to do this. We need to keep going so the bad men don't find us." Her eyes grew even bigger. Annabelle waited for the tears to come. To her surprise, the tiny girl reached for her daddy's hand and let him lead her across the bridge.

The bridge was every bit as rickety as she had feared. She trembled as she watched her husband and child slowly cross over the vicious water flowing below. Her heartbeat was heavy in her chest as she kept up a constant litany of prayer. She stepped onto the bridge when they reached the middle. A blast of wind hit them suddenly. Was the bridge shaking? Or was it just her? The bridge quivered below her feet. She placed her hands on the rails and took a step. The rails and the wood beneath her feet vibrated with each and every step she took.

Don't look down. Don't look down.

She looked down. The sight of the water rushing below nearly brought her down to her knees. Her stomach heaved. She jerked her head up, striving to keep her eyes on the bridge and her husband's back. He was right in front of her. He and Bethany had almost reached the other side.

Even as she watched, he took another careful step. His foot went through the rotting wood. Bethany screamed. Annabelle's heart stopped.

"Shh. It's okay, Bethany. Just a bad piece of wood. Let's keep going."

Where did he get it from? The man had nerves of steel. He'd been shot at, several times, seen his boss murdered, been brought into hiding and now was walking across this death trap of a bridge, and still his voice was calm and reassuring. As if this was a normal afternoon walk for him. A feeling of admiration spread through her.

She was frozen. They made it to the other side. She

stood where she was, feeling the bridge sway and hearing each individual creek.

She drew in a deep breath and edged forward. One step. Another. Partway across, she saw the place where Tyler had lost his footing. Holding her breath, she stepped around it. She was almost to the other side, when she heard Tyler shout.

"Behind you! Get down!"

A shot rang out. It bounced off the tree next to his head.

She looked behind her. Jim and his friend had figured out that they were being tricked. She dropped to her hands and knees, feeling the bridge give a slight bounce as her weight hit it.

She couldn't believe she had just done that.

Another shot. This time, when she looked ahead, she saw that Tyler had shoved Bethany behind the tree. He was kneeling at the other end of the bridge, hand outstretched. Desperation stood out starkly in his eyes.

With a burst of speed she hadn't known she was capable of, she scrambled across the bridge on her hands and knees. If she was going to die, it wasn't going to be because she had waited for death to come and get her.

As soon as she was close to him, Tyler reached out and grabbed her, pulling her the rest of the way over. Together, they ran to where Bethany was.

Another shout behind her made Annabelle swing around. Her mouth dropped open. There was a gap in the bridge. Jim was lying flat on the bridge, his Illinois baseball cap nearly falling off his head. The other man was nowhere to be seen. Right in front of Jim, though, there was a gaping hole. She knew immediately what had happened. Jim and friend had obviously decided to follow after them across the bridge. They had also apparently lacked the sense to move slowly.

"We can't stay here."

Urgency colored Tyler's voice. Bethany was in tears.

Tyler picked up Bethany in his uninjured arm. "We have to get away from here. Far away."

Tyler couldn't believe how close they had come to getting caught. The look on Annie's face when she had frozen on the bridge had terrified him. Then he had spied the men running up behind them. He didn't think he'd ever forget that image—a man holding a gun, aimed right at them, while Annie's back was turned to him.

She could have been hit. Maybe injured. Or worse.

He couldn't let himself be drawn into thinking about that right now. He had more important things to do. Such as locating the marshals.

"Let's get that cell phone set up and try the marshals."

She searched him with her eyes. "I am going to have nightmares about that bridge for the rest of my life."

He glanced down at her. "Me, too. I think my heart stopped when you fell to your knees. The way it bounced! Not to mention watching those men run onto the bridge, shooting." He shook his head fiercely as if trying to shake off the memory.

Bethany hiccupped into his shoulder. Annie tightened her lips and grabbed the phone out of her bag. "I am not even sure if the thing is already charged. We may have wasted our time."

He thought about it. "Yeah, but it's worth a shot."

Shrugging, Annie unboxed the phone and turned it

on. It took ten minutes, but she was able to get it set up and add the airtime.

"It doesn't have a lot of battery." She showed him the phone. The battery icon was almost empty.

"It's better than nothing." He hoped it was enough.

Pulling out Karl's number, she quickly punched in the digits and hit Send. She put it on speaker, so Tyler could hear it, too. It was answered almost immediately.

"Hello?"

"Karl? It's Annabelle." Tyler could see the tears welling in her eyes.

Hearing the voice of the marshal relaxed something inside of him. At least they knew he had survived. He had not allowed his mind to go there, but the thought had been constantly in the background the past day and half.

"Annabelle? Where are you? Are Tyler and Bethany with you?"

"Hey, Karl. Tyler here. Yes, we're all fine. Although we have had a few close calls. We saw Rick was hurt. How is he? And Stacy?"

"Rick will be out of commission for a few weeks, but he'll be fine. Stacy is here with me. We've both been concerned about you."

Annie and Tyler gave as clear directions as they could. The bridge they crossed was actually a landmark that Karl recognized. "I know that bridge. Crossed it a few times myself when I was hiking in the area as a teen. I used to live around here. I'm only about an hour from you. Keep heading east. If you hit Garman Road, follow it. We'll track you dow—"

Karl's voice was cut off. Annie looked at the phone

in her hand. It was no surprise when she informed Tyler
that they had no battery left.

"I guess we keep walking." Tyler wanted nothing
more than to slow down, but that wasn't a choice.

Twenty minutes later, they hit Garman Road. Both
Tyler and Annie let out sighs as they spotted the name.
It was a two-lane highway with a constant stream of
traffic. They continued walking until a dark Ford Tau-
rus pulled out of the line of traffic onto the narrow
shoulder beside them. He had never seen the car before. Tyler was ready to grab his family and bolt when
the window rolled down and he saw Stacy looking at
them. Karl was in the driver's seat.

"Care for a ride?" Stacy's words were casual, but the
skin around her eyes was tight. They were the eyes of
someone who had been worried.

Tyler nodded and opened the back door. A booster
chair was sitting in the middle for Bethany. He let his
daughter in, then gestured for Annie to follow her. Once
they were both inside, he jogged around to the other side
of the vehicle. Karl turned on the blinker. It might be a
minute or so before there was a break that would allow
Karl to merge back onto the highway.

Nothing had ever felt as good as sinking into car
seats in the back of an air-conditioned car. He barely
had the energy to strap himself in before he slumped
down in the seat and closed his eyes, letting out a sigh.

"I was expecting a different car," Annie said softly.

He opened his eyes a crack. That's right. They had
left Iowa with three distinctly different vehicles.

Stacy turned partially around in her seat. "Our other

vehicles have obviously been made. We still don't know how they found us."

Tyler straightened in his seat. "We do."

Briefly, he told the marshals about the past day, including the conversation that he and Annie had overheard while they were hiding in the tree house. "I wondered about that. But no one was spotted following us. The good thing is, they have no idea where you are headed, and this is a totally different vehicle."

"I'm just relieved that Rick wasn't killed," Tyler said. "I think I would have felt guilty for the rest of my life if he had died."

To his surprise, Annabelle reached around Bethany and touched his shoulder. "You had no control over this situation, Tyler. I know it's awful, but you are as much a victim of it as we are. I can't even think about what you went through, seeing your boss killed that way."

He grabbed on to her words like a lifesaver. Could she really mean it? "But my job—"

"Does not give anyone the right to harm you or anyone connected to you."

"She's right, Tyler." Stacy shifted so she could turn in her seat and see them. "None of this is your fault."

A glance flickered between Karl and Stacy. He could see Karl's arm move. And Stacy blush. Was he holding her hand? Tyler peered around Bethany at Annabelle. He grinned. Her eyes were narrowed as she gazed speculatively at the two in the front seat. So she saw it, too.

The silence that fell was heavy, thick with the emotions of the adults in the car.

Karl broke the silence. "It's time we told you about where you will be going. There's a little Amish community in Ohio. It's in a small farming town called Harvest. There's a large number of Amish and Mennonite families settled there. You will be going in the program as Ty and Annie Miller. You need to start thinking of yourselves that way. There is no more Tyler and Annabelle."

Things were starting to feel real very quickly. Karl continued to speak.

"You are going to be a young married couple who have decided to join the Amish church but have not yet been baptized. That should help you out of situations where you come across a cultural tradition or taboo. Plain folk will be forgiving since you are still learning. You will be staying with Abraham and Julia Beiler. They will supposedly be old friends of yours who have invited you to stay with them while you make the transition to Amish life."

"How much do they know?" They had to know something, obviously. US Marshals were asking them to house people in their home. Complete strangers.

Stacy replied. "They know that you are in the witness protection program. And they know that you are not really Amish. We didn't tell them the entire story. But they wouldn't be surprised. They, too, are in the witness protection program."

Tyler felt his jaw come unhinged. They were being placed with other program members? That seemed a bit unusual.

"What else?" Annie asked.

"Well, let's see… Julia has two children. Her son, William, is fourteen. He's a nice young man, responsible and very helpful. Her daughter, Kayla, is seven. I think she'll be a good friend for Bethany."

Bethany's ears picked up this last comment. She lifted her head from the toys that she had found on her seat. "Does Kayla like to swim? I am learning to swim this summer."

Stacy grinned. Tyler understood. His daughter was too cute to resist. "I have no clue if she swims, honey. You'll have to ask."

Nodding, Bethany lost interest in the conversation and returned to her toys.

"Where was I?" Stacy tapped her chin. "Well, Abraham was a police officer for about a decade or so. Although he was raised Amish, right, Karl?"

The blond man at the wheel nodded. "Yup. He was recently wounded. Oh, and the bishop knows that you are in the program. He is a rather forward-thinking man. He agreed to allow you to have sanctuary in his district. I promised him you'd try to conform as best as you could."

Tyler expected as much. Annie had a hesitant look on her face. "Everything will work out, Annie. We can do this."

She rolled her eyes. "You have no idea, Tyler. But I promised to try. So I will."

"We'll be there in a few hours. It's a nine-hour drive from where we were staying in Iowa. We're in Indiana right now."

"I should be able to pull onto the road after the red truck passes." Karl craned his head to watch the progress of the truck, his hands starting to turn the wheel.

Before he could pull back onto the road, a bullet hit the side of the car. Bethany screamed. Annie put her arms around her daughter in an attempt to shelter her.

Tyler was dimly aware of Stacy calling in the attack on her radio.

The shooter was somewhere off to the right, staying out of sight.

Suddenly, Tyler realized that their heads were above the back seat. Within sight of anyone with a gun. Without pausing, he reached over and unbuckled Bethany.

"What are you doing?" Annie screamed at him.

"Guns! Annie, they have guns."

Horror replaced the surprise on her face. Without another word, she snatched open the latch on her own seat belt. Then she pulled her screaming daughter onto the floor with her. Tyler ducked down.

The back window shattered.

Bethany started sobbing. "I scared, Daddy! I scared!"

He reached over and ran his hand down the top of her head. "I know, baby. I need you to be brave. Hang on tight to Mommy."

That wasn't going to be a problem—he could see that she had a death grip on her mother. And Annie obviously was holding on to her as hard as she could. He knelt beside them on the floor, covering them as much as possible with his own body.

Please, God, protect them. Keep them safe.

The spontaneous prayer was a cry from deep within his soul. He would do whatever he could to spare them as much pain as humanly possible. If that meant taking a bullet for them, then that's exactly what he would do.

The tires squealed as Karl yanked sharply on the wheel, pulling the car out onto the road. A bullet smashed through the rear passenger window, sprinkling glass over the back seat and the three people crouched on the floor. Stacy screamed.

"Stacy!" Karl yelled, the car jerking.

Stacy sat up. "I'm okay. It missed me."

"Stay down," Karl yelled. Tyler could hear the fear in his voice. It had to be hard for him, seeing the woman he had feelings for in danger. Tyler knew exactly how he felt. He pulled Annabelle and Bethany closer. Karl's jaw was clenched as he kept driving. A minute later, they heard sirens. Sitting up, Tyler looked back and saw two police cars driving along the shoulder. Tyler and Annie relaxed their positions. The top of their heads touched, right above the daughter they were trying to protect. For a moment, neither moved. Tyler needed this connection with her right now. Knowing how close they had come to being injured, he needed to know that Annie and Bethany were unharmed.

Five minutes later, Karl had pulled off the road. The marshals quickly took stock of their situation. Stacy had a spot of blood on her left shoulder where a piece of glass had nicked her, but she was fine. Karl looked at the wound, his face pale and tense, while she talked to him in a calming voice. Several times, her right hand moved to touch his cheek. Karl hugged her briefly. When he released her, he turned to them, his calm marshal face firmly back in place.

Tyler could still see the shadows in the man's eyes. Shadows brought by seeing a loved one in danger. He peeked at Annabelle and Bethany out of the corner of his eye. They were fine, sitting huddled together. He knew how Karl felt, all too well.

* * *

Karl might look unmoved by the events of the past hour, but Annabelle had seen his reaction when he'd thought Stacy had been hurt. No matter how calm he was now, it was obvious that the tall blond marshal was in love with the brunette Stacy. Watching their interactions as he took care of her shoulder, Annabelle was certain that the woman returned his feelings.

How would she feel if anything happened to Tyler?

It was not a comfortable question. Not too long ago, Annabelle was sure that she wanted no part of Tyler back in her life. She had the reasons memorized. He was unreliable. He put his work above his family. He didn't care enough.

The Tyler she was seeing now, however, was not that way. He had put himself in harm's way for them several times. His care and concern for them was real. She knew it was. The way he had protected her and Bethany several times already proved that. He had changed in the time they had been separated.

What would she do if anything happened to him?

She recalled the way she had felt when she saw the blood on his arm earlier. Granted, it was not a serious wound. But if it had been? If she lost him, how would she react?

She had to be honest with herself. If something did happen to Tyler, no matter how angry she was, she would be devastated. Not just because he was Bethany's father, either. She had to take care. It would be far too easy to find herself falling for him all over again.

And that thought terrified her.

Chapter Ten

Tyler had thought that they would never make it to the Amish community. At least, not alive. Karl had been mostly silent for the past few hours, only talking to answer questions or to give necessary information. Stacy had tried to talk with him, but his answers were mostly single-word replies. Tyler didn't envy the man. He clearly had feelings for Stacy. He obviously hated that Stacy was in danger, but he also respected her as a marshal. Tyler recalled his own reaction when Annabelle had been hurt. His response had been to emotionally and physically withdraw from his family. A decision that he was now regretting. Knowing what Karl might be going through, Tyler had allowed the man his privacy. Several times, he'd exchanged concerned glances with Annie. She'd obviously noticed Karl's withdrawal. And though she hadn't said anything about it, he had no doubt that Annie was aware of the full reason behind it. She was a very observant woman, his Annie was.

Except that she was most definitely not his Annie.

Not anymore. A fact that was getting harder to remember the more time they spent in one another's company. She fascinated him in so many ways. He had to keep reminding himself of why he had needed to let her go in the first place.

He could change jobs if they ever got out of the witness protection program.

The thought stunned him momentarily. And it was tempting. Very tempting. He did not let himself dwell on the thought, however, knowing that he had an obligation to fulfill. His current job was his best way of going about that. No matter how much he was growing to hate it.

Karl pulled up a long driveway. It was gravel, and Tyler could hear the rocks crunching beneath the wheels of the car. Dust billowed around them. It had been a few days since it had rained. A large white two-story farmhouse loomed before them. Alongside the driveway, wood was stacked. The family was already preparing for the harsh months of winter. A clothesline on a pulley system ran from the edge of the porch to the top of the garage. Sheets, dresses, shirts and trousers snapped and waved in the breeze.

Near the top of the drive, Karl parked the vehicle. Beyond it, Tyler saw an enclosed buggy in the barn.

When he'd envisioned Amish communities, he'd somehow pictured houses closer together. These houses were on large plots of land. Not only that, but it was also obvious that while most of the houses on the street were owned by Amish, not all of them were.

"Are all the Amish homes white?" he asked in a low voice.

"Around here they are," Karl responded. "I am not one hundred percent sure, but that may be one of the things decided by their bishop. Things like color of clothing and such can be decided by him. So, you might have two districts side by side with different rules."

"Hmm." Interesting information to tuck away in the back of his mind.

Karl and Stacy opened their doors and Tyler followed suit. Then he jogged around the car and opened Annie's door for her. She unfastened Bethany and helped the child out of the car. The solemn group approached the house.

As they walked up onto the porch, the door was opened by an attractive woman of around thirty. Her lovely golden-brown hair was tucked beneath a white bonnet-type hat. He couldn't remember the name of it. The strings were untied and hung over her shoulders. The little bonnet reminded him of a teacup, with the flat back and the round shape of the sides. The woman was dressed in a calf-length blue dress with a white apron on it.

"I am happy that you have arrived. Please come in. I am Julia. My husband will be here shortly."

The tired family moved inside the house. The late afternoon was warm, but the house was surprisingly cool.

It was a beautiful house. All wooden floors and handcrafted furniture. There were, of course, no lamps or electric appliances. The light streaming into the kitchen was all natural. The walls were bare, except for a few oil lamps. No pictures were hung on them. Nor were there any curtains on the windows. But still the place felt like a home. The floor plan was open, and the living room was larger than he was used to seeing in a house. There was a large china cabinet with a full set of china situated near the side wall in the combined kitchen-and-dining area. And he could see quilts on several of the chairs.

"You have a lot of open space here," he commented.

"We need the space," Julia said. "It's for when we have church."

Tyler raised his eyebrows. He looked around at the others in the room. Apparently, Karl and Stacy both understood what she was saying because they nodded. He felt foolish for asking, but if he was going to pretend to be Amish for a while, he should probably know about this, as well. He glanced at Annie and saw the same blank look on her face that was probably on his. So he wasn't the only one. When she turned her head, their eyes met. And held. Electricity shimmered in the air between them. She broke the connection first, cheeks reddening.

He rubbed the back of his neck, feeling uncomfortable. His neck was warm. His cheeks and ears were probably red, too. He pulled his mind back to what they had been discussing. There were so many things about the Amish culture he didn't know. It was like he was in school and didn't know the material the day before the test. He felt ridiculous needing to ask about the most basic things. But he didn't let that stop him. This was too important to let pride stand in the way. He could literally risk his family's life if he didn't have some sort of understanding of the Amish culture.

"I hate to sound ignorant," he said. "This is all very new to me. You have church in your house?"

Julia didn't seem to mind all the questions. In fact, she grinned at him.

"I know it seems a little bit strange." She chuckled a little. "When I first came to an Amish community, I was a little startled by it, as well. Now, it seems natural. Just as it should be. Amish homes are built with a wide-open floor plan so that every family in the district can host the church service at least once a year. There are almost twenty families in our district. We have church every other week. On the weeks that we don't have church, that's a visiting day when we can go and visit relatives and friends."

"Where do all the people sit?" Bethany asked, joining the conversation. Her face scrunched up as she thought of something that she didn't care for. "Does everybody have to stand during the whole church service?"

Julia laughed again. Annie covered her mouth so she wouldn't laugh at her daughter. Tyler ruffled the soft blond hair on top of her head. He got such a kick out of listening to the way her mind worked.

A pout started to form. She must have thought the adults were laughing at her.

"Don't feel bad, bug. I want to know that, too," he told her with a wink.

Julia was shaking her head. "No, we don't stand for the whole service. There is a set of wooden benches that are brought around and set up in the house on Saturday evening. We have what is called our church wagon and that is the trailer that carries the benches. Church Sundays are always a fun time."

Bethany didn't look like she was convinced.

The child continued to pepper Julia with questions. It soon became clear that Julia had a lot of practice handling an inquisitive five-year-old. She answered the questions with patience and good humor.

The back door flew open and another little girl dashed into the room. She was three inches or so taller than Bethany. The girl crashed to a stop when she saw that they had company. Her eyes popped with excitement.

"Mommy! Who are they?"

Julia turned to Tyler's family. "I would like you to meet my daughter, Kayla. Kayla is seven years old and in second grade. My son, William, will be home soon. He is fourteen. He and my husband are out working on chores in the barn."

Kayla had apparently lost interest in the conversation. All of her attention was focused squarely on Bethany. She walked over to stand beside the younger girl, giving her a quick inspection.

"I'm Kayla," she said, forgetting that her mother had already introduced her. "What's your name?"

Bethany ducked her head, shy for once. "I'm Bethany. I'm gonna be six."

Tyler and Annie exchanged laughing glances. "Bethany," Annie said, "you just turned five a few months ago."

Bethany heaved a dramatic sigh and rolled her eyes. "I know that, Mommy. But that means that I'm going to be six next."

A few minutes later, Abraham Beiler arrived with William. Tyler liked them right off. Abraham was not the most talkative fellow one could meet, but Tyler could tell that he was an intelligent man. He tried to imagine the man in the dark Amish trousers and the full beard as a cop. It was there in the eyes, he decided. Those eyes said that he had seen far more pain and despair than he had ever wanted to in his lifetime. Tyler would never ask. He respected the man's privacy. Not to mention the fact that he had seen his own share of grief.

Before he left, Karl pulled Annie and Tyler, or Ty, aside. "I'm giving you guys a phone to use in case of an emergency. It is for emergency use only. This placement will only work if you two do your best to fit in. That means phones are out. Do not try to contact anyone from your old life."

He glanced over at Annie when he said that. Ty grimaced. Probably because she had someone worth contacting. Everyone he had was here in the program with him. That was a little sad to think about, but it worked out well, considering the circumstances.

"Will we see you again?" Annie asked.

"Oh, yeah. I will check in on you. And if you ever feel that you are in danger, I will come, or Jonathan or another marshal. You are not in this alone."

Karl's phone buzzed. He pulled his phone out of his pocket and read the text. Tyler was startled to see a huge grin break across the man's face. And relieved. The man had been so somber for the past few hours, the expression was a welcome change.

"I have some good news," Karl announced to the group at large. "Jonathan texted me to say that he and his wife, Celeste, have a beautiful baby girl, and Celeste is doing wonderful."

The mood of the group lightened after that information. Putting his phone away, Karl appeared more relaxed than he had been. He talked to Tyler for a few minutes more. Tyler let his gaze drift over to Annie for a few seconds. Stacy was with her. Whatever they were talking about, it looked intense. Realizing that Karl was still speaking, he yanked his attention back to him.

Karl and Stacy left. Julia showed them to their rooms. Tyler's room was on the first floor, but Annie and Bethany were both on the second floor. Abraham handed Tyler some clothes similar to what he and William were wearing. Annie and Bethany followed Kayla and Julia upstairs to try on some Amish clothes.

Abraham invited Ty to go out to the barn with him and William to start getting him acclimated to his new life. Karl had said that they weren't alone. And it was true.

But at the moment, surrounded by people and a way of life he wasn't familiar with, it sure felt like he was.

Annabelle woke up the next morning feeling disoriented. It took her a few moments to realize where she was. She reached over on the bedside table for her phone out of habit. *Oh, right*, she remembered as her hand touched an empty surface. No technology.

This was going to be interesting.

Not that she was glued to her phone or anything. She was just used to being able to look up the time and the weather anytime she wanted to. Or search the internet for obscure facts if she had time to kill. Or catch up on whatever was trending on Facebook.

Okay, maybe she was a little too attached to technology.

She lay still for a few minutes, thinking back on her conversation with Stacy. It had been strange. She'd asked the female marshal how she was feeling. The other woman had given her a smile.

"I'm fine, really. Don't worry about me."

"Karl seemed to be concerned," Annabelle had blurted without thinking.

Stacy had grinned, her cheeks growing pink. "I should have known we wouldn't be able to hide it. Karl and I have been seeing each other for a while now."

"Isn't it hard, dating someone when you have such dangerous occupations?"

When Stacy had laughed softly, Annabelle had realized just how rude her questions might sound. "I'm sorry. I shouldn't—"

"No, I understand. Look, yes, our jobs are dangerous. One of us might get hurt someday. Or worse. I believe that when you are blessed enough to have someone you love in your life, you shouldn't waste it. Love is too precious."

She had given Annabelle a significant look. What was her message? Annabelle felt uncomfortable with the memory now, sure she didn't really want to know.

She dragged herself out of bed and looked at the dresses that Julia had found for her. There were several in various pastel shades. She picked up the first one. It was a plain lavender-colored dress. Although she normally went for brighter colors, it was a lovely hue. She put it on and then tied the white apron over it. It felt strange wearing a dress after so many years. And a dress with elbow-length sleeves, too. She usually wore sleeveless tops in the summer. Or T-shirts.

Warily, she glanced down at her feet. The dress came to three inches above her ankles. Her scars didn't show. Mostly. But if she stretched up, the dress might ride up enough to show them.

Black stockings it was. Grimacing, she pulled the stockings on her feet. Immediately, she felt less self-conscious. There was no way the scars would show now. Not dressed like this.

The hair. What had Julia said about her hair? She would have to put it up. Apparently, Amish women never cut their hair. Julia had told her she could braid it and put it up or wear it in a bun. Annabelle chose to wear it in a braid. She knew how to make a neat braid. Her buns were always messy and tended to come undone.

After a frustrating ten minutes, she had her hair up and the starched white *kapp* that Julia had given her perched on top. She wished there was a mirror to see herself. She felt like she was playing dress-up. With a sigh, she realized that she had no reason to delay any longer. She went to Bethany's room to help her daughter get dressed for the day.

It soon became apparent that Bethany thought dressing Amish was great fun. She was going to look just like Kayla. Bethany was bouncing with glee as Annie fixed her hair like Kayla had worn hers the night before. When she saw the little *kapp*, Bethany squealed and clapped her hands.

"Really? I get my own little hat? I'm gonna look just like Kayla!"

Laughing, Annie put it on her head. "Yes, you get

your own little hat. You look like Kayla and like Bethany."

"Hurry, Mommy! I want to go see her!"

There was nothing more that needed to be done.

Holding out her hand to her daughter, she said, "Let's go and join the others, shall we?"

"Whee!" Bethany caught her mother's hand and skipped to the door, pulling Annie along with her. Annie allowed her daughter to drag her down the stairs and into the kitchen. The poor thing had been through a rough few days. She couldn't find the heart to try and temper her excitement.

"Bethany!"

"Kayla!"

The two girls embraced each other like they were best friends who hadn't seen each other for months. All the adults smiled.

"Let me look at my Amish girls." Tyler strode forward, grinning. Annie couldn't help it. An answering grin tugged up the corners of her mouth. She turned away so he wouldn't see it. Or see how affected she was by the sight of him. Why was her heart pounding?

"Look at me, Daddy!" Bethany twirled for her father.

Tyler picked her up and cuddled her close, placing a kiss on her bonneted head. Annabelle's heart melted. Whatever issues they had in the past, she could no longer deny that Tyler truly loved his daughter. What had happened to change him all those years ago?

"You sure do look plain," Julia commented.

She couldn't get over the change in Tyler. It suddenly struck her that he was growing a beard. Of course, he had not been able to shave in the past few days.

She hadn't even really noticed the extra growth. But now, as he stood before her in dark trousers and a blue shirt with dark suspenders on, she could see it. He had shaved the mustache that had also started to come in. And sometime between last night and this morning, his hair, which he had always worn on the longish side, had been cut. Not the usual cut, either. He now had the same haircut that Abraham sported. Part of her wanted to giggle. The other realized that it didn't matter how Tyler dressed or groomed himself, he was still a very handsome man. One that had the ability to make her pulse skip. Even after everything they'd been through.

That was not the way she wanted to be thinking.

The group sat down to eat a light breakfast. After breakfast, the men left to go to the barn. Tyler paused on his way out. He put a hand on her elbow and led her over to the window.

"How are you doing? I have been worried about you."

She blinked. "Worried about me? Why? I'm doing fine. It was nice to get a full night's sleep in a real house."

He smiled, but she could see the worry was still there. "Annie, I'm serious. I know that this is a safe place for us. Even so, I keep thinking of all the close calls we've had. Those people coming for me have been relentless. And I am feeling horrible dragging you and Bethany into this whole mess."

"Hush." She placed her fingers over his lips. The skin where they touched tingled. She snatched her hand away, face heating up. For a second, she forgot what she had been planning on saying. "I know that we could still be in danger. And I know that I was really angry with you just a couple of days ago. But, Tyler, this mess is not your fault. You didn't know that your boss was working with criminals. Nor did you have any idea what you were walking into. That's life."

Her heart thudded in her chest as the look on his face warmed. "You are amazing, you know that?"

Embarrassed, she decided that they were getting just a little too serious. She placed a hand on her hip and gave her head a saucy toss, which probably looked silly with a *kapp* on. "Yes, I am amazing, mister. Glad you finally caught on."

Tyler grinned at her antics. She relaxed a little, happy that she had chased some of the seriousness from his face. Then, before she knew what he was about, he bent and placed a warm kiss on her cheek.

"Oh, I always knew that you were amazing. I was just making sure you knew it, too."

With a last wink, he sauntered away and grabbed the straw hat that was hanging on a hook by the back door. Then he was gone, off to find Abraham in the barn. Annie stared after him, her mouth hanging open in surprise. Without thinking, she reached up and placed her hand over the spot he'd kissed. It still felt warm.

Julia bustled by, tossing Annie a smirk as she passed.

Annie blew out a breath, hard. She placed a hand on her heart, feeling the heavy beat.

So much for not letting herself be affected by his charm. Oh, she was in so much trouble.

Chapter Eleven

"I don't wanna." Bethany folded her arms across her chest and pouted.

Here we go again, Annabelle thought, frustration beginning to stir inside her. They had been living in the Beilers' home for a week now. Bethany had been enchanted with the old farmhouse for the first few days. Her first buggy ride had thrilled the little girl. Bethany felt like a grown-up as she helped her mother and Julia with the chores around the house. Annie sighed. She'd never enjoyed helping with laundry and baking so much. She understood it. Bethany must have felt like she was on an extended camping trip. Plus, Kayla, Julia's daughter, was helping. And Bethany adored Kayla. She also loved the cows and the horses.

And the chickens. Annie was tempted to roll her eyes at the thought. Her daughter had discovered that the chickens didn't mind being carried around. She had adopted one of them as her own. She'd named the hen Mrs. Feathers.

Julia and Abraham were very gentle and understanding when Bethany would run after the large white bantam and carry her around like she was an overgrown cat. Of course, the line had to be drawn when Bethany wanted to bring the chicken into the house with her.

"*Nee*, we do not have chickens in the house," Julia had told her gently when the child first brought her inside.

Annie was sure she'd see a temper tantrum. Instead, fourteen-year-old William had coaxed Bethany and her new pet outside with him. Annie and Julia had laughed about it after they had left the house.

This morning, however, Bethany had announced that she was ready to go home. No amount of pleading or arguing with logic would work. Nor would bribing her daughter. She'd tried everything she could to gain her child's cooperation, but Bethany wasn't having it.

"Come on, Bethany. You've worn a *kapp* every day we've been here. You know that Kayla and Julia wear one, too. And I have been wearing one, too. You said you liked it. Remember?"

She held out the offending white *kapp*, the strings dangling over the sides of her palm. Bethany had put on her dress and let her braid her hair. And that was as far as she could get her to budge.

Annie wanted to rip off her own *kapp* and pull her hair out. A soft knock at the bedroom door interrupted the stalemate.

"Come in," she called.

Julia opened the door and entered, a smile on her pretty face. Today she was walking around without any stockings or shoes on her feet. For a moment, Annie felt a tug of jealousy. What would it feel like to allow herself to not wear stockings, to allow the scars to show? She remembered Tyler's words, how he had told her she was beautiful, scars and all.

But was she brave enough? Someday, she promised herself. But not yet.

"Can I help you, Julia?" She smiled back at the other women. Her warm brown eyes were filled with kindness and joy. Julia had been busy. Annie could smell the rich aroma of coffee, and the warm smell of biscuits floated in the air. Her stomach rumbled. It was breakfast time. She'd eat as soon as she convinced her daughter to put on the *kapp*.

"I wanted to let you know that breakfast is ready. Ty and Abraham have already gone out to the barn. I believe that they were discussing things that they were needing at the market in town. They might be planning a trip."

Her interest piqued. The market, from all accounts, was a street of small family-owned shops and vendors. It was a popular spot for Amish and non-Amish alike to shop and gather. She'd been wanting to go there herself, just to see it.

She sighed. "That sounds like fun."

Bethany blurted out, "I don't wanna wear the little hat this morning. Kayla wasn't wearing it yesterday."

Julia smiled, a flash of sympathy in her eyes. "Yes, it's true that she wasn't wearing the *kapp* in the house. But she couldn't go outside without wearing it. If you want to eat breakfast without it on, that is fine. You will not be able to go and see Mrs. Feathers without it, though."

Bethany's pout grew less pronounced. She looked outside several times. The lure of the lovely summer weather and the chicken were strong inducements. Annie bit back her smile. She had a feeling the chicken was going to win.

Finally, Bethany raised her big blue eyes to her mother. "Can I eat breakfast without the little hat, Mommy, please? I will put it on before I go see my chicken."

Annie nodded, flashing a grateful smile at Julia. The other woman nodded. Happy again, Bethany ran out of the room, calling Kayla's name.

"Thank you." Annie sighed. "She doesn't understand why we can't go home."

"It's not an easy thing." Julia paused. "You know that I was in witness protection, too?"

Annie nodded.

Julia continued. "My son witnessed a gang shooting." She nodded when Annie gasped and covered her mouth with her hands. "It was terrifying. The gang members were literally in our apartment. We had to hide in a bathroom. When we went into witness protection, I worked as Abraham's housekeeper. He had left the Amish community and married but returned once he was a widower. I know how it feels to be running for your life with children who are resistant to the Amish way of life."

"Did Kayla—"

"Actually, it was William. But he grew to appreciate Abraham and the life we have here. And I thank God every day that he is no longer involved with the wrong people." She sighed. "It's been a while since I have talked about my past. That's one of the harder things about being in the program."

"I know." Annabelle frowned. "I am dreading someone asking me questions about my life before I came here. It's hard, knowing I can never tell anyone outside of the program anything about my real past. I can't talk about my parents or my brother—" Tears filled her eyes as she thought of her family.

"It can be difficult. Remember, though. Everyone inside this house understands what you're going through."

Reflecting on Julia's words, Annabelle walked with her to the kitchen. It was nice to be around people who understood. Just to be on the safe side, she decided she would still refrain from talking about her family. It hurt, knowing that no one would truly know who she was while she was in the program.

Tyler would. She blinked at the thought. No matter how long they were in the program, as long as they were together, she would have one person who knew who she was. One person who would know the past she couldn't talk about. She shrugged away the thought. But as she followed Julia downstairs, her steps were lighter.

The children were already inside the open kitchen. The table was long and wooden, obviously handcrafted. So were the chairs. They had sat to eat. Following the Amish custom, the children and the women bowed their heads to say a silent blessing over their food. Annie still felt odd not praying out loud as she had done at home with Bethany.

The biscuits were light and flaky, absolutely delicious. Especially drizzled with warm honey. The children had just been excused when the men entered the house. Both men took off their wide-brimmed hats and hung them up on the hooks right inside the door. Ty had continued to grow a beard, but no mustache, as a sign that he was a married man, though in name only.

Annie had trouble getting used to it. She had known him for over eight years. In that time, he had never worn a beard. Not even a goatee.

"Good morning, Julia. Annie," Ty greeted the women as he sat himself at the table. Abraham joined them shortly, a mug of hot coffee in his hands.

"Ty and I have been planning, isn't that right, Ty?" Abraham's face, which had been rather serious, lightened considerably when creased with a smile, the way it was now.

"Yes, indeed we have." Ty winked at Annie. "We have things we need from the market. What say you, Annie, my girl, to a trip to the market?"

"Could we?" She hadn't meant to squeal, but judging from the grins on the other faces, they didn't mind. She hadn't left the property since they'd arrived. She was beginning to feel a bit closed in. A trip to the market might not be much, but it would get her out of the house for a while. Then her enthusiasm dimmed. "But I'm not sure. I don't know that I want to bring Bethany—"

"Leave her with Kayla, William and I," Julia interrupted. "You need a break, Annie. This would be perfect. And we really do need some items from the market."

She bit her lip. Could they really do it? "But what if we are recognized? I don't want to lead anyone back to you."

Abraham nodded. "We have talked about this. You cannot spend your time imprisoned here. But I understand your concern. Wear your own clothes. That way, if you are recognized, no one will be led here. I will take you in the buggy and drop you off before the market. That way you won't be seen leaving here *Englisch*."

The more she considered the idea, the more excited

she became. To leave the farmhouse, to go into town, even if only for an hour, would be wonderful. And she had to admit, if only to herself, she wanted to have some time away with just Tyler. Time where she could explore the idea of whether or not she could allow herself to truly give him another chance.

"Can you wait for fifteen minutes?" She spun to see the smile break across his face like a ray of sunlight.

"I can even give you twenty." He winked, and her stomach fluttered.

She spun again to face Julia. "You don't mind? Really?"

Julia laughed and waved her hands at Annie. "Go. We will watch the child."

She needed no other encouragement. Forgetting to be dignified, she sprinted up the stairs. Moving quickly around the bedroom, she gathered her clothes and changed. She decided to leave her hair up and her *kapp* on for the time being. She didn't want to give herself away to anyone looking inside the buggy.

When Tyler saw her in her normal dress, but with a *kapp* on her head, he smiled so wide the corners of his eyes crinkled. That was a smile she hadn't seen in a long time. She had missed it but didn't realize it until this very moment.

Tyler looked more like himself in his jeans. "I guess I should wear my hat in the buggy so we match."

She giggled. "I feel like a teenager. This is ridiculous."

His smile faded, but his eyes remained soft. "It's not ridiculous, Annie. You have been a trouper through all of this. You deserve a break."

They both did. She just hoped they could get one.

* * *

When was the last time he had heard Annie laugh? It had been too long. He was enjoying the silly mood she was in on the way to the market. The buggy swayed slightly due to an uneven patch in the road. Their shoulders touched. He wished he could stretch his arm across the back of the seat and wrap it around her shoulders.

He didn't think she was ready for that. Actually, he wasn't sure he was ready for it, either. The feelings that were starting to rise were messing with his judgment. The past week had been amazing. The simplicity of the Amish life had allowed them to spend time together as a family without the distractions that normally surrounded them. Even while they were sharing a table with Abraham's family, he could gradually see her relaxing more this week. Bethany had been able to be a kid again, and he had seen the pleasure glowing in Annie's eyes and smile as she had stood watch over the little girl that held both of their hearts in her small hands.

But as much as he enjoyed this respite, he could never quite forget that somewhere, men were searching for him. Because of his job, he was again in a killer's sight. He just didn't know how he'd walk away from her again when this was all over. Being in her presence, day after day, he could feel her inching her way back into his heart.

As the buggy drew closer to town, a conviction grew in his chest. Annie needed to know the truth about what had happened. Every time he saw her wearing stockings when Julia walked around her house barefoot, he was filled with guilt. He knew that he was the reason that she hid her legs.

He could never forget that.

Would she forgive him? He hoped and prayed that she would, but honestly, he didn't know what she would say, or do. He had hurt her so many times in the past, he wondered if this would be the one that would break their connection for good.

The buggy jerked as it halted. They both jolted forward slightly. They had arrived. Annie carefully removed her *kapp* and set it gently on the seat. She reached up and unpinned her braid so that it swung freely past her shoulders. He took off his hat and set it next to her head covering. Both of them put on baseball caps, pulling them on securely.

Nervously, they exchanged glances. This was it.

Getting out of the buggy, they both cast furtive glances around. No one was about.

"I will pick you up here at two," Abraham said.

"Sounds good. Thanks for the ride."

They watched their friend drive away, then they started toward the market. Without thinking about it, Tyler reached out and grabbed Annie's hand. The moment they touched, he felt her stiffen. Now she would pull away. But she didn't. After a moment, he felt her relax again. He smiled, swinging their hands between them.

They reached the edge of the market. It was bustling with activity. Many of the shops had brought some of their merchandise outside and set up displays on the sidewalks. Amish and *Englisch* alike mingled in the warm June morning. It was going to be hot by the time noon rolled around, but right at the moment the weather was warm with a light breeze. Tyler flicked his gaze over to Annie. He grinned. She was looking everywhere she could, her eyes wide as she took in everything. He had known she'd react this way. Annie loved seeing new places and watching people. To her, this was more fun than any fancy restaurant or going to a show. He'd missed that in his life these past few years.

They wandered around to the different shops. Tyler didn't buy anything. Whatever they bought, they'd have to carry with them. Knowing that someone was after them and might show up at any moment meant that they had to be ready to run and could not be hampered with nonessential items. Abraham would be purchasing whatever was needed back at the farm. Anything else was just a useless material possession. Not worth the trouble.

At lunchtime, they grabbed hot dogs and sodas at one of the food stands that dotted the sidewalk.

Every now and then, he looked around. He could never get over the feeling that disaster was about to strike. Maybe coming to the market had not been a good idea, after all. He had done it to get Annie away from the farm, knowing that it would please her. Now he felt like they were wearing targets on their backs.

He looked at his watch. It was one thirty. They had half an hour to go before they were to meet up with Abraham again. Although they had enjoyed their outing, he felt like he would be glad to get back to the Beiler home.

He was probably being foolish. Still, he remained on alert.

A few minutes later, he was glad that he had not completely let down his guard.

"Ty." Annie nudged his side with her elbow, her voice a tense whisper. "We're being watched."

His pulse hiked. She was staring off to the left a bit, her brow wrinkled. He noted that she was tugging at her braid. Although she looked calm enough to the casual observer, the increased pressure on his hand told him clearly that she was becoming agitated.

Stay calm. Look casual. Pulling her closer, he pretended to kiss her head, angling his face so he could peer over her. A young man with cold dark eyes was staring straight at them, his gaze narrowed. It was a calculated gaze. The stare of a man trying to figure something out.

Or maybe he was trying to imagine what Tyler looked like without his slight beard.

"Turn away," he whispered out of the corner of his mouth. "Pretend nothing is wrong. Like we are just any other couple here to look at the shops. We are just going to casually walk away. Stay close. We may need to run."

She nodded and turned with him.

They didn't talk. His ears were hyperfocused now, listening for any sign that they had been recognized. They skirted their way past two buildings successfully.

"We'll just wander around the side of that next building," he decided. "Then we will have to run. Do you—"

Whatever he was going to ask was forgotten.

"Tyler!" a voice yelled behind him.

Instinctively, he whipped his head in the direction of the voice. Screams followed as the man dropped the fliers and pulled out a gun.

"Run!"

Annie didn't need the urging. They bolted. Tearing past the shops, they both kept as close to walls as they could. They cleared the store and tore up the hill.

A shot rang out. Then another. Metal clanged. Something dropped behind them. Right where they had been.

They couldn't stop to look.

Tyler tugged Annie toward another group of buildings.

"No!" Annie gasped. "Too many people!"

She was right. The man chasing them probably wouldn't care if he hit someone else.

They darted behind an empty tourist bus that was parked along the side of the road. Tyler peeked out, keeping himself low. The man who had been chasing them was still there, but he seemed to have lost them in the crowd.

That wouldn't last for long. Sooner or later, he would head their way. Then what? When the man paused to turn and search, Tyler waited until he was turned in the opposite direction. Then he pulled Annie out from behind the bus and into the building that the bus was parked in front of. It was a large auction house. There were rows upon rows of vendors set up inside with their crafts and wares. And there was a door out the other side.

Sirens shrieked and drew closer. Tyler could have wilted where he stood in relief. Still, he wasn't going to let down his guard. Even if the police were on the scene, he couldn't assume that the danger following them was over.

They hurried through the building at a swift walk, trying not to be too conspicuous. The noise level in the place was over the top. Tyler kept looking back. No sign of the man.

They made it to the other side of the building without anyone calling out to them.

A few seconds later, the sounds of gunfire could be

heard in the background. He heard people screaming. Someone—no doubt an officer—shouted for people to get down.

Tyler's mouth was dry. He put his hand against Annie's back, silently encouraging her to walk in front of him. If bullets went flying toward them again, he wanted to keep her from being hit.

There was a path leading away from the building. It was convenient. But far too visible. Tyler pulled Annie off the path. A smaller building, probably for storage, was off to the side. He pulled them behind it. The good thing was that no one could see them there. Of course, that meant that they would not be able to see anyone coming, either. It was a chance he had to take.

The shouting and the gunfire behind them stopped. He wished he could go back and check it out, to be sure. That was a chance he couldn't take, though.

They needed to regroup and consider their options.

"We have twenty minutes until Abraham comes for us."

He heard Annie's breathing. There was a small gasp. Annie was in pain.

"I think I've been shot."

Chapter Twelve

Shot?

Feeling like he was moving in slow motion, Tyler pivoted to face his wife.

Her face was pale and pinched with pain. His chest tightened as he looked over her. Then his glance fell on the gravel at their feet. It was a mixture of various shades of white and gray. There were some almost black patches.

And every few inches, a splotch of red.

Blood.

His wife, his Annie, had been shot.

Feelings of remorse and self-recrimination threatened to overwhelm him, but he shoved them aside. He didn't have time for that.

He couldn't see where she was bleeding from.

"Where, Annie?" His voice came out harsh with fear.

"My leg."

He could see it then. Her right lower leg. There was a hole. A dark circular stain was slowly growing, creeping out across the faded denim of her blue jeans.

He had to stop the bleeding. But with what? He had nothing on him that would be useful. He had to go and find something. He clenched his teeth and peeked around the corner of the shed. No one was coming toward them. He had to take a chance, although he hated to leave her by herself. She'd be safer here than coming with him, though.

"Wait here."

She protested, but he was too focused to stop. Running back inside the auction building, he let his eyes adjust to the sudden dim light after being out in the blinding sunlight. No sign of the man who had shot at them. Quickly, Tyler purchased two bottles of water and a T-shirt. He didn't even stop to look at the design.

Picking up his purchases, he hurried back to Annie. She was right where he had left her, sitting behind the shed with her back up against the brown wall. Her legs were stretched out in front of her.

Kneeling at her side, he slowly began to inch up her jeans toward her knee to expose the wound.

"Wait," she cried, a thin thread of panic running through her voice.

He frowned. "Annie. I don't want to hurt you, but I have to stop the bleeding."

He met her gaze. He didn't like the resigned look that entered her eyes. Her lips tightened, meshing together to form a straight line. After a few eternal seconds, she nodded.

That was all he needed. He resumed his task. Thankfully, she had chosen to wear looser-fitting jeans this morning. If she had opted for skinny jeans, he would have had to have cut them. And he didn't have anything on him to do that. Finally, he could see the wound. He let out the breath he was holding. It was not as bad as he had feared. More of a graze than a full-on hit. He would not have to worry about a bullet still in the leg. He opened one of the waters and poured it gently over the wound. Taking the T-shirt, he patted the wound. More blood welled. He would need to put pressure on it. Placing his left hand on her leg to hold it steady, he held the shirt against the bleeding side of her calf with his right hand. He felt her flinch once. She trembled. He winced. He had to be hurting her. It couldn't be helped, although he wished it had been him and not her who had been wounded.

"Are you okay?"

Her face was turned away from him. She nodded, but didn't say anything.

He checked the wound several times. After about ten minutes, he was satisfied that the bleeding had stopped. He gripped the shirt at a seam and pulled. After a second, he heard the gratifying sound of fabric ripping. He kept pulling. He ripped until he had enough material to make a bandage, one that could be hopefully covered by her pant leg.

"I think that's good. Do you think you can walk on that?" Tyler pulled the pant leg back down, completely covering the emergency bandage, and slid his gaze up to her face. To his astonishment, tears were streaking down her face. "Annie! Did I hurt you? I'm so sorry. I tried to be as gentle as I could."

She shuddered. "It's not that." The words sounded like she half swallowed them. She gulped.

He was confused. "If I didn't hurt you, why are you crying?"

It could have been a reaction to the stress, but he didn't think so. Her eyes, even though tear-filled, were luminous, staring at him almost with awe. That was not a sight he was used to seeing.

"You touched them." The whisper was soft.

Huh?

"What?"

"My scars. You put your hand right over them as if you didn't even see them."

Oh. He so didn't want to have this conversation sitting here, vulnerable. They needed to get moving.

"I didn't see them. Annie, they have never bothered me like they do you. Look, I need to tell you something, but we need to get walking first. We can't be sitting here. We're too out in the open."

She nodded once, then held out her hand for him to assist her to stand. She braced herself against him and let her weight gradually fall on her injured leg. "I can walk."

Keeping to the edge of the woods, they circled the street where the market was set up, deliberately going the extra block so as not to lose the cover the trees gave them. Several times, they stopped to give Annie's leg a chance to rest. It was a painstakingly slow journey.

"We should call Karl," Tyler said.

"Oh, yes." Annie stopped, and searched through her purse for the phone that the marshal had left with her. "Here, you talk to him. I'm going to sit down for a few minutes."

Quickly, he called Karl and left a voice mail when the marshal didn't answer.

Tyler turned and watched Annie with concern.

Something was going on in her complicated mind. It had something to do with her scars. He had always known that she felt they were ugly. And he had tried to convince her that they weren't as bad as she thought. But maybe there was more to it than that. Something deeper.

He remembered something his old pastor had said after his mother had lost hope and died soon after his father was gone. *Not all scars show up on the skin. Some are soul-deep.*

Was this one of those cases? He remembered how embarrassed she was to let him see her scars, even though he had seen them before. And he remembered her reaction when he had touched them. Did she think that the scars were what drove him to withdraw? He had kept silent to protect his family, but had his silence also led to his wife's loss of self-confidence? It was years too late, and maybe his timing was off, but he needed to let her know the truth. If something happened to him, he didn't want Annie to continue believing a lie.

Even if she despised him for the truth.

It didn't take long before Annie's leg was throbbing intensely. Every step shot pain up her leg. She didn't complain. She didn't want to appear weak. But there was no way she could keep herself from limping. What if she had to go to the hospital? Would Karl put a guard outside her door?

Suddenly a thought occurred to her. What if the man who had shot her had escaped the police? Did he know that he hit her? *What if he searches the hospitals?*

Her breathing quickened. The only place she would feel safe was back at the Beiler farm. She nearly cried when they finally found Abraham. The buggy might have appeared more fragile than a car, but to her, it was beautiful and a sign of God's grace and protection.

For his part, Abraham looked like he had been pacing back and forth. There was a frantic look about his eyes. It was a bit startling. He looked like such a calm fellow. So strong and quiet. Seeing him so obviously on edge was odd.

He and Julia had been part of the program, though. Which meant that he knew all the dangers that went along with it. Not to mention, she reminded herself, he had been a cop for ten years.

Relief flashed across the older man's face when he saw them racing, or in her case limping, toward him. He frowned as he watched her approach.

"What happened?" Abraham asked the moment they appeared. "Two police cars passed me on the way. When I arrived, people walked by me talking about someone shooting at the police in the market."

Tyler scanned the area, his mouth grim. "Let me tell you when we get back to your house. I don't think it's safe here. The sooner we can leave, the better."

Abraham didn't ask any more questions. He hopped up on the seat. The moment that Tyler and Annie were settled in the buggy, he flicked the reins and clicked his tongue, and the horse started forward.

Annie and Tyler quickly put their headwear back on. They sat side by side, the tension vibrating off both of them. Tyler reached over and grabbed hold of her hand. She not only let him hold it, but she also squeezed his and kept a tight grip on it, as if she was concerned that he would be ripped away from her.

Annie couldn't stop shaking. "What if the police didn't get him? He could still be out there, watching."

Tyler nodded. Letting go of her hand for a moment, he reached down and pulled a lightweight blanket over them. "Get down."

They both sank below the thin blanket. Soon, Annie felt sweat beginning to trickle down her neck. It was a toss-up whether it was more from the heat or the fear.

The moment they reached the house, Tyler helped her inside. "We need to check your leg. I am worried that it might get infected."

She was too tired to argue. She changed back into her Amish dress, knowing that it would be easier for him to see to her leg without her jeans getting in the way. This time, when he looked at her leg, she didn't feel the embarrassment that she did earlier. She was still touchy about the scars, but he'd already seen them and hadn't acted like they repulsed him.

She had to rethink a lot of things she'd thought over the years. The idea made her squirm. As much as he had done or not done in their marriage, had she made the mistake of being overly judgmental toward him?

The idea bothered her. A lot. She had always considered herself a forgiving and merciful person. But now she wondered if she had withheld those qualities from the one person in her life she had vowed to show them to.

Julia came to assist before Annie could get too far into her own examination of conscience. She brought clean bandages and some antibacterial ointment. "We can have the doctor out tomorrow if it starts to look infected. Right now, it looks sore, but it really is not that much more than a skin wound."

Annie sank back against the chair, relieved. Tyler did not look convinced. "Ty, let's leave it until the morning."

Reluctantly, he nodded.

He was still looking pensive. Something else was on his mind.

"What's up?"

"I need to talk with you," he muttered. Julia and Abraham melted away. Julia said, "William has the girls. I will tell him to keep them out until you're done."

When they were alone, they looked at each other. Annie waited for him to break the silence.

Finally, he sighed. "I have a confession to make. I'm not sure if you will hate me or not when I'm done. At least, more than you do already."

She cringed. "I don't hate you, Ty. I never did. I was hurt and confused."

He looked off in the distance. It was as if he didn't even hear her. He seemed to be lost in his own memories.

"I don't think I ever really told you what happened with my father." He looked down, rubbing the toe of his shoe against some imaginary piece of dirt. "I know that you were aware that he had died when I was fifteen, but there was more to it than that. You see, my dad was a good man. He tended to believe the best about everyone. Even when they didn't deserve it."

She could already tell that this was going to be a story that broke her heart. She would hear the story through, though—she could tell that Tyler needed to tell her.

Tyler seem to have trouble finding the words to say what happened. She tried to help him along.

"Did someone take advantage of your dad?"

He nodded. "My uncle—his brother. He had gotten into it with some very bad people. When my dad tried to help him by going to the cops, those people decided to try and ruin him. And they did."

Her hand went to her throat—she was horrified.

Tyler continued his story. "My parents went to the police again. By this time, they had lost almost everything. And I don't just mean material things. They had lost their self-respect. Friends had stopped calling. My best friend's parents even told him that he couldn't hang out with me anymore. Unfortunately, my parents couldn't afford a good lawyer. And the court-appointed one just didn't seem to be taking the case seriously. So no one was ever punished except for my dad and my mom."

He caught her eyes with his, and the breath stuck in her throat. The pain she saw reached out and grabbed her.

"It killed him." His voice was so low, she had to lean forward to hear him clearly. "Oh, I know it was officially a heart attack, but this tragedy is what killed my dad. And it broke my mother's heart and she died, too. When I was offered a scholarship, I knew that I wanted to be a lawyer. I wanted to put people like that in jail. I took great pleasure in putting them in jail, too."

His head dropped into his hands. "And that's when my trouble started. I became so obsessed with putting the bad guys in jail, that I neglected you. Eventually, though, I paid for my arrogance. One of the men I put behind bars had a son. A son who promised to make me pay. I could never prove it, but a week later, a truck ran through a light and into our living room window."

Her heart stopped. The accident. Her scars. They led back to Tyler and his job.

Annabelle didn't know what to think. Or how to feel. To know that the accident that had caused her so much misery and pain was, in fact, no accident at all. If she could believe Tyler.

And she did.

It all made sense now. The way he'd started to pull back after her accident. The way he had suddenly not wanted the family to go anywhere.

"That's why you didn't go to my father's funeral." It wasn't a question.

He nodded. "I never wanted to hurt you. I was afraid that if I showed up, he would go after your family. I was terrified that you or Bethany would be hurt or killed. I knew that my job was a danger to you. The man who wanted me to pay died of a heart attack. Then, two days later, you walked out. When you left, I wanted to go after you. But I knew it was for the best. I had many enemies. I couldn't guarantee another wouldn't have come after me."

"I can't believe you didn't let me know what was happening!" She shook her head. "And what if we were in danger because you weren't there to protect us?"

Tyler sighed and dropped his head into his hands. "I made sure that people knew we were not together in any sense. I stayed away from Bethany so it would appear that I was an uninterested father. And I have a friend who is a detective. He checked up on you now and then. I did whatever I could to make sure you were safe. I was pretty sure that the danger had been eradicated, but I couldn't risk it."

Annabelle felt like she was watching some poorly written soap opera. Any moment now, something would pop out of nowhere to save them. But, of course, it would not. "I thought that you were pulling back because my scars disgusted you."

Had she really just told him that? She was a bit embarrassed by her vanity.

His shocked face told her more than his words could that the thought had never entered his mind. "Annie, you're beautiful. You always have been. I thought your scars were beautiful, too."

She ducked her head. That was hard to believe.

"It's true. Every time I saw your scars, I remembered running to find you and lifting your lifeless body in my arms. I thought you were dead. I looked at your scars, and I remembered the gratitude I felt at knowing that you were alive."

Their conversation was interrupted when Abraham entered the room carrying a cell phone. She recognized it as the same kind of phone that Karl had given her and Tyler.

"Is it Karl?" Tyler asked, accepting the phone when Abraham held it out to him.

"Yes."

When Tyler answered the phone, she knew that their conversation was over. Frowning, she rapped her knuckles against the side of the chair. Her stomach was unsettled. Partly from the conversation they had just had, and partly from the events of the day. She remembered how gentle Tyler had been as he had seen to her wound. She had been so angry with him for so long, she had forgotten how sweet he could be.

Was she still angry with him? Now that she had an explanation, she understood what had happened between them. If she was honest with herself, she probably had let her insecurities caused by her scars keep her from fighting for their marriage.

Tyler had pushed them away to protect them. She got that. She even could respect it, although she felt he was wrong.

What she didn't know was whether she could ever trust him not to do the same thing in the future if they were in danger.

Chapter Thirteen

The doctor came out to see her the next day. He cleaned her wound with a solemn expression and then told her that the next time she helped clean her husband's hunting rifle, they needed to make sure it was not loaded first. Blinking, she agreed. Cleaning a hunting rifle? She probably couldn't tell him that someone had shot at her.

Tyler and Abraham had gone to the barn to work by the time the doctor had finished and left. Sighing, she realized that there would not be an opportunity to talk with him more about what had happened in the past until later.

Did she want to talk more? Because if she didn't talk to him, then she didn't need to deal with the emotional bulldozer he had hit her with the day before.

Did she blame him for her accident? Could she allow their relationship to continue to grow, knowing what she knew?

It was fine while they were here, hidden in Amish country. But what happened when they returned home, if they returned home? She knew that he regretted missing out on their lives. She also believed that he did what he could to protect them.

What she didn't know, and what she had been afraid to ask, was whether or not he would make the same choices again. Would he, if they returned to their lives, again bury himself in his work at the price of their family?

He had felt driven by what happened to his father. She got that. But she could not go through the emotional wringer he had put them through again.

A car drove into the driveway. It was Karl. She moved toward the door to let him in, but Julia beat her there.

"Karl!" The Amish woman greeted him with a smile. "I did not expect to see you again so soon. Although, you are always welcome."

"Good morning, Julia. I didn't plan on visiting so soon." His gaze found Annie. "Ty said you had been attacked and that you had been shot."

She nodded. "That is true. I don't think it's serious, though."

"The whole situation is serious. I need to talk with you both."

"He's working with Abraham in the barn. I'll go get him." Julia hurried off. Less than ten minutes later, she returned, Tyler striding in behind her.

"Karl!" The men shook hands.

"Ty. As I was telling Annie, your situation is serious, but I do have some good news. Someone had heard gunshots and had called the police to the market. When they arrived and surrounded him, the man refused to surrender and began shooting at the police. They returned fire, and the man in question was killed. Although I never take someone's death lightly, I am relieved that he never had a chance to reveal that he had seen you."

"How do you know that?" She clenched her fists tight enough for her short nails to dig into her palms.

"The police identified him as someone local. He had a long rap sheet, mostly minor crimes. His computer and his phone have been checked out. He apparently got word of the bounty on your head. As far as we can tell, he was at the market and recognized you from the pictures that had been circulated."

"It seems odd that he would recognize us." Tyler narrowed his eyes, his lips tight.

"Not really. This guy was known for his memory. What we used to call a photographic memory. The fact that he recognized you isn't odd, but it isn't exactly something most people can do, either. He made no phone calls after he saw you. Were you dressed Amish?"

"No, and we didn't arrive at the market in the buggy. Abraham dropped us off before we got there."

"Good. That should help." He frowned. "I think you should still be safe here. This scenario could have happened anywhere we placed you. But I am going to start planning for a new placement for you. Just in case we need to move quick."

Her heart sank. She had just started to get comfortable with the Beilers. And Bethany would be difficult. The only reason her daughter really tolerated their situation was because of Kayla and her chicken. She knew that her daughter was becoming anxious to return home. He hadn't said they had to move, though. Only that it was a possibility.

Unwillingly, her eyes moved to Tyler. He had been quick-thinking during their ordeal. Had he always been that competent in dealing with a crisis? She was discovering new depths to him.

Karl continued. "For now, your cover is safe. I just would ask that you avoid the market until things settle down."

He glanced around. "Are the kids here?"

"William took them out to the neighbors'. New kittens."

"Ah. Well, that sounds great. I want to talk with Abraham as long as I'm here."

Disappointment settled over her. She had enjoyed the market. Well, until the man started shooting. Knowing that she would not be able to go again anytime soon made her feel like the prison bars were coming in tighter.

"I'll show you where he is," Tyler said. "He was going out in the woods to check on something."

Karl walked outside with Tyler. Annie sighed, discouraged.

"Annie, it will work out."

Annie slowly rotated on her stockinged feet to face Julia. "I'm not sure it will. I feel like everything is coming unglued. Things I have known for years are not as they seem. My husband has someone after him, and therefore us, and now I can't even go into the market."

She needed to stop talking because she sounded like a teenager. Any moment she'd say, "It's not fair!"

"Come, sit." Julia brought two coffee mugs to the table. She joined her. "Have you talked with Ty about how you are feeling?"

A flush crawled up her neck and into her cheeks. "No. Julia, Ty and I, well, we're married. But we have been living separate lives for several years now. I had always believed it was because he chose his job over us. Now, I'm not sure what to think."

Briefly, she outlined what Tyler had told her, skipping over the part about his father. When she told the other woman about the accident that had nearly killed her and had left her with so many emotional and physical scars, Julia covered her mouth with her hand.

"Oh, that is so terrible!"

Annie realized there were tears on her cheeks. She dashed them away angrily. She was crying way too much lately.

"I don't know what to do. I am afraid of the fact that we seem to be growing so close. I don't want to get hurt again." She wasn't worried about him abandoning Bethany again, though. He'd said he wouldn't, and despite everything that had happened in the past, she trusted him to keep his word.

Julia considered. "Sometimes life is hard. Before I met Abraham, I was struggling to raise two children alone. William, he's such a wonderful young man. And he is such a joy to me. Now. A year ago, though, he was in trouble. Well, you remember what I told you, about him getting involved with a gang. He even ran away."

"No!" Shocked, Annie stared at her new friend.

"It is true. Abraham, his story was equally harsh. His first wife and child were murdered, killed by a car bomb. I do not know how he survived that."

Neither did she. The thought of anything happening

to Bethany turned her stomach. How did one pick up the pieces after such devastating events?

She asked the question out loud.

"The only way I know to survive is through my faith."

Annie bit her lip. "I'm afraid I haven't relied on God as much as I should through this. I tend to leap and think of going to God afterward."

A brief smile flickered across Julia's face. "That is human nature. But I think the more we trust in Him, the more resilient we will be when the hard times come. Because they will come. Having faith does not mean we have an easy path."

The truth of the statement hit her. She had acted as if things should be easy, because she had faith. When she left Tyler, she had expected him to come after her, and then pouted when he hadn't.

And despite his distancing himself from them, he wasn't the one who left.

That was all on her.

Karl excused himself to take a phone call, leaving Tyler and Abraham alone. As they usually did, they began to talk and debate current issues. Abraham Beiler was one of the most interesting men that Tyler had ever met. The man had lived a very hard life, and had managed not only to survive, but also to thrive. Tyler shuddered even to think about losing his family so violently.

The one thing that made Tyler uncomfortable was how unreserved Abraham was when it came to talking about his faith. Tyler realized he had kind of given up on his faith when things had turned sour. He hadn't even given God a chance to work before he had pushed

Him out of his life. Instead, he had just accepted things as they were. His life stalled.

When was the last time he had a real friend to talk to? Even when he was supposedly happily married to Annie, on some level he always kept his emotional distance from her. It was almost like he had always known that one day she would leave him.

No, that wasn't true. Her leaving had shocked him. But what had shocked him even more was that he hadn't really even noticed how far apart they'd gotten. He hadn't noticed how much pain she was in. Was it by choice?

"Ty, how is Annie feeling today?" Abraham asked. It was almost as if he knew whom Tyler was thinking so hard about.

"Oh, I think she's doing all right. She's strong." He paused, then blurted out, "I hate that she was hurt because of me."

Now what on earth had made him say that? Abraham was going to think he was off his rocker. That's not the sort of conversation one has with a virtual stranger.

Except, Abraham and Julia didn't really feel like strangers. It was probably because Tyler knew that they were in the witness protection program, as well. And lived to tell about it. Abraham had told him about the deaths of his wife and child, as well as the gang members who had been hunting down William. Now, they were a family, living a simple life far from where they had started out.

That made him pause again. The Beiler family was still in the witness protection program. And they probably always would be.

What if he and Annie were always in the program, too? They couldn't go on as they were. Deep inside, he knew that he still had feelings for her. They had never really died out. He had just shoved them aside so that he could carry on doing his job. A job, if he was honest, he had come to despise. He felt no joy inside when he was working. Only a sense of never-ending duty.

Could they be a couple again? But what would happen if they left the program? He didn't know if he even wanted to go there.

Abraham was staring at him, an expectant look on his face. He was no doubt waiting for Tyler to explain why he had been avoiding his wife. Tyler laughed to himself, although there was no humor in the sound. He'd been doing a lot of explaining himself lately. He wasn't exactly sure that he enjoyed that.

"Hey, Ty! Abraham!" Tyler was grateful to see Karl approaching. "I have some news for you."

Tyler was glad to know that the man who'd been shooting at them hadn't found out where they were.

But Annie wouldn't be happy about having to stay away from the market. He knew that she had enjoyed the experience, minus the shooting, of course.

"What I really wanted to tell you," Karl said, his tone catching Tyler's attention, "is that the judge has moved up the trial date. And Billy Clarke, our resident technology whiz kid, has stumbled on information that the bounty out on you has increased. Tyler, I don't need to tell you that you and Annie have to stay under the radar. Now, more than ever. Every bounty hunter and petty thief in the continental US will be after you. They won't care if they bring you in dead or alive."

* * *

Karl stayed through dinner, then he departed with a final warning for them to be careful and to stay alert. After he left, Tyler asked Annie to take a walk outside with him. Her eyes widened. He'd caught her by surprise. She said yes, to his relief.

They stepped outside and moved away from the house. Not too far away. Just far enough away where their conversation would not carry through the windows to the people still inside. As they walked, he laced his fingers through hers.

"Annie…" He couldn't bring himself to look at her. Not yet. "Karl brought some news today."

She halted and tugged him to a stop with her. "Is it about the man who shot me? I know that Karl said that he doesn't think our cover has been blown."

"Yes, and no." He caught her other hand and leaned toward her. Their foreheads touched. *Just for a moment*, he thought, *let me pretend that she still loves me and that everything will be fine.* "You already know that he's no longer a threat. What Karl just told me is that the trial date has been moved up."

Annie pulled back. He managed to mask his disappointment. "That's good, right? The sooner the trial ends, the sooner people will stop chasing us."

"Not if the bounty is still there. Some people will do anything to make money." Reluctantly, he released her hands and took a step back. Immediately, he wanted to grab them again.

He heard her harsh breath.

"Karl thinks that the number of people out to get me has increased. Exponentially."

She was silent for a minute. He waited.

"Will we ever be safe? Or will we have to stay in witness protection forever?"

He wished he knew the answer to that question.

Chapter Fourteen

"Annie!" Tyler walked toward her, waving something.

Wait. Was that the newspaper? She grinned as she grabbed at it. Julia and Abraham read the local Amish newspaper, but they didn't get the *Englisch* one on a daily basis. She missed reading the comics.

"When did you get this?" She held the paper close to her as she stared up at him. My, he looked pleased with himself.

"I remembered how you enjoyed reading the comics, so I asked Abraham if he could pick up a newspaper while he was in town."

"Oh, thank you!" Stretching up, she planted a kiss on his cheek. Their eyes met. Unwilling to decipher the emotions flashing in his eyes, or flooding her system, she took the paper and escaped to her room, feeling his eyes following her.

She flipped through until she found the comics. They were as funny as she remembered. Maybe even more so because she had not had access to them.

She flipped the page again. And froze, bile rising in

her throat. A picture of a block where three houses had been decimated by fire was in the center of the page. Her mother's house was one of the three destroyed! She would not have known it if it was not for the undamaged houses surrounding the destroyed buildings.

Feverishly, she read the rest of the article. No mention of people dead, although the article did mention several injuries. Her hand went to her throat. Swallowing hard, she forced herself to read on, blinking back the tears. The local police believed that the fires might have been started by a serial arsonist, one that had hit houses in several states. That was probably why it made the paper in Ohio. Normally, fires in Southern Illinois wouldn't be reported this far east.

Her mother had gone to stay with Ethan. She wasn't even there. Annabelle kept telling herself that she was being silly.

It didn't matter. No matter how much Annabelle tried to convince herself that her mother was safe and had not been inside the house at the time of the fire, every time she looked at the newspaper and saw the charred remains of her childhood home, a chill went down her spine.

A new thought occurred to her. Her mother had been very resistant to the idea of going to stay with her son. What if, despite all of Ethan's persuasion, her mother had remained stubborn? Ethan would have had no method by which to contact her. What if her mother had been inside when the house had gone up in flames? Images of her mother wounded and lying in a hospital bed tormented her.

She could not endure not knowing the truth!

Annabelle read the article again. All it said was that it was a house owned by a widow in her late sixties. It did not mention anything about anyone being inside the house when it caught fire.

There was no doubt in Annabelle's mind that the police were wrong. This was not the work of a serial arsonist. No, this was the work of someone who was searching for Tyler and her. Someone who didn't know where they were, but who hoped that she would see the news coverage on the fire.

They're just trying to draw us out. She knew that. Deep in her bones, she understood that attacking her mother was just a way of getting at her and Tyler. But no matter how much she tried to convince herself that it would be foolish to contact her mother, she could not get that house out of her mind.

She stewed about it all day long. Several times, Tyler asked if she was all right. Even when she said she was, she could tell that he wasn't convinced.

I should show him the article.

But she didn't. She knew that if she showed him the article, Tyler would know that she was thinking of contacting her mother. He would also, most likely, put the blame upon himself. He held himself responsible for way too much as it was.

Wait a minute. She didn't have to contact her mother. Although she very much wanted to be the one to contact her mother. She needed to hear her mother's voice. But she also knew the rules. She could not contact her mother. But she had the phone that the marshals had given her so that she could contact them.

She could contact Karl or Jonathan.

At the first opportunity, Annabelle excused herself to go upstairs to her room. It was after suppertime, but due to the extended summer daylight, she still had plenty of light in her room. She took the cell phone out of her bag and dialed Karl's number with fingers that shook. Now that she was actually taking steps to find out the truth, she was terrified of what she might discover.

The phone rang once. Twice. After four rings, it went to voice mail. She should leave a message. She knew he was busy and would call her back.

She didn't. Instead, she ended the call, knowing that she wouldn't have been able to stand it any longer. She couldn't call from the house phone. That was too risky. Abraham and Tyler were working in the barn. They wouldn't be back for another few hours. Kayla and Bethany were at a neighbor's house. What should she do?

"Annie?" She quickly hid the phone as she heard Julia calling.

Opening her door, she met the other woman in the hall.

"Ah, there you are!" Julia flashed her a warm smile. Annie smiled back, hoping her smile wasn't as wobbly as it felt. "I was thinking about going to the quilt shop for a few supplies. It's not as elegant as going into town, but maybe you would want to go with me?"

"Absolutely!" She jumped at the opportunity. If she found someone with a cell phone, maybe she could make the call. That way, she wouldn't have to conceal a phone on her person.

When they arrived at the quilt shop, her heart sank. The only person present besides Julia and herself was the woman running the store. They got into a lengthy discussion regarding patterns. Bored, Annabelle wandered outside. She started walking around the building, when a van pulled up. Two women and five children spilled from the van, all chattering in loud voices. She winced. She'd gotten used to the quiet manner of Julia.

Seeing her chance, she approached the woman on the far side of the van and asked if she could use her phone. The woman stopped talking and stared at her, her mouth dropping open. Flushing, Annabelle explained that a non-Amish friend's house had burned down and she wanted to check on her. Softening, the woman held out her phone.

"Of course."

Thanking the woman, Annabelle walked a bit apart. For privacy, but also so that Julia would not see her through the window.

She was making a mistake. She needed to wait. But her fingers were already dialing the familiar cell phone number. She held her breath. There was still time to hang up. Her mother would not even recognize the number.

She didn't, though. She was too close to give up.

Clenching her fists, Annabelle waited for her mother to answer her phone.

Come on, Mom. Answer the phone. Come on. She pounded her fist lightly against her thigh as she waited. Every second she grew more tense, trying to keep the thoughts of why her mom might not be answering from creeping into her mind. Finally, after what seemed an eternity, her mother picked up the phone.

"Hello?" Her mother sounded annoyed. Ah! She

probably thought it was a telemarketer. Her mother could never be convinced that it wasn't rude to ignore calls from unfamiliar numbers. For once, she was glad.

Annabelle tried to answer her mom but found herself choking up too much.

"Hello?" Now her mom sounded angry.

"Mom!" she blurted out. "Are you all right?"

Just the mere sound of her mother's voice was enough to bring the tears spurting to her eyes. She sniffed and did her best to blink them back. She never cried. For years, she had prided herself on her strength. On her ability to handle anything. Now, it seemed all she ever did was cry.

"Annabelle? Is that you?" There were tears in her mother's voice, as well. "Oh, honey! I am so glad to hear your voice!"

"Mom, I saw the newspaper article. Your house! I was so scared. I was afraid that you were in it. They were saying it might not have been an accident." She had to sit down. She sank down on the bench outside the store. The emotional roller-coaster ride she had been on for the past week was getting to be too much.

"Honey, I'm fine. It's just a house. No one was inside of it. I did what you asked and I'm staying with your brother. We both know that my house did not accidentally go up in flames."

"It had to have been arson." Annie had never been as sure of anything in her life. "Mom, you know that they were out to get me. Hoping I would come home to see you."

"That's what we think, as well. Whatever you do, do not come home. I want to see you, you know that. I think, though, that one of the people trying to find you will be watching me and your brother, hoping to get you. And through you, Tyler." Her mom's voice held no blame. Annie knew that her mother held no rancor against her son-in-law. In fact, she had often told Annie that she prayed that somehow they would get back together someday. Until recently, Annie had thought the idea was ludicrous.

There was a pause on the other end of the phone. When her mother spoke again her voice was softer, smaller somehow. Annie knew that she was not the only one feeling the effects of the separation. "Annabelle, how are you doing? And how is my granddaughter? I have been praying so hard for you. I feel like part of my heart has been ripped apart."

Annie took a deep breath to steady herself. "I know. But we're safe."

Julia would be out any second.

"Mom, I gotta go. Love you."

"Okay, baby girl. Be safe." Her mom hung up the phone.

Annie smiled. Then she frowned. What was that click?

Uneasy, she disconnected the call and returned it to the woman, thanking her for her understanding. Julia came out as they were talking. Fortunately, she didn't appear to have seen what Annabelle had done. That didn't make her feel less guilty for breaking the rules.

She had thought that she would be at peace once she talked with her mother. She did feel better, knowing that her mother was safe. Worry continued to eat at her, niggling itself into her mind long after she went to bed.

She knew that the marshals had good reason to tell clients not to contact people from their past. Her call could get them kicked out of the program. Karl and Jonathan had clearly explained the rules.

And she had deliberately disobeyed them.

Had she just betrayed Tyler?

They had been living with the Beilers for three weeks. Every morning, Tyler woke up wondering if today would be the day that they were discovered. The day that all of their attempts to hide failed.

Whatever happened today, it would be a new experience for them. For the first time, Tyler, Annie and Bethany would be joining the Beiler family at church. He would be meeting the other nineteen families in the district. That was a whole bunch of people who didn't know that they weren't really planning on becoming Amish.

Of course, they might not have a choice.

He shrugged away the thought.

Annie, however, was almost dancing with her excitement. She was so thrilled to finally be meeting more people and getting the chance to get out and be social. Tyler could not help the smile that came to his face as he watched her. She had been so tense lately. Not that he could blame her. It was difficult knowing that people were searching for them. For the first time in days, though, he could see her natural exuberance.

Tyler had helped the men unload the church benches from the wagon. The men had accepted him as part of their group, although some of them had ribbed him about choosing to join the church at such an old age. He scoffed. Old. Yeah, right.

He actually enjoyed being part of the group that set the benches up.

The church service was interesting. It had been so long since he had been to church. He expected to be uncomfortable. And he did squirm a bit. But he was busy experiencing all the new and unexpected differences. Oh sure, he had known from what Abraham had told him that the women and the men would be seated separately. What he hadn't expected was to connect so much with what the bishop was saying. Part of him wondered if the bishop was giving his message for the sake of Annie and Tyler. Tyler remembered that the bishop knew who they were. The bishop's message centered around trusting God even when they were in the desert.

An apt description.

After the service, there was the meal that the community took together. Again, the men and women were seated separately.

For some reason, Tyler was uneasy. He liked being able to see exactly where his wife and daughter were. At the moment, though, they were here surrounded by other people. He really just needed to relax and enjoy the day.

As the men were gathering outside after they had eaten, Tyler overheard a group of the boys talking about a couple of men in town.

Tyler didn't pay too much attention until he heard one of the boys talking about the man who was wearing an angry expression and an Illinois baseball cap. He froze where he was. Could it possibly be someone searching for them? There was no way to tell. Wearing an Illinois baseball cap wasn't exactly unusual. He was probably overreacting.

But what if he wasn't? Suddenly, he remembered the men who had chased them down after Rick had been shot. The one man, the one called Jim, had worn an Illinois baseball cap. Tyler felt as though ice water was sliding through his veins. How would he have found them?

"Levi said he had a gun. I did not see it, but he looked mean enough to have one. Right?" The boy nodded at his friend.

The other boy, who had to be Levi, agreed. "*Jah.* It wasn't a hunting rifle, either. It was a gun like an *Englischer* would carry. Maybe a police officer. But I don't think that man was a police officer."

Neither did he.

His anxiety spiked. He needed to get his family out of there now. He walked around, searching for his wife and daughter, doing his best not to run. He didn't want to call attention to himself. Nor did he want anyone else to panic.

Abraham was ahead with William. He lengthened his stride to catch up with them. Putting his hands in his pockets, he walked beside them, trying to act as if he had not a care in the world. Inside, he was breaking apart at the seams.

"Abraham, would it be possible for us to leave soon?" he asked the other man quietly. His eyes darted to the side to make sure no one else had heard.

Abraham raised his eyebrows, but otherwise gave no other indication that it was an odd request. "I assume something happened?"

Although his manner remained calm, Tyler knew that was his cop voice. He'd heard similar tones from other cops he'd worked with. This was the first time that it was so personal, though.

"I heard a group of boys talking. There was a suspicious man in town with a gun. A man who may or may not be searching for us. The description, though, sounds a lot like a man who had chased us when we were traveling through Indiana. They don't know we are hiding here, and I know that I am probably overreacting. But I don't care. I want my family where I can see them."

Abraham rubbed his bearded chin. "I do not blame you in the least. I would want the same thing. Let's gather up our wives and the *kinner*, and we can leave in a few minutes. I need to let the bishop know what's happening."

Tyler winced. He understood completely. He was concerned, though, that the bishop might decide that the Everson—or rather the Miller—family was not worth the trouble. He would hate to be the reason any of these good people got hurt.

Within minutes, they were headed back to the farm. Kayla and Bethany were the only ones who talked on the way home. It was clear that the events had put a damper on the adults' moods.

Tyler constantly peered out of the buggy, expecting to see Jim or some other bully with a gun prowling along the streets. He didn't see anyone suspicious. That didn't relax his tension. He knew better that to let down his guard. These men were out there, and they were vicious.

The next morning, he stayed home and helped on

the farm as much as he could. Abraham was going into town to grab some needed supplies. As he was getting the horse hitched up to the buggy, Tyler jogged out to him.

"Abraham, can you do me a favor while you're in town?"

"Maybe so," Abraham replied. Although he was not smiling, there was a definite twinkle in his eyes.

Tyler lowered his voice. "I want to see today's newspaper. There might be some mention of the man the boys saw in town. Hopefully, there will be information about him being arrested, but I want to see if there is anything useful."

"I can scan the paper for you," Abraham offered.

That was true. Tyler thought about it. "No. That's okay. I think I would feel better reading it myself. Sorry. I know you just bought one for us last week."

"I don't mind picking up another for you," Abraham replied.

When Abraham returned with the paper later that day, Tyler read through it. On page three, there was the mention that the police were looking for a suspicious man carrying a gun. It might have nothing to do with them.

Deep in his gut, Tyler couldn't quiet the feeling. Jim had somehow traced them to Ohio.

How long would it be until he found them?

Chapter Fifteen

What had she done?

Annie couldn't escape the feeling that disaster was pending. She prayed as hard as she knew how, but she still could not shake the dread that had taken hold of her. She replayed the conversation with her mother multiple times. Each time, she cringed. Why had she called her mother? Karl had called her back, and she had told him about the fire. He had assured her that her mother was fine.

Annabelle hadn't told him about the phone call.

She needed to tell Tyler what she had done. He'd be upset. And rightly so.

Hopefully, he would be better at the forgiveness thing than she had been.

She looked again at the newspaper. She had so many great memories at that house, but her mother was right. It was just a house. People were more important. That was why she had made that phone call.

"Annie?" She heard Julia calling.

"I'm coming," she answered.

Leaving the newspaper on the desk, she headed
down the stairs. She was halfway down when she realized something. She had left her stockings off. It was
a warm day, so her feet were not cold. It felt strange
knowing that, for the first time in several years, she was
not going to cover up her legs. Granted, no one in this
house would care about the scars. But it still felt like a
huge step for her.

Feeling lighter than she had in days, Annie waltzed
into the kitchen. Julia was getting ready to leave. She
had her stockings and her shoes on. She had also placed
a black bonnet over her prayer *kapp*.

"I need to go out for a bit. I should be back within an
hour. Will you be fine here by yourself?"

Annie nodded. "Of course! You go and run your errands. I will see you when you return."

She watched Julia as she headed out the door. It had
been a while since she had been on her own. It was
kind of nice.

Bethany found her a few minutes later. She had some
books in her arms. "Mommy, will you read to me?"

"Of course I will."

Annie sat at the table with Bethany at her side. They
read the first two books together. They had just opened
the third book, when Annie looked up. She shuddered
and the blood drained from her face. Jim, the man with
the gun, was sneaking down the field toward the house.
She could run, but what if he shot at Bethany?

She had to save her daughter.

How? With terror blazing through her veins, she realized that the only thing she could do was distract him.

"Bethy, I want you to listen to me." The little girl

looked at her with wide eyes. "The bad man is coming. I can see him. I need to make you safe."

She hated the frightened expression that slid over her daughter's face, but she needed to make sure she understood the gravity of the situation. She needed Bethany to remain hidden until Tyler found her. Only then could she be sure that her daughter was safe.

Quickly, she brought Bethany into the pantry. It was hard to breathe around the terror that filled her system. Dragging Bethany over to the far wall, Annie pushed two shelving units apart just enough for her daughter to squeeze between them.

Helping her fit into the small space, she had her crouch down. "Okay, Bethany. I need you to stay here and not make a sound, do you understand?" She waited for her daughter to nod. "Good girl. Mommy is going to lead that bad man away from here so that he can't hurt you. Stay here and keep quiet."

Leaning forward, she kissed the blond head. She loved Bethany so much. She prayed that her daughter and Tyler would be safe. The question of whether or not she would ever see her daughter again popped into her mind, but she shoved it out. She couldn't give up. There was too much at stake.

As soon as she was sure her daughter was safe, she left the kitchen. She had not made it far into the house when a rough arm grabbed her and a calloused hand covered her mouth. The scent of old tobacco and sweat filled her nostrils. She gagged.

"Look who's here. I have searched for you and that sneaky husband of yours for weeks. I should have burned down your mama's house earlier. I would have had the reward money half spent by now." She cringed as a low chuckle filled her ears. Her call to her mother had led him right to them.

Jim forced her out of the house and down the street a short ways. There was a beat-up pickup truck parked along the side of the road. He grabbed some rope from inside and tied her hands. Then he forced her into the truck. He slammed the door behind her. "If you try to escape, somebody will die. And it will be your fault."

She believed him. Twenty seconds later, he hauled himself behind the wheel and started the truck. He didn't go far. He pulled the truck behind the empty house down the street and parked it. Then he took her inside. The house was falling down around them. The roof had holes in it. She could see the light from outside filtering through. The clouds were starting to gather up above. She had a feeling that the roof would leak like crazy once it started to pour. Then what?

Jim pushed her down onto the floor. She didn't want to look down to see what was covering the floor. It couldn't be good. She stared at Jim, waiting for him to tell her exactly what he planned.

He swung a decrepit chair around and sat facing her. The chair creaked.

"Your man, he's gonna be searching for you real soon. When he does, I'll catch him. I have a reward to get. Do you know how hard it was to figure out how to get it for myself? Kory was planning on getting his share. Tossing him off the bridge took care of that problem. I hadn't planned to kill him, but when I saw him almost fall through the bridge, I knew it would be easy to accomplish."

She had thought the other man had fallen. He had pushed him. The acid in her stomach churned.

"I decided that your mama would be the perfect lure, and I was right. I followed her to your brother's house. She likes to leave her phone in her unlocked car. I had a buddy put a bug in her cell phone, then I burned the house. I haven't had so much fun since I was kid. Always did like fire. When you called to check on your mother, we got to listen in. It took us a while to find you. But I was able to force someone at the cell phone company to look up her call records and where the calls came from. It was only a matter of time after that. We just had to talk to the right people to learn about a new family in the area."

Her phone call to her mother was going to cost Annie her life. And possibly Tyler's, too. Thankfully, she had been able to hide Bethany before Jim had gotten into the house. At least her little girl was safe. She couldn't believe how dumb she'd been. But she had been acting on pure nerve at that point.

The clip-clop of horse hooves made the foul man fall silent.

Jim stood and walked to the door. "Good, that other woman just pulled in the driveway. Soon, the whole crew should be home. When your man finds you gone, he'll come to find you. As soon as he's on his own, I'll make my move."

Jim gave a rusty chuckle and rubbed his hands together in glee.

"This is going to be so much fun," he gloated.

The dread that was roiling inside her went up a notch.

* * *

Where was Annie?

Tyler and Abraham had returned from helping the neighbor. Abraham immediately headed out to the barn to check on a project he'd set aside earlier. Tyler entered the house, but no one seemed to be there. Maybe she had gone somewhere with Julia. No, they wouldn't have left Kayla. Kayla was out in the front yard, playing by herself. That was odd. The girls had been each other's shadows ever since they had moved in with the Beiler family.

Maybe she knew where Bethany was. He sauntered to the child and crouched down so that he was at eye level with her.

"Hi, Kayla. I was wondering if you knew where Bethany was. I need to find her."

Kayla blinked at him. "Nope. I looked for her. She wasn't inside." The seven-year-old shrugged her slim shoulders. In her world, not being able to find her friend one day didn't seem like a big deal.

Tyler had every reason to believe that it could be a very big deal. He jumped up and ran inside the house. Julia was baking something that smelled delicious in the kitchen. It barely registered with Tyler.

"Julia! Have you seen Bethany or Annie?"

She must have heard the fear threading through his voice. Stopping what she was doing, Julia shook her head. Her face paled slightly. She wiped her hands on a dish towel and started toward the door. "I'll check upstairs. I saw Annie about an hour ago, right before I left for town."

She ran lightly up the steps to Annie's room. He

wasn't surprised when she came down a minute later. Her face was distressed. "She's not there. And there was no note or any sort of clue as to where she might have gone."

Julia's expression was becoming concerned.

Between the two of them, they searched the house for clues. Tyler was ready to scream. He heard a sniffling noise from the pantry. Walking in, he looked between two shelving units. Crouched down on the floor was Bethany, her face wet with tears.

Heart pounding, he pulled out his daughter and lifted her into his arms. He buried his face against the side of her *kapp* and held her tight. His baby girl was alive. He could not stop shaking.

Finally, he managed to walk out of the pantry, still holding her in his arms. Julia ran in and saw the child. She immediately wiped her eyes.

"Bethany," Tyler rasped out of a throat too tight. "Why were you in the pantry?"

The child gulped back another sob. "Mommy put me there. She told me to stay still and not move." A tear broke free. "I didn't move, Daddy. I didn't. I heard you calling, but Mommy said don't move."

His poor girl.

"Why did Mommy put you in there? Did she say?" His chest was tight. He knew that something horrible had happened. And he also knew that Annie had done all she could to protect the little girl.

"Mommy saw the bad man coming. She told me to stay so he wouldn't find me."

"This bad man," Julia said. "Did he come?"

Bethany nodded. "He made Mommy go with him. He said something about hurting Grandma if she didn't."

Of course Annie would do whatever she could to protect her mother. Really, to protect any of them.

Bethany started to cry again in earnest. "I want Mommy. Daddy, go find Mommy."

He kissed her, blinking back his own tears. "I will, bug. I'm gonna get Mommy as soon as I can."

He had no idea how. But he would find her. He went up to her room, to search and see if there was something that Julia might have missed. The room was spotless. The only thing out of place was a newspaper on the desk. He nearly walked by it without taking another look, but something about it made him glance down again.

The newspaper had obviously been handled a lot. It was wrinkled in various places and looked like it had been folded back to a specific page. The picture facing up was a burned-down house. At first, he almost missed it. Something about the picture caught his eye, though. When he looked closer, he realized that he knew the neighborhood. He had gone there frequently when he and Annie were still together.

It was his mother-in-law's house. All at once, he remembered how Annie had been on edge for the past week or so. Ever since he gave her the newspaper. He should have questioned her more. Maybe then she might have confided in him what had happened.

They had used her mother to draw them out.

He knew what he had to do. Searching the room quickly, he located the phone that Karl had given them. He dialed Karl's phone number, impatiently tapping his fingers on the table while he waited for it to be answered.

A deep voice answered. "Karl here."

"Karl. This is Tyler Everson." Tyler spit the words out so fast, he wasn't sure that the marshal would be able to understand him. He forced himself to slow down and speak at a normal rate. "I think that someone has taken my wife."

He quickly explained that Annie was missing. When he mentioned the newspaper opened on her desk to the article about the fire, Karl was concerned.

"She told me about the fire. My guess is that she contacted her mother." Karl's voice didn't betray any judgment.

Tyler had already concluded the same thing. He also concluded that she had regretted her ill-advised actions. But it would have been too late. If only she had come to him. He would have helped her figure something out. At least, they should have called the marshals.

"I will send someone to check on the mother and brother. In the meantime, I will be there as soon as I can. If you hear from them, contact me at once."

Tyler agreed. The second he hung up, he headed outside. He was going to try and see if there were any hints outside. Bethany had said that Annie had seen the man coming. Tyler decided to walk the perimeter of the property, see if he could find any clues that might lead him to discover the whereabouts of his wife.

If she was still alive.

He had never in his life felt such despair. Reaching the barn, he looked inside and then around back. Nothing. Giving in, he let his knees buckle. Falling to the ground, he knelt on the fresh grass. And for the first time in his adult life, Tyler Everson truly poured out his anguish and his fears to God.

He had no idea how long he knelt there behind the barn. When he finally stood, he felt renewed in purpose. He recalled a verse from his childhood. He thought it was from the Gospel of Matthew, but he wasn't sure. He didn't even remember the entire verse. The only part that he could recall was Jesus saying that He would be with them always. When all this was through, he was going to find a Bible and look up that verse.

Right now, he was going to find his wife.

He continued along the perimeter of the house. Abraham and William had joined in and were searching in another section of the property.

A drop of water hit him squarely on the cheek. Tyler glanced up at the sky. The clouds were dark and rolling through the sky at great speed. In the distance he saw a bright flash of light. Lightning. A few seconds later, thunder rumbled.

Great. He'd be searching in a thunderstorm.

He hoped that Annie was out of the elements.

He continued looking. He wanted to call out her name but restrained himself. She might hear him, but so might her kidnapper. He would lose any advantage he might have. Not that he had any. The kidnapper had to know that he was searching for her.

He kept going. Every now and then, he'd see a movement. It was always an animal or something blowing across the yard. He was trying not to lose hope.

Would he ever be able to tell her that he still loved her? He hoped so. He needed to move faster. The rain was starting to fall harder. If it fell much harder, it would soon be hard to see anything more than a few inches in front of his face. His teeth chattered. The rain was cold. Within minutes, his clothing was soaked and his hair was plastered to his head. He shoved his hands in his pockets and kept his arms close to his body in an attempt to stay warm. He didn't even consider going back inside the house. Not while Annie was in the control of a madman with a gun. He said another quick prayer under his breath.

His ears strained. What was that? He listened. There it was again. There was a rustling sound. It was somewhere behind him. He started to pivot to locate the sound. Something hard was shoved into his back. He didn't have to look down to know that it was a gun.

He had been found.

Chapter Sixteen

Jim shoved the gun harder into Tyler's back.

"Don't try anything funny, you hear? I got your pretty little wife, and I have no problem with killing her to make you mind your manners."

Tyler did not doubt that the man would do just that. At least he knew that she was still alive. He allowed the man to push him away from the house toward the street. Every step would bring him closer to his wife. As they walked, he fought the urge to try and overpower the man forcing him along. He knew that there was a good chance that the gun would go off if he did. The other thought that kept running through his head was that this man was the only person who knew where Annie was.

The thunder boomed directly overhead. Lightning was now flashing in the sky with a vengeance, illuminating the surrounding landscape. It was frightening and awesome at the same time. The rain continued to pound on them. Soon the ground had turned into slippery mud. Tyler slipped once. The man behind him showed him no mercy. He smacked at Tyler with the gun. Tyler cringed, expecting the gun to go off. When it didn't, he straightened. Jim pushed at him again. They continued slogging through the summer storm until they reached their destination.

Jim pushed Tyler into the darkness of the falling-down house. Tyler had noticed the house in the past week or so. Abraham had told him that it had been standing deserted for two years now. There was no running electric. There was talk that the local government was going to tear down the building one of these days. It was a hazard and an eyesore.

Tyler heard someone ahead of him. His steps quickened. He was pretty sure that he would find Annie if he just kept moving. A light speared through the shadows. Jim had turned on a flashlight.

Sitting on the floor, her back against the wall, was his Annie. Her hands were tied in front of her. She looked uninjured. Momentarily forgetting the man walking behind him, Tyler skirted around the chair sitting in the middle of the floor and knelt down in the dirt beside his wife.

She was the most beautiful sight he had ever seen.

"Annie, are you hurt?" Was that hoarse croak his voice?

She stirred. Opening her eyes, she stared at him. "Tyler? Oh, Tyler." Her voice became a wail. "I am so sorry. I didn't mean to lead him to us."

"Hush, none of that. Remember what you keep trying to tell me? You are not responsible for someone else's bad choices. If I saw my mother's house had burned down, I would have called her, too."

"I didn't want you to come. I was hoping that you would be safe."

Another voice joined in, ruining their reunion. "Aw,

ain't this sweet? I hate to interrupt this little party, but I have some business to take care of."

Jim stomped over to him and took out a pair of handcuffs. Who knew where he had gotten them. By the faint light of the flashlight, he ordered Tyler to put them on himself. He didn't dare argue, as the man was holding the gun aimed right at Annie's head.

At first, Tyler thought he meant to kill them right then and there. To Tyler's surprise, he merely walked over and sat down on the chair, keeping his gun trained on the pair of them. "As soon as this rain lets up, we'll be on our way. I will collect the money for killing you, make no mistake, but I am wondering if there is a way to make this whole business more profitable for myself."

Whatever the man was planning, Tyler wanted no part of it. He'd had a difficult afternoon. He was trying to keep his calm so that he could be cool-headed when the opportunity to escape and save Annie arose.

A clamor of voices outside caught his attention.

Abraham's voice was calling out his name. Annie's name.

The man holding the gun started muttering angrily. Tyler smiled in the darkness. He suddenly realized why the man hadn't just shot them. Any shots made would immediately lead people in this direction. The man didn't want to shoot them, then be forced to make a run for it without his proof that he had killed Tyler. He wouldn't be able to collect any money for that.

He could just take a picture with his phone. Tyler was a little amazed he hadn't done that yet.

Unless he planned to take them with him. That seemed like it would be more hassle. Why would Jim want to haul two grown adults across the state with him if all he needed was proof that he had killed Tyler? The men's voices came closer. Tyler felt his hopes rise. Maybe the men would see their footprints in the mud. The hope faded as the voices continued past.

Jim laughed. Tyler felt Annie shudder beside him. He understood. That harsh bark was more of a bitter cough than a sound of humor.

He wished he could somehow comfort Annie. There was nothing he could do, though, except sit beside her in the dark and wait for the rain to stop. He still had one hope. Since Jim was waiting for the storm to break and light to return, they still had the chance that Karl or Abraham would arrive and intervene.

He held on to that hope for the next few hours. At some point, he must have drifted off to sleep. He awoke when someone kicked at his legs with steel-toed boots. The pain shot through his legs and into his hip. He didn't give the man the satisfaction of hearing him complain, though. Nor would he give up hope.

Karl and Abraham would keep looking for them. They just had to hold out a little longer until they arrived.

The early morning light was starting to stream through the holes in the roof.

"We need to get out of here," Jim growled. "Before people start moving around. Stand up."

Tyler stood, then helped Annie to stand as best as could with the handcuffs on. She was moving stiffly this morning. Between her still-healing wound and sitting on the floor all night, it was no wonder.

He wished there was something he could do for her, but Jim wasn't a man of patience. As they left the building, Annie and Tyler went ahead of Jim, who kept his gun on them the entire time. He continued to push them to move faster.

Outside the building, the ground was slick with mud. Annie and Tyler both managed to sidestep the biggest patches.

Jim slipped. As he fell, the gun hit the ground and went off. Annie and Tyler both dove for the ground. Tyler heard a thunk as Annie hit her head on a rock. Jim scrambled to his feet, wild-eyed. He aimed the gun at Tyler.

Tyler took one look at the man and knew that he was going to shoot.

Annie felt Tyler's sudden stillness and forced herself to look up, blinking past the blinding pain in her head. Everything was blurry. After a few seconds, the blurriness faded enough for her to see the gun pointing straight at her husband.

"No!" she screamed.

A shot rang out.

Jim crumpled to the ground. Shouts and the sound of pounding feet headed their way. Arms gently lifted her. She saw that Tyler was on his feet, too.

Karl was there. His face was grim as he put a gun back into its holster. It made sense suddenly. Jim hadn't shot Tyler. It was the marshal's gun she had heard going off. The monster who had held her captive and had burned down her mother's house was dead.

The darkness was swirling around in her head.

She passed out.

When Annie woke again, she knew that she was in a hospital room. She could feel a bandage on her head.

That was where she had hit her head on a rock. A doctor was leaning over her, flashing a light in her eyes.

She grimaced.

"Well, Mrs. Miller, I must say you are doing surprisingly well for someone who has been through your ordeal. I think you missed getting a concussion from that fall, although you did hit your head rather hard. You have five stitches in your head." He tapped the bandage on her left temple lightly.

Although she argued, the doctor insisted she remain overnight so that the staff could watch her for complications.

He came in to check her first thing the next morning. She wanted to dance when he said she could go home.

"Try to take it easy for the next few days, please," he cautioned, walking toward the door. "I am going to go write up some care instructions. Then you will be free to go."

She slumped back against the bed as he left. Five seconds after he left, the door opened again. She frowned until she saw who it was. Tyler walked in and her mood immediately picked up. He sauntered over to her bedside and kissed the tip of her nose.

"Come to spring me?"

He grinned, but she could see the shadows on his face. "Yes, ma'am. I am to bring you back to the house so that Julia may spoil you and Bethany can see that her mother is well."

Remembering what had started the awful experience, Annie dropped her eyes in shame. "I betrayed you, Ty. I saw that picture of my mom's house, and I called her. I needed to hear her voice, but in doing so, I led him right to us." She explained how Jim had traced them. "Because of me, my mom was put in danger, and we were almost killed."

Tyler tipped up her chin with his finger. Reluctantly, she met his eyes. "Sweet Annie, it's not your fault. Who could blame you for wanting to check on your mom? I can't. I would have wanted to do the same."

She searched his eyes. He seemed sincere.

Her eyes widened. "We came in here dressed in our Amish clothes!"

He shook his head. "They made me change before I could enter. And they kept you covered up. No one was allowed to see you except the doctor and the marshals."

"And Karl? Is he kicking us out of the program?"

Even with Jim out of the way, she knew they weren't safe. Not while the trial was still in the future.

He sighed. "Karl's not happy. But he has decided to give us another chance. Especially since that Jim character is dead. He thinks that Jim died without telling others where we were. So for now, our cover is safe."

She closed her eyes briefly. When she opened them, she caught her breath at the intensity of his stare. "Don't—" he brought his head closer to hers "—ever do that to me again."

She knew he wasn't talking about the phone call. He was referring to her getting kidnapped and almost killed. After all that had happened between them, some feelings had remained. They might have even grown stronger. She really should keep her distance. Especially since they were both feeling so emotional after all that had happened.

Annie stayed where she was, anticipation zinging

through her as her husband moved nearer. He was giving her a chance to back out, she realized. He was letting her make the choice.

Well, she'd already chosen. Looking at his face, she felt the emotion welling up inside her. The love that she had tried not to feel had grown back against her will. Only this time, the feelings were deeper, more mature than before. Knowing that danger was following them put a new perspective on things. She remembered Stacy's words to her and understood what the woman had been saying. Love was too precious to take for granted. Annie finally admitted to herself that she loved Tyler.

Reaching up, she put her hand on the back of his neck and pulled his lips to hers. She caught his grin the moment before their lips touched. It had been three years since they had kissed. Now, as he gently pressed his lips against hers, she felt as if those years had never happened.

He lifted his head. Scanned her face. One of his hands stroked her head. Then he bent and kissed her again.

That evening, she went back to the Beiler home feeling optimistic, about her marriage, and about life in general. As the evening grew late, though, she could sense that Tyler was withdrawing into himself. And she couldn't understand why.

She went to bed, praying that it was all in her imagination.

Even though she knew it wasn't.

Chapter Seventeen

He shouldn't have kissed her.

Tyler was still brooding about his poor judgment the following day. Tyler had seen the look in Annie's eyes. He knew that she was developing feelings for him again. Instead of filling him with joy, the notion filled him with dread. If she loved him, it would be difficult for her when they left witness protection and went their separate ways.

His heart ached to stay with her and Bethany. He knew that the love he had tried to deny feeling had just been dormant. Being with her, those feelings were coming to life again.

But they couldn't be together. The image of her lying in the hospital bed flashed through his mind. He squeezed his lids shut and clenched his teeth. He couldn't let that happen again. It was all his fault that she had been hurt. If he hadn't been so selfish and demanded that they stay together, she and Bethany might be somewhere on the other side of the country, safe and living their lives.

He knew that Annie was aware something was wrong. She'd been watching him for the past hour. When she'd tried to talk with him, the despair had bit deep into him. What he wouldn't give to be able to enjoy her company and tell her what was on his mind. He was done being selfish, though. As soon as he could, he had escaped to his room. Seeing that bandage on her forehead felt like an accusation. Every time he saw it, the guilt and fear cut deep into him.

He knew what he had to do. Remaining here was no longer an option. He would go. Once he was far enough away, he'd call Karl and plan to meet him. Karl could find him a separate placement.

It wouldn't be fair just to leave, though. He couldn't let her wonder what had happened to him. Going to the desk in his room, he pulled out some paper and sat to write a letter. His shoulders slumped. Shaking off his sorrow, he bent over the paper and wrote the hardest letter of his life.

Dear Annie,
I know that you are worried for me, and I am sorry for that. I can't stay and let my presence continue to endanger you and Bethany. I thought we could be a family. I was a fool.

As long as I am with you, then you are in danger.

I am leaving. Not because I don't care, but because I do.

I love you and Bethany with all my heart. I pray that you can forgive me. When she forgets me, can you remind Bethany about me? I know

I have no right to ask, but I also know that your heart is too generous to deny this request.

Be well and be happy. With all my love,
Tyler

Feeling like his heart had shattered in his chest, he quickly packed a bag and let himself out the window. His mouth twisted. It was a good thing his room was on the ground floor. Hefting his bag, he started off. Alone.

When Tyler didn't come out for lunch, Annie went to look for him. He had been acting strange all morning.

It was the kiss. He was regretting kissing her. She sighed. Tyler still felt overly responsible for their situation. She paused outside his door. It was time she told him she loved him and, just as important, that she forgave him. She had been carrying her anger and hurt around with her for so long, but it was time to let it go. It was time to reconcile with her husband.

Determined, she knocked on his door. He didn't answer. Acting on a hunch, she opened the door.

He wasn't there. Seeing the paper propped up on the desk with her name on it, she moved inside the room to get it, her feet feeling like they had cement blocks tied to them. She had a bad feeling about this.

Reading the letter, she felt the blood drain from her face. Shaking, she sank into the desk chair.

Oh, that stupid man! To go off and leave them without telling her, as if she didn't have a choice in the matter! She had loved him and lost him once because he decided to play the hero. She wasn't about to lose the man she loved a second time without fighting for their love and trying to save his life.

Clutching the letter in her hand, she ran out of the room and down the stairs. Bursting into the kitchen, she crashed to a stop in front of Abraham. Wordlessly, she handed him the letter. Honestly, she was so rattled she wasn't sure if she could speak right now. The anger at his high-handedness mingled with her very real fear for his life.

Abraham's face paled. "When did you last see him?"

"About an hour ago." She clasped her hands in front of her.

Abraham looked at his stepson. "William, go and look and see if any of the buggies or horses are missing."

Annie protested, "He wouldn't take any of your things."

"I know that, Annie. I need to check."

"Mommy?" Bethany's scared voice caught her attention. What did she tell her little girl?

"Bethany, sweetheart, eat your lunch and then I will take you and Kayla to the barn to see the kittens," Abraham announced.

Bethany brightened. She glanced at her mother before she agreed, though. Annabelle flicked a grateful look at Abraham. "That sounds like a great idea, Bethy!"

Satisfied, the child turned her attention back to her lunch.

Annabelle turned back to Abraham.

"I am going to get in touch with Karl." She kept her voice low. "He needs to know about this." She rushed out of the room and back up the stairs. Once in her room, she rifled through her clothes until she found the cell phone that was buried there. It was a flip phone. The one she'd been given specifically to contact Karl if there was trouble.

Fumbling with the phone, she opened it and called the number that he had programmed into it. It rang once. Then it rang again. The anxiety in her mind spiked. When she got the voice mail, she hung up. Jonathan Mast. She would call him. Abraham gave her the number. The second ring was cut off abruptly. "Jonathan Mast speaking."

Annie wilted and sat on the bed. She felt too heavy for her legs to hold her up.

"Hello?"

"Jonathan, this is Annabelle, Annie Miller." Which name did she refer to herself as?

"Annie, yes. What's wrong?" His voice came back at once. The tears she'd been holding back spilled out of her eyes and rolled down her cheeks. A harsh sob welled up and burst out of her throat. It hurt. "Annie?" His voice was sharper.

"It—it's Tyler," she gasped out. "He's gone."

A pause.

"What do you mean he's gone? Where did he go?" Jonathan demanded.

"I don't know. He left me a letter. He blames himself for everything that has happened and went off. He wrote that he thinks Bethany and I would be safer without him here. I'm so scared. He's going to get himself killed."

"Annie, I want you to listen to me. I am on my way to you. I will be there as soon as I can. I am going to be calling the police near Harvest, and they will be searching for Tyler, too. If you hear from him, think of anything that will help us to find him, I want you to call me immediately. Do you understand?"

She nodded. Then grimaced at herself. "Yes. I understand."

The small click on the other end of the phone let her know that he had hung up. He was on his way. She caught her lip between her teeth. A sharp pain made her wince. She had bitten through the layer of skin. The metallic taste of blood hit her taste buds.

How long would it take him to get there? It all depended on where he was. It could be hours yet before he arrived. Hours in which Tyler could be caught and tortured. Or killed. And she was supposed to sit here while her husband was out there somewhere risking his neck? She knew why he had gone. He thought that if he left them, the marshals would continue to hide Annabelle and Bethany. No doubt they would get a totally new placement. Tyler, though, he seemed to believe that if he weren't with them, they would be safer. It was crazy thinking. They would be in danger no matter what as long as Barco was still a menace.

Tyler, however, seemed to be allowing his emotions to cloud his judgment. Like he'd done before. She should just let him go.

She could not do it. No matter how many times she told herself she was being foolish, Annabelle knew that she was going to have to go after her husband. No one else knew him like she did.

No one else loved him like she did.

And she had never even told him that she still loved

him. She read his letter again. All the guilt, all the concern. No, she couldn't stay here while the husband she loved risked his life for her.

But she couldn't just leave. What about Bethany? Torn about what to do, she wavered.

Strengthening her resolve, she went downstairs and found Julia. "Julia, I need your help."

Julia fastened her concerned gaze on her new friend. "Anything. You know that."

She nodded. She felt guilty, because she was about to willfully deceive her friend. "Listen, Jonathan Mast is on his way. So are the police. They are all going to help find Tyler. Can you keep an eye on Bethany?"

She went back upstairs to change into her own clothes. She shoved the phone into the pocket of her jeans. As she was putting on her tennis shoes, her eyes fell on one of the scars that marred the smooth skin on her legs. Those scars had embarrassed her for so long. Why? She remembered Tyler's face when he touched the scar. The tenderness. The gentle care. She saw none of the disgust she had felt so often when she looked at them. Why? Because the scars did not—should not—define who she was as a person.

She was done hiding behind them.

A few minutes later, she was out the back door and going in search of her husband. She had no idea where she was going. But she remembered that Harvest had only one bus station. That seemed to be the most likely direction to go. Tyler was only an hour or so ahead of her. Hopefully, she could find him before he boarded a bus.

She walked for an hour. No sign of him. She started

to pray. Every once in a while, her mind would wrangle with the notion that she might have taken the wrong road, or that she might have been headed in the wrong direction. If she had her own phone, it would have a GPS on it.

She shook the ideas away. She needed to keep going. She knew that she was going the right way.

A loud click on the left startled her. Spinning, she found herself staring into the face of a stranger. A handsome young man with a winsome face and a wealth of curly black hair. The man had a charming smile. He also had a gun, aimed right at her.

"Well, hello, Mrs. Everson," he said, almost pleasantly. "How nice of you to join me."

Tyler had left the house an hour and a half ago. He'd changed out of his Amish clothes and back into his own stuff and slipped out. He had walked for about an hour when he had come to his senses and realized that leaving his family would not make the danger go away. It would only cause three people pain. He turned back, intent on returning and begging his wife to take him back. He hadn't gotten far when he heard Annie's voice just around the bend. She must have found his letter almost immediately. And, in typical Annie style, she must have stormed out to find him. Did she call the police? The marshals? He had no idea. When he had talked to Karl almost an hour ago, he didn't mention a call from Annie.

Karl hadn't been happy with his decision to leave. He felt bad, knowing the marshal was even now on his way to pick Tyler up. Hopefully, he wouldn't be too annoyed with him.

Strolling around the bend, he saw Annie struggling with a stranger. The man was doing his best to drag her along with him.

"Let her go!" Tyler yelled.

Annie gasped his name as he stepped forward. He glanced at her. Was she hurt? She didn't look hurt; she looked mad.

The man didn't let her go. Instead, he barked a harsh laugh. "Let her go? No way, man. I got a tip that you were seen down this road an hour ago. I never dreamed I would run into the missus here. She's my insurance that you will do exactly what I want."

He didn't protest when the man forced them to get into his truck. Tyler was at the wheel. Annie was in the middle, her leg touching his. The dark-haired man sat on the other side of Annie, his gun pressed into her side. Tyler had no doubt that if he made the wrong move, this man would casually pull the trigger and end his wife's life. Tyler had to think of a way to get her out.

It was clear in his mind that the smiling stranger had no intention of letting either of them live. Not after he'd let them both get such a clear image of him. Why hadn't he just shot them where they were? That was the question. Tyler knew that the bounty on him was for his death.

"I'm guessing you're wondering why you are still alive, aren't you?"

Tyler jerked. Having this savvy young man echo his thoughts was disconcerting, to say the least. "I know that you've figured out that I don't really have a use for you. But here's the thing. You have caused my family a lot of grief, Mr. Everson."

His family? Who was this kid? "My father is sitting in prison because you couldn't mind your own business. My mother, she's inconsolable."

"You're Barco's son." His voice was flat. Honestly, he couldn't even say he was surprised. Now that he thought of it, he could see the resemblance. Until that moment, he'd never seen Wilson Barco Jr.

"Obviously," the kid sneered. "I would have thought a lawyer would be smarter."

"So if you're not going to kill us—"

Annie's words broke off with a gasp. Tyler jerked his eyes around to see Junior pushing the gun harder into her side. Her face paled even more, gaining a waxy cast to it.

"Hey!" The truck swerved slightly as he reacted to the sight of his wife suffering at the man's hands.

"Careful!" Junior snarled. "You crash and she dies."

He straightened the truck, his knuckles going white as his grip on the steering wheel tightened. He had to keep his wits about him. As soon as he saw a chance to rescue Annie, he would take it. It no longer mattered what happened to him, as long as he could save her. And give her a chance to be returned safely to their daughter.

Junior was apparently only too happy to tell them all about his plans for them. "In answer to your question, Mrs. Everson, of course I'm going to kill you. I don't plan on letting someone else claim money that should go to me as my inheritance."

Charming. The family devotion boggled the mind.

"I think, however, that my mother would be comforted to know that you are suffering for what you have done to our family. The loss of business. You have no idea how much money has been lost because of you."

This was like a bad gangster show. He could hardly believe people actually thought this way. Except that this warped young man held a gun to Annie's side.

"How did you find us?" Annie asked.

"I've been keeping an eye on this situation. I know, for example, that your mother was used as bait. And that you bit and called her. When the man who burned down her house obtained records of your mom's phone calls, he told me about it. I think he thought I would up the bounty. It wasn't that hard to trace the phone you used. I was able to get a rough idea of where you were calling from. Flash your pictures around, and that's all it took."

Annie looked at Tyler out of the corner of her eye. He glanced down. Somehow the phone the marshals had given them was open on the seat beside him. She had called someone. Who? He sent up a prayer that the phone signal would be tracked.

He hoped it worked. Hoped someone found them, although it was unlikely.

One positive thought ran through his mind.

The man had no idea that they had been living with the Amish. That much was clear. He had no idea where to go to get to Bethany.

He drove for forty-five minutes, going through so many twists and turns that he could barely keep them straight in his mind. Every time they shifted, he checked the compass on the dashboard. The majority of the time, they were headed west. Back toward Chicago. Surely, they weren't going to drive this way for the next five hours, were they? Flicking his eyes to the gas gauge, he saw that they only had half a tank of gas left. Lifting his head, he had just enough time to see the police cruiser swerve in front of the truck. He turned the steering wheel and stomped his foot on the brake. The truck careened over to the side of the road, the right front tire going up over the embankment on the side of the road.

Wilson Barco Jr.'s head slammed against the passenger side window. He slumped, stunned. Tyler could hear the man breathe, so he knew that he wasn't dead. Who knew how long he'd been dazed, though.

Now was his chance. Yanking the gearshift, Tyler put the truck into Park. Then he threw open the door and jumped out, pulling Annie with him. She threw her legs over the side and made the small hop down before the two of them started to run, hand in hand, toward the police.

"Hey!"

Tyler turned and looked back. Barco's son was standing on the road taking aim. Tyler jerked Annie to his side and tried to hide her from Junior's view. A shot rang out. A burning pain seared into his shoulder. He didn't care.

"Keep running, Annie!" He followed her, waiting for the second shot. It went wide. The cops took aim, but they didn't fire. He and Annie were between them and Barco.

"Annie, get down," he told her.

The moment they were out of the way, the guns began to fire. He knew without looking that Barco was hit when they stopped. He wanted to look up, but found that his strength was gone.

"Tyler? Tyler! Get up!" He heard Annie's voice. It sounded like it was coming through a tunnel. It had an odd, echoing sound to it.

"Annie?" He couldn't make his mouth work right. His voice was muffled. He was going to pass out. His head was full of buzzing. The voices around him faded away.

When he came to, he was lying on his back. Annie was kneeling at his side. He'd never seen anything more beautiful than her pale face. Her brown eyes were flooded with tears. *Aww.* He hated that he had made her cry again. Actually, he hated that he had put her through everything she'd gone through in the past few weeks. When she'd asked if they could go into separate placements, he should have agreed. His gaze zeroed in on the bandage on her forehead. Another wound on his wife that he had to accept responsibility for. He regretted his selfishness.

How could he ask her to take him back after this?

"Ma'am, you need to move so we can treat him."

Annabelle's face was replaced by a paramedic's long face on one side. Jonathan Mast looked down on him from the other side.

"She was prettier." What was he saying? The paramedic rolled his eyes. Jonathan laughed quietly.

"I'm sure she was, Tyler. We have to get you to the hospital."

"Where—where's my daughter?" It was so hard to talk. He'd never felt so weak in his life.

"She's fine, Tyler," Annie said from the side. He moved his head back and forth, trying to crane his neck to see her. "Julia is watching her."

Julia. Exhausted, he sank back down, allowing the paramedic to care for him. He didn't protest when he was lifted gently onto the stretcher and placed in an ambulance. His eyes closed. He heard the door shut.

A warm hand took hold of his and held it. He pulled his lids open with an effort. Annie had come with him in the ambulance. His eyes devoured her face. "Are you all right?"

She smiled at him. It did funny things with his heart rhythm. "I'm fine, Tyler. You don't need to worry about me."

"Barco?"

Her smile dimmed slightly. "He didn't make it. He was killed at the scene. I told Jonathan what he had said about his mother. The marshals are going to check into whether or not she had any part in the illegal activities of her husband and son."

He certainly hoped not. "I hate that she has lost a son."

Annie sighed. "I do, too, but that is not your fault. Nor is it mine. The man made some really bad choices."

That was the truth. His eyes closed. He couldn't keep them open any longer. He let the darkness slide over him, knowing that Annie was beside him, holding his hand.

Chapter Eighteen

Tyler hated hospitals. He couldn't step inside one without being reminded of Annie almost dying. Annie crying for him, in pain. Confused by the accident. That memory had haunted him for the past few years. Even though he was coming to terms with the fact that he wasn't completely to blame for what had happened, it still pained him to recall his beloved wife's suffering.

And yet here he was, lying in a hospital bed, a large bandage across his chest.

The memory of what had happened surged through him. His pulse spiked. Where were Annie and Bethany? His last memory was of Annie's face, pale and drawn with concern, as she leaned over him. But what if something had happened after he had blacked out? He couldn't just lie here! He had to go and find them, make sure they were safe!

Tyler struggled to sit up, desperate to discover what had become of his family. The stitches in his shoulder pulled. A slight twinge in his arm caught his attention. He looked down. For the first time since he woke up, he realized he was hooked up to an IV. A grimace twisted his face. He was a mess.

"Good afternoon, Ty. Glad you're awake."

His head jerked up. He hadn't even heard the door open. Jonathan Mast sauntered in. "Hey, Jonathan."

Jonathan stopped at the edge of his bed and narrowed his eyes. "You took quite a beating out there. I certainly hope you weren't planning on doing anything foolish. Like getting out of bed."

"I need to make sure that my wife is okay."

Jonathan reached out and placed a calming hand on his shoulder. The one without the stitches. "Relax. Annie is fine. Bethany is fine. Wilson Barco is still in jail. His son is dead. For now, the threat has been neutralized."

"For now." Tyler set his jaw. He had to do the right thing. No matter what it cost himself. "Look, Jonathan, I want you to find me a new placement."

The marshal's eyebrows moved closer together as he furrowed his forehead. "I can see why you would feel that way. You have to give me time to find a new placement. And to get the new identities together. And—"

"No." Tyler shook his head. Each word he said was like a chisel being hammered into his heart. "Not identities. Identity. I think that my girls would be safer if I wasn't with them."

The frown on Jonathan's face grew more pronounced. "Tyler, man, you don't want to do that. Do you? You know what it would mean. It could be years before it's safe for you to come out of the program. It's possible it may never be safe. If you go this route, then you will be separated from them. Maybe even for the rest of your life. I don't think you want to do that."

He didn't. Not even for a second. But it was the only way he could think of protecting them. "I do know that. But I also know that criminals like Barco are relentless. If I'm not around Annie and Bethany, maybe they would be easier to keep hidden. I will do whatever I need to do to keep them safe. Wouldn't you do whatever you could to protect the family you love?"

He could see that Jonathan was wrestling with the subject in his mind.

"Don't I get a say in all this?"

Annie. Tyler turned his head. His breath caught in his throat at the lovely woman standing in the doorway. Her large brown eyes were shadowed. She had seen so much in the few weeks that they had been hidden with the Amish. He had never loved her more. It killed him to think of giving her up. She never took her eyes off him as she spoke to the marshal.

"Jonathan, may I please have a moment alone with my husband?"

The marshal hurried to the door. "Of course, Annie. Take your time." He was out of the room in a flash.

The silence stretched between them, awkward and tense with longing.

"I can't believe after all we've been through that you would even consider leaving us again. Tyler, I thought we could finally be a family. And now you're thinking of ripping us apart? Why?" She stepped up close to his side. If he wanted to, he could reach out and touch her. He curled his fingers into the bedsheet, controlling the impulse.

He sighed, wilting back against the pillow and closing his eyes briefly. When he opened them, she was still there, still staring at him with hurt on her face.

"Annie, we were building something. And for a short time, I actually thought it might work out. I love you, Annie. I never stopped loving you."

"Then why—"

He held up a hand. Not a command. A gentle plea. Surprisingly, she paused and waited for him to speak. "Annie, you know why I let you go the first time. I know you said there was nothing to forgive, that it wasn't my fault. But here we are in the same position again. My job has once again put you and Bethany in danger. If I leave, then maybe you could go on. Be safe and happy."

She was already shaking her head, a challenge in her flashing brown eyes. "You are not God, Tyler Everson. Even if you left, who is to say that these people wouldn't still come after us, to try and use us to bring you out? But even if no one ever tried to do that, Tyler, you can't let them decide how you live your life. All the bad decisions, those are things we can't help. And maybe you're right. Maybe we would be 'safer.'" Annabelle made air quotes with her fingers. "That doesn't mean we'd be happier. Tyler, I don't know how long we will have together. All I know is that I really do want to spend ''til death do us part' with you. With my husband. The husband I am choosing for a second time. And I want Bethany to have her father near as she grows up. And maybe a couple of brothers or sisters, in time."

He watched the color rise in her cheeks. How he loved this woman! And to think of raising a family with her, well, it would be his dearest wish. Would it be selfish?

"No, it wouldn't be selfish."

He blinked. He must have said that out loud.

"And you were wrong about another thing." Her words were soft, almost a whisper. "We might go on without you, but I don't feel like I could be happy. Not really. I would forever wonder where you were, if you were safe, if you were well. I wouldn't be able to stop myself. That's how this love thing works. Even if we try to convince ourselves we're fine, deep inside we're just lying to ourselves."

He already knew that. Hadn't he spent the past few years trying to keep busy just to fill the hollow void left by his family's absence? Could he even bear to go back to that lifestyle again, especially knowing she still loved him and had forgiven any wrong he'd done?

"I don't want to leave you," he admitted. "It breaks my heart to even contemplate taking that step. I would willingly give my life if it spared yours and Bethany's, though. You know that, right?"

She nodded, her eyes deep. They pulled him in. "And I feel the same. If you want to, we can ask Jonathan to relocate us. The whole family. I will move as many times as we need to. Just say we can stay together."

"Annie, it might mean that you can never see your mother again. Or Ethan."

"After what just happened I know very well that I cannot risk talking to my family until this is over. And I choose to believe that someday God will make the situation right."

Suddenly, it occurred to him that in all his planning,

he had neglected the most important step. He hadn't prayed about it, hadn't involved God in his plans. Who was better equipped to keep his family safe than the Almighty?

"I think we should trust God with the whole problem. Just hand it over to Him." Annie's words hit him like a confirmation. How arrogant he'd been! Closing his eyes, he said a silent prayer, asking God to forgive him. *Lord, I put my family in Your hands, knowing they are far more capable than mine. Please protect us and teach us to follow Your will.*

Peace flooded his soul in a gentle wave.

The door swung open. Jonathan Mast reentered the room. He looked between the two of them. "Okay, Tyler, here's the deal. I can move you to a different placement by yourself. But once I do, I can't change it. We have already made more changes than are normally allowed."

Feeling happier than he had since he woke up in the hospital, Tyler grinned. Jonathan looked taken aback by the expression. Annie's face tensed. He understood. He was, in essence, deciding his family's future. "About the new placement, Jonathan. I'm not going to be breaking up my family. We'll move together. We're in it together, until the end."

With a happy cry, Annie launched herself into his arms. He winced as her hand bounced off his wound. He didn't complain, though. Having her in his arms again was worth the pain. Over her head, Jonathan smiled at him and gave him a thumbs-up before he backed out of the room and closed the door softly behind him, leaving Tyler alone with his wife.

Annie raised her face, tears pooling in her eyes. One

spilled over and streaked down her cheek. He caught it with his finger.

All at once, a look of horror crossed her face. "Oh! I forgot about your injury."

She started to pull away. He wouldn't let her go. "I'm fine. In fact, I'm more than fine."

His eyes searched her face. He tugged her closer.

"Tyler, I don't want to hurt you."

He traced a finger down her jaw. "A little pain I can deal with. What was really hurting was the idea of leaving you again." His finger paused as he searched her eyes. "I love you, Annie. Even more than I did when we got married."

Her face grew soft. "Oh, Tyler. I love you, too. I don't want us to be separated anymore."

He couldn't help the grin that spread across his face. "You know what I really need right now?" She shook her head. He lowered his voice. "I really need to kiss my wife."

She stilled, her face softening. "That can be arranged."

Annabelle shifted so that her face was close to his. He lifted his head and closed the remaining distance between them.

Annie stood in front of the sink, washing dishes. Her eyes searched the street every so often, watching for a car. Stacy had come to stay with them while the trial was going on. Karl had called her the night before to tell her that Tyler would be coming home the next day.

Annabelle couldn't wait to see her husband.

"Mommy, is Daddy here yet?"

Annabelle dried off her hands and faced her daughter. Bethany was carrying a large chicken. Rolling her eyes, Annabelle decided not to say anything, for now. When they had left the Harvest community, Bethany had missed Mrs. Feathers. Fortunately, their neighbors in their new community in Spartansburg, Pennsylvania, had plenty of chickens. They didn't care if Bethany carried one around.

"He'll be here today, honey. That's all I know."

The little girl sighed. "Me and Chicken are gonna go watch for him."

"I'll go with you," Stacy said. "We'll stay on the front porch since it's muddy from this morning's rain."

She placed her left hand on the child's shoulder. A gorgeous solitaire ring flashed in the light coming through the window. Annabelle was so happy for Karl and Stacy.

Jonathan had moved them almost immediately following their decision to stay together. For the most part, she was content. She was with her husband and her daughter. The only thing that made her sad was knowing that she would probably never see Julia and Abraham again. To keep them safe, Abraham and Julia had been moved to a new location, as well.

Annabelle shrugged off the momentary sadness. They were alive. They were together. For now, she'd be good with that. They were living with a new Amish couple in a different community for the time being.

Her memories were interrupted by Bethany's squeal. "Daddy!"

Flinging the towel onto the counter, she ran out to the porch to greet Tyler and Karl.

Bethany and Annabelle both ran to be embraced by Tyler. The little family approached the porch together.

"Did the trial go well?"

Tyler nodded. "Yes. Barco was found guilty of all the charges against him. He's not going to be getting out of prison, probably for the rest of his life."

"And," Karl said, "we were able to seize his assets. Which means the bounty is no more."

Annabelle's heart stopped. "Does that mean—"

"We can go home." Tyler hugged her tight.

She hugged him back. They would go home. Together.

Epilogue

"The ceremony was lovely, Annabelle."

Annabelle turned and smiled as her friend and neighbor, Danielle Johnson, moved to stand beside her. Danielle had saved her life when she'd called Annabelle three months earlier to warn her that someone had been watching her house. Annabelle's heart was full, seeing her friend here to celebrate with them.

She allowed her gaze to wander across the lawn. The trees were vibrant with changing hues of red, orange and gold. She loved autumn. Bursts of color were everywhere you looked. The air even had a different smell to it, fresh and crisp. It was her favorite season. And now it was even more special. Today was Tyler and Annabelle's eighth anniversary. To celebrate, they had decided to bring their friends and family together so they could renew their vows to show their renewed commitment to each other.

Danielle's husband, Mike, and Tyler were standing near the barbecue grill, deep in conversation. Maybe Tyler was telling Mike about his new job. Annabelle

sighed, content. Tyler had given up criminal law alto-
gether. He now worked in an up-and-coming firm that
specialized in family law. And even better, after today,
he would be moving in with Annabelle and Bethany.

Stacy and Karl were talking to her brother, Ethan.
They were holding hands.

Jonathan Mast and his wife, Celeste, joined them.
Rick was with them. Tears stung her eyes—she was
grateful that he had recovered so well.

Laughter drew her attention back to the group. Celeste was laughing at something Jonathan was saying
to their daughter. Celeste seemed to be one of those
women who took to motherhood naturally. And their
new daughter was precious. She'd slept through the entire ceremony, cozy and warm in her mother's arms. As
she watched, Jonathan reached out and took his daughter from Celeste's arms. The look of love on his face as
he looked down at his baby girl made her sigh.

Her eyes sought out Tyler. When she found him, a
sigh of content left her. He winked at her, the warm look
in his eyes bringing a flush to her cheeks.

"Uh-oh." Danielle gave her a pointed look. "You guys
are so cute, the way you keep watching each other."

She shook her head but couldn't stop smiling. "I
thought what we had was dead. To find love again with
him, it's been amazing."

"You look happy," Danielle stated.

"I am happy." Annabelle shielded her eyes against
the glare of the sun with her right hand. "I'm amazed
at how close Tyler and I have grown. I loved him when
we first got married, but now, the feelings are even

stronger. More intense. It's almost like we are different people." She shook her head. "I can't explain it."

"Aren't you different people, though?" Danielle cocked her eyebrow at Annabelle. "God is part of your relationship now. And I think, going through what you guys have just survived, it really made you look at what was important."

That made sense. A commotion out on the lawn distracted her. Both women turned as shouts and giggled erupted.

Laughter bubbled up inside Annabelle and spilled forth as three very wound-up little girls chased each other around the lawn, followed by a small puppy, who was happily yipping as she played. Annabelle's brother had gifted them with the black Labrador soon after they returned home for good. He claimed that nothing said stability and home like a dog. Bethany had taken one look at the dog and it was instant love.

Annabelle hadn't wanted a dog just yet. Even Tyler had been doubtful. Until Bethany had handed the squirming puppy to her father. Annabelle had watched, amused and resigned, as he immediately melted and announced that they needed a good name for her.

"You know that she just manipulated you, right?" Annabelle had told him. "You're wrapped around her finger and she knows it."

Tyler had just shrugged with a smile. "I don't care. I won't let it go too far. But I am just so glad to have you both back in my life."

So was she.

Annabelle raised her left hand and took a sip of the Pepsi she was holding. The sunlight glinted off the rings on her hand. She couldn't help but marvel at how blessed she had been.

Her mother had hosted the reception that followed the simple ceremony where Tyler and Annabelle had renewed their wedding vows.

"This has been a beautiful day, hasn't it?" She closed her eyes and lifted her chin, enjoying the cool breeze that played with her hair. She'd left it down today, the way that Tyler liked it. She enjoyed the feeling of the sun on her bare head. Although, sometimes she missed the simplicity of the life they'd experienced briefly when they were living with the Amish.

"Not as beautiful as my new-old wife," a warm voice whispered in her ear. She shivered.

Tyler. Her smile edged into a grin. He wrapped his arms around her from behind and pulled her back against him. She sighed as she leaned back into him. Gratitude for the love they had rediscovered filled her. She could barely speak through all the emotions whirling inside her.

"Walk with me?" Tyler asked, rubbing his chin against the top of her head.

"Anywhere."

Holding hands, they wandered amid their guests, talking and laughing. Every once in a while, Annabelle squeezed Tyler's hand, just for the pleasure of feeling him squeeze back in response. A few times, he raised their joined hands so that he could place a kiss on her knuckles. She sighed when he did. And she noticed that some of the other women did the same.

Sorry, ladies. He was all hers.

"You good?" He leaned down to whisper in her ear.

The love she saw in his blue-gray eyes sent a thrill trickling down her spine. She was so blessed that they had found each other again.

"I'm fine," she whispered back. "Just feeling emotional."

"I meant it, you know."

She quirked an eyebrow at him, confused. "Meant what?"

"I love you and our daughter more than anything. I won't let myself be blinded again."

Turning slightly, Annabelle raised her free hand to gently cup his cheek. The soft whiskers of his beard, now neatly trimmed up, tickled her palm. "I know that. I was just thanking God for giving us another chance. I love you so much."

The intensity of his eyes deepened. The world shrank to the two of them. When he leaned forward to kiss her, she rose up on her toes to meet him halfway.

The crowd around them burst into applause. She jerked back, startled.

Tyler laughed and pulled her close again. "They'll have to get used to it," he said before capturing her lips again. Annabelle melted into the kiss, smiling against her husband's lips.

* * * * *